D0498129

Praise for *The Guilty Plea*

"A compulsive page-turner. . . . His humanizing of seemingly obvious killers raises doubts in the reader at the same pace as it does for the jury." —*Maclean's*

"The book's page-turning twists and relatable, personable characters are sure to thrill mystery lovers and lit elitists alike." —*Precedent*

"Rotenberg's . . . courtroom drama is terrific." —Ian Rankin

"Not since *Anatomy of a Murder* has a novel so vividly captured the real life of criminal lawyers in the midst of a high-stakes trial." —Edward L. Greenspan, Q.C

"Rotenberg juggles the many plot elements with aplomb, unveiling each new surprise with care and patience." —*Quill & Quire*

"A great book for summer." —*The Globe and Mail*

"Rotenberg has crafted an idealistic but gripping—and distinctly Canadian—portrait of how justice does and does not get done." —*The London Free Press*

"It's a solid whodunit." —*Winnipeg Free Press*

"A dock-chair novel . . . the book has local buzz galore." —*National Post*

Praise for *Old City Hall*

"Loved it! Rotenberg's *Old City Hall* is a terrific look at contemporary Toronto." —Ian Rankin

"Breathtaking . . . a tightly woven spiderweb of plot and a rich cast of characters make this a truly gripping read. . . . Robert Rotenberg does for Toronto what Ian Rankin does for Edinburgh." —Jeffery Deaver

ALSO BY ROBERT ROTENBERG

Old City Hall

The Guilty Plea

STRAY

BULLETS

ROBERT ROTENBERG

A TOUCHSTONE BOOK
PUBLISHED BY SIMON & SCHUSTER
NEW YORK   LONDON   TORONTO   SYDNEY   NEW DELHI

Touchstone
A Division of Simon & Schuster, Inc.
1230 Avenue of the Americas
New York, NY 10020

This Touchstone export edition May 2012

TOUCHSTONE and colophon are registered trademarks of Simon & Schuster, Inc.

For information about special discounts for bulk purchases, please contact Simon & Schuster Special Sales at 1-800-268-3216 or CustomerService@simonandschuster.ca.

Manufactured in the United States of America

10   9   8   7   6   5   4   3   2   1

ISBN 978-1-4516-4235-3
ISBN 978-1-4516-4238-4 (ebook)

For my three children,
Peter, Ethan, and Helen,
who mean everything to me

Where are the vile beginners of this fray?

—William Shakespeare, *Romeo and Juliet*, III, 1

PART ONE

NOVEMBER

It was bad enough working in the kitchen of a doughnut shop for mini-mum wage, but having to wear a hairnet was even worse. Especially since the Tim Hortons uniform they made Jose Sanchez wear was at least a full size too big. Made him look ridiculous. Made it hard to talk to Suzanne, the pretty young server who worked out front. Not that it mattered. She had a boyfriend, a punk named Jet. And why would she be interested in an illegal immigrant to Canada whose real name wasn't Jose Sanchez but Dragomir Ozera. And who wasn't a chef from Portugal, as he'd told his employer, but was a Romanian linguistics student with a warrant out for his arrest. Fucking hairnet.

Suzanne and Ozera liked to hang out together on their breaks. He'd sneak her a doughnut from the baking tray, she'd snag him a coffee, and they'd head out back for a smoke. This afternoon it was almost five o'clock, and the mid-November sky was already losing its light. Suzanne was sitting in their usual spot on one of the overturned milk crates with a pack of Players in her hand. He bent down to take a ciga-rette, and it took three tries to light the bloody thing. The wind was strong and chilling.

He stood up, took a deep puff, and exhaled into the scant light. Then he saw it.

"Shit," he said.

"What?" she asked, looking around.

"It's snowing. I can't believe it."

Six years ago, when Ozera first arrived in Toronto from Romania, he was excited about the idea of experiencing a real Canadian winter. But now all he could think was, November fourteenth. December four-teenth. January fourteenth. February fourteenth. March fourteenth. Somehow he had to get through another four months of ice and snow.

"I guess winters aren't like this in Portugal," she said.

"I never saw snow once before I came here," he said.

Of course he'd been born in the mountains of Romania and was in fact an excellent skier. These days he was having fun pretending to be Portuguese and had even grown sideburns to fit the part. At his last job he was Argentinean, complete with a long twisty mustache. Luckily, his facial hair grew real fast.

She handed him the coffee and he took a sip. He winced. At Timmy's they served something called a "double-double." Watery coffee with two creams and two sugars. He didn't have the heart to tell her how horrid it tasted. Who in the world would put cream in anything you'd want to drink? he thought as he struggled to keep the coffee down.

She reached for his cigarette and took a long drag. Her shift was over. She was waiting for Jet, who always picked her up at five in his big, old Cadillac. Guy was never late. She seemed fidgety.

"What's up?" he asked.

"It's my ex, Dewey. Got out of jail three days ago, and I hear he's looking for me." She twirled her long, curly hair between her fingers.

"Jail?"

She returned the smoke, and Ozera took a puff.

"He just finished three years for a drugstore robbery. I took the bus out to Kingston every third weekend for eighteen months." She rolled up the sleeve on her right arm to show him a tattoo on the underside. It read: "DeWEy." A red heart was drawn over top of the "WE."

He offered her back the cigarette, and she grabbed it.

"I couldn't take it anymore. Those stupid trailer visits made me feel like a sex slave. And he was calling me collect every night. Cost a fortune." She exhaled a line of smoke that danced in the wind. "Dewey's a jealous asshole, and he's smart. He already knows I work here, my shift, everything. And he hates Jet. We all grew up in this little place called Pelee Island."

The name of so many things in this country ended in the "ee" sound, Ozera thought. Timmy's. Harvey's, a hamburger chain that competed with Wendy's. Hockey. The manager of the Toronto Maple Leafs was named Burke, but everyone referred to him as Burkee. Now there was Dewey.

"What's he look like?"

They shared the smoke as she described her former boyfriend. Real short. Spiky red hair and a squished-in face. Scary dark eyes. Usually hung out with his buddy Larkin, who was a foot taller and had long hair all the way down to his ass.

"I'll keep my eyes open for them." He butted the cigarette on the curb and headed back inside. In the kitchen, two fresh racks of cinnamon crullers were ready. He pulled them from the oven and headed out front.

Dewey and Larkin must have come in while Ozera was outside with Suzanne because he saw the two guys she'd just described to him right away. They were sitting by the door. Larkin, the one with the long hair, was chatting up some black girls at the next table. Dewey, short and red haired, stared out through the front windows at the dimly lit parking lot. He wore a blue-and-white striped British football scarf around his neck and was rubbing the tassels at the end between his fingers.

The place was busy. Line-ups at both cash registers. Off to the side, the shift boss was dealing with some Chinese customers who didn't speak English. He was trying to explain to them that the owners, Mr. and Mrs. Yuen, weren't in today.

Nobody noticed Ozera. He looked through the front windows into the parking lot and saw a pair of headlights approach as Jet's Cadillac drove in.

Dewey was watching it too. Ozera saw him tap Larkin on the elbow, say something to him, point out the window, and jerk his head in that direction.

Ozera dropped the cinnamon crullers on the counter and rushed out back. He opened the door and looked around. No one was there.

"Suzanne," he yelled.

No answer.

"Suzanne, Dewey's here with his friend."

Silence.

He closed his eyes. *Be smart, Dragomir, and stay out of this,* Ozera told himself. The last thing he needed was more trouble.

Back home, after he'd graduated from university in Bucharest, there'd been absolutely no work. He was the oldest of five kids, and his mother was alone. His father had left long before. Ozera joined the Romanian International Football Team, a fake team that had never played a game of football—or soccer, as they called it in North America—and was a perfect way for twenty men to sneak into Canada. At the time Toronto was booming, and there were tons of construction jobs, even for a linguistics student who'd never picked up a hammer in his life.

Things were fine until the recession hit. Overnight the work dried up. He scratched out a few jobs, and then he got stupid. Got caught stealing some food. It wasn't something romantic as in *Les Misérables* when the guy stole a loaf of bread to feed his family. He'd hidden some imported French brie, lovely-looking goose pâté, and two thin boxes of expensive Belgian crackers in his satchel. That's what you get for trying to impress a girl. The cops released him, and gave him a piece of paper with a date to go get photographed and fingerprinted, and another date to go to court. He never went. Couldn't risk it with immigration.

Ozera turned to head back inside. Out of the corner of his eye he spotted the milk cartons where he'd just been sitting with Suzanne. He thought how nervous she looked smoking her cigarette. Her tattoo, the "WE" and the heart above those two letters. Her ex-boyfriend Dewey staring out the window, tapping his buddy Larkin on the elbow to go outside.

He heard male voices coming from around the side of the building nearest the parking lot. He sighed and closed the door quietly. He tiptoed to the corner and peered around it.

Dewey and Larkin had their backs to him. They were standing in the shadows, beside a row of low bushes that ran all the way along the wall, watching the Cadillac. Ozera took a few silent steps closer.

Out in the corner of the parking lot, Jet was standing beside the front door of his Cadillac. Ozera couldn't see Suzanne anywhere.

A fat man holding the hand of a little boy walked up through the middle of the lot. "Daddy, daddy," the boy said as they walked toward the front door. "It's snowing." The child's sweet voice carried well in the early-evening air.

"First time in your life," the father said. He sounded ecstatic.

Ozera braved a few more steps forward. He could hear Dewey and Larkin talking.

Suddenly Suzanne emerged from the other side of the building, running across the lot behind the father and son, rushing toward Jet.

Ozera looked back at Dewey and Larkin.

Then he saw the gun.

It happened so fast.

Bang. Then *bang*. Then *bang*.

Ozera's ears were ringing from the sound. He couldn't believe what he'd just seen.

For a moment there was this weird silence. Like that space in sound and time after the lightning, before the thunder rattles down on your head. The air filled with an acrid smell.

He jumped back, stepped through the bushes, and slammed his shoulders against the nearest wall.

"Oh God! Help!" the father screamed from near the front door.

Car doors slammed. Wheels squealed.

"What the fuck," Dewey hissed.

"My son!" the father cried out. "He's been hit!"

Jet's Cadillac peeled out of the lot.

Ozera wished he could disappear into the wall behind him. The rough bricks dug into the back of his head and neck. He tried to not even breathe.

He watched Dewey and Larkin in terror. A shot whistled past him and slammed into the wall over his head. He ducked down. Should he run?

"Stash it," he heard Dewey say. "You know where."

"But . . ." Larkin said.

"We got to split up," Dewey said.

Ozera covered his face with his hands. He thought of his mother. Footsteps ran past him. He peeked through his fingers just in time to see Dewey scoot into the back alley.

He breathed. It felt like for the first time in hours. But Larkin was still there. Standing in the same spot by the bushes, with the gun in his hand.

Voices were shouting.

Ozera stopped breathing. He tried not to move. But he couldn't take his eyes off Larkin, and the gun.

Larkin shook his head. Then he turned toward Ozera. There was just enough light for their eyes to meet.

Ozera froze. Please, he prayed, please.

Somewhere in the distance a siren screeched, the sound cutting the air like a piercing arrow.

Still looking at Ozera, Larkin stumbled back and was illuminated by the parking lot lights. He teetered on his feet like a drunk college kid coming out of a bar, then pulled up his shirt and stuffed the weapon down the front of his pants.

Ozera's heart was pounding like a freight train.

"Call 911," someone yelled.

This seemed to jolt Larkin. His head jerked toward the front door, where the father was screaming. Then he bolted, running across the front of the lot out onto the street, his hair trailing behind him like a comet's tail.

Ozera stepped out from his hiding place. Right in front of the door, the fat man knelt down beside his little boy, who was lying motionless on the ground.

"My son! Help!" the man pleaded.

Up the street he heard the siren approaching. *Run,* Dragomir, *run,* he told himself.

A second siren was coming from the other direction.

If he left now, he would lose six days' pay. Plus his fake ID. He'd need to get another name. Whole new identity. Better than getting caught. Better than Dewey and Larkin finding out who he was. He pulled off his name tag with "Jose" on it and stuffed it into his pocket. The snow was starting to really come down. A frozen shiver skittered through his whole body.

His head felt itchy. What was it? Oh, he remembered, the damn hairnet. He ripped the stupid thing off his head, threw it into the bushes, and ran toward the clustering darkness.

2

Location, location, location.

Where to meet an ex-lover whom you hadn't seen or even spoken to for a couple of months? Homicide detective Ari Greene had been forced to ask himself this question a few hours before, when he got a call on his cell phone from Jennifer Raglan.

"Hi," was all she said.

"Long time no talk," he said.

"Ari, I need to see you today."

Raglan was married, with three kids. A year before she'd separated from her husband and soon after that started seeing Greene. She was a Crown Attorney, he was a cop, so they'd made sure to keep their affair secret. Things lasted a few months until she'd cut it off and gone back home.

"What's wrong?" he asked.

"Better if we talk."

"Let's have a coffee," he said. "How about the city hall cafeteria? I'm in court until four thirty. Meet me at about ten to five."

Lots of lawyers, cops, and judges met up in the cafeteria at the end of the day and since Raglan and Greene had done a number of cases together, meeting there would seem normal. Besides, Greene didn't like fancy restaurants. Best to hide in plain sight.

He arrived at quarter to five, and the place was busy. He got a tea and found a booth in the corner that would offer them a modicum of privacy.

"Nice to see you, detective," Raglan said a few minutes later when she walked over to him. She had hot coffee in one hand and extended the other toward him.

He stood and shook it. She held on for a few extra seconds.

"Nice to see you too." He felt like an actor on the first day of rehearsal of a new play, reciting lines he didn't have a handle on yet.

"How's work?" she asked as they sat across from each other.

He pulled the special-issue beeper off his belt, the one used

exclusively for emergency homicide calls, and plopped it on the For-
mica table. "I'm back on the top of the batting order," he said.

"Never ends, does it?" She blew steam off the top of her mug in his
direction.

"Keeps us both employed." He took a sip of his tea, which had
cooled down. "How're the kids?"

She filled him in on family matters. Her oldest son had quit hockey
and was spending most of his time in his room playing bass guitar
and doing God knows what else. The middle boy had been picked to
be the team goalie, and the equipment cost a fortune. Her daughter
wanted to go to camp again next summer. That would mean another
three thousand dollars.

"How's your dad?" she asked.

"Dating." Greene's mother had died two years earlier, after a seven-
year fight with Alzheimer's, and his eighty-six-year-old father was making the most of his remaining time. "No Jewish woman over the age of
seventy-five who lives within a mile of Bathurst Street is safe."

She laughed. A real laugh, one that he liked a lot.

"I'd love to meet him one day." She stared right at him. Raglan always said her eyes were nothing special. Called them "boring brown."
He didn't think they were boring at all.

"He'd like you," Greene said.

She blushed. Neither of them spoke. She'd called the meeting, and
he was a good enough detective to wait her out.

Raglan reached out her hand, the one closest to the wall, and
touched his arm. "My mother's sick," she said.

He knew that her mom had been a widow for many years. She lived
in the house where Raglan was born in Welland, a small town about
two hours away. Raglan, like Greene, was an only child.

He intertwined his fingers in hers. "How serious is it?"

"Very. Throat cancer. She never smoked a day in her life."

"Damn. When did you find out?"

"Four and a half weeks ago, the day after her birthday. She waited to
tell me. She's only sixty-seven."

He looked back at Raglan's brown eyes. She was tough. This was
the first time he'd ever seen her tear up.

"Ari, I keep trying not to call you. Not to see you." She tightened
her grip on his fingers. "But it's just so . . ."

The beeper started to buzz. A loud, distinctive yelp. It bounced on
the table like a Mexican jumping bean.

Their fingers flew apart.

He clapped his other hand on the beeper. Didn't move to look down at it.

She covered his hand with the beeper in it. "You have to answer it," she said.

"We have to talk," he said back.

The beeper was shrieking.

"Ari." She pushed his hand toward him.

"I know." He tore his eyes from her and read the urgent message in his hand.

3

"All available officers in Quadrant D. Sound of gunshots in the area of Elm Street and University Avenue, at or near the Tim Hortons on Elm."

It was a "hot shot." An extra-loud emergency call that blasted through Officer Daniel Kennicott's police radio, overriding everything else. It meant a major crime was in progress: drop everything and go.

Kennicott started running full out. He unclipped the radio from his hip.

"PC Kennicott. Badge 8064, D Post," he shouted. "Corner of University and Armoury, heading north. About thirty seconds away."

"You'll be first officer on scene," the dispatcher said. "Be careful."

University Avenue was a European-style boulevard, the widest street in the downtown core. On a Monday night, the sidewalk was packed with office workers streaming to the subway. A cold wind was blowing through the city, bringing with it the first snow of the season and covering the rain-soaked sidewalks with a sleek layer of ice. He bobbed and weaved through the crowd, careful of his footing, like a halfback racing toward the goal line.

"Child hit by bullet," the dispatcher said. Her dispassionate voice was a strange counterpoint to the terrible news. "One suspect seen fleeing on foot. Backup and ambulance on the way."

Kennicott got to Elm Street and cut to his left. "Almost there," he said.

"Second suspect not accounted for," the dispatcher said.

"Ten-four." He unhooked the top of his leather gun holster. His feet slapped against the pavement, making a loud pounding sound. He could feel his heartbeat accelerate. Despite the descending darkness, his vision seemed almost supernaturally clear. A few more strides and the doughnut shop came into view.

In his four years on the force, he had got two other hot shots. Both had been relatively static domestic situations—a wife stabbed to death in a bathtub, a husband dead on his kitchen floor. But this was gunplay right in the middle of the city. People all around. The shooters on the loose.

He was a good runner. It came from years of competing in marathons while he was at law school, bored to tears by the endless books. That was one of the things he liked about being a cop. The job could throw anything at you at any time. He pulled out his gun.

Then he slipped on the ice, tumbled to the ground. Shit, he thought, yanking himself back up. Thank God I still have the safety on. He rushed down the sidewalk.

The Tim Hortons was located on a long rectangular lot, tucked in between two tall office towers. The front half was a parking lot, which extended all the way to the back on the right-hand side. The doughnut shop was located in the back left corner, the light pouring out into the darkness from its glass-fronted windows.

He tried to take in the scene all at once. People were rushing out, dispersing into the night. A few stood outside near the doorway, screaming at 911 on their cell phones. On the ground in front of them, a large man was bent over a young boy. Somewhere over the din he heard a siren. Then another. Please, let one of them be an ambulance.

He stopped running and made himself walk toward the child. The wind was fierce. His gun felt hard and cold. He held it in front of him, pointed downward. His head swiveled back and forth, looking for signs of danger. The missing second suspect.

"Sir, Toronto police," he said when he got to the man beside the child.

"My son is hardly breathing," the man said.

He holstered his gun and knelt down. "Ambulance is on the way." He felt the side of the little boy's neck. The pulse was faint. He searched the body for an entry wound where he could apply pressure to stanch the bleeding.

"It's his head," the father said.

In the light from the doughnut shop he saw a tiny red mark behind the left ear. My God, he thought.

He listened for the sirens. Willing them to get louder. Closer.

There was something in the child's hand. A toy cell phone, still in its plastic wrapper.

At last the sirens were behind him. He turned. The low revolving lights of the ambulance shrieked down Elm Street. Right behind raced two television news trucks, their huge antennae rising in the air as they pulled up.

A crush of people had started to gather around. Reporters appeared out of nowhere and started taking pictures. Crowding in.

He jumped up, grabbed the flashlight off his belt, and waved it at them like a madman. "Toronto police! Toronto police! Everyone out of the way!" he hollered at the top of his lungs. "Everyone out of the way!"

It took a few more seconds for the ambulance to pull in. The *whoop, whoop* of its siren bounced off the office buildings on both sides of the lot, the echoing making the sound louder, more urgent. Two attendants got out. Shut their doors. Looked around. It seemed to take forever for them to start walking toward the boy. Why the hell didn't ambulance drivers ever run? It felt like hours.

But it was enough time for him to catch his breath and think. He was the first cop on the scene. Step one: save life. He'd done all he could on that score. Step two: capture any suspects. Nothing more he could do about that right now. Step three: preserve the evidence.

He knew that months from now, in a staid downtown courtroom, everything he did in these first crucial seconds would be subject to microscopic examination. Critiqued down to the last detail.

Behind him, a little boy was fighting for his life. In front, people were drifting away in all directions. Trampling on evidence. Disappearing as witnesses. He was alone, and the tide was rushing out. He started to move.

4

"I'll call you when I can," was all Ari Greene had time to say to Jennifer Raglan before he jumped out of his seat at the city hall cafeteria and headed outside into the freshly falling snow. He thought about rushing over to his car but decided it was faster on foot.

Homicide detectives often bragged about how they always walked, never ran. But, despite the slippery sidewalks that had turned to sheer ice as the temperature dropped, he ran. Across the plaza in front of the new city hall, under the arch at the side of the high court—where this case was sure to end up—through the rush-hour traffic on University Avenue, and down Elm Street to the Tim Hortons.

Three squad cars were there already. Two constables were stringing up police tape across the front of the parking lot. Other officers were talking to witnesses. Four television trucks had pulled up, their long antennae high in the darkening sky, like metallic giraffes looking down on the chaotic scene. Hordes of people were farther back on the street, keen for a view, talking on their cell phones.

Greene flashed his badge at the officers with the police tape.

"String it wider, much wider, I want an outer perimeter," he said. "Cover the whole street and buildings on both sides. I want everyone and everything moved back. Police cruisers, TV trucks. Now."

"Yes, sir," both the cops said in unison.

Greene ducked under the tape. He'd spotted a cop he knew, Daniel Kennicott, who looked as if he was in charge.

"Hi, detective," Kennicott said as Greene approached him.

"When did you get here?"

"I was the first officer on scene," Kennicott said. "The ambulance left about two minutes ago with his father. They're going to Mount Sinai up the street. Mother is there, having complications with her pregnancy."

"The boy?"

"I got a faint pulse. He's four years old."

"You find the entry wound?"

Kennicott pointed just behind his left ear. Didn't say anything.

"You get the boy's name?" Greene asked.

"Kyle. Kyle Wilkinson. Father's name is Cedric. He says the family just moved up to Canada a few months ago from California. I've detailed all the officers here to round up every possible witness. More squad cars are on the way."

The snow was coming down, thick and heavy. Greene felt the cold for the first time. "Good. We'll need to get a mobile police unit here fast so we can interview people."

"I ordered it. Should be here in ten."

"What about protection for the family at the hospital?"

"I've got two officers there already. I used my cell when I called it in to the dispatcher so the press wouldn't pick it up on the police radio."

"Okay. Make sure the cops there understand that no one gets in but me."

"Will do."

"What about the forensic officers?"

Kennicott pointed back to the street, where the two cops with the tape were moving people and cars back. "Look who just arrived."

Greene saw a tall Asian man in jeans and running shoes, with two backpacks slung over his right shoulder, approach the tape. The man looked like a cross between a street person and a graduate student. When the cops tried to stop him, he flashed his wallet at them. One of them lifted the tape and he marched right up to Greene and Kennicott, his hand extended for a handshake.

Officer Harry Ho was smart, thorough, and dedicated. For Greene, there was only one drawback to working with him. Ho was a nonstop talker, eager to impress everyone with the breadth of his arcane knowledge and the wryness of his dark humor.

They'd worked together on cases for more than a decade, but Greene had never seen an expression on Ho's face like the one he saw now. Lips pulled tight. Body stiff. All color drained from face. His quick eyes scanned everywhere.

"Hi, Harry," Greene said, shaking hands.

Ho grasped his hand hard. Did the same with Kennicott. He didn't say a word.

In the five years Greene had been a homicide detective and the twenty he'd been a cop, he'd never worked on a child murder. His colleagues had warned him that there was nothing like it. That the cases always ripped a piece out of you. That it was one of those things in life you just had to live through. Or try to live through.

"The ambulance just left," he said. "Kennicott was the first officer on scene. The boy had a faint pulse."

Ho was staring at the ground. Examining every inch of concrete. He got down on his knees to get a closer look. "I heard," he said.

Some light was coming from inside the doughnut shop and the outdoor parking lot lights were on. But it wasn't bright enough. There were still too many dark corners. "We need more lights," Greene said.

Ho snapped his head up. "Get everyone and everything out of here as fast as you can. I need ten, no, twenty portable klieg lights. Canopies to keep this snow out."

"Done." Greene looked at Kennicott, who nodded.

"My team is going to scour every inch of this scene on our hands and knees," Ho said. "Every damn inch."

Yes, Greene thought. Every damn inch.

5

" . . . *is known to police and considered armed and dangerous. The four-year-old boy was downtown with his father, walking into a Tim Hortons to get a doughnut when gunshots erupted . . .*"

Click.

"Fuck that noise."

Nancy Parish snapped off the clock radio by her bedside and lay back on a pile of feather pillows. She turned to the other side of her queen-size bed. The empty side. This talking to herself was a habit she had to break, she thought, running a hand through her thick brown hair. She yawned. Then she smiled. Tomorrow morning she wouldn't wake up alone. At last, after three months, there'd be a man in her bed. Not a moment too soon.

She threw back the covers. Fresh clothes hung on the exercise bike she'd bought four years before, the day her divorce settlement came through. It now had a permanent home in the bay window, where most days she used it to dry off her bras and panties. She hadn't pedaled the stupid thing for two years. On the floor beside it, a black wallet with her airplane ticket and passport was stacked atop of a pile of *New Yorker* magazines. Beside them was a sketch pad and a plastic pencil case, with an old color photo of Niagara Falls on the cover. She'd had it since grade six.

Parish reached for her BlackBerry. There were nine calls from the same number starting at four in the morning. In the cab on the way to the airport she'd call her partner, Ted DiPaulo, and he'd deal with them. Thank God for Ted. It was almost impossible for a criminal lawyer to get away. The phone calls and e-mails, faxes and letters never stopped. But to hell with it, seven days on the beach in Mexico with Karl, the guy from Cleveland she met three months before in the Dominican Republic. Boy oh boy.

Downstairs on the kitchen counter, the message button on the phone said six calls had come in overnight. She'd told her best friend, Zelda, who usually phoned about five times a day, not to call on pain of death. It must be a client.

"Not my problem," she said, filling the kettle with hot water from the tap. Zelda always bugged her to use cold water to make coffee, but who had the time? "I'm off duty."

Late last night when she'd left the office, DiPaulo had made her swear she wouldn't answer the phone or check her voice mail. It felt great to watch that light blink, on and off, on and off, and ignore it. As a backup, they'd set up an emergency system. If DiPaulo really needed to get hold of her, he'd call her cell. It had a special ring tone—the Mexican hat dance—just for him.

"Da da, da da, la da da, la da da. Da da da, la da da, la da da," she sang to herself as she danced around the kitchen and yanked open the fridge. The kettle began to churn, adding a backbeat to her singing.

"Mex . . . i . . . co, here I come." She pranced to the front door. There was just a hint of light in the dark morning sky. The first snow of the season had blown in last night, leaving a white layer on everything except the newspaper perched on the front steps of her semidetached house. It was wrapped in a blue plastic bag. She slid it under her arm, waltzed back to the kitchen, and tossed a handful of coffee beans into the grinder.

"Grrrr," she sang along with the chopping sound, her mind drifting to thoughts of Karl. Karl hugging and kissing her at the airport. Karl in a bathing suit. Afternoon siestas with Karl. "I love you, Nancy," Karl had said their last night together. Karl, Karl, Karl. "Mmmm, mmmm, mmmm . . ."

She scooped the coffee grounds into the French press pot, poured in the boiled water, and burst out laughing. A whole week of sun, sand, and sex. Get out of Toronto in November, the darkest damn month.

The instruction booklet said you were supposed to let the coffee sit for five minutes, but fuck it. She palmed the plunger down, poured out a nice hot cup, and sat at her narrow kitchen table. She pulled the paper out of the bag and was about to take her first sip when the phone on the counter rang.

"No, no, no." She wagged her finger at it, like an angry grandma in some fairy tale. "I'm out of here."

Her cell rang, playing the Mexican hat dance.

"Shit." She stared at the newspaper as she answered her partner's call. "Ted?"

"Did you talk to him?" DiPaulo didn't even say hello. Not his usual polite style.

The front page was dominated by a mug shot of a young man with

a screaming headline on top: ARMED AND DANGEROUS—FULL POLICE
MANHUNT FOR SUSPECT IN TIM HORTONS BOY KILLING. Staring back
at her was the face of Larkin St. Clair, her client for the last ten years,
since he was twelve years old, when he'd started his life of crime by
stealing from *Toronto Sun* newspaper boxes.

"No, Ted, I . . ." Parish was reading frantically now. "Wait."

She lunged across the kitchen for the home phone.

"Nancy Parish," she said, breathless, her lawyer's way of answering
the phone clicking in automatically.

"Where the fuck you been?"

It was St. Clair. He never introduced himself. No need. She often
joked that she'd known him longer than any other man in her life, including her ex-husband.

"I just saw the paper." She was carrying on the unspoken code—
never use a client's name on the phone when he's on the run.

"Fuck, man, I've been calling and calling—"

"I didn't know it was you." She started to pace.

"This time, I'll turn myself in." He sounded shaky.

"Good."

"Meet me where we were going to have that beer," he said. "Just
you."

That beer. For years, as he had careened from halfway houses to
juvenile jails to provincial institutions to federal penitentiaries, they'd
had an ongoing mythical conversation. How one summer night the
two of them would go to a restaurant on the Danforth, around the
corner from her house, sit on the outdoor patio, St. Clair no longer in
jail, finally off parole so he didn't have to piss into a cup twice a week.

Of course it never happened. But they had the restaurant all picked
out. Information that no one else would know.

"I'm leaving on holiday in half an hour," she said. Out the back window a swirl of fresh snow was coming down against the dull gray sky.
"My partner Ted DiPaulo's—"

"No way, Nancy. Where you going?"

"Mexico."

"Mexico? You don't get it, man. I'm front-page news."

"I can't do it."

"Nancy. Listen. This isn't what it sounds like. I need you."

"The cab's going to be here soon." She eyed the packed bag in the
front hall that she'd carried downstairs last night.

"Then I'm gone," he said. "No way I'm going into the cops with anyone else."

"I haven't had a holiday in—"

"Fuck it."

"But Ted's . . ." She looked back at the newspaper. Beside the mug shot of St. Clair was a color photo of a young couple with a beautiful dark-haired boy.

"I'll disappear, man."

"He's a former Crown Attorney and—"

"They won't find me for a hundred fuckin' years."

Her eyes went to the father in the photo, a fat man with jowly cheeks. His eyes were soft and sparkling.

"Nancy, what's going on?" she heard a distant voice say. Who was talking to her? Then she realized Ted DiPaulo was screaming at her through the cell phone in her other hand. She looked over at her cup of coffee, growing cold.

"How long do you need?" she asked St. Clair.

"Half an hour," he said.

"Make it forty-five minutes," she said. St. Clair had never been on time for anything in his life. "I'll drive by our place real slow and pop open the back door behind me. You jump in and keep your goddamn head down."

"I love you, Nancy," St. Clair said before he hung up.

She looked at the home phone in her hand. Then again at the eyes of the little boy's father.

"I love you, Nancy," she said to herself, not quite sure whether or not she'd spoken out loud.

6

Ari Greene should have been tired. It was a quarter to seven and he'd been up all night interviewing witnesses in the big police mobile command unit truck stationed down the block from the Tim Hortons. Twenty-two patrons and passersby had been there when the shots rang out. He'd spoken to them one after another without a break because he wanted to get their recollections down on tape as fast as possible. While their memories were fresh.

But fatigue was the farthest thing from his mind. The case was a giant jigsaw puzzle and he was thinking overtime trying to stitch it together. Most of the witnesses had seen bits of what happened or heard snippets of conversation, and only a handful would be useful at trial. Not one of them had witnessed the actual shooting.

Still, they were consistent enough on key points that a story emerged. At about five o'clock two young men, one short with red hair, the other tall with very long hair, were at a table inside the door of the Tim Hortons. A large car—one witness, a South African businessman who'd been standing across the street, said it was an old Cadillac—pulled into the far corner of the lot. The two men went outside. A woman ran from the opposite corner of the coffee shop across the lot to meet the driver, who had gotten out of his car, and seconds later there were gunshots. Just how many shots wasn't clear. Estimates ranged from as few as three to as many as nine. Greene wasn't surprised by these inconsistencies, which were typical with civilian witnesses. One of the bullets hit a little boy who was walking into the shop with his father. No one saw where the short red-haired guy went, but many saw the tall one with the long hair sprint across the parking lot and run out onto Elm Street.

As Greene's night wore on things had become even clearer. Just after ten, Detective Officer Ho walked into the command unit with the surveillance footage from the doughnut shop. The inside camera caught the two young men seated at a table near the door, drinking coffee. The camera angle was from on top, making it impossible to identify them. The one with the long hair all the way down to his waist was chatting to some girls at the next table. At 5:00:34, according to the counter in the corner of the video, the shorter one tapped his partner on the arm and pointed out the front window toward the parking lot. The two exited at 5:00:58. The first 911 call reporting gunshots came in at 5:03:01, and seconds later, at 5:03:49, the tall guy could be seen rushing into the parking lot. He looked over to the spot where the child had fallen, stuffed something into the front of his pants—it wasn't clear enough to identify as a gun—and ran out onto Elm Street. Just before he took off, he turned and looked right into the camera, which captured his face perfectly.

"Stop it right there," Greene said to Ho, who was playing the video on his laptop. "I recognize that face. Looks like a younger version of Austin St. Clair, who I've arrested six times. He's still in jail on a jury-tampering charge.

"Excellent guess. It's his son." Ho chuckled for the first time all night. He pointed to the screen. "These two young geniuses left their coffee cups on the table. I rushed them up to the lab and the overnight operators lifted two sets of prints."

"You get a match?"

Ho pulled some police reports from his bag. "We got a definitive for Larkin St. Clair, your old pal Austin's only son. Take a look at his latest mug shot."

It was the same guy. "And the short one?" Greene asked.

"Got a partial that's probably Dewey Booth. Wouldn't stand up in court but take a look at their file. These two jerks have a long history of committing crimes together. Last time they robbed a pharmacy late at night. Booth punched a female pharmacist in the face when she hesitated handing over the money. Broke her jaw. He got three years. St. Clair was standing six outside and he only got a year plus probation. Booth just got out of jail four days ago and the next day St. Clair's probation officer reported him as AWOL. He missed his weekly appointment."

Greene called headquarters. The front desk back at Homicide was going crazy fielding calls from the media, who wanted a news update for their morning editions. He dictated a press release with Larkin St. Clair's most recent police photo on it, not the image from the video. He didn't want to reveal that St. Clair was captured on tape. That would lead to questions about whether the police also had pictures of his partner. And right now, he wanted to keep Dewey Booth's name under the radar.

Just after seven in the morning, minutes after he'd finished interviewing his last witness, a call came in on his cell.

"Detective Greene?"

"Yes."

"This is PC Darvesh. I'm one of the officers guarding the Wilkinson family at the hospital."

Greene closed his eyes. "Yes."

"The child. Kyle. He died."

Breathe, Greene told himself, breathe. He wasn't quite sure how long it took him to say, "I'll be there in ten minutes."

The icy walk up the snow-covered street only took a minute or two and when the elevator opened on the ninth floor of the hospital, the sun, which was climbing over the downtown skyline, hit him square in the eyes. He squinted involuntarily.

"Sir, I'm afraid only authorized personnel are allowed on the floor this morning," a young female police officer said, stepping in front of him. She had dark hair, blunt-cut tight to her head. Her face was stern, her eyes tired.

Greene had his badge in his hand, and he flashed it at her.

"Oh," she said. "Sorry, detective."

"Don't be sorry, that's good work." He extended his arm to shake hands. "Ari Greene."

"PC Albright," she said. Her fingers were tense.

"Where's the father?" he asked.

"Room 908. He just told his wife."

"I heard she's pregnant," he said.

"Due in about two weeks. Started bleeding a few days ago. Has had two miscarriages since their first son was born." She spoke in a clipped staccato, like she was reading from a notebook.

"Who's your partner?"

"PC Darvesh. He's outside the room."

"Good," he said. "The press are all over the lobby downstairs. I've got officers covering every elevator and the stairwell. Still they'll try to sneak up here. No matter what, don't let them anywhere near them."

"I won't."

He took a few steps down the hall, then turned back. "Remember, you're not just protecting this family," he told Albright. "Being here, they see people care."

Her tight lips turned up into a wan smile. "Thanks, detective."

The door to room 908 was open. Another young officer, this one a male Sikh wearing a blue turban with a Toronto police insignia squarely in the center, was standing guard, his back to the wall. He glanced at Greene's badge and nodded. From inside the room Greene heard crying, great sobs of shock and sorrow.

The officer gave Greene a firm handshake. "PC Darvesh." He kept his voice low.

"Ari Greene." He stood beside Darvesh.

An old clock hung crookedly on the opposite wall. It was 7:18.

"How long you been here?" Greene was almost whispering.

"Since midnight."

"Tough assignment," Greene said.

"Yes." Darvesh's eyes were straight forward.

Greene folded his arms and concentrated on the sweep of the second hand. He was impressed with PC Darvesh. The man's stillness. Patience. Learning how to wait things out was the toughest thing to teach young cops. He reached into his inside pocket and pulled out a business card.

"Don't go home when you get off shift," he said. "Call me. I might have an assignment for you."

Darvesh took the card and didn't say a word. Greene liked his quiet confidence.

Footsteps approached from inside room 908.

"You must be Detective Greene," a large, rotund man said. He reached out his hand.

Greene shook it. "Hello, Mr. Wilkinson."

"Thanks for watching out for my wife." Wilkinson's eyes were puffy.

"What else can we do?"

Wilkinson shook his head. "What can *I* do?"

Greene looked down at his hands. "I need to take a statement from you as soon as you're ready."

Wilkinson wiped a tear off his big cheek. "Okay."

"There's a lounge down the hallway. It should be empty this early in the morning," Greene said.

The two men walked shoulder to shoulder through the hospital corridor, neither saying a word.

Greene heard a ringing sound.

"Damn cell phone." Wilkinson jammed his hand into his pocket. He turned it off without even pulling it out to look at it.

They continued on in silence. "Do you have any brothers or sisters or relatives who live in Toronto?" Greene asked as they neared the end of the hall.

Wilkinson shook his head. "Head office moved us up here three months ago and we're still getting settled. Both of our families are back in California. Why?"

"We'll worry about it later," Greene said.

"I heard you identified the shooter."

"We've got a suspect," Greene said.

"Someone said there were two guys."

"It's early yet."

Tempting as it was for the police, and frustrating as it was for the victims, telling the family too much at this early stage was a huge mistake. Wilkinson seemed to sense this and changed the topic. "Kyle lived for almost fourteen hours. The doctor said he was a real fighter."

"I heard that."

The lounge was empty. The big man stopped just inside the door and turned to Greene. "You need someone to identify the body. That's why you asked if we had other family here."

"It has to be done," Greene said. "Is there anyone. A neighbor? A nanny? A friend?"

Wilkinson's jaw clamped tight like a vise. "You don't have capital punishment in Canada, do you?"

"No, sir."

"What do these bastards get? A few months at a hobby farm?"

"Twenty-five years for first-degree murder."

Wilkinson slumped down into the chair nearest the door. "My wife is crushed. If you don't catch these guys . . ." He slammed his big fist into his open palm so hard that it sounded like a slap.

7

Driving her nine-year-old Honda along the north side of Danforth Avenue, Nancy Parish slowed to a crawl at the traffic light, which was turning red. The snow from last night still covered the sidewalks. Pappas Grill, the restaurant where she was supposed to pick up Larkin St. Clair, was on the next corner, but there was no sign of him.

She scanned the street.

At this early hour the wide avenue was stirring to life and the round red traffic signal glowed against the brightening sky. The sun cut low on the horizon, speeding through its limited late-autumn trajectory. To her right, a man dressed in a white uniform was shoveling off the space in front of his bakery. To her left, a merchant came out of his all-night fruit market and turned the spotlights off a table of outdoor produce. A group of women joggers dressed in sleek running-wear crossed in front of her car, determined looks on their reddened faces.

I'm pathetic, Parish thought. She'd been so busy trying to get everything tied up at the office so she could get away that she hadn't done any exercise for a week.

But where was St. Clair?

The light turned green, and she accelerated slowly. Fortunately hers was the only car on the road. She was almost at the restaurant and still nothing.

Then she saw a flash of color. St. Clair rushed out from a recessed doorway. She threw the car in park, reached behind her, and cracked open the back door. He ran around the rear of the car and in a second was inside, slamming the rusty door shut behind him.

"Keep your fat head down," she hissed, hitting the gas.

"I'm down," he said. "I'm down."

She'd seen him toss a cigarette butt on the road before he jumped in the car, and he reeked of tobacco. His long hair, which he always wore far down his back, had been hacked off to shoulder length.

"Get under this." She threw a blanket that she'd grabbed on her way out of her house at him.

"I'm covered."

"What the fuck did you do to your hair?"

"I'm on the run, man," he said.

She laughed. "Larkin, you're really lousy at this. You wanted to change your appearance, why didn't you shave it all off?"

"You crazy? Chicks love my hair."

"Glad to see you've got your priorities straight." She checked her rearview mirror. Still no traffic on the road. "We're going to police headquarters."

"Why not fifty-five?"

Fifty-five was the local police division that had been a second home for St. Clair since he'd been twelve.

"The division will just transport you downtown to the homicide bureau. Congratulations. You've made it to the big leagues."

Up ahead, a truck had pulled up outside a Greek butcher, and a man wearing a white apron was hauling out a sheep carcass on his shoulder. She felt thankful that, despite the invasion of high-end coffee shops, designer cookware stores, and white-walled hair salons, Danforth Avenue still had its share of tacky bridal shops, dry cleaners who actually did repairs, and places like this butcher's, with a row of carcasses across its broad front window.

"You'll be fresh meat for the press," she said.

"See that picture of me in the *Sun*? Whole fucking front page."

"Don't sound so proud of yourself." She handed him an envelope. "Take this. The letter inside says you've been informed of your right to remain silent and that you don't wish to make any statements at this time."

"Me talk to the cops?" St. Clair chuckled. He had a deep, engaging laugh. "Not this time, not any fucking time. 'We don't rat, we don't crack,' that's our motto, man."

"Just show it if you need it."

"I'm zipped," he said.

"Ha." She knew St. Clair had a near-pathological need to talk. Befriend everyone. Showcase his larger-than-life personality.

In a few blocks she crossed the bridge across the Don Valley and the city burst into view, the downtown office towers a forest of gleaming glass. The sunshine glistened off a gold-plated building and spangled across her windshield.

"And watch out for the phone. No blabbing to one of your girlfriends the minute you're in jail," she said. "They're going to have you wired for sound. And don't yak to your cell mates."

"Yeah, yeah, yeah," he said. "How's your knee?"

This was classic St. Clair. Just when you wanted to punch him in the face, he turned charming. Knew the right button to push.

"I was back on the ice this week for the first time." Parish was a hockey player and had won a full scholarship in the States for university. She loved to play. Last winter she'd had a major injury, and, Larkin being Larkin, he had caught her at a weak moment and she'd told him about it. Now, whenever the temperature was rising between them, he asked about it just to show how damn much he cared. "Knock it off, Mr. Master Manipulator. I'm not kidding about keeping off the phone."

"Hey, don't tell me how to handle my women."

She was over the bridge now. She slammed on the brakes. Hard. He smashed up against the front seat.

"What the fuck," he yelled.

"Get out of my car." The street was deserted. She clambered out of the driver's seat and yanked open the back door. "Now."

"No one tells me what to do." He threw off the blanket and sat up, his eyes blazing.

"Wrong. I'm telling you. Out. You want to be the Man? Face on the front page? Brag to your girls? Be my guest. I'm not losing a murder trial because my client wants to showboat."

"But—"

"But nothing." She checked the street. Still no one was around. The wind was whipping up through the valley. She pulled the top of her coat tight around her neck. "I'm going to Mexico. You can talk yourself into a first-degree murder conviction all by yourself. Call me in twenty-five years."

He bent his head between his legs and stomped his feet like a child. "Fuck. Fucking fuck, fuck."

"Larkin, out."

"I'll keep my trap shut. I promise."

"Larkin."

"You can't dump me now. I'm your original client."

This was his trump card, and he played it when he really needed her.

On a Monday morning ten years before, St. Clair was in custody for the first time. Parish had just been called to the bar and it was her first day at work at Grill & Partners, a criminal law sweatshop filled to the rafters with young, underpaid, overworked juniors. Alvin Grill, the senior partner, walked into the bull pit—the huge room where six defense lawyers were hemmed in like cattle.

"Who's free to run down to Jarvis Street and interview a kid?"

The other five lawyers were grinding away, with a fistful of trials set for that day.

"I am," she said.

"Lucky you. His name's Larkin St. Clair," Grill said. "I've represented his father for decades. Kid's going to be some lawyer's legal aid ticket for life. Every shark out there will want to get their hooks into him."

That first meeting, St. Clair had sensed right away how green she was. "I've already had three lawyers try to sign me up," he said, looking right at home in jail. "You look like a rookie. How many trials you done?"

She met his eyes. "None. Believe it or not, this is my first day. You're my first client ever."

He was taken aback by her honesty. She could tell he liked it.

"Why should I choose you?" he asked.

"Because I'll work harder than anyone you'll ever meet," she said. "And I'll always tell you the truth."

He hired her, she beat the charges on a technicality, and they'd never looked back through a decade of trials. In every case, they'd either made the best possible plea bargain or won outright. Never lost an actual trial.

Parish looked at him, hunched over in her car. He'd grabbed the blanket and pulled it up to his neck. Her hands were freezing. She couldn't believe it was this cold already, and only the middle of November. Last winter she'd splurged and bought a real nice pair of leather gloves that, inevitably, she promptly lost.

A taxi passed, and more traffic was on the way. She closed the back car door halfway. "Larkin, you've never kept your mouth shut."

"I will, you'll see. So will Dewey."

"Dewey?" St. Clair had met Dewey Booth years before when they were in juvie, the name all the kids had for the young offenders' detention center. St. Clair was sixteen and already about six foot four. Booth was a fifteen-year-old pipsqueak. Hardly five feet. He'd been in jail for a week when St. Clair arrived and hadn't eaten a thing. Everyone was stealing his food. Larkin was enraged. He beat up three or four guys on the range, made sure Dewey got double portions, and their lifelong bond was formed.

"What was Dewey doing there?" she demanded.

"He's like my little brother. One hundred percent rock-solid," he said.

"This just keeps getting worse."

"Anyhow, the cops'll never find him."

"Spare me," she said.

"If they do, he'll keep his mouth shut."

"Yeah, right."

Parish couldn't stand Booth. At least with St. Clair, despite all his bluster, all his lying and half-truths, he had a code. She had never known him to fire a gun or wield a knife. He hated bigots in jail and guys who hit women. Just before his eighteenth birthday, the two of them broke into some rich people's house one weekend when they thought the family was skiing up north. They were surprised to find the nanny's teenage daughter in the basement, studying for her exams. They tied her up and Booth wanted to rape her. The girl's statement to the police made it clear that St. Clair, who loved to brag that he'd never lost a fight, kept his young partner in crime off her.

Over the years, Parish read the statement many times to remind her of why, despite all the trouble he caused her, she remained so loyal to Larkin St. Clair. She knew it by heart:

> *"I was studying chemistry and they came in and tied me up with a rope. The tall one with long hair went out to get some duct tape for my mouth. The short one was real scary. He just went crazy. Panting like a dog. He grabbed my breast and started ripping off my skirt, but the tall one ran back in and pulled him off me. Threw him against the wall. 'You just go nuts, don't you, every fucking time,' he said. 'Don't lay a hand on her again.' He was very angry at his short friend but he smiled at me real nice. Said he was sorry they had to tie me up and told me not to come to court. Said no one would hurt me. I knew he was telling the truth. They left the room and I heard them breaking things all through the house but I never saw them again."*

Parish's coat wasn't heavy enough and her body wasn't accustomed yet to the cold weather. The wind seemed to cut right through her.

St. Clair rubbed the blanket under his chin. His eyes were bloodshot. His badly cut hair was ragged. "How old was the kid who took the bullet?" he asked.

"Four years old," she said.

"My aunt's son Justin is five."

St. Clair had been living with his aunt, Arlene Redmond—the only person in his family without a criminal record—since he'd got out of jail. Did some cooking and gardening for her, babysat her son.

She got into the backseat and shut the car door. It felt good to get out of the cold. He put his head on her shoulder.

"Fuck," he said.

She stared at him.

"Nancy," he said.

"What?"

"You're not going to believe me."

"You lie to me all the time, especially at the beginning of a case."

His always-hyper body didn't move. "For once in my life," he said, "I'm not guilty."

In her head, she didn't want to believe a word St. Clair said. But in her gut—that intangible thing that Parish knew made her a good lawyer—she could feel it was true.

8

Morning was finally coming, and Daniel Kennicott hadn't stopped working for a moment. Yesterday afternoon, when Detective Greene arrived at the Tim Hortons, he had quickly taken charge of the scene. With so many witnesses to deal with, he'd told Kennicott to bring Tim Hortons employees back to police headquarters to interview them.

Kennicott knew Greene assumed they'd all been working behind the counter when the shooting happened and probably didn't have much valuable evidence to give, so he was giving him the assignment more for the experience than anything else.

Goes to show, you never know what you'll find. He'd spent the night following up on what he'd learned and was glad was when Greene finally called.

"Any luck with the employees?" he asked.

"Yes. There's more to the story than we realized," Kennicott said.

"Okay, come on over. You still in uniform?"

"No, I changed."

"Good. The press are crawling all over this place, looking for coppers in police cars. Just walk down, and they probably won't notice."

It was cold out, even though the sun was coming up, but Kennicott was glad to be outside. The fresh air felt good. He counted six television trucks parked across the street from the doughnut shop, nose to nose, like cattle at a trough. Technicians were outside, setting up their cameras and lights.

Overnight a spontaneous shrine of cut flowers and cards of condolence, many of them clearly handmade by children, had burgeoned on the sidewalk and a tentlike police canopy had been erected to protect them from the elements.

Greene must have been watching for him, because when Kennicott approached the big police mobile unit, he walked outside.

"Let's get out of here before the press sees us." He blew warm air into his bare hands.

"I brought you a hot tea, extra-large," Kennicott said. He knew Greene didn't drink coffee.

"Thanks," Greene said, cradling the paper cup. "You hungry?"

"Sure, but—"

"If we're not going to sleep we need to eat," Greene said. "We'll walk and talk. How did you do with the employees?"

"Four staff were working when this happened. Three were serving customers and didn't see anything. Fourth was a baker in back named Jose Sanchez. He didn't stick around."

Greene stopped in his tracks. "He left?"

"Gone." Kennicott had been a cop long enough to know that it was highly unusual for people to not stay to help the police when something horrible like this happened. Especially employees.

"Any idea where he went?"

Kennicott shook his head. "No. I interviewed the owners of the Tim Hortons, a Chinese couple named Yuen. All their employment files were in the office. I got Detective Ho to retrieve them for me. This Jose Sanchez only gave one phone number. A cell."

"And?"

"Line's out of service. One of those cheap throwaway phones like all the drug dealers use. He could have bought it anywhere. Impossible to trace."

"Address?" Green started walking again, east from the hospital down an alley by a parking lot.

"He gave the Waverley Hotel."

"Great." The Waverley was a flophouse that rented rooms out weekly, for cash. "Let me guess, the hotel has no record of a 'Jose Sanchez.'"

"None."

"Does Tim Hortons pay his salary into his bank account?"

"I asked that. He just takes a check."

"Which he cashes at some money mart. Could be anywhere. Jose Sanchez. Sounds like John Doe to me."

"He's probably illegal," Kennicott said.

"And wants nothing to do with the cops. Top priority, we have to find him. You get a description?"

"Thin, dark hair, about five-seven. According to his file he's twenty-five years old. Everyone mentioned he had a small birthmark beside his left eye, about the size of a thumbnail."

"Any of them know him personally?"

"No. They said he was friendly with a server who worked there named Suzanne Howett. Used to go out back and smoke with her all the time."

They headed south on McCaul Street. The air filled with the smell of baking bread. Kennicott felt his stomach churn. An involuntary reflex.

"Where is she?" Greene asked.

"Her shift had ended. She has a boyfriend named Jet. Sounds as if he's the real possessive type. Drives her to work and picks her up every shift, here and at her other job she's got at a gas station. Owns an old Cadillac. One of the staff saw her run across the parking lot to him before the shooting. The car took off as soon as the shots ended."

"You get in touch with her?" Greene asked.

"I checked her out on the police computer first. Twenty-two years old, doesn't have a record, but a few years ago she was charged as an accomplice in a late-night robbery. Allegation was she was the getaway driver. The two young guys who went with her pled guilty, and the charge against her was dropped."

They walked by a long brick building, where the words "Silverstein's Bakery" were written in flowing red script over the first-floor windows. Greene turned at a beat-up orange door with a sign that said AUTHORIZED PERSONNEL ONLY and yanked it open.

"Where we going?" Kennicott asked.

"I thought you were hungry," Greene said.

Inside, they descended a few concrete steps and Greene directed Kennicott to the baking floor, where loaves of bread were cooling on a huge, circular metal rack. The smell of yeast filled his nostrils. Out of the wind, the air was luxuriously warm.

A tall, balding man looked up from his clipboard and smiled when he saw Greene. "Ari, what can I get you?"

"Brian, this is Officer Daniel Kennicott," Greene said.

"You have to work with this guy?" Brian asked, shaking Kennicott's hand.

Kennicott smiled. "Sometimes."

"We're on the Tim Hortons shooting around the corner," Greene said.

"Un-fucking-believable," Brian said. He hauled up a handful of bagels from a deep plastic bin and tossed them into a paper bag. "City's going to rat shit. Take these for the crew, they're hot."

Greene gave him a five-dollar bill.

Brian shook his head, took the bill, and rang up five dollars on the old brown cash register by the wall. Underneath a handwritten sign that said CASH ONLY. He looked at Kennicott. "Only known this guy since we were on the basketball team together in high school. Do you think he'll let me give him a stupid bagel?"

Outside in the wind, they both ate. The bagels let off steam in the cold air.

"Tell me more about this robbery," Greene said. "You have the names of the two co-accused."

Kennicott swallowed down a chunk of fresh dough. "Happened at a pharmacy late at night. I saw the press release you put out a few hours ago. Larkin St. Clair was one of them. The other was named Dewey Booth."

Greene let out a loud whistle. "Booth was almost certainly the other guy there last night, but I'm not releasing his name yet. What did the report have on the getaway car?"

"An old Cadillac. There was a license number. It's registered to a James Eric Trapper."

"Jet," Greene said.

"Pardon me?"

"His first initials, they spell Jet."

"I didn't see that." Damn, Kennicott thought. "He's got a minor record. Mostly fencing stolen goods. One possession-of-a-gun charge. Lives in an apartment in the Beaches with a woman named Rosie Lazar. She had a baby five months ago and he's on the birth certificate as the father."

"Jet's a busy fellow," Greene said. "This means Larkin and Dewey knew Suzanne."

"Especially Dewey. I contacted Kingston Pen, where he spent the last three years, and dragged the records guy out of bed. She visited Mr. Dewey Booth for the first year and a half he was there, then stopped."

Kingston Penitentiary was the oldest and nastiest jail in the country. Kennicott had gone there often to visit clients when he was a lawyer.

"That last visit Dewey beat her up real bad," Kennicott said. "She snuck in some cigarettes for him and apparently he burned the baby finger on her left hand with it."

"He sounds like a lovely young man," Greene said, shaking his head. "So she takes up with Jet. Same old story. Guy goes to prison and some other guy moves in on his girlfriend. First guy is pissed, big-time."

"It's even worse. Jet isn't just some guy. The three of them grew up together on Pelee Island, down in Lake Erie."

They turned onto Elm Street. The TV hosts were getting ready for their live reports at the top of the hour. The men were having their makeup applied, the women were putting on lipstick.

"That would make Dewey even angrier," Greene said. "You should be able to get Suzanne's phone and cell number from the Tim Hortons people. Set up a tap on it."

"I've done it," Kennicott said.

"Anything useful yet?"

"No. Just a lot of 'OMG I can't believe this happened' to a girl who sounds like her best friend."

"Good work," Greene said.

In the five years he'd known Greene, Kennicott could count on one hand the number of times he'd given him a compliment. There was a complicated history between them. They'd met the day after Kennicott's older brother, Michael, was murdered. Greene was the officer in charge of the case and after a year, when it looked to be going nowhere, Kennicott quit his promising legal career to become a cop and help solve the crime. Gradually, Greene had become his unofficial mentor, but the unsolved homicide hung heavy between them.

Officer Ho was waiting for them across the street from the Tim Hortons. Greene gave him a bagel.

"My parents were from Shanghai," he said. "They used to buy bagels on a string and put them over their bicycle handlebars," he said.

"Take the whole bag for everyone out here," Greene said.

"Thanks."

"The little boy didn't make it," Greene said.

"I heard."

"What have you got?"

Ho had hand-drawn a diagram of the lot. A large rectangle divided into four quadrants with the doughnut shop in the back-left quarter and the high-rise buildings on the sides. Exactly as it looked from their vantage point.

"We got four bullet hits. First mark is here." He pointed to a spot on the walkway around the corner from the front door, on the parking lot side. "Direction of the shot is almost straight down, fired from close range."

"How can you tell?" Greene asked.

"The dimensions. It's wider at the top and tapers down. Plus there are burn marks right on the cement. I've sent scrapings off to be analyzed."

"Second bullet?"

Ho pointed to the high-rise building on the side of the lot farthest from the doughnut shop. "There's an indent about twenty feet up. Bullet just missed a window. Angle is on a rise, about sixty degrees."

"Third?" Greene asked.

"The side wall of the Tim's. Behind the spot where that first bullet went into the walkway. This one is also at an angle, rising up."

"And the boy took the last one," Greene said.

Ho looked down at his drawing. "The little boy was almost at the front door."

"Find any shells for comparison?"

Kennicott knew that smart shooters had learned to pick up their shell casings, so they couldn't be traced back to a specific weapon.

"Only recovered one but it was crushed," Ho said.

This was another trick criminals used. Smash the shell and they were no good for a comparison with a gun.

"After the autopsy we'll have the bullet in his brain," Ho said.

There was a grim irony here. Because the boy had died they'd be able to recover the shell and have a much better chance of proving their case. But why would a shooter grab some of his shells and crush others? Unless there was more than one shooter.

"Where was the crushed shell?" Kennicott asked.

Ho pointed to the corner of the lot, farthest from the doughnut shop. "Down there."

"That's where the witnesses put Jet when he picked up Suzanne in his old Cadillac," Greene said.

"Look at this." Ho placed a ruler on his sketch. "If you draw a line from where the shell casing was found to the spot in the wall of the Tim Hortons where the bullet hit, it's straight."

The implication of all this was clear. There'd been one shooter beside the doughnut shop and a second one down at the end of the lot.

Before anyone could say anything Greene's cell phone rang. He pulled it out and looked at it before answering. "Excuse me, this is headquarters," he said.

Kennicott and Ho exchanged glances.

"Greene," he said into his phone. "What have you got? When? Just now. Good. We'll be there in ten minutes. Put him in the video room on the third floor. And whatever you do, don't let him wash his hands."

He hung up and looked Kennicott right in the eye. "Larkin St. Clair just walked into police headquarters."

9

Ralph Armitage was smiling so hard his cheeks hurt. This had happened every morning for the last nine years that he'd awakened next to his wife, Penny Wolchester. She was without a doubt the most beautiful woman he'd ever dated, and he had gone out with plenty of attractive women. That all came to an end on his thirty-fifth birthday, when his four older sisters took him out for dinner and, as they now joked, read him the "Ralphie, it's time to grow up" riot act.

He slid over to the side of their new, eight-thousand-dollar, horsehair-filled organic mattress and silently swung his legs onto the floor. Something stirred behind him, and a moment later he felt the light touch of a hand on his broad back.

"Best day ever," Penny whispered. Her long fingers felt good on his skin.

"Best day ever," he whispered back.

Since their fairy-tale wedding—on a crystal-clear evening in late June, with five hundred people assembled on the back half of the Armitage family estate north of the city, the vast backyard where as a boy Ralph dammed streams, built forts, and found secret hiding places—they'd said the same words to each other every morning upon waking and every night before falling asleep.

Best day, best wife. As usual, everything was perfect in the life of Ralph "Hey, everyone calls me Ralphie" Armitage. His mother and his older sisters all said that he was born grinning and never stopped. He'd spent his summers at the same all-boys camp his father and grandfather had gone to and, like them, had worked his way up to head counselor. In so many ways his life had always been a boyish, endless summer.

Now he had the best job, as the new head Crown Attorney in the sprawling downtown Toronto office, presiding over forty-seven lawyers, the busiest prosecutors in the country. "Crime Central," he called it, keeping his ever-present grin in place through the endless tales of drugs and violence and injury and death.

With his sunny disposition, to say nothing of his six-foot-four athletic frame, impeccable pedigree, and overall savoir faire, he had risen seamlessly through the prosecutorial ranks. Picked to be the youngest head Crown ever, to the outside world it seemed to be the logical next rung on Ralphie's ladder of success.

But this last step hadn't been easy. He'd taken over from Jennifer Raglan, an experienced, hands-on Crown who was immensely popular with the lawyers in the office. Last June, Jennie, as he called her even though she found it annoying, gave up the job for personal reasons: burnout, marriage on the rocks, never getting to see her kids. Blah, blah, blah. He was thrown into the fray during what came to be known in Toronto as "the Summer of the Gun," when the murder rate spiked and he had had to scramble to cover the flood of serious new homicides.

Even worse, he was viewed with suspicion by the other Crowns, in part because he'd never cut his teeth on a long, tough murder trial, a rite of passage he'd managed to avoid. Even when assigned the hardest cases, Ralphie found a compromise, brokered a deal to get a guilty plea, and charmed the toughest defense lawyers with his smiling persona. The upshot was that he'd developed a reputation for being a back-room, not a courtroom, lawyer.

He won the job in part because the government bureaucrats wanted someone who could keep things in line, smooth out the paperwork, stick to a budget. For all of his predecessor's skill in the court and her pizzazz with the staff, Jennie Raglan wasn't a great organizer. Ralph was. This was not surprising given that his father had been taking him to the office to review the balance sheets and employee flowcharts of various Armitage companies and charities since he was thirteen years old.

He kissed Penny on the side of her neck and started to get off the bed. Her fingers caressed the underside of his arm.

"Honey," she said, her voice still sleepy, "you haven't looked at the guest list yet. You keep promising."

He reached for her hand. For the last forty years, the Armitage family had held a massive outdoor charity ball on the Victoria Day holiday, always the third Monday in May. Every Canadian child had pleasant memories of staying up late to watch the big fireworks displays held across the country. Queen Victoria, the English monarch for whom the holiday was named, was born on the twenty-fourth of May, and the three-day weekend was also referred to as the "May Two-Four" long weekend. A "two-four" being slang for the most popular way to buy beer in Canada, in a case holding twenty-four bottles.

"I'm bad," he said.

"Your sisters keep warning me that we must get the invitations out before everyone goes south for the winter. I need to get them designed and printed."

"Today, I promise." He took her hand and gave each finger a kiss.

In the kitchen he poured out his morning glass of fresh-squeezed Whole Foods orange juice, then went to the front door of their downtown condominium to pick up the four local newspapers. His regular routine was to read all the Toronto crime news, and this morning one story had knocked all other news off the front page.

ARMED AND DANGEROUS. FULL POLICE MANHUNT FOR SUSPECT IN TIM HORTONS BOY SHOOTING, said the usually staid *Globe and Mail*. POLICE HUNT FOR TIMMY'S SHOOTING SUSPECT, shouted the populist *Toronto Star*. HAVE YOU SEEN THIS MAN? demanded the aggressive *National Post*. The best was the *Toronto Sun*, the only tabloid in the bunch, most famous perhaps for its front page after the 9/11 attacks, which featured a picture of the burning Twin Towers and one word in huge type: BASTARDS!

Today the *Sun* had outdone itself: LARKIN: WE SEE YOU, its headline blared. The whole front page was dominated by a mug shot of the suspect, Larkin St. Clair, distinctive with his long hair parted down the middle.

Armitage gulped his juice as he stared at the photo. Larkin St. Clair. He remembered those eyes. Years ago he'd worked in youth court—kiddie court as the Crowns all called it—at the 311 Jarvis Street courthouse. He believed that most youth crime was a function of broken homes and a failed education system, and aggressively cut deals that allowed kids to avoid prosecution if they provided heartfelt apologies and did substantial community service.

His strategy worked. The long trial list shrank, and most of the young offenders disappeared from the system. But every once in a while he would come across someone like St. Clair who played him for a fool.

St. Clair's father, Austin St. Clair, was a con artist and a swindler. His mother, a natural-born beauty who'd gone to seed, was a drug addict. Larkin started his life in crime when he was twelve, by stealing from newspaper boxes. Instead of fishing a magnet down the money slot and yanking out a few quarters, as most kids did, he devised a system of cracking open the cash box using a pair of specially modified pliers. Soon, he had ten teenagers working for him. When he was arrested, he had more than a thousand dollars stashed under his pillow, all in loose change.

At fourteen, he started stealing lottery tickets from a series of corner stores and selling them through his team of teens at a 50 percent discount. Fifteen was his year of joyriding, hot-wiring cars, and barreling around the city late at night. That bought him his first stint in juvie, where he hooked up with a short kid named Dewey Booth and the two became an inseparable team. When Larkin was seventeen, his last year as a juvenile, they broke into a mansion in Rosedale, thinking the family was away on vacation. But the teenage daughter of the live-in nanny was in the basement studying. They tied her up and ransacked the place.

The trial had been set for three days, and, for once, Armitage wasn't offering any deals. On the first day the girl didn't show up. He sent out a squad of police cars to find her, but her mother had sent her back to Grenada to live with her grandparents.

He would never forget the smirk on St. Clair's face the day the case collapsed. "Nice try, Mr. A," the asshole muttered as he'd sauntered out of the stuffy second-floor courtroom, his jeans halfway down his thighs. By now, he was well over six feet, and he wore his hair far down his back.

"Larkin." Armitage shook his head when they were in the hallway. "I gave you so many chances."

St. Clair flicked his hair back over his shoulders. "Innocent until proven guilty, man."

Armitage felt a dart of anger race across his skin, grabbed St. Clair, and rammed him against the wall. "There'll be another case. And I won't lose it," he muttered. This was the first and only time in his legal career he lost his cool.

Sitting at his kitchen table, gripping the front page of the *Sun,* staring at Larkin St. Clair's manipulative eyes, Armitage's shoulders stiffened. He started to read the article.

A four-year-old boy walking with his father into a Tim Hortons was hit by a gunshot to the head as slugs flew through the parking lot on Elm Street west of University Avenue late yesterday afternoon. Police believe the child was an innocent victim caught in the middle of a deadly argument. They've issued a warrant for twenty-three-year-old Larkin St. Clair, pictured above, who they say was caught on video and is considered armed and dangerous.

Chief of Police Hap Charlton stated he was "livid at the total disregard for human life." A spokesperson for Mayor Scarlett, who is on holiday with his family in Nashville, echoed the same sentiments and sent his condolences to the little boy's family.

Police haven't said if they are hunting for anyone else. A witness, who only described himself as Vikram, says he saw two young men, one tall with very long hair, one short with red hair, walk outside the doughnut shop together moments before gunfire erupted.

Got you this time, Larkin, Armitage thought. And he was sure the other suspect would be St. Clair's buddy, that little punk Dewey Booth.

Footsteps approached from down the hallway. "Honey, I'm getting in the shower," Penny said.

He turned to see his wife leaning on the door frame. She wore his old tennis club T-shirt, which came to the top of her thighs. Six feet tall, she was a top fitness trainer, and those legs of hers went on forever.

"I'm meeting your sister Rachel at the club to talk about printers for the invitation, then I've got a late class," she said. "I can't wait for our cooking class tomorrow night."

She was talking about their weekly Thursday night date. Right now they were learning to make sushi, or was it sashimi? He always got them mixed up. The first night of their honeymoon, they'd pledged to each other that no matter what was going on at work, they'd never miss one of their evenings together.

"Great," he said.

She rubbed a bare foot up against her calf. "I bought some new herbal body wash," she said.

He drank in her sleepy body. "You don't know how much I wish I could join you," he said.

"So?" She yawned and stretched her arms above her head, lifting the T-shirt higher.

He flicked the newspaper. "A little boy was killed last night during a shooting downtown."

"I just heard about it on the news." She ran both her hands through her cascading hair. "It's horrible."

"It is horrible," he said. "And it's going to be my case."

10

There was an all-night grocery store near police headquarters and Ari Greene took Daniel Kennicott there for a little shopping expedition. He bought two Cokes, a bag of chips and a bag of popcorn, and two blister packs of gum, and at the cash register asked for a plastic bag.

Something was bothering Kennicott about what Greene had done when the phone call came in about St. Clair surrendering himself, but he wasn't sure if he should mention it.

"You're wondering why I didn't have St. Clair's hands bagged right away, aren't you," Greene said when they were back outside in the cold.

"Well, yes." Kennicott felt like he'd read his mind. "Isn't it standard procedure with a suspect in a shooting case to wrap their hands up immediately?"

"Sure is," Greene said.

"So?"

"Instead we're going to give him all this junk food." Greene had a grin on his face for the first time all night.

Up on the third floor in the homicide bureau they found the officer on duty.

"I want you to bring this in to Larkin St. Clair and his lawyer." Greene gave him the bag of goodies. "Make sure the video camera's turned off."

"But, detective, we can tell them it's off and still keep it on," the officer said.

"The camera is off. Is that clear?"

"Yes, sir."

Greene took Kennicott into a quiet back room. "You're going to be my scribe," he said. "Everything will be recorded on video, but I also want you to take notes."

"No problem."

"Do not, I repeat *not,* shake hands with St. Clair."

"Got it."

"When I give you the signal, pick up all the food wrappers and pop cans around his chair. Get a pair of latex gloves and a brown paper bag from the evidence room, and stick them in your back pocket. Tell the camera operator to turn the video on the moment we walk in the room, and I want it off the second we leave." Greene stood up. "I'm going to clean up."

In the men's room, he rolled his sleeves up past his elbows and washed and dried his arms twice. The same with his face. He looked at himself in the mirror, he wasn't sure for how long.

He checked to make sure the washroom was empty before he pulled out his cell phone. "Officer Darvesh, it's Detective Greene," he said when the officer who'd been standing guard at Ms. Wilkinson's hospital room answered the phone.

"Hello, sir."

"You off shift yet?"

"Yes, sir. I'm back at the division."

"Where do you live?"

"Not far. On Gerrard Street. Near Coxwell."

The intersection was right in the heart of Little India, four or five city blocks packed end to end with East Indian restaurants and shops. He wondered if Darvesh lived with his parents. "Go home and put on the most beat-up clothes you have. Old jeans, a sweater with holes in it, a T-shirt, running shoes. The dirtier the better. And get over to headquarters fast. I've got an assignment for you. Undercover."

"Yes, sir. And I'll change out of my police turban. But one small problem." Darvesh's voice had a sarcastic lilt to it. "All my clothes will probably be very clean, and I have no sweaters with holes in them."

The guy's mother must be doing his laundry, Greene thought. "Tell your mom not to worry, she might not hear from you for a while."

"There's no point in saying that," Darvesh said.

"Why not?"

"No matter what I say, she always worries."

Greene laughed. "Just like mine used to."

Beneath his stoic exterior, Darvesh had a good sense of humor, Greene thought. Good. He was going to need it.

Kennicott was waiting for him outside the room where they'd put St. Clair and his lawyer. He opened the door and they went in together.

"Ms. Parish, haven't seen you for a while," Greene said.

Nancy Parish was slouched in one of the two wooden chairs. She popped up and shook his hand. "Morning, detective," she said. Parish had been on a murder trial Greene did last year and was a real pro to deal with.

"Mr. St. Clair." Greene didn't extend a hand to Larkin, who looked as if he'd fallen asleep on his seat.

St. Clair raised his eyes to look at Greene. Instead of his hair coming all the way down his back, as it did in all his recent photos and video from the Tim Hortons parking lot, his long locks had been hacked off at about the shoulder. This was a very stupid move. Now the Crown Attorney would tell the jury that this obvious attempt to change his appearance displayed Larkin St. Clair's consciousness of guilt.

"I'm Detective Ari Greene. This is Officer Kennicott."

Kennicott nodded, staying back.

"Did you get everything you need while you were waiting?" Greene asked Larkin, as courteous as a friendly waiter.

"I guess." He looked at a Coke can and the crumpled-up bag of potato chips on the floor beside his chair. "I've got to piss but they won't let me."

"I want to make sure you know what will happen today." Greene ignored his comment. "Right now I'm going to arrest you. After that Officer Kennicott and I will leave and you can speak with your lawyer. When you're done, two forensic officers will come in and do GSR tests on your hands."

St. Clair twitched and rubbed his hands on his pants. The kid was experienced enough to know that GSR meant gunshot residue.

"They'll take away all your clothes to test them too." Greene pointed up high to the far corner of the room. "I had the camera turned off when you were alone here with your lawyer, but it was put back on a few minutes ago when Officer Kennicott and I came in."

St. Clair stared at Greene.

He looked over to Kennicott and nodded. Kennicott pulled out the gloves and bag from his back pocket and collected St. Clair's Coke can and chip bag.

No one said a word.

Greene looked over at Parish. She was doing her best to keep her face neutral, which was tough to do after seeing her client try to rub his hands clean on his clothes.

Everyone in the room knew that gunshot residue was like thousands of tiny pieces of Velcro. If St. Clair had fired a gun, or even handled one after it had been fired, there'd be traces of it on him. And Greene intended to shake them out.

11

Ralph Armitage's corner office was enormous and he loved it. There was the credenza behind his desk that he'd filled with photos of himself and Penny on their various vacations—skiing at Whistler, scuba-diving in Costa Rica, trekking in Nepal. The law books that lined two whole walls. And the wide windows on the last wall that looked out onto Nathan Phillips Square, the wide-open space in front of city hall named after one of Toronto's most progressive mayors, where right now sleety snow was pelting down.

Best of all was his long and wide desk, the center point of the room, which he kept meticulously clean except for the current file he was working on. This was in stark contrast to his predecessor, Jennie Raglan. Her desk had been a flurry of papers, constantly getting shuffled and lost. She never closed her door, which made her office a Grand Central Station of Crown Attorneys rushing in and out at every moment.

When Armitage took over, he'd tried to establish a less chaotic way of running things. He closed his door and made a point of meeting with lawyers one at a time. He forced them to schedule their appointments and expected them to arrive promptly.

At precisely ten o'clock there was a knock on his door. He slipped the guest list for the party that Penny wanted him to approve into the top drawer. Two pages done, ten to go.

"Albert, come on in." He swung the door open and made way for Albert Fernandez, an ambitious young Crown Attorney whom he'd picked to work with him on the prosecution team.

Fernandez wore a well-tailored suit, and his black shoes were polished to a shine worthy of a four-star general. The guy was a bit stiff, Armitage thought. Maybe because he was born in Chile and came to Canada as a kid. But he was the hardest worker in the office. Was up on all the most recent court decisions. Exactly the type of lawyer he needed on this case.

"I've updated Larkin St. Clair's criminal record," Fernandez said, sitting in one of the two clients' chairs facing the big desk.

Armitage came out and sat beside Fernandez. Albert wasn't a name you could easily make a nickname out of, he thought. All his nick-names ended in the "ee" sound. He tried to imagine calling Fernandez "Fernie," but it just didn't work.

"There's a full page of convictions and another two and a half pages of charges he beat," Fernandez said, passing over the papers.

Armitage looked over St. Clair's criminal history with a practiced eye. Possession of stolen property. Fraud. Joyriding. Theft under five thousand dollars, then later theft over five thousand dollars. The home-invasion case that Armitage had lost was on the last page: mischief and theft over five thousand dollars, robbery, sexual assault— charges withdrawn.

"In about an hour, Detective Greene will have the wiretaps set to go at the East," Fernandez said.

The East was the Toronto East Detention Centre, the jail that would be St. Clair's home for the foreseeable future. Greene wanted everything in place before he arrived. It was incredible how recently charged prisoners couldn't resist yakking their head off on the phone. Even experienced criminals. Drove their defense lawyers to distraction.

"Where's St. Clair now?" Armitage asked.

"Greene's still interviewing him," Fernandez said.

"Perfect. I prosecuted St. Clair when he was in kiddie court. The guy can't keep his trap shut. What else?"

"St. Clair's friend, Dewey Booth." Fernandez handed over a second set of papers. "His record's even longer. Got out of the Kingston Pen four days ago. St. Clair missed his appointment with his probation officer the next day."

"I remember Booth," Armitage said. "He's the quiet one."

"Probation officer says St. Clair was actually doing alright until Booth was back on the street."

"Buddies in crime. Anything put Booth at the scene?"

"Witnesses have St. Clair drinking coffee with a short red-haired guy in the Tim's minutes before the shooting."

"Anyone see him outside?"

"No. And no one sees where he goes after the shooting."

"What about an outdoor video?"

"There is one and St. Clair's on it, but not Booth."

"Too bad," Armitage said.

"Detective Greene said they're looking for him."

Armitage stood and stretched, his long arms well above his head. "Good work, Albert." He had to find a way to loosen Fernandez up if they were going to be stuck together on this trial for the next six months. He checked his watch. "I've got to chuck you out of here in five minutes," he said. "A reporter, Awotwe Amankwah, from the *Star* wants to talk to me."

Fernandez looked at him. "About this case?" he asked.

Most Crowns were terrified of the press and Armitage thought this civil-servant mentality was ridiculous. "No, no, he just wants to discuss the rise in shoplifting as the Christmas season approaches."

"Really?" Fernandez looked relieved.

Did this guy have no sense of humor? "I was kidding," Armitage said. "Of course he wants to talk about the case. There's no other news in the city. The press is going nuts for this story."

"What are you going to tell him?"

Armitage was tempted to say "Members of the Crown's office are upset because this is going to interfere with their Christmas holiday plans," but he didn't want Fernandez to have a heart attack right there. He turned his face serious. "That we're outraged. That this type of crime touches everyone in the city. That we're not going to lose Toronto to gun violence. That we'll work night and day to prosecute those responsible for this horrible crime." As he spoke, his own words sank in with real meaning.

He could see they had an impact on Fernandez too.

"Good," the young Crown said.

"Who's St. Clair's lawyer?" Armitage asked.

"Nancy Parish. She's represented him forever."

"That's right." He remembered her from St. Clair's home-invasion case. When the nanny's daughter didn't show up for court, Parish didn't gloat, as some counsel would have done. Class act.

His phone rang. He popped out of his chair and looked down at the call display on his desk. "Sorry," he said to Fernandez, "I have to take this."

"Go ahead."

"Ralph Armitage." He listened for a few moments and then gave a series of answers: "Yes, sir." "I understand." "I agree." "Believe me, I know." "Yes, I've decided on the prosecutor." "Me." "That's right." "Thanks." Then he hung up.

He turned back to Fernandez. Maybe I could call him Albie, he thought.

"That was the mayor. Before you came in, the premier called too." He lowered his voice. "This is not to leave this room. They both said the same thing: No matter what, no deals for St. Clair. We're going all the way. Get this rat convicted of first-degree murder."

12

"Jesus Christ, Larkin." Nancy Parish was alone again in the room with her client, sitting in the chair beside him. Out of an abundance of caution, she placed him with his back to the camera. Detective Greene had assured her it would be turned off again. Parish knew he was an honest cop who played by the rules and would respect solicitor-client confidentiality. But still.

"What'd I do?" St. Clair asked.

"Rubbed your hands on your pants the moment Greene mentioned the GSR. It's all on tape. Why didn't you just say 'Yeah I fired the gun'?"

Larkin's jaw dropped. He reached back to collect his long hair, a nervous tic of his. But nothing was there. "Damn it," he said.

"We're not going to talk about it now. Not here," she said. "But remember, all you have to do is be near a shooter. Or touch the gun after it's been shot. GSR sticks to everything like crazy glue."

He bent forward and rubbed his hands together between his knees, like Lady Macbeth trying to get rid of the blood, she thought.

"The newspapers say there's a video of you running from the scene, jamming something in the front of your pants," she said.

"It wasn't the gun."

"What was it?"

"A pack of smokes. I swear."

"Great. Where's the gun?"

"I don't know. Honest, I don't."

She knew St. Clair too well. Telling the truth, even to her, never came easily to him. And the more he protested that he was being "honest," the more likely it was that he was lying. She shook her head. "Larkin."

"Don't you believe me?"

"You got one chance. The cops and the Crown are going to be wild to find that gun. You got anything I can use?"

"Use? Use for what?"

"Information. Cut a deal. Right now you're trapped. And Dewey's

God knows where. But trust me, last night while you were having some happy time with one of your girlfriends, he was changing his fucking clothes and taking a long hot shower. Once they find that GSR on you, it's all over."

St. Clair jumped out of the chair and paced around her in a wide circle that gradually narrowed, as if he were a dog looking for a place to lie down. He came to a stop, his back to her. "I don't rat, man, I told you."

"This is murder." She believed Greene when he said the camera was turned off, but still she was whispering. More like hissing, she thought. "Not some stupid break-and-enter. Twenty-five years."

"So what?" St. Clair lowered his voice, echoing her. "Dewey was in the pen for three years. He's connected now. I won't last five days if I rat him out."

"It's your call," she said.

"I just made it."

He sat on the chair across from her. All she could do was stare at him. *I knew he was telling the truth.* That's what the nanny's daughter had said about St. Clair when he saved her from being raped by Dewey Booth.

"Greene's going to interview you," Parish said. "I can't be in the room. He's going to feed you all sorts of reasons to talk to him."

"Such as?"

"Who knows. They have a witness. They already found Dewey and he's ratted you out."

"No fucking way that's going to happen."

Parish squeezed her fists in frustration. "I'm not saying it happened. They're allowed to tell you any fairy tale they want to trick you into talking. Where's that letter I gave you in the car?"

He reached into his back pocket. "Here."

She took it and tossed it on the floor beside his chair.

"Why'd you do that?" he asked.

"Because for the GSR test they're going to bag your hands. You won't be able to reach it."

"Smart."

"Hah. I wish I had some duct tape."

"What, you want to tie me up?"

"No," she said. "Seal your lips. Look, when I say 'nothing' I mean absolutely nothing."

"Fine."

"Okay, practice time. Pretend I'm Greene."

She stood up, went to the door, and walked back to the chair beside him. "Hi, Larkin." She pointed to the camera in the corner. "I turned the video back on, that okay with you?"

"No problem," he said.

Parish smacked him on the arm. Hard.

"What?" he said.

"I said say nothing, that means nada. Zip. Tape it up. Not a word. Got it?"

He bit down on his lip.

"I said: 'Got it?'"

He shook his head.

"Don't even do that. I want you to do nothing."

13

Daniel Kennicott sat beside Ari Greene and watched Larkin St. Clair on a monitor. They'd turn the camera back on once his lawyer had left. He stood on a bedsheet—there to collect any GSR flakes that dropped off his clothes and body—and stripped off his clothes. Two male forensic officers were at his side, and they gave him fresh underwear, an orange jumpsuit, and paper slippers, then put bags over both of his hands and taped them around his wrists.

After Greene and Kennicott were done interviewing St. Clair, the same officers would come back in, remove the bags, and test his hands for GSR. This could have been done before they talked to him, but Greene thought St. Clair would feel more vulnerable with his hands bound up.

The forensic officers packed up their gear and left the room, closing the door behind them. Kennicott got up to go back inside.

Greene didn't budge. "He can wait for a while," he said.

Kennicott sat back down. St. Clair fidgeted like crazy. Shook his head, rocked back and forth, and finally got up and walked in a tight circle. Sometimes he reached back behind his head in search of his shorn-off long hair, the bags over his hands causing him even more frustration.

Greene's eyes were riveted to the screen, and they watched together in silence for about ten minutes.

"Let's go," he said at last. "Take the chair beside him. I'll stand by the door. It will make him think I don't care if he talks or not. Larkin's a kid who needs attention."

Back in the room, Kennicott took the chair beside St. Clair. Greene propped himself against the wall by the door, his legs crossed. Relaxed, like a patient porter waiting for a train.

"You need anything, Mr. St. Clair?" Greene's voice was polite.

St. Clair scowled but didn't say anything.

Greene flicked his head toward Kennicott. "Officer Kennicott's here as my scribe. He'll record everything you say. I've turned the video recorder back on. That okay with you?"

St. Clair clamped his mouth shut.

Kennicott got out his pad and pen.

"We've seen you on the Tim Hortons video." Greene looked down at his fingernails as he spoke.

St. Clair's jaw was so stiff it quivered.

"Picture of you sticking the gun down your pants is clear."

It wasn't, but Kennicott knew trickery like this was commonplace.

"Next we'll have the GSR tests."

St. Clair crossed his arms, burying his covered hands in his armpits. Even under the bulky jumpsuit, his forearms looked big. Prison-gym muscles. "I'm not saying shit."

"And twenty-two eyewitnesses. Including the baker from the Tim Hortons who was standing right behind you," Greene said, his voice a flat monotone. No need to tell St. Clair the witnesses' evidence was all over the map and only five were of any use, or that Jose was missing in action. "The guy saw everything."

"Take a look at that," St. Clair said at last. He kicked his leg out at an envelope that was on the floor. "It's from my lawyer, Nancy Parish. A love letter for you guys telling you I'm not saying shit."

Greene's face showed no emotion. He walked over, picked up the envelope, read the letter, put it back in the envelope, bent down, and replaced it on the floor. He retreated back to his position on the wall by the door. The law was clear. St. Clair could keep silent, but that didn't prevent the cops from questioning him. The key, Kennicott knew, was to keep him talking.

"You sure you don't want anything? Another Coke? Chips?" Greene asked again. He made no mention of the lawyer's letter he'd just read.

"How about you pick my nose?" Larkin held up his bagged hands, like a kid wearing winter mittens. "Want to do it for me?" He laughed.

"We know your buddy Dewey got out of jail four days ago. You didn't show up for your appointment with your probation officer the next day."

St. Clair whipped his head up. Greene had his attention now.

For the first time since he'd come in the room, Greene stared back at St. Clair. He pointed a finger at him and raised his voice. "Just like old times, isn't it. Dewey and Larkin back together."

Kennicott saw St. Clair's body go rigid. Greene's getting to him, he thought.

"You got about five minutes to decide if you want to help us find Booth or not." Greene was back to looking bored. Even checked his watch.

"You read my lawyer's letter. I'm not saying squat."

"Story we've got, Dewey's the shooter," Greene said, as if he hadn't heard what St. Clair had just said. "You're not the gun type."

St. Clair closed his eyes and turned his head skyward, like a blind man searching the air for sound.

"I'm guessing Booth takes a few potshots at Jet, because he's going out with his old girlfriend, passes the gun to you, and takes off," Greene said.

Kennicott knew what Greene was doing. Trying to feed St. Clair a story, with the hopes he'd latch on to it. If he said Booth was the shooter, then, when they arrested Booth, he might put the blame back on St. Clair. When two defendants point at each other, it's known as a cutthroat defense, and it almost always backfired on both parties. A prosecutor's dream, and a defense lawyer's nightmare.

St. Clair was shaking his head hard now. His eyes were still closed. Greene pantomimed a writing gesture with his hand to Kennicott, who nodded and started making notes. He made a point of loudly flipping over a page.

It caught St. Clair's attention. He opened his eyes and stared at Kennicott. "What the fuck you doing?" He pointed up to the camera with one of his bagged hands. "It's all on tape. I told you guys, I'm not saying shit."

Kennicott kept writing.

"You probably owe Dewey a favor," Greene said. "He took the three-year rap for that drugstore thing, and you got just twelve months and probation. Least you could do is hide the gun."

St. Clair started breathing hard. "You got no crap putting me and Dewey together."

"Actually," Greene said, "the manager who was on shift has already picked both of you out of a photo lineup. You two left behind your coffee cups and we printed them. Bad move. Came out clear as day."

Again Greene was stretching the truth.

St. Clair swallowed hard.

"We know Dewey's heading home," Greene said. "I'm sending Officer Kennicott down to Pelee Island."

A smart guess by Greene, Kennicott thought.

St. Clair swiveled to look at Kennicott and laughed, like a schoolkid with the giggles. "Good luck. No one knows the island like Dewey. He's got a million places there to hide."

Kennicott put his head down and wrote.

It took a moment for St. Clair to realize that he'd just confirmed Booth had been with him at the shooting and had gone back home. "Fuckin' cops!" he screeched.

Greene shrugged and reached for the door handle. "Don't worry," he said. "We'll tell your best friend you told us where to find him."

St. Clair bolted to his feet. "I didn't say a goddamn thing. This is all bullcrap. I don't know where the fuck he is."

Kennicott got up to follow Greene out.

"Officer Kennicott will be on the ferry this afternoon," Greene said. "Thanks for the info."

"Shit." St. Clair raised his hands, looked at the bags on them, and in frustration kicked over his chair.

Greene left without turning around.

Kennicott stopped at the door.

St. Clair glared at him. Fury in his eyes. With his back to the camera he mouthed, "You better watch your ass." The words were crystal clear, as if he'd shouted them at the top of his lungs.

"Are you completely out of your crazy-ass criminal mind?" Zelda Petersen, Nancy Parish's best friend, said the moment she walked into the Pravda Vodka Bar and spied Parish seated alone at a table in back. The Pravda, a trendy bar on Wellington Street, was one of the many downtown watering holes that Petersen frequented. When she found out Parish hadn't left town, she insisted they meet here at noon for a drink. Amazingly, for Zelda, she was only twenty minutes late. "You could be getting laid on a beach in Mexico right now."

"Coulda, woulda, shoulda," Parish said. She was already on her third shot of vodka, and her words were slightly slurred.

Petersen tossed her Burberry Prorsum fur-lined aviator jacket, which cost her two thousand dollars at Holt Renfrew, on a stool and revealed what Parish thought of as typical Zelda work wear: an incredibly short black skirt and outrageously patterned stockings, both of which accentuated her ridiculously long legs, and a terrifyingly tight low-cut top that exposed a wide expanse of her La Perla bra. Not your typical outfit for a top tax lawyer at one of the most conservative firms in the country, but Petersen could get away with it. She was one of a handful of people in Canada who knew the Income Tax Act backward and understood equity derivatives, whatever the hell those were, making her exceedingly valuable. "Instead you take the worst possible case on the planet. Defending a child killer."

"*Alleged* child killer." Parish caught the eye of the cute young waiter who'd been serving her.

"What did your boy toy Kenny from Detroit say?" Petersen asked.

"You mean Karl from Cleveland." Parish had some vodka left in one of her shot glasses. She downed it in one gulp. "I finally reached him on his cell about an hour ago. I said I could be there in three or four days, and he said don't bother."

The young waiter was back at the table. Petersen turned on him before he could say a word. "Two more shots for her and four for me. I've got to get caught up."

He smiled and reached down to pick up the glasses. Parish liked his blue eyes, which he was trying real hard to avert from her friend's bulging breasts.

"If you can't get laid, at least you can get hammered," Petersen said when the waiter was barely out of earshot.

The two friends had met fifteen years ago, on their first day of law school. Students were divided into groups in alphabetical order and led on a library tour. Petersen was a farm girl from a small town, Biggar, Saskatchewan. Her husband, Horst, whom she'd met in high school, was back home planting barley and milking the cows. She hadn't been on a subway before coming to Toronto and was the only woman who wore a dress.

Halfway through the tour, Petersen shocked Parish when she whispered in her ear: "Want to split and get a drink?" Their unlikely friendship was formed over a bottle of Grey Goose vodka, which they drank all afternoon sitting on the floor of Petersen's new apartment. She didn't have any furniture, but she had two tall tumblers with logos on them that read NEW YORK IS BIG BUT THIS IS BIGGAR.

"What are you doing with a name like Zelda?" Parish had asked as they worked their way through the bottle.

"Blame my mom," Petersen said. "She was an English teacher who got stuck in a shit-ass prairie town. Named me after Scott Fitzgerald's wife, who, by the way, also loved to drink."

"And who went mad," Parish said.

They laughed the intoxicating laughter of new friendship. Within a week Petersen had a whole new wardrobe, within a month she'd given Horst the heave-ho, and by Christmas break she'd slept with two professors and a couple of the married men in the class. She drank copious amounts of alcohol, stood third in the graduating class, and now at the age of thirty-eight was billing out at seven hundred dollars an hour.

"Did I want a boyfriend in Cleveland anyway?" Parish said, throwing back another shot of vodka. She looked around the bar. Where was that waiter? I mean that cute waiter, she thought.

"Boyfriend, shmoy-friend," Petersen said. "You take on a case like this, you got to be on your game. How can you do that without regular sex?"

Petersen's definition of "regular sex" was at least three times a week. Absolute minimum. She loved to brag that fucking, drinking, and billing were her three favorite activities, in that order. A few years before she'd branched out to women. Said it was like having a second car. And it drove her nuts that since Parish's divorce, Nancy's sex life had been practically nonexistent.

The waiter was back. He was maybe twenty-five, Parish thought. No, probably younger.

"We're going to need two more shots each," Petersen told him. "My best friend's had a tough morning."

"Sure." Mr. Very Cute Waiter smiled.

Parish found herself admiring his butt as he walked away. She tossed back the next drink—what number was that? Fumbling around her six-years-old-and-counting, always overstuffed leather bag, she pulled out her beat-up BlackBerry. "After we talked, Karl, aka Mr. Fuckhead, wrote me an e-mail." She struggled with the scroll button until she found the message, cleared her throat, and read:

11:15 a.m. Nancy, I understand your devotion to your work, and I admire you for it. But I only get three weeks' vacation a year and by the time you get down here the week will almost be over.

"I keep telling you, guys are assholes," Petersen said.

Lately, she'd been trying to convince Parish to switch teams, or just switch-hit. Even offered to set her up with a few women "friends."

"Can you believe it? He writes me a 'Dear Nancy' letter and doesn't even write 'Dear,'" Parish said.

"You're a hopeless romantic," Petersen said.

"I mean how the fuck can I go out with a guy like that?" The vodka was tasting better and better. Good move, Zelda, ordering two more each. It had been a long time since she'd gotten hammered like this. Larkin was being arrested and processed so there was nothing else she could do. And she sure as hell wasn't going to go back to the office when she was supposed to be in Mexico.

She checked her watch. Only about one thirty. Look at all the people in this bar. They know how to go out and have fun. She couldn't remember the last time she'd left the office before nine at night and here it was the middle of the day and the party had already begun. Why the hell did she work so hard anyway?

The very cute young waiter guy with the great bum arrived with four more shots. Or was it a great butt? Bum. Butt. What was the difference anyhow?

"Why don't you take him home?" Petersen asked, watching Parish watch him as he moved on again after delivering the drinks. "Girl, you're going to burn out all those toys I bought you."

Last March, on Parish's thirty-eighth birthday, Petersen had given her a hundred-dollar gift bag of assorted sex toys. It had come from a store called the Red Tent Sisters, which described itself in its brochure as "an independent, pro-woman, pro-sex Toronto boutique and wellness centre."

Parish's cell phone rang. She looked at the display. It was Awotwe Amankwah, her journalist pal at the *Toronto Star*. Nobody, not even Zelda, knew about her friendship with him.

They often did each other favors. She'd be an unnamed source when he needed some inside information for a story about a case and he'd plant something in the press to help her out with a trial.

"Hi, Ted. I'm in a very loud bar and can't talk," she said into the phone. Amankwah would understand that she was using her partner's name as a cover. Her head felt woozy.

"Short and sweet," Amankwah said. "There's a warrant out for Dewey Booth, your client's best friend. Cops have got a very good lead."

The alcohol seemed to drain right out of her. In a second she felt sober as a stone. "Shit."

"Gets worse for your guy. Last month, Dewey had a new lawyer for his parole hearing. Phil Cutter. Guy's a snake. You better watch out."

Cutter and Parish had had a major run-in when he was a Crown Attorney. Now he was a defense lawyer and widely regarded by all as a king-sized asshole. "Thanks." She felt as if she was going to throw up. She couldn't tell if this was because of the alcohol or the news. "See you tomorrow at the office."

"Got another child-killer client?" Petersen asked when Parish hung up. "I'm going to be the last friend you have left before this is over."

"I've got to go," Parish said.

"Great. Next time you're leaving that fucking cell phone at home."

Parish waived Mr. Cutesy Waiter over and insisted on paying the bill. For all her pizzazz, Petersen went through money like water and was constantly, secretly, broke. The waiter processed the bill right in front of them. He angled himself so Petersen couldn't see what he was doing, wrote something on a card, and passed it to Parish with her receipt.

It said: *I'm Brett. Here's my cell number. I'm off shift at eight.*

"I don't know how you go home alone night after night," Petersen said.

Parish sneaked the waiter's card into her back pocket. Bye-bye, Karl from Cleveland; hello, Boy Toy Brett. Petersen was right. This case was about to ramp up another notch, and she was going to need some distraction. To say nothing of the money she'd save on batteries.

15

The downtown bus depot was a place from another time. Steps away from soaring new condos, trendy coffee shops, and high-ceilinged gourmet food stores, it was a remnant of the 1950s Toronto still standing in the spanking downtown core. The tired old building was all gray walls and ceilings, harsh fluorescent light, and the lingering smell of exhaust fumes. Daniel Kennicott took a seat on a hard-backed plastic chair. The place didn't have one redeeming quality, as far as he was concerned.

Most of the passengers looked tired, the staff worn down. The only real signs of life were the pigeons who fluttered about inside, avoiding the mesh netting and spiked ledges designed to keep them out. The sound of tinny rap music drifted in from the sidewalk, where a bejeweled guy was playing a radio at full volume in his illegally parked Camaro, all his windows down despite the cold.

Kennicott, out of uniform, wore jeans, boots, and a windbreaker, with a lightweight bulletproof vest on underneath. He was waiting for the bus down to Kingsville on the north shore of Lake Erie. There he'd get the boat across to Pelee Island and try to catch up with Dewey Booth.

"You could run down there in a police car," Greene told him this morning, handing him a large file of background information on Booth. "But a few more hours won't make a difference. Dollars to doughnuts, he took the bus. Follow in his footsteps." An open-ended assignment such as this was typical of Greene, who always pushed and challenged him.

Kennicott had sent a copy of Booth's picture to every bus and train station, airport, and police service in Ontario. Booth didn't have a passport, but Kennicott alerted the border guards anyway. So far, no one had spotted him. Booth didn't own a car or have a driver's license, but to be sure he sent officers to every car rental place in the city armed with Booth's latest prison photo. No one recognized him.

On the other side of the grimy station windows, his bus pulled into one of the open bays. Toting his knapsack over his shoulder, he headed out the door and joined the line of travelers. The wind whipped through the breezeway and black soot spewed from the rear tailpipe. He found an open seat near the front, and fortunately, no one sat beside him. This made it easier to read through Booth's file, which he settled into once they were on the road.

Dewey Booth's mother had been an eighteen-year-old crack addict, and his father was a nasty piece of work who burned the baby with cigarette butts. When he was three years old, Children's Aid swooped in and he lived in a succession of foster homes, causing more and more trouble as he grew. He had a particular penchant for torturing animals, and left a succession of injured kittens and puppies in his wake. Then, rather miraculously, when he was nine years old a gay couple, Richard Booth and Aubrey Cooper, who ran a bed-and-breakfast on Pelee Island, stepped in and adopted him. In a report that Kennicott found buried deep in the file, one of the social workers characterized this move as a "Last chance, Hail Mary pass."

Booth first showed up on the police radar when he was eleven for smashing pumpkins and throwing eggs at neighbors' windows on Halloween. By the time he was thirteen, he'd already been charged three times. When he was fifteen one of his fathers died swimming offshore when he got caught one night in the undertow. After that his life of crime ramped right up.

At seventeen he was caught slipping out of a high-up window at a youth detention center. Apparently he was a good climber and an even better fighter. He broke the guard's jaw in three places. "Mr. Booth is suspicious of authority and fearful of abandonment," the pre-sentence report for the case said. "His personality features uncontrollable anger and rage." No kidding, Kennicott thought as he flipped through the rest of Booth's sordid story.

The one positive in Booth's life seemed to have been his parents. "Yeah, I had two dads," he told one of the probation officers who prepared yet another report. "Now I've just got Rich. He always takes me in."

Kennicott put the file down and looked out the bus window. Yesterday's sudden snowfall had petered out, replaced by a dull, sleety rain. A hundred miles south and west of Toronto, the bus left behind the last hint of the Canadian Shield, the great glacial rock that covered much of the northern part of the country. Everything had flattened out. Farms and fields dotted the tabletop landscape. The earth was lying fallow, preparing for its winter hibernation.

In the small town of Chatham, he got off to change buses. They were farther south and the weather was turning milder. Even the rain had stopped.

Before the American Civil War, this town had been the northern terminus of the underground railroad and was the "home of Uncle Tom's Cabin Historical Site," according to the brochure he read in the one-room station. A plump woman whose face was set in a permanent scowl sat behind the counter. He showed her his police identification and then Booth's photo.

"You seen him in the last twenty-four hours?" he asked.

"Don't recognize him." She barely glanced at the picture.

"Were you working yesterday?"

"Work every day." She shrugged. "Most of 'em don't even come inside. It's only a ten-minute wait."

He went back outside just as his bus pulled into the parking lot. He was the only one to get on board.

"Where you headed?" the driver asked. He was a chipper man with a big smile.

"Kingsville, then the ferry over to Pelee Island."

"Cold time of year to go island-hopping," the man said. "You should come back in the spring."

He showed the driver his police identification and the photo of Booth. "Recognize him?"

"Yesterday. Morning run. There were four Mexicans going to work at the winery, and him. Surly little kid. Sat in the back with his hood up."

"He say anything to you?"

"Nope. I even drove them all the way to the ferry launch. Not supposed to. The little runt didn't even say thanks."

Sounds like our boy Dewey, Kennicott thought. He took a seat by the window, pulled out his cell phone, and called Detective Greene.

16

Ari Greene timed it so he got back to the Tim Hortons a few minutes before five in the afternoon. He wanted to be there exactly twenty-four hours after yesterday's shooting. Get a sense of the place at the same time of day. And the light. Which was diminishing fast, like a film of a sunrise that was being fast-forwarded .

The parking lot was still cordoned off by police tape. The impromptu memorial shrine had grown exponentially since early that morning. More flowers, more cards. Candles were burning. Some people had written notes in colored chalk on the sidewalk.

Only two television news trucks were left. A steady rain had melted all the snow, but the dampness made the air even colder. The reporters looked miserable. The story was completely dominating the news and Greene knew they were just waiting for a shot of the police taking the tape down for the evening news.

Officer Ho and his forensic team had packed up and gone a few hours before. One cop remained on duty, a squat, Polynesian-looking young man.

Until about fifteen years ago, the Toronto Police Service had a height restriction. New recruits had to be more than five foot eight and weigh one hundred and sixty pounds. It made no sense. Especially since the city attracted an unprecedented number of people from everywhere in the world, including many nationalities that were just plain shorter. Thankfully the rule was dropped, and the formerly all-white face of the police was starting to change.

"I'll be here about half an hour," Greene said after he'd introduced himself to the officer, who was named PC Bambridge. "Then you can take the tape down. I'm sure you're tired."

"Comes with the job," Bambridge answered.

He pointed to the shrine. "Get a squad car here and have them package up all the flowers and cards and candles. I want these carefully preserved for the family."

"Right away."

"I always take one last look around. Important to do before you close a major crime scene."

"I'll remember that, sir."

He went inside the empty doughnut shop and took a seat at the table by the window where the video showed Larkin and St. Clair had sat. He pulled out the twenty-two witness statements, which he'd had transcribed during the day, and read over the most helpful ones carefully. Next he looked at Kennicott's interviews with the Tim Hortons employees on shift at the time. The thing that had bothered him all day was this missing employee, Jose Sanchez. The other staff said he must have left by the back door.

During the day he and Kennicott had run Sanchez's name through the police computer and twenty hits came up. They went through every one and clearly none of them was the guy working in the kitchen here. Immigration was no help; neither was motor vehicle licensing, nor OHIP medical records. Nothing matched. There were thirty-four Jose Sanchezes listed in the phone book and they called them all. Dead end.

I have to find this guy, Greene thought.

He looked at his watch. Exactly five o'clock. He walked outside. Dusk had fallen, softening all the distances. In many ways, this was the hardest time of day to see, even worse than at night, when streetlights took over and created contrast between dark and light.

He walked down to the corner of the lot where Jet had parked his Cadillac and looked back at the spot by the side of the building where there was a chip in the walkway. Booth and St. Clair had stood there in the dark and from Jet's vantage point, it would have been impossible to see them.

Greene clicked on his flashlight and, following the route that Officer Ho had shown with his ruler on his diagram of the scene, walked in a straight line to the chip in the walkway. When he got there he shone it up on the wall behind, following the same line. The bullet mark in the wall was right in the middle of his circle of light. And perfectly in line with the place where Jet's car had been.

Greene tried to picture the scene twenty-four hours ago. The Cadillac pulls into the front corner of the lot and Jet gets out of his car. At the same time, Cedric Wilkinson and his son Kyle walk up from the street through the middle of the lot. When they are steps from the front door Suzanne Howett runs out from the other side of the building, crosses behind the Wilkinsons, and greets Jet. Gunshots pierce the quiet of the night. Young Kyle is hit in the head and goes down. His father starts to scream. Howett jumps in the car and Jet takes off. Larkin St. Clair stumbles out of the dark; stuffs something, almost certainly the gun, down his pants; and takes off across the front of the parking lot toward the street. No one sees Dewey, but the back of the lot leads to an alleyway. Obviously that's where he goes.

Jose, Jose, or whoever you are. Where were you? What did you see? What made you run?

Picture it, he told himself. Try to see it.

If Jose went out the back door before the shooting, maybe he heard Dewey and St. Clair talking. It's dark here. The employees say he and Suzanne used to smoke out back. Officer Ho had found some cigarette butts there.

He lowered his flashlight so the beam was level with the row of bushes that lined the side of the building and walked with care toward the back, like a suspicious night guard in a cheap noir film. Halfway along, something cast a spiderweb-like shadow on the wall. He pulled a pen out of his pocket, reached over, and plucked out a black hairnet.

17

"You're lucky to have such a nice day this late in November," the uniformed woman on the ferry said to Daniel Kennicott. He'd just strolled off the boat, down the ramp to the wharf on Pelee Island. "And it's never as cold over here. You should come back here in the spring."

She was right. The air was noticeably warmer than on the mainland and the clouds had cleared. He'd read that the island was famous for its temperate climate due to the moderating effect of the surrounding lake. One of the reasons it was such a good place to grow wine.

"I first heard about Pelee Island when I was in grade five," he said. "Always wanted to come here."

"Can't get any farther south in the whole country," the woman said.

The big boat held space for a number of vehicles in its hold. When they cleared the parking area, he made his way down the gangplank. He heard squawking sounds when he got on shore. Overhead a flock of Canada geese gained a graceful curve in the blue sky. Outside the perimeter fence, an unmarked police car was waiting for him.

"You know the Hawk Haven Inn Bed-and-Breakfast?" he asked the dark-haired police officer who was driving once they'd introduced themselves. Her name was Françoise Gelante. She had wavy auburn hair and a smile that exposed a row of perfect white teeth.

"It's in the southwest corner. Down the road from the lighthouse." She drove slowly on the narrow road. There was only room for one car, and when a vehicle came at them from the other direction, both of them had to straddle the shoulders to pass.

On the boat ride across, he had bought a little replica of the Pelee Island lighthouse in the gift shop and attached it to his key chain. "Take me close, but I want you to stay back out of sight."

The island was big, more than sixteen square miles, and remarkably flat. Farmers' fields were interspersed with stands of brush and trees, most of which were bare.

"Is this the only police cruiser on the island?" he asked.

"This is it. I like to say on the island there are two cops, one cruiser, and no secrets. I can hardly sneeze here without someone offering me a Kleenex."

"It's pretty."

"You should come back here in the spring."

"So I've been told," he said.

After a few minutes they slowed to a gentle stop.

"Around this bend, it's the fourth place on your right." Gelante raised her cell phone. "I'll wait for your call." They'd traded numbers on the short drive over.

"Thanks." He got out and walked along the narrow paved road. There were traces of smoke in the air. He passed a few houses on his right before he saw the Hawk Haven Inn Bed-and-Breakfast. A beat-up For Sale sign was staked on the lawn. At the top of the driveway, a man with his back to the road was tending a fire of leaves and branches with a metal pitchfork.

"Good morning, sir," Kennicott said, walking uninvited up the stone path. The man turned his head around in alarm. There was a small gold earring in his left ear.

"I'm afraid the inn is closed," the man said.

Kennicott stopped at the edge of the fire. Along with the foliage, a shirt, a pair of pants, a coat, and a long blue-and-white striped piece of cloth were smoldering.

The man tried to scoop some leaves over the clothes. "I said we're closed."

"I'm aware of that, Mr. Booth," Kennicott said.

The man twisted the pitchfork and it fell from his hand. Up close, although Richard Booth was well-groomed, his age showed. Kennicott estimated he was in his late sixties or early seventies.

"My name is Officer Daniel Kennicott. I'm from the Metropolitan Toronto homicide squad." He pointed down at the fire. "I'm looking for your son."

He had thought long and hard about how to phrase this. Saying "I'm looking for Dewey Booth" sounded too official, but just saying "I'm looking for Dewey" was too informal. "Son" seemed to carry with it the weight of responsibility he wanted to convey.

Booth's shoulders slumped. He made no effort to retrieve the pitchfork. "I've been looking for Dewey for so many years." He had the fatigued look that builds up over a lifetime.

"We know he's on the island," Kennicott said, deliberately switching to the plural "we" to emphasize that he wasn't alone. "If I have to call out the emergency task force, it'll be very messy."

Booth refused to meet Kennicott's eyes.

"Dewey was last seen leaving the scene of a shooting, wearing a long blue-and-white English soccer league scarf." Kennicott kicked at the fire and exposed the striped cloth. "Gunshot residue doesn't usually last more than twenty-four hours because of the lead in it. It's so heavy it falls off. But there can be traces. The only way to be sure to eliminate it is to burn your clothes."

Booth bent down for the pitchfork.

"Don't touch that." Kennicott moved in his way. "I have to warn you, Mr. Booth, the charge of accessory after the fact for a first-degree murder charge could get you five years in jail. Easy."

"Aubrey and I tried so hard with the boy. We were getting somewhere, we really were. Then he got swept away in the undertow." Booth covered his face. Kennicott could hear him crying. "The last seven years have been a nightmare."

"I need to find Dewey," Kennicott said.

Booth flicked his head to his left.

Kennicott wasn't sure what he was doing.

"He loves to climb," Booth said. "Can get up on anything."

Kennicott was confused, then it hit him. "The lighthouse. That's the only place to climb here, isn't it?"

"Dewey's favorite spot on earth. Where he could be alone with the sand and the waves and the big lake."

"How far is it?"

"Hundred yards down the road, then you hit the path."

Kennicott took off. He sped past a historic plaque at the end of the road on his way down a wooden walkway, the sky almost invisible now under the overgrown hanging vines and trees. A plague of small airborne bugs hit him in the face. One went down his throat, and he gagged on it as he ran. It was sunset. Bug hour. Just like when he and his brother were kids at the family cottage.

The path turned and in few seconds he was on the beach. An old sign that warned swimmers of the danger of the undertow was attached to a lifesaving station with a long pole and a buoy. The sand was littered with broken shells. To his left the tower came into view, surrounded by rocks and boulders. Dewey Booth, his red hair tossed by the wind, was leaning over the metal railing that ringed the top of the lighthouse. A thick climbing rope hung down, threaded through three round spikes on the way up.

"Who the fuck are you?" he yelled when he spotted Kennicott.

"Toronto police, Homicide," Kennicott said, not wanting to get too close in case Booth had the gun.

"Who ratted me out?" he said. "My fucking father?"

"Actually it was your pal Larkin. He told us you'd be down here."

"Bullshit. We don't rat, man."

"How do you think I knew how to get down here this fast?"

Booth shook his head in the wind and looked south across the lake.

"Just now I caught your dad trying to burn your scarf," Kennicott said. "I'm going to arrest him for accessory after the fact to first-degree murder."

"Leave the old goat alone."

"It's worth five years in jail," Kennicott said.

"Fuck you, cop."

"You don't want me to arrest him? Throw the gun over the edge and climb down nice and slow."

"I don't have the gun."

"That's what Larkin said too." In fact, St. Clair hadn't told them a thing about the gun.

"Ha!"

Even from this distance, he could see that Booth was glaring at him. He reached for his phone. "You've got ten seconds, then I call in backup."

"If I come down, will you leave the old fag alone?"

"One hundred percent."

"And I get my call to my lawyer as soon as I hit the ground."

"No problem."

"Okay, here take this." He reached both hands to his belt.

Kennicott ducked. A moment later something came flying off the top of the lighthouse. It was his shirt. Next came Booth's shoes, socks, and pants. When all he had left was a pair of underwear, he hopped out over the edge, grabbing the rope monkeylike, and effortlessly walked himself down.

Kennicott ran over with his gun out and arrived just as Booth got down.

"See, copper, totally unarmed." He had his bare arms stretched out in front of him. "Here, cuff me in front, give me that cell, and back off. I need to call Phil Cutter, my friggin' lawyer."

18

Not one snowflake was left on the ground this morning, but a damp cold rain was falling hard, and dark clouds hung low over the city. Ari Greene put his hands into his overcoat pockets, lowered his head, and walked toward the Tim Hortons.

It was a quarter to nine. Despite the chill in the air, a line of customers spilled out the front door and snaked around the corner. There was a new pile of cards and flowers three times the size of the one he'd had PC Bambridge pack up for the Wilkinsons yesterday. The bright colors of hope were muted by the clouds and rain, but none of the caffeine-craving customers seemed to even notice. Greene was always amazed how quickly life went back to normal at a crime scene once the police had packed up their gear, taken down their yellow tape, and departed. Even after a horrible murder such as this one, which had made the whole city stop and mourn, the relentless flow of commerce shoved everything aside with uncanny speed.

The TV cameras were back in full force. The reporters were interviewing the customers for comments, asking a series of inane questions: "How do you feel about the shooting?" "Are you afraid to come back here?" "What words do you have for the family?"

Greene pulled his scarf tight around his neck. He took his place in line and ten minutes later was inside. Behind the counter, the harried staff worked at breakneck speed. Are they this busy every morning? Greene wondered, until he saw a handwritten sign that hung crookedly from one of the cash registers. It read:

WE THANK YOU MOST LOYAL CUSTOMER
THEREFORE TODAY MAKE SPECIAL OFFER
FREE DONUT WITH COFFEE PURCHASE
PROPRIETORS MR. AND MRS. YUEN

A middle-aged Asian man was behind one of the tills, and a middle-aged Asian woman was behind the other one. All the other employees' uniforms were dark brown, but theirs were light beige.

Greene's turn came and he approached the woman. "What you like, sir?" she asked with her head down.

"Mrs. Yuen," he said.

She looked up at him. Her eyes were ringed with fatigue. "Yes?"

"I'm Detective Greene, the officer in charge of this case. I'm glad to see you're back in business."

"You do not wear uniform?" Yuen was an unusually large Chinese woman.

"No. I didn't want to alarm anyone."

She smiled, as if it were a real effort. Her good manners were battling with her evident exhaustion.

"I need to meet with you and your husband," he said.

"Fifteen more minute please." She looked at her watch. "At nine o'clock, line be shorter."

"That's fine. I'll take a tea with milk, no sugar."

"Which free doughnut?"

Greene shook his head. "Give the next customer two."

She handed him the tea. "No charge."

"Yes." Greene gave her a two-dollar coin and tossed another one in the charity box for a kids' summer camp.

Just as Mrs. Yuen predicted, at nine o'clock the place emptied out like a schoolyard after the bell had rung. She signaled for one of the employees to take her place at the till, went over to her husband, and tapped him on the shoulder. He was about half a foot shorter than she was. She pointed discreetly at Greene.

The man smiled and motioned to a gap on the far side of the counter.

"Hello, hello," he said as Greene approached. Mr. Yuen pumped his hand with real enthusiasm. His smile broadened, but he said nothing else.

"My husband English very bad, but he understand everything," Mrs. Yuen said. "Please come to office in back."

The office was a cubbyhole, with a small desk jammed into one corner and a steel chair in front of it. A mop and bucket were in the other corner.

"This is most terrible tragedy," Mrs. Yuen said the moment she'd closed the door behind him. "Poor family."

Above the desk Greene saw a formal photograph of a much younger-looking Mr. and Mrs. Yuen, with two daughters by their side. They were flanked by two older sets of parents. Also on the wall were four cheaply framed "Certificates of Excellence" from Tim Hortons headquarters, congratulating the Yuens on their work as "Top Franchisees."

"We put life saving into business," Mrs. Yuen said. "Have won many award. Follow every rule in franchise agreement. This very clean store. We work every day. Seven days every week. We are Hong Kong Chinese. Parents care for children. What happen now?"

The words spurted out from the woman like water bursting through a hole in a dam.

"In my experience, people tend to forget this kind of tragedy very quickly," Greene said. "Your business might suffer for a few days, but I hope not long after that."

Husband and wife traded looks.

"The best thing you can do is help us with our investigation," Greene continued.

"Yes," Yuen said. "My husband and I both pass citizenship exam with perfect mark. He no speak English much but he read very well. No problem with police ever."

Greene smiled and pulled out a sheaf of papers from the thin briefcase that he usually carried with him. "These are the initial statements taken by the police two nights ago. We interviewed every employee and customer we could find. The manager on duty said neither of you were here."

The couple looked at each other again. "My husband insist we both leave for two daughter ballet recital. First time in three year we not here during day."

"My father came to this country with nothing," Greene said. Young cops were taught at Police College to never reveal personal information about themselves to the public. They were supposed to remain cool and aloof. Greene broke the rule all the time. "He made many sacrifices, but he never sacrificed his family. You didn't do anything wrong."

Mr. Yuen looked at Greene and smiled.

"One of your employees, Jose Sanchez, we can't find him. I understand he was the baker."

"Donuts not baked at this location," Mrs. Yuen said. "Dough made at factory. Delivered five thirty in morning and we reheat. Everything preset so real chef not required. We pay minimum wage. Not look very carefully at qualification."

Or their immigration status, Greene thought. Everyone had their own fears when the police showed up, and he could see Mrs. Yuen break into a sweat. The air in the small room felt close.

"I'm not from the Labour Department. Or the Immigration Department. My only concern is this murder investigation. Did Mr. Sanchez show up to work today?"

"No. And no call. Tried to reach through cellular telephone many time. No answer."

He reached back in his case and pulled out a file. "I've looked at his employment records you gave Officer Kennicott."

"Yes," she said.

Greene sat in the chair and opened the file. It had almost nothing in it. Jose Sanchez, or whoever he was, claimed to be twenty-eight years old and born in Lisbon, Portugal; had a high school education; had experience as a chef and a baker working in restaurants; spoke English, Portuguese, French, Italian, and Spanish; and came to Canada six years ago. He was hired seven months before, passed his three-month probation period, and was now a full-time employee. The only piece of identification he'd given was a photocopy of a social security card with his name on it. No picture. Greene was sure it would be a fake. They were ridiculously easy to get.

"He said that he spoke five languages."

"Talk to many customer," Mrs. Yuen said. "We speak only English and Cantonese. He very good worker."

"I don't imagine you ever saw where he lived?"

They shook their heads.

"Meet any of his family members? Wife, girlfriend, children?"

"No," Mrs. Yuen said.

"Do you have any photos of him? Maybe from a company party?"

"Tim Horton regulation. Only one celebration each year. Must be in December."

Greene stood. "I'm going to send a composite artist over here later today. Nothing to be afraid of. He'll talk with you and the staff for a while and draw up a sketch of what this man looks like." He reached back inside his briefcase and pulled out a sealed plastic bag. Inside was the black hairnet that he'd found in the bushes outside last night. "Do you recognize this?" he asked.

"Hairnet," Mrs. Yuen said. "Kitchen staff must wear. Is regulation. Ten-dollar deposit. We return when they leave company."

"We need to keep this for evidence." He reached into his wallet, pulled out a ten-dollar bill.

"No. Okay," Mr. Yuen said, speaking for the first time. He had his hands up, anxious to reject the money.

Mrs. Yuen flashed her husband another look.

"Please," Greene said. "Take it."

She reached for the bill and folded it squarely into her hand. "Have given away four hundred and twenty-four dollar of doughnut today."

Greene stood up. "I'll be back in touch."

"We will be here," Mrs. Yuen said.

Greene shook both their hands. He had no doubt the Yuens would be hard at work at their franchise no matter what day he showed up. And that the man who called himself Jose Sanchez wasn't coming back.

19

"My client Dewey Booth can lead you to the gun," Phil Cutter said, staring straight at Ralph Armitage. He was a short, high-strung man with an oversized, shiny bald head and almost no neck. "I assume that's what you want."

Half an hour before, just as Armitage was about to leave his office for lunch, Cutter, a former prosecutor turned defense lawyer, had called and insisted they meet at the Plaza Flamingo, a huge Latin restaurant and nightclub on College Street. The two men were sitting at a round table. Four televisions were blaring different soccer games, and all around them people were cheering.

He could see why Cutter wanted to meet here. No one in this place would recognize them. He'd also insisted that Armitage come alone.

"Of course I want the gun." He met Cutter's dark eyes. What prosecutor wouldn't want to recover the murder weapon? he thought.

"Good." Cutter kept staring. "Here's the deal. Dewey takes you to the gun in a place where only Larkin St. Clair could have put it. In return, you drop all charges against him."

Even though Armitage was much taller than Cutter, the man had always intimidated him. In part, this was because of Cutter's unparalleled track record in court as a Crown. He'd prosecuted forty-three murders, and thirty-nine had ended in convictions. In part, it was Cutter's take-no-prisoners attitude toward everything he touched. But most of all, Armitage knew that Cutter was one of the few people in his life he couldn't charm.

"That's ridiculous." Armitage chuckled. He could hear how hollow his laugh sounded.

"No." Cutter's eyes didn't move. They bored into Armitage like black nails hammered into concrete. He didn't blink. "What evidence have you got? That grainy video is a load of crap. Larkin St. Clair stuffing something down his pants. Could be a doughnut for all you know. Even if you put Dewey with him at the scene, how do you know which one pulled the trigger? Witnesses told the newspapers there were all kinds of shots. How about that guy in the old Caddy who took off? Maybe he fired first and killed the kid, and then picked up his own shells and disappeared. Face it, Armitage, you need the gun that fired the bullet so you can match it with the one in that boy's brain."

Despite himself, Armitage nodded. Cutter was right. Unless he could prove St. Clair had the actual gun, the case had a huge hole in it. Especially with some witnesses saying they'd heard as many as nine gunshots, which would be too many rounds for one handgun. They were almost certainly wrong. Only four bullets could be accounted for, and probably the sound echoing off the buildings on both sides was the reason for the higher number. But words such as "almost" and "probably" were the building blocks for defense lawyers to raise a reasonable doubt.

"What if I told you Dewey can tell you the type of gun that was used?" Cutter asked.

"That certainly would bolster his credibility."

"Desert Eagle semi-automatic revolver," Cutter said.

Armitage tried to keep his face blank. But forensics had already established that the bullet recovered from the autopsy of the boy had come from a six-shot pistol, such as the Desert Eagle. He turned away and reached for his cell phone. "I need to make a call."

Cutter's arm flashed out at lightning speed, stopping him. "No way," he said. "We both know how the Crown's office works. You start consulting and this whole thing takes days. Dewey's not going to wait. It's a one-time offer: you get the gun, my kid walks."

Armitage needed time to think. This deal could blow up in his face. But if he didn't make it? He looked around the room. I must be a head taller than all the Mediterranean men here, he thought. And the only blond guy here. He faced Cutter. "I need a statement under oath. On video. Dewey tells us exactly what happened, that he wasn't the shooter, that Larkin St. Clair pulled the trigger, and you've got a deal."

Cutter turned away. He looked at one of the televisions that was playing a highlight reel of spectacular soccer goals.

Armitage waited for him to respond. Cutter kept staring at the screen, one minute, then two. What's he up to? Armitage wondered. Four minutes, five minutes. Cutter didn't say a word. The final goal was scored and a Coke ad in Portuguese came on. Without even a glance back, Cutter grabbed his briefcase and jacket, and stood up.

"Well?" Armitage asked.

"Euro Cup finals start in June," Cutter said, slipping into his coat.

"Wanted to watch a few goals from the qualifying rounds. This meeting was a complete waste of time." He turned to leave.

"What did you expect?" Armitage wasn't sure if he should stand or not. He decided to stay seated.

Cutter spun around and glared down at him, like a tiger about to manhandle his prey. "Listen, this case has this city in a total uproar. I've lived in Toronto my whole life and never seen people so angry. I just handed you a first-degree murder conviction on a silver fucking platter and you don't want it. News flash, Ralphie boy, this isn't summer camp. You might be good at playing office politics, working out plea bargains on cases with dump-truck defense lawyers when no one gives a shit. Face it, you're a desk jockey, not a trial lawyer. The whole country is watching this case and you better be prepared. This is hardball right from the get-go. After today, I'm throwing straight at your head."

Armitage felt the blood drain from his face. He wasn't used to looking up at people. He thought again about standing, but Cutter was too close. "I need to hear from your client, or no deal," he said.

"He's not saying a word unless we have a deal. And good luck finding the gun." Cutter moved in inches from Armitage's face. The overhead lights glistened off his hairless head. "I was a prosecutor for twenty years. You don't make this deal now, Larkin and Dewey will keep their mouths shut tighter than a pair of old whores too tired to give another blow job."

Armitage tried to swallow but his mouth was dry. "We have witnesses who put them together inside moments before the shooting. Then they both flee. They're both parties to this offense."

"Hah!" Cutter's face was red with anger. "No way. There's not one stick of evidence of two guys working with a common purpose. Unless you can prove who pulled the trigger, both of them are going to walk." He straightened up, buttoned his jacket, and extended his hand. "See you in court, counsel. I'm sure you'll do the Armitage name proud. Your daddy will be most pleased."

Armitage grasped Cutter's hand and held it tight. "Phil, you know I need to get approval for something like this. Give me two hours."

"Approval? You? The new head Crown, Ralph Armitage, superstar prosecutor, needs to get approval?" Cutter yanked his arm back as if Armitage's hand was infected. "I thought you were the big cheese now."

Cutter had spent his whole professional life in the Crown's office and until about two years ago he had been next in line for the top job. Then he pulled some dirty tricks on another murder trial and made the mistake of bragging about it to his fellow Crown Attorney Albert Fernandez while they were talking in a quiet restaurant. Fernandez was Mr. Goody Two Shoes and reported Cutter. Ratted him out, as the criminals called it. It occurred to Armitage that this was why Cutter had wanted to meet in this noisy place. To prevent himself from being taped again.

"Don't get personal," Armitage said.

"Oh no, I'm going to get very personal. I bet you remember how it felt when you prosecuted Larkin and Dewey for that home invasion in Rosedale and these two clowns walked right out of kiddie court, don't you?" Cutter had switched into full cross-examination mode.

"The witness went back home to the islands." Armitage felt sick.

"I heard you lost your cool out in the hallway."

He remembered throwing St. Clair up against the wall. The punk's long hair all over the place. His voice, mocking him. *Innocent until proven guilty, man.* "That was a long time ago," he told Cutter.

"Keeps you up at night, doesn't it?"

Armitage's mind was spinning. "It wasn't the highlight of my career."

"Now, imagine these two clowns strolling out of court free as birds. Everyone's going to see you fall flat on your face. How's that going to feel?"

Armitage was pinned down by Cutter's laser stare, like a kidnap victim tied to his chair.

"What are you going to say to the parents?" Cutter asked.

He's never going to let up, Armitage thought.

"'Sorry your son was shot and I lost the case'?" Cutter demanded. "Maybe you'll invite them to your annual family party next spring. Watch some fireworks. I'm sure that will make them feel better."

Cutter was right. No way he was going to let St. Clair walk away scot-free again. "I need a statement." He tried not to come across as being desperate but knew he probably did.

Cutter flicked open his briefcase. "Here's an affidavit signed by my client, Mr. Dewey Booth, dated this morning, sworn by my partner, Ms. Barbara Gild, barrister and solicitor. Booth says he didn't fire the gun. That Larkin did. That he knows where Larkin hid it and is willing to take the police there in return for the charges against him being dropped. All on one neat page." He shoved the paper in front of Armitage.

"I want this on video," Armitage said.

"Forget it. My client swore this under oath to a member in good standing of the Law Society of Upper Canada. If that isn't good enough for you, I'm out of here."

Armitage scanned the page. "Booth is going to say all this on the stand under oath?" he asked.

"Every word."

"That St. Clair fired the shot that hit the boy."

"Yes. And he'll lead you to the gun."

Armitage stood at last. He looked down at Cutter. "If this is a lie, if he's perjured himself, then all bets are off."

Cutter reached out and shook Armitage's hand. "We have a deal on pain of perjury. Right?"

"Yes," Armitage said. "We have a deal."

For the first time since they'd met, Cutter smiled. He reached back into his briefcase and laid a typed document under Armitage's nose. It was entitled: "Agreement Re: Mr. Dewey Booth." With a flourish he produced a gold pen with his initials on it. "I knew you'd agree," he said. "Now sign on the dotted line."

20

Daniel Kennicott's second-floor flat was hot. His landlords, Mr. and Mrs. Federico, who lived downstairs in their house on Clinton Street, treated their only tenant like he was the son they never had. It was the middle of November, and they'd turned the heat on, which was a good thing, considering the unusually early cold weather this month. Right now the rain, which had been beating down all day, was turning to snow. It looked as if another big storm was on the way.

But the radiators in his place were old and noisy. Unless he was there to open a window it got stuffy real fast, and despite his running a humidifier full-time, the air was always too dry.

He opened the window in the kitchen in the back and the one in his bedroom at the front to create a cross-breeze, tore off his clothes, and stepped into a warm shower. He let it run over him for a long time. Hard to believe it was almost forty-eight hours since he'd got the hot shot and taken off at a run. He started to replay those first crucial moments: slipping on the ice on the way to the Tim Hortons, the father's ashen face in the doughnut shop light, the tiny hole in the back of his son's head, the pulsing red ambulance light. The echoing sound of its siren pounded in his brain.

Greene had sent him home with a treasure trove of intercepted communication between Suzanne Howett and her boyfriend Jet. He'd gone through it all at the station, and now he had to put it in chronological order and highlight the key points.

Out of the shower, he got dressed in a pair of jeans and a T-shirt and unpacked his briefcase on the kitchen table, where he preferred to work. In the four years since he'd joined the force, new technology had radically changed policing. Now it was impossible to imagine a major criminal investigation without gleaning evidence from texts, tweets, Facebook entries, and cell phone calls. Especially when it came to young people, who had an almost pathological addiction to all things virtual.

Suzanne Howett fit the profile of a prolific user. And she'd created a torrent of text messages, which started about an hour after the shooting. Kennicott had everything transcribed. He made himself a latte in the little Italian espresso machine he'd bought down on College Street and sat down to sift through it all. It took him a few hours to pick out the handful of intercepts that mattered the most. All those years as a lawyer had taught him how to get down to the nub of things.

First came a text Howett had sent to a friend named Cindy, who they'd learned was a fellow gas station employee.

November 14, 5:42 p.m.

Howett: OMG. OMG. U wont believe w jst hppnd. Jet picked me up @ Timmys and Dewey wuz thr nd a little boy was shot. OMG. OMG.

Cindy: What? What hppnd? OMG jst on the news. U wer ther???

Howett: Ya. Dewey and hs frnd Larkin. The jerk who tried 2 pick u up.

Cindy: Who ws shooting???

Howett: 2 crzy. Jet jst droppd me off.

Cindy: Can I com ovr?

Howett: Pleeeeessse. gtg. Jet calling I need my bff.

END OF TRANSMISSION

A wiretap on Howett's phone came next.

November 14, 8:05 p.m.

Howett: Can you talk?

Trapper: Yeah. The baby's in bed. I'm outside. The cops come by yet?

Howett: No. The news says the boy is still in the hospital.

Trapper: I know.

Howett: What did you tell your wife?

Trapper: Nothing.

Howett: The cops are going to find out I worked there and, like, they're going to talk to me. What should I say?

Trapper: Tell them you didn't see anything. Nothing else.

Howett: But I didn't see anything.

Trapper: Try to stay calm. I've got to go.

END OF CONVERSATION

They had records of all of Howett's Internet searches on both her old laptop computer and her iPhone. She'd spent the night checking news sites and searching for updates on the story. The only exception was at 11:20 P.M. when she'd logged onto Hollywood.com and read two articles about Leonardo DiCaprio.

At midnight the surveillance team reported a young black woman arrived at the building in a taxi and went up to Howett's place. She was seen hugging Howett in the doorway by an undercover cop posing as a pizza delivery guy for an apartment down the hall. The officer didn't catch what they said but he could hear Howett crying. The woman was later identified as Cynthia Burlington, age twenty-two, fellow employee at the Petro-Canada station. No criminal record. No police contacts. She stayed until eight the next morning.

At five to nine in the morning the police issued a press release, which stated that, after a brave fight for his life, four-year-old Kyle Wilkinson had died from the gunshot wound he'd received the night before. It expressed their condolences to the Wilkinson family. Within seconds this news was everywhere.

Howett made another call a few minutes later:

November 15, 9:08 a.m.

Howett: (crying) Did you hear?

Trapper: I just heard.

Howett: I can't stop crying. That poor little boy. Cindy was here last night but she's left.

Trapper: I told you not to talk to anyone.

Howett: I didn't say anything.

Trapper: (laughs) Right. Why did you tell her to come over?

Howett: Well she knew about the shooting at Timmy's. Like the whole world knows. But I didn't tell her anything else. I swear.

Trapper: There's one thing I don't get.

Howett: What?

Trapper: How come Larkin's face is all over the TV and there's nothing on Dewey?

Howett: I know. I can't figure it out either.

Trapper: I've got to go. Make some deliveries. The cops come, don't say anything. Got it?

Howett: Yeah. Bye.

END OF CONVERSATION

There was only one more call.

November 15, 10:15 A.M.

Trapper: Did you hear?
Howett: What?
Trapper: Larkin's been arrested. It was on the car radio. He walked into the police by himself.
Howett: What about Dewey?
Trapper: Nothing about him at all.
Howett: Aren't they going to arrest him?
Trapper: I don't know.
Howett: How come?
Trapper: I told you. I don't know. Right. Now listen, we have to stop talking on phones and everything. The cops could be getting wiretaps and that kind of shit.
Howett: But what about Dewey and you and me and—
Trapper: No. Don't tell them anything.

[Note—Howett starts to cry. Continues for twelve seconds.]

Trapper: Suzie.
Howett: What should I do? Like, I'm supposed to be at the Petro-Can for the afternoon shift for the next two days.
Trapper: Right. Go to work. Act normal. I'll pick you up like always in twenty minutes.

[Note—a pause. Five seconds.]

Trapper: You okay?

[Note—a pause. Ten seconds.]

Trapper: Suzie?
Howett: Jet.
Trapper: What?
Howett: Dewey's crazy.
Trapper: What else is new?
Howett: I'm scared.
Trapper: I know.

END OF CONVERSATION.

Kennicott cut and pasted all the transcripts, put them all into one file, and e-mailed it over to Greene. He was tired.

He fished through the collection of CDs of the conversations between Suzanne and Jet, found the last one, and brought it with him into the bedroom. He put it on his CD player and listened to it as he went to the window and watched the storm coming in. The snow was heavy now. Hearing the words was much more chilling than reading them.

He played the final part of the conversation again:

"Jet."

"What?"

"Dewey's crazy."

"What else is new?"

"I'm scared."

"I know."

The cold air blew over the top of the hot radiators.

I'm scared. I know. I'm scared. I know.

It echoed something inside him.

His last conversation with his brother. Making plans to meet for dinner. *Daniel, for once, don't be late,* Michael had said and laughed. But his voice had an edge. A hint of fear.

He had arrived late. Too late to protect his brother.

There was a truth here that maybe he'd been hiding from himself for a long time. He hadn't just become a cop to try to solve the mystery of Michael's murder. He'd become a cop to protect people. So they wouldn't lose what he'd lost.

He kept watching the snow. As exhausted as he was, there was no point in trying to go to sleep.

21

It had been more than forty-eight hours since Ari Greene had gotten the emergency call about the shooting, and he'd barely had time to go to the bathroom. Sleep was a distant memory. He'd tried lying down for a few hours last night in the downstairs sleep room at police headquarters, but had just lain in the dark with his eyes half-open, his mind whirling in overdrive, like a car engine when the gas pedal got stuck. Finally, he'd gotten up, grabbed a quick shower in the gym, changed his clothes, and headed back to work.

But now it looked as if he had enough things in place and he could go home for the night. The weather outside had turned nasty, and it would be nice to get back before the snow piled up. He wanted to shovel his father's walk.

There were holes in the case. Always were. They hadn't found the gun yet, despite searching all the garbage cans, Dumpsters, and sewer grates near the Tim Hortons and going through Larkin St. Clair's aunt's house, where he was living on probation. They'd probably never recover it. His main concern was to track down Jose Sanchez, the baker who'd disappeared. And their surveillance of Jet and Suzanne was in place. Key decision was going to be when to pull the plug and bring them in.

He cleaned up the papers on his desk and stifled a yawn. He hadn't had a moment to call Jennifer Raglan to ask about her mother and now she'd probably be home with her family. He'd get in touch with her tomorrow.

His phone rang.

All he wanted to do was go home. He hesitated before answering. "Detective Greene," he said.

"It's Ralph Armitage again. I need to talk to you about something."

"Go ahead." He'd been updating Armitage for the last three days on the progress of the investigation.

"Has to be in person," Armitage said.

Greene closed his eyes for a moment. "I'll be over in ten minutes."

"Actually, could you make it at seven o'clock?" Armitage said. "I've got a six o'clock scheduled."

Armitage was such a bureaucrat. And he'd probably slept in his nice warm bed the last two nights.

Greene used up an hour at his desk doing more paperwork and arrived outside the head Crown's office at a quarter to seven. The waiting room was empty. A few minutes before seven Awotwe Amankwah, a reporter who worked at the *Toronto Star,* emerged. The criminal courts were his beat.

"Tough case, detective," he said.

"You have young children." Greene knew Amankwah had been involved in a bad custody fight with his ex-wife for the last few years.

"I can't imagine what that family is going through."

"I know the press is going to be after this story, but I'm keeping everyone away from them."

"Understood," Amankwah said before he left.

Greene knew that with this kind of case he had to control the media. Even use them sometimes.

At exactly seven o'clock, Armitage came out and ushered Greene inside his neat and organized office. When Jennifer Raglan was in charge, this had been a messy, bustling place. Now it felt sterile, except for the photographic shrine of Armitage and his equally tall, equally athletic-looking wife stacked on the credenza behind his desk.

"This is important," Armitage said after he shut the door behind them. They were both standing. "If we don't find the gun that fired the fatal bullet, we're in trouble in this case. Agreed?"

Something about the question made Greene feel uneasy. He was tired. And pissed off that Armitage was such a press hound that he made him wait an hour so that he could do yet another media interview.

"Not really," he said. "In most shooting cases the gun is the first thing to disappear."

"Okay then," Armitage said. "But if we could find the gun and match it to the bullet that killed young Carl, that would be great, wouldn't it?"

"Kyle."

"What do you mean 'Kyle'?"

"The boy's name was Kyle, not Carl."

Armitage shrugged. "Okay. But you agree, matching the gun to the bullet is crucial. Right?"

Greene felt as if he was being cross-examined. It made him careful with his words. "Crucial, no. Helpful, yes."

"Very helpful, right?"

He had an arrogant, shit-eating grin on his big face and Greene wanted so badly to reach over and wipe it off.

"Probably," Greene said.

"What if," Armitage said, puffing himself up, "I was to tell you that someone has been found who is prepared to identify the shooter, under oath? And that this same person will tell us where the shooter stashed the gun? What would you say to that?"

Greene wasn't happy about being treated as if he was a witness on his own case. "I'd say, 'How do you know about this?' and 'Why the hell wasn't I informed?'"

"I'm informing you now." Armitage gave his patented Cheshire-cat grin. Real proud of himself.

Greene had hit only one person in his life. That was back in high school, when a bully insulted his father in the school cafeteria. Right now he was thinking a good hard slap would do it. He was sick of Armitage's game. "What's this all about?"

"I know where the gun is," Armitage said.

Greene's first thought was: You fool. You found the location of the gun in a first-degree homicide case and made me wait almost an hour and a half before telling me?

"Where?"

"St. Clair's aunt's house. You guys missed it in your original search. It's stashed in a tree trunk."

Forget the slap. Greene wanted to land a punch on Armitage's square jaw. "Who told you this?" he demanded.

"Booth's lawyer."

"Phil Cutter?" There were few lawyers in the whole province Greene respected less.

"I made a deal with him."

"You made a deal with Cutter?"

"Had to. This was a one-time offer."

"On my homicide investigation? You made a deal without asking me?"

"I've got a sworn statement from Dewey Booth saying that Larkin St. Clair was the shooter." Armitage reached onto his desk for a piece of paper that had been lying facedown. "Describes where you can find the gun."

Greene grabbed the one-page affidavit and read it through in record time. He waved it in Armitage's face. "You dropped a first-degree murder charge, and this is all you got?" He tossed the paper toward the desk but it didn't reach, just fluttered down to the floor, like a rudder-less kite.

Armitage rushed over to pick it up. "Yes, and it was the right move."

Greene could feel the waves of fatigue and anger coursing through his body. Stay calm, he told himself. "Why in the world would you do this without telling me?"

"Cutter called me. Insisted we meet alone. At some place over on College Street. The Flaminco . . . something."

"You mean Flamingo."

"Flamingo?"

"Yes, the Plaza Flamingo, west of Bathurst," Greene said.

"Yeah. Look, there's a key point you missed." Armitage picked up a pad of blank paper from his desk and drew a large rectangle that took up most of the page. "This is the crime scene," he said. In the top left-hand corner he drew a second rectangle about half the size and wrote "Tim Hortons" inside it. In the surrounding white space he wrote "parking lot." At the front entrance he put two X's and wrote under them a capital "W" and a small "w." "This is where Wilkinson and his son were when the boy got shot," he said.

Greene looked at the drawing, shaking his head.

On the parking-lot side of the doughnut shop he marked two X's and wrote "L" and "D." "There was a fresh chip on the sidewalk here. Let's assume Larkin and Dewey were standing at this spot."

"I know that," Greene said.

Armitage pointed to the bottom right-hand part of the page. "James Eric Trapper, aka Jet, drove his old Cadillac in and stopped here." He drew a small rectangle and wrote "Caddy" beside it. "Right?"

"There's nothing new here."

"We have five half-decent witnesses, and not one of them sees the shooting. Their evidence as to the number of shots fired ranges from four to ten."

"Nine," Greene said. "Evidence of Adela Dobos. She'd just walked outside when the shots started."

"Still more than six," Armitage said, "and that's why it's a problem. Could mean there was more than one gun. Plus the flattened shell case was found here." He tapped the Cadillac in the drawing. "Jet's got a bad criminal record, including possession of an unregistered handgun. If he was shooting, he could have picked up his own shells before he took off but missed one that he drove over." He drew a curved line in front of the car that showed it driving out of the lot. "Possible, isn't it?"

Greene stared at Armitage.

"I'm sure that's what the defense is going to say. It's possible. No proof beyond a reasonable doubt," Armitage said.

"Tell me something I don't know," Greene said at last.

Armitage dropped the pad of paper and opened the only folder on his desk. He passed over a sheet of paper. "Take a look at this."

Greene recognized it right away. A set of stick-man drawings of a body, one from the back and one from the front. "This is from the autopsy report," he said, giving it back. "Shows the bullet hit Kyle in the side of the head. So what?"

"But did you notice which side of the head took the bullet?" Armitage asked, trying to get into cross-examination mode.

Greene didn't need to take a second look. "The left," he said without missing a beat.

Armitage retrieved his drawing of the crime scene. "But Larkin and Dewey were to the Wilkinsons' right, not their left." His voice was rising in excitement. "You didn't notice that, did you?"

"Of course I did."

"You did?" Armitage asked. "And it didn't bother you?"

Big mistake, Ralph, Greene thought. Never ask a question in cross-examination if you don't know the answer. "Not one bit."

"Well, how could we prove Larkin was the shooter if the bullet comes from the wrong direction? How do you explain it?"

Mistake number two, Greene thought. Never give a witness an open question in cross-examination. Gives him the chance to take control of the story.

"Happens in every murder case," Greene said. "A homicide's not a jigsaw puzzle. Pieces never fit perfectly. They're not supposed to. You remember the Wray case back in the early 1970s? When Wray knew where the gun was, and that was used to convict him of murder?"

"We studied it in first-year law school," Armitage said.

"I know. I went to law school for a year," Greene said. "My professor was an Aussie and used to talk about the difference between the 'law' and the 'lore.' He had such a thick accent that the two words sounded the same, so he spelled them out. The l-a-w said that because Wray knew where the gun was, it was good evidence that he fired it. The l-o-r-e was that Wray was covering for his brother."

For the first time since Greene had come into the office, Armitage didn't look quite so cocky.

"The point is, the same facts can lead to all sorts of different conclusions. Some of them wrong. Kyle Wilkinson could have turned around for a million reasons," Greene said. "Maybe he heard the car coming in the lot. Or noticed Suzanne Howett running behind him. Father said it was just starting to snow; he could have looked up at the sky. So what? Kids are always turning in circles."

"But his father doesn't say anything about it in his statement you took from him, does he, about his son turning around?"

"So what?" Greene said. "Man was in shock. The mind blanks out on small, unimportant details, especially at first. All the dad says is they were walking into the Tim Hortons, he heard a bang noise, and the next thing he knows Kyle is lying on the concrete."

He didn't feel like hitting Armitage anymore. He just wished he never had to deal with this fool again. "We have Suzanne Howett and her boyfriend Jet under around-the-clock surveillance. We've tapped their phones, their cells. Everything. Once we move in on them, they'll probably shut right up. This is our best chance to find out what they know. See if Jet had a gun. You may have noticed, I'm keeping Dewey's name out of the press. I want to put pressure on them. This deal you just made has to be kept confidential. One hundred percent."

Armitage gave him a blank stare. Shrugged and pointed to the door.

Greene turned to the door then back at Armitage. Confused. Then it hit him. "Amankwah? You told the reporter about this?"

"I said the story was embargoed and he agreed. He won't use it until I say so."

Greene grabbed the phone on Armitage's desk and shoved it in his face. "You call him right now, tell him if this gets out he's never going to interview another Toronto cop for the rest of his career."

"Okay, okay," Armitage said. "But we both know it's hard to keep these things quiet. Cutter's a blabbermouth and—"

"Call Cutter too. Tell him to keep his trap shut or the deal's off." Armitage was right. Something like this wouldn't stay secret for long. "Tell them both I need twenty-four hours." He was already at the door. He couldn't wait to get out of there.

"I made this deal because I thought it was the right thing to do," Armitage said, the phone hanging limp in his hand. "I'm the one who has to stand up in court and try this case."

"And I'm the one who has to has to tell the Wilkinsons that we've dropped the charges against one of the two guys who probably killed their son." He slammed the door behind him as hard as he could and hoped he'd broken off the hinges.

22

The thing Nancy Parish hated most about her job was visiting clients in jail. And the worst place of all was Toronto East Detention Centre, an industrial-size prison in a barren part of Scarborough, the poorest and most remote suburb of Toronto. It was especially horrible coming here at night, when the rest of the world was doing normal things, such as spending the evening at home.

Pulling into the windswept parking lot, she turned off her car and braced herself. On the news she'd heard that another big snowstorm was coming in and already there were flakes falling onto her windshield. What lay ahead was a walk along the broken-down, freezing-cold concrete path; check-in procedure at the steel desk; passage through two security doors; an inspection by the guards; and a ride up the gray elevator to the third floor, where Larkin St. Clair had been housed since his arrest.

She hadn't talked to him yet about what had happened at the shooting. This was by design. He always told her so many half truths and outright lies at the start of the case, she wanted to give him a chance to cool down.

She had actually planned to take the night off. Amazing as that sounded. But just half an hour ago her pal Awotwe Amankwah, the reporter at the *Star,* called on her cell while she was in her car.

"I just got out of an interview with your friendly Crown, Ralph Armitage," he said.

"Bet he's all pumped up about taking on the highest-profile case in years."

"Where you going?"

"Believe it or not I'm headed home. Hard to imagine, isn't it."

"Think again," he said. "You're going to want to go see your client after you hear this."

"I don't like the tone of your voice," she said.

"Pull over, because this will knock your socks off."

She turned into an empty parking lot and couldn't believe what Amankwah told her. The cops had arrested Dewey Booth and within hours Armitage had made a deal with his lawyer, Phil Cutter. Booth claimed St. Clair was the shooter and was going to lead the police to the gun that fired the fatal bullet. In return the charges against him would be dropped. Even worse, the weapon was stashed at St. Clair's aunt's place, some secret spot the cops had missed when they'd initially searched it.

The prison elevator opened on the third floor, and Parish went to the sterile interview room, where she sat on a steel seat, seething with anger. St. Clair had told her a big fat lie about the gun, and she was so pissed she wanted to throttle him.

"Hey, Nancy, meet Rachel, my favorite prison guard," St. Clair said minutes later as he was led into the small interview room by a squat, gum-chewing woman in uniform. "She's tougher than my aunt Arlene."

Rachel the prison guard rolled her eyes in Parish's direction.

Larkin's aunt was the only person in his dislocated life who'd stood by him through thick and thin. His mother's younger sister, the two siblings were polar opposites. Whereas Larkin's mom was beautiful and lazy, Arlene was fat and hardworking. She'd had a job as a mechanic at the subway rail yards for decades, doing the night shift. Now, on top of that, she was raising her son, Justin.

"Larkin makes friends wherever he goes," Parish told Rachel. "Each and every prison."

He was wearing the standard-issue orange jumpsuit and looked as comfortable in it as a movie star in a silk bathrobe. "You'll see, Rachel baby. I'm the inmate of your dreams."

"Sit down." Rachel tried to sound stern, but Parish saw her smirk.

Bloody Larkin could make anyone smile, she thought.

He made a show of pointing to the bolted-down steel chair at the other side of the table and directing Parish to it. "Ladies first," he said, doing a mock bow.

"I'm ready to kill you," she said once the guard was gone and they were alone.

"What's wrong?"

"Everything."

"Meaning?"

"Meaning your so-called best buddy, Dewey."

"They find him?"

She kept her eyes on him. "It gets worse."

He pulled his remaining hair back from his face and held it with both hands.

"Forget about 'we don't rat, we don't crack,'" she said. "Dewey completely fucked you over. Told the cops you were the shooter. Made a deal. He's going to walk."

His head jolted back. He gaped at her.

"And get this," she said. "He's taking the cops back to your aunt's house. He says the gun's hidden in some secret place that only you could stash it. I assume your aunt would kill Dewey on sight with her bare hands."

He began to shake his head. Wordless for perhaps the first time in his life.

"Then he's going to testify against you at trial."

St. Clair's eyes bulged. "Shit," he whispered.

"That's an understatement." She could feel her anger at him rising. "Why the hell did you lie to me about the gun? If you'd told me, I could have found a way to return it. It would have been a perfect bargaining chip, but now this is a disaster."

"How could Dewey do that?"

"Easy. Maybe he doesn't tell his lawyer a bunch of lies."

"I'm going to be sick." He jumped up and rushed out the door.

Parish stayed seated in the bolted-down chair. She heard him retching in the hallway, the vomit making a splat sound as it hit the concrete floor. A vile smell wafted in through the open doorway.

23

Ari Greene drove into the self-serve Petro-Canada service station and got out of his car. The blizzard that had started last night had been building all day, gaining in ferocity this afternoon. The wind was whipping the snow in a near-horizontal line right in his eyes.

He opened the gas cap, removed the hose, and filled his car. The 1988 Oldsmobile had a big tank, and his hands were freezing by the time he'd finished. He looked around at the two other drivers also filling their cars and nodded.

Inside the station, the young woman behind the counter rotated on a stool behind the cash register. She hadn't changed very much from the photo in her work file at Tim Hortons, he thought, except her hair had grown. It was long and wavy.

"You that old car at pump seven?" she said without making eye contact. There was an opened bubble pack of Nicorette on the counter, and she was chewing gum.

"That's right."

"Petro-Points card?"

"No." He handed over his personal credit card, not his Metro Police one. He wanted to talk to her a little before he told her who he was. "Can you believe this weather?" he said.

She shrugged. "And it's only November."

"Probably will be a slow night for you."

"My shift's almost over."

She processed the payment and tapped her pen on the credit card machine while waiting. "Sign here," she said, tearing the slip of paper off with her right hand when it came through and handed it over to him with a pen using her left. He noticed her baby finger remained curled inside her palm.

He signed the receipt, then opened his wallet and showed her his badge. "Detective Greene from the homicide squad," he said. "Suzanne, I need to talk to you."

Her jaw froze. He could see the piece of gum resting on the tip of her tongue.

"I . . . I . . . can't."

"You don't have much choice. We know you left work at Tim Hortons just minutes before the shooting. We know you grew up on Pelee Island with Dewey, and we have the records of each time you visited him in jail."

He had his briefcase with him, and he took out the composite drawing of the baker who called himself Jose Sanchez, a handsome, youngish-looking man, with a glint in his eyes and a small birthmark by his left eye. "You recognize him?"

Suzanne stared at the drawing. Transfixed. "I'm . . . I'm at work now."

"Like you said, your shift is almost over. We know it ends in twenty minutes, at four. We know your boyfriend Jet is going to come and pick you up. We know he does that every night whether you are working here or at the Tim Hortons. We know he picked you up on the night of the shooting. We know you live at 144 Easterbrook Avenue, apartment 204. We know your cell number and your e-mail address, and we've listened to all your calls and read all your texts and e-mails for the last three days."

Her face flushed, turning her skin beet red. She flicked back her shoulder-length curly blond hair and pointed to the two customers behind him. The men who'd been outside a minute ago filling up their cars. "I need to serve them."

"No you don't," he said. "They're both undercover cops. With me. We've already talked to your boss. He knows you're going to leave early today."

"But . . . but Jet—"

"It will be much better for you if you're not here when Jet shows up. He doesn't have a job, does he?"

"Well. Not right now. But he's looking for work as a stunt driver."

Greene motioned for Daniel Kennicott, who'd also come inside, to stand by the door. He reached into his briefcase again and pulled out a long piece of paper.

"This is a warrant to search your apartment," he said to her. "We have reason to believe you and Jet are in possession of substantial amounts of stolen property. Flat-screen TVs, iPhones and iPads. Espresso machines. We have video surveillance of Jet for the last two days doing deals all over the East End."

She didn't seem to know where to look.

"The apartment is in your name." He pulled out a photocopy of the lease and pointed to her signature on the last page. "That's you.

Suzanne Howett. Even if Jet's the one bringing the stuff in and out, by law you're in possession of all this stolen property."

She started to cry. "I don't have a record."

"Jet does. Want to see it?" He reached back in his briefcase again.

"No. Jet hates being in jail."

"You have two choices," he said. "Come with me now, and I won't execute this warrant. Or go home with Jet, and then you'll both be arrested."

She reached for a Kleenex and dabbed her eyes. The heavy black mascara she wore was starting to run. "There's no one to bail me out," she said. "My parents don't give a shit."

He pointed to the composite drawing back on the counter. "You recognize him, don't you?"

She curled her lips inward and nodded.

"Jose's not in trouble," he said. "We just want to find him, talk to him."

"But I don't know him except at work."

He slipped the drawing back into his briefcase. It had a noisy zipper and he began to close it. Out at the gas pumps new cars were driving up. "You have one minute to decide. Wait for Jet and get arrested or come with me and tell me what you know."

She jerked her head up at him, her look of sorrow replaced by defiance and fear. "Where the fuck is Dewey? Why haven't you arrested him?"

He wasn't going to tell her about Armitage's deal. "You're afraid of him, aren't you? That's why Jet drives you to and from work."

She started to shake.

"Dewey burned you, didn't he?" He reached out, took her left hand, and uncurled the baby finger. She didn't resist. The whole outside layer of skin was scarred and leathery.

"He hurts people, animals too," she said.

"Come with us." Greene said. "That's the only way I can protect you."

She punched another Nicorette out of the blister pack, popped it in her mouth, and let him guide her down from her stool.

24

Daniel Kennicott was freezing. After Detective Greene drove away with Suzanne Howett, he'd positioned himself outside the Petro-Canada station, waiting for James "Jet" Trapper to show up. He couldn't stay inside and risk being seen.

The snow was pelting down even harder now and the wind had churned up a notch. He checked his watch. Five after four, and there was no sign of the Cadillac. He stomped his feet and dug his hands in under his armpits.

Jet was late. Had he figured out something was up? Or was it just the bad weather and the terrible traffic? The street they were on, O'Connor Drive, had two lanes going both ways and the cars were piled up, barely moving.

At a quarter after four, the Cadillac finally pulled into the lot. Kennicott took a step back, keeping himself out of sight. Jet drove slowly. The only legitimate work record he'd been able to find about Jet was some jobs he'd gotten as a stunt driver for a few of the film companies in the city. He handled the big car well. Crawled up to the front door of the station but, instead of stopping, went through and made a wide circle around the pumps. Kennicott saw him pick up his cell phone.

Not good. Suzanne wasn't there and now that she was with Greene, she wasn't going to answer his call. Kennicott had tucked his cruiser in back of the building, about thirty feet away. Should he run and get in it?

Jet did another loop and parked at the edge of the lot, the nose of his car pointed toward the street. He got out of the car, put the phone in his pocket, and walked through the snowstorm, looking around. He stopped at the front door and peered in through the glass.

Come on, come on, Kennicott thought. Go inside, then I've got you.

Jet pulled his phone back out and tried another call.

The snow was so thick that Kennicott could hardly see. He got on his police radio. "Move onto the street," he whispered to the officer whose unmarked police car was at one of the pumps, pretending to gas up.

"Ten-four," the cop in the car said.

"Drive out of his line of sight. But stay close."

Jet turned and watched the unmarked drive away. He waited until he couldn't see it anymore. He still hadn't gone inside.

He knows something's up, Kennicott thought.

Suddenly, Jet jammed the phone back in his pocket and started running to his vehicle.

Shit. Kennicott grabbed his radio again. "He's going to the Caddy. Cut him off! Cut him off!"

Jet jumped in and threw his car in gear.

Kennicott ran across the snowy ground. But it was slippery. Treacherous.

The Cadillac lurched forward and was almost out of the lot when the unmarked reversed at it on the road and slammed into its side, sending the big car skittering. It spun sideways and smashed into a minivan. The two officers in the unmarked were both flung back in their seats by the impact. They looked stunned.

Kennicott was charging ahead as fast as he could get traction, just a few feet away.

Horns started blaring. Above the din, he heard the cracking sound of a car door opening. In a flash, Jet was out in the snow and racing through traffic, crossing the crowded street.

"Stop! Police!" Kennicott yelled.

Jet glanced over his shoulder, then kept going.

Kennicott danced his way through the cars on the road.

Jet got to the other side of the street and ran into a driveway beside a house, heading toward the backyard gate. He flung it open and dashed out of sight.

Kennicott plowed after him. Behind the house fresh footprints in the snow led to the fence at the end of the yard. He scaled it and came down in a forest of trees. The house backed onto the Don Valley, a large ravine that ran through the city's East End.

He stopped to catch his breath. "Jet, you're only making this worse for yourself. Talk to us and I don't have to arrest you."

Listening hard, he heard the crash of branches. A distant voice yelled back at him: "Fuck you, cop."

That's an original line, Kennicott thought as he took off after the tracks. The woods were unexpectedly thick, considering they were in the middle of the city, and the snow surprisingly deep. All those years of marathon running meant he had a great store of strength in his legs.

And he was angry, which helped fuel his drive. He crashed through the branches, releasing the smell of fresh pine. Jet's footsteps were getting shorter. Means he's getting tired.

At the bottom of the hill, the land flattened out and there were only a few trees. The snow was coming down hard and the wind was fierce. He caught a glimpse of Jet, gaining speed on the easier terrain as he reached the river and crossed a little footbridge. A smaller hill rose on the other side, and on top were houses and streets. If Jet made it to there, he could go in any direction. There'd be car tracks he could follow without leaving a trail in the snow.

Kennicott grabbed his radio and called dispatch. "I've followed the suspect down into the valley," he shouted. "He's headed for the other side. The north part of Rosedale. Get some cars over there."

"We're trying," the dispatcher said. "But with this storm, everyone's tied up on the main streets. Traffic's a horror show."

He clicked off the radio and tore ahead. When he hit the bridge he felt himself getting a second wind. Jet was starting up the other side, his pace slackening.

Keep steady, he told himself. Knees high. Breathe.

Halfway up the hill the trees grew thicker again. He was only about twenty feet back.

"Jet, last chance to stop."

"No . . . way . . ." Jet was huffing.

The hill was steeper as they neared the summit. Jet reached for a branch to hoist himself up, and it broke in his hand with a loud snap. His feet slipped. "Shit."

Kennicott was steps away now. Sweating despite the cold.

Jet scrambled to his feet. He was climbing again with speed. Almost at the top, kicking snow into Kennicott's face.

Kennicott planted a foot on an exposed root and jumped, reaching blindly for Jet's leg. I missed it, he thought. But then he felt his hand brush against the side of a shoe.

It was just enough to break Jet's stride. He landed on his back, puffing up a cloud of snow underneath him.

Kennicott grabbed his ankle.

Above him he saw Jet was sitting up with a rock in his hand. "Here, cop, take this," he said and flung it.

Kennicott tried to duck, but it hit him square in the forehead. Blood spurted out into his eyes. He wiped it away with his free hand just in time to see Jet hurl another rock down at him. He ducked again and took the impact on his shoulders, still holding on to Jet's foot.

Jet started to kick at his fingers, smashing them against a tree trunk. Pound, pound, pound.

He couldn't hold on much longer. If he let go, he'd tumble backward down the hill.

In desperation he braced his foot on a tree root, and when the next kick came, he grabbed Jet's other ankle and yanked it down with all his might.

It worked. They both tumbled back down the hill. Jet landed on his face.

Kennicott was almost on top of him. He went to his belt, grabbed his handcuffs, and slapped them on Jet before he could move.

"I told you," he said, gasping for air. The cuffs made a grinding sound as he tightened them. "I didn't need to arrest you."

"I'm not saying shit!" Jet screamed.

He must be reading from the same script as Dewey, Kennicott thought. "Just give me a statement and I won't have to arrest you." He lifted him to his feet. "Dewey and Larkin were shooting at you and Suzanne," Kennicott said. "Why won't you help us?"

Jet shook his head. "Help the cops?"

"Okay, help yourself."

"Well where's Dewey? I don't see in the papers that he's been arrested. Has he?"

"No, he hasn't been," Kennicott said.

"Where's Suzanne?"

"In a safe place."

"Yeah? For how long?"

"We'll take care of her," Kennicott said.

"Go ahead and put me in jail. Just make sure I'm in protective custody. With Dewey on the loose, I'm not saying squat. He's a fucking psycho."

In the fading light their eyes met. Kennicott could see this was not false bravado. Jet looked scared.

25

"We caught your pal Jet," Ari Greene said to Suzanne Howett. "He took off from the gas station and we had to chase him down into the valley. Now he's facing additional charges of escaping from police and assaulting police to resist arrest."

"Great," she said with an exaggerated frown. "I know Jet. He'll never say a word to you guys."

Greene was sitting alone with Howett at an old wood table he'd had put into the same bare room in the homicide bureau where he'd interviewed Larkin St. Clair two days before. In the corner, the ubiquitous video camera was turned on, and a few minutes ago, it had recorded her being cautioned that the statement she was about to make was being taped, that it would be transcribed and she'd be asked to sign it, and that it was a criminal offense to give the police false information. He'd spread out three file folders on the table. Each had a large typed label, big enough for Howett to read.

He picked up the one that said SUZANNE HOWETT—EARLY YEARS.

She clasped her hands in front of her mouth and scratched between her front teeth with a fingernail. Watching him intently.

"You and Jet were in kindergarten together," he said, looking in the file, although he didn't have to. "Same class until grade eight, then both of you went to the mainland for high school."

She pulled her hands away from her mouth. "There's one school on the island. Twenty-four students in the whole place. Stupid."

"Dewey showed up in grade four."

"I remember. Both his dads brought him the first day."

"All three of you were in high school together too."

"Until Dewey quit," she said. "After one of his dads died."

He picked up another folder, entitled SUZANNE HOWETT—JAIL VIS-ITS. "Dewey's first year and a half in Kingston Pen, you went to see him twenty-four times. Then you stopped. How come?"

She shook her head. Her blond curls rippled across her face. "It sucked taking the bus out there all the time."

"That the only reason?"

She stared straight at Greene for the first time. "Stupid trailer visits are, like, gross."

He looked down at her left hand, with the baby finger curled inside.

"He got pissed when I told him I was breaking up with him." She pulled out her finger and rubbed it. "He's never going to forgive me."

He picked up a third file, labeled SUZANNE HOWETT/JAMES ERIC TRAPPER WIRETAPS & SURVEILLANCE. He made sure she saw it. "It didn't take us long to make the connection between you and Dewey and we started listening within a few hours of the shooting," he said.

She hid her finger again. "So you know everything."

"I know you are scared of him."

"Wouldn't you be?"

"Probably." He'd left the composite drawing of Jose Sanchez face-down on the table. He turned it over. "What do you know about him?"

She shrugged her shoulders very high. "Like I said, he's just a guy I know at work. What's he got to do with this?"

"That's what we're trying to figure out. He left after the shooting and didn't come to work the next day. Not answering his cell. We're searching for him."

She gave Greene a sullen look.

"When's the last time you saw him?" he asked.

"We always had a smoke out back at the end of my shift. We were there just before everything happened. I think he liked me. He's from Portugal. Real smart, speaks a whole bunch of languages."

"Where does he live?"

"I don't know."

"What else do you know about him?"

"Nothing. I swear. I've never seen him anywhere but work."

Greene thought about how Jet drove her to and from both her jobs all the time. The guy probably never let her out of his sight. "Okay. Can you describe him to me?"

"Jose's funny. Changes his look all the time. Said he could grow a beard in a week. Sometimes he had long sideburns, or a mustache, or a goatee, or nothing. When he was clean-shaven he had a baby face."

This guy is smart, Greene thought. "Give me the basics. How tall was he?"

"A little taller than me, about five-six, five-seven. Skinny."

"Skin color?"

She flicked her hair out of her face. "Dark. Like Portuguese guys. Brown eyes. That's about it. He hated wearing the Tim Hortons uniform."

"How old would you guess?"

She bit her lower lip. "I don't know. Like he could look real young, but I think he had to be older. Late twenties maybe."

"Glasses, tattoos?"

She giggled. "I never saw his tattoos." She pointed to the drawing. "See? He has this little birthmark thingee by his eye."

"That night, what did you talk about?"

"I told him about Dewey. How I'd heard he was out of jail and that he'd found out where I worked. That he hung out with that jerk Larkin."

"Did you tell him you were afraid of Dewey?"

"It was pretty obvious."

"Then what happened?"

"We finished our smoke and Jose went back to work. I went around the side of the building away from the parking lot to wait for Jet. It's dark there. A few seconds later I heard Jose yelling to me from the back door. He warned me that Dewey and Larkin were inside. Then Jet's Cadillac drove in. I ran across the lot and told him we had to get out of there fast. I didn't even notice the father and his kid. Never saw them."

"What happened next?"

"Someone said, 'Here, take this,' then I heard the shots. We jumped in the car and took off."

"How many shots?"

"I don't know. A lot."

"Did Jet have a gun?"

"No. He didn't have a gun."

"You sure? You're under oath now and I'm going to get this statement typed out and have you sign it."

"I'm sure. Jet didn't have a gun."

"Where did the shots come from?"

"Behind me somewhere. Near the Timmy's, but . . ." She put her head in her hands. "I didn't know anyone was hit. I didn't see anything. We heard about it on the radio driving home. I couldn't believe it. I totally freaked. If it wasn't for me that little boy wouldn't have been . . ." She started to cry.

He thought of how dark the spot was where Booth and St. Clair had been standing. How Suzanne had told Jet on the intercepted phone call that she hadn't seen anything. And her story was consistent with the witnesses who saw her running across the lot. He passed her some tissues and waited. "You've been thinking about this, haven't you?"

She sniffed and nodded. "I'm telling you the truth. This is what happened."

"That night, did you see Dewey?"

She blew her nose hard. "No."

"Larkin?"

"No."

"Did you see Jose outside again?"

"Not after our smoke."

"Where do you think Jose went?"

She balled the tissues in her hand. "I have no idea."

"We need to find him."

"He was just a guy I worked with. There's nothing else to tell you."

"You said you thought Jose liked you."

She laughed. "I'm blond. He's Latin. Happens all the time, believe me."

Greene laughed too. "Think. What did he tell you about himself? His family, friends, school?"

"I guess he's illegal or something, because he was paranoid about the cops. He loved reading. Always had a book in his back pocket. Once he said he had wanted to be a professor before he came to Canada."

"Of what topic?"

She shrugged.

This conversation wasn't going anywhere, Greene thought. He started to put the folders together in a neat pile. "What else? You talked to him every day for months."

"He knew tons of languages. The Yuens—they're the owners—really liked him because he could speak to all sorts of customers."

"I'm sure that was useful working downtown." He was just making conversation now. Time to wrap up this interview.

"I remember one day these people came in looking for the Eaton Centre. They were so lost. Jose started yakking away with them. I had no idea what language he was speaking."

"Did you ask him?" There were probably about a hundred thousand illegals in the city, Greene thought. A million ways for this guy to hide. He squared the bottom of the folders on the table.

"When we went for our smoke. He said it was Romanian. I said, 'How do you learn Romanian in Portugal?'"

Greene dropped the folders. They landed with a smack.

"He gave me that cute little smile of his," she said. "Put on a fake accent: 'Comrade. Please. No further questions.' We both laughed. He sounded just like one of those bad guys you see in the movies. Know what I mean?"

Romanian, Greene thought. Of course. It's a Romance language. Jose had put on his job application that he spoke French, Spanish, Portuguese, Italian, and English, which made sense. But he hadn't mentioned that he spoke Romanian. Which also made sense if this guy really wanted to hide.

PART TWO
DECEMBER

26

Dragomir Ozera recognized the guy on the front page of the newspaper right away. He was Ralph Armitage, the prosecutor in the Wilkinson case, whose picture had been featured in every Toronto paper for weeks after the little boy had been shot at the Tim Hortons. The guy was a publicity hound, and here he was again, a huge grin on his face under a big banner headline: FEATURE STORY: CROWN ATTORNEY RALPH ARMITAGE AND THE DEAL BEHIND THE TIMMY'S SHOOTING CASE, BY STAR COURT REPORTER AWOTWE AMANKWAH.

Ozera had been working for a month as a dishwasher at the Le Petit Déjeuner, a hip restaurant down on the old part of King Street. His new fake name was Arkadi Denisovich, and he'd told his employer he was Russian. He was having fun making up all these new names and stories about himself. Now he sported a full beard, with no mustache, Alexander Solzhenitsyn style.

It was two days after Christmas and yet another big snowstorm was hitting the city. Already it had been a hell of a winter. Meant there were hardly any customers. That made it easy for him to grab the paper, slide downstairs to the bathroom, lock the door, sit on the toilet, and read.

He kept thinking about that horrible night. Everything he'd seen. And that little boy shot dead, his father calling for help. All the sirens. How he'd panicked and run. What else could he do? There were more than enough people there to help. He figured there'd be a lot of other witnesses. If he'd waited for the cops they'd have arrested him, probably deported him. But even worse, his name and picture would be in the papers and Suzanne's ex-boyfriend Dewey would know who he was.

The original newspaper reports didn't give much detail about the police investigation, other than the arrest of Larkin St. Clair and some comments by witnesses that they'd seen him with a shorter guy. Ozera had been watching the newspapers closely. No one had identified Dewey by name, but he assumed the cops were looking for him. Ozera kept hoping they'd catch the guy and put him behind bars. Then he wouldn't have to lie awake at night, sweating and afraid.

Today's article started out by profiling Armitage. Talked about his wealthy family, his father, grandfather, and even his great-grandfather, the original Ralph Armitage, who created the family fortune in Toronto exporting lumber back to England. Now the Armitage family was famous for their civic pride and philanthropy.

That's why the name sounded familiar. Ozera often took books out from the Ralph Armitage Memorial Library. Once he broke his arm and had gone to the Armitage wing of Toronto General Hospital. From time to time he picked up a shift as a cleaner at the opera house Armitage Hall. The job paid cash and he could listen to the singers from the locker room in the basement.

The guy had four doting older sisters, who all worked for the various family-run charities. And he had a beautiful wife who was a fitness trainer at one of the city's top gyms and this year was planning the family's huge, annual, May Two-Four fireworks display for poor city kids.

"We lead very busy lives," Armitage told the reporter, Amankwah. "Thursday nights are sacrosanct. We call it our midweek date. Right now we're taking cooking classes together."

The article tracked his rapid rise in the Crown's office, talked about how charming he was, how he insisted on being called Ralph, "or Ralphie," he said, "which is what most people call me once they get to know me."

"Ralphie" suggested to Amankwah that they have lunch at a nearby dim sum restaurant in a basement on Dundas Street. Apparently he knew half the people they passed on the street, the Chinese family who ran the place, and just about every judge and lawyer who came in to eat.

"Why do you bother with such a tough job," Amankwah asked him in the interview, "when you could take the easy route and work in the Armitage financial empire?"

"My family imbued us all with a passion for public service," Ralphie replied.

"Bullshit," Ozera muttered under his breath.

The second part of the article described the man accused of the murder, Larkin St. Clair. How his father was a career criminal, his mother a drug addict. It talked about Larkin's own criminal record and how he'd befriended a short guy in prison named Dewey Booth. A source had told the writer that a number of witnesses saw a short young man who fit Booth's description sitting with St. Clair at the Tim

Hortons minutes before the shooting. The source also claimed that Booth had led the police to the murder weapon, which was found in the backyard of St. Clair's aunt's house.

At the end of the article, clearly relishing the moment, Armitage told the writer he'd made a deal with Booth's lawyer. Booth had showed them where to find the gun. Now he would testify against St. Clair, and in exchange he wasn't going to be charged with murder.

By the time he finished reading the article, Ozera was shaking. He flushed the toilet and staggered out of the stall to the sink. An old EMPLOYEES MUST WASH THEIR HANDS sign hung beside the corroded mirror. He looked at himself. He had turned thirty years old a few weeks earlier, and all of a sudden he looked his age. Gone was any trace of boyishness. His skin was pale and sallow. His dark hair was starting to thin. His eyes were red. He'd been crying and hadn't even realized it.

What was he going to do now?

He ran the cold water, filled the sink, and lowered his face into it. It hurt. Stung real hard. That was the idea.

27

The concierge in the lobby of the apartment eyed Ari Greene with suspicion. A metal label on the counter he sat behind said his name was Iqbal.

"Good morning," Greene said. "I'm here to see Mr. and Ms. Wilkinson."

Iqbal shook his head. "We do not reveal the names of our residents. No visitors are allowed unless I have a specific request." He jutted out his jaw, like a bulldog.

Greene pulled out his badge and business card. "I'm glad you are protective of the family."

Iqbal made a show of checking his various security screens before he looked at Greene's identification. He shrugged. "Police or no police, without an invitation, I cannot let you in."

Greene dialed his cell. "It's Detective Greene," he said when Cedric Wilkinson answered. "I'm in your lobby and am very impressed with your concierge. If it's not a bad time, I'd like to drop up and pay a quick visit."

"I'd appreciate it," Wilkinson said. "I'll call down to Iqbal. He's been great at keeping the press away. My wife and the baby are having a nap. I'll meet you at the elevator."

Iqbal picked up his phone a few seconds later, and then, with little enthusiasm, unlocked the glass door that led to the marble-lined main lobby.

"I'm glad you stopped by," Wilkinson said to Greene when he opened the door to their apartment. The place was on the thirty-third floor, a corner suite facing southwest. It was spacious and sparse. Wilkinson had told Greene that before the shooting they they'd been looking for a house to rent, but there was nothing decent on the market. They would normally have had a sweeping view over a big valley named Hoggs Hollow, but right now the snow was so heavy the windows were covered in white.

"That night was the first time in his life Kyle had ever seen snow," he said once he'd hung up Greene's coat. They were standing together, looking outside. "He was so excited. I'd bought him a Toronto Maple Leafs hat, and he told me the kids at day care told him it was called a toque."

Greene watched the blizzard with Wilkinson. There was nothing to say.

"We're not used to having doormen, elevators, underground parking," Wilkinson said. "Back home we had a huge backyard."

Greene saw a plastic Christmas tree with a few unenthusiastic decorations in the corner of the living room. A big double stroller was in the hallway. A blanket covered only the front seat. The throw rugs on the hardwood floors didn't quite fit the space. "How's Kieran doing?" He made a point of asking about the newborn by his name, not just referring to him as "the baby."

"Colicky. Kyle spoiled us. He was such a sleeper. Poor Madeleine, she's up all night with the breast-feeding and then I walk him. She's resting now, and I don't want to wake her."

"Please don't."

"We wanted to go home for the holidays, but she's had all these problems with the stitches and then the bleeding. Doctor doesn't want her to fly yet. I've already told the company I want to transfer back to California once the trial's over."

"I understand."

Wilkinson's big face looked drawn. He seemed to have lost some weight. "I'm not being very polite. Do you want some coffee?"

"No, thanks."

"Tea, juice, water. Anything else?"

"I'm fine."

"Well, I need some coffee."

They went into the kitchen, and Greene sat at the table in the breakfast nook. Wilkinson had a full pot in the coffeemaker. He poured himself a cup and sat down.

"I've tried to take your advice, detective, and haven't read the newspapers. Haven't followed the news online. And I'm not responding to any of the reporters' requests."

There was a buzzing noise. Wilkinson reached into his pocket and turned off his cell phone without even taking it out. "I promised Madeleine I'd try to stay off this stupid thing. They called me 'Cedric Cell Phone' at work, because I was on it all the time."

Greene waited until Wilkinson looked at him. "The grooves on the bullet that killed Kyle were a perfect match with the ones on the gun we found at Larkin St. Clair's aunt's house," he said.

"What will that mean?"

"Means the case against Larkin St. Clair just got stronger."

"And that deal the prosecutor made with Dewey Booth's lawyer?"

Greene had told the Wilkinsons about Armitage's agreement with Cutter back in November and they had been upset.

"Charges are going to be dropped. He's a Crown witness now. As long as he follows through and testifies that St. Clair was the shooter, he'll never be charged."

"Never?"

"Unless we can prove he committed perjury, that's it."

The big man's body slumped. "Damn it," he said.

Greene took a copy of the *Toronto Star* out of his briefcase and tossed it on the table. "I wanted to show this to you before you stumbled on it. Slow news time between Christmas and New Year's, and the story hit the front page."

Wilkinson looked down at the picture of Ralph Armitage, smiling back at him in full color. He scanned the headline and read the first few paragraphs. He shook his head. "Bastard. He just loves getting his name in the press, doesn't he?"

Greene heard a loud crashing noise down the hallway.

Wilkinson jumped out of his chair with alarming speed for such a big man and rushed out of the room.

Greene went to the door of the kitchen and waited. From his angle he couldn't see down the hall.

"Honey, it's okay," Greene heard a woman's voice say. "I slipped in the bathroom."

"Is Kieran—"

"He's in the crib. He's fine," the woman said. "Everyone's okay."

Greene heard a door close. He sat back down at the kitchen table and turned the newspaper over so Ralph Armitage wasn't grinning at him anymore.

About five minutes later, light footsteps came back along the hall. He'd only met Madeleine Wilkinson once, the day after the shooting when she was in the hospital. In stark contrast to her husband, she was beanpole thin, even after giving birth. She stopped at the doorway and leaned her lithe body against the frame.

"Cedric told me the other suspect won't be charged," she said. "He's real upset."

"I don't blame him. We got some tests back on the gun that confirmed the story he'd told us. The press has gotten wind of it, and I wanted you both to hear it from me first."

She nodded. "Good of you to come."

"Least I could do."

"Cedric doesn't blame you for this. We know you're doing your best. Really, we do."

Greene got up. "I should be going," he said.

She didn't move. "It's much worse for him. He was there. He had to tell me."

He stood still. "I know."

"Cedric was just buying Kyle a doughnut. We used to fight about it. Him feeding our son too many sweets. And now he feels like it's all his fault."

He took a few steps. As he passed her in the doorway, Madeleine Wilkinson put her hand on his shoulder. "Cedric says you're the only one who's honest with him," she said. "The only one he can trust."

28

Nancy Parish was sitting in the same chair she'd sat in most of her life, in front of the family dining room table, with her father to her left, her mother to her right. Everything as it had always been, except this year Rick and Roger, her younger twin brothers, weren't in their seats across from her. The rascals had managed to be away for Christmas— Rick out west working as a chef and skiing in Banff, and Roger in graduate school down east in Halifax.

Which meant she'd been forced to face her parents all on her own for three endless days. Somehow they'd survived Christmas without a fight, and on Boxing Day she'd run out to the stores to shop. This afternoon was their last meal together, the kind of formal family feast her mother loved to prepare. The main course was always the same: roast lamb, honeyed yams, and broccoli with toasted almonds. Not the type of food Parish ate anymore, especially for lunch, but she had to admit it tasted good.

They'd made it all the way through to dessert, her mother's signature apple pie with Kawartha Dairy vanilla ice cream, without anything erupting. But it was brewing, like the winter storm up from Texas that had arrived with a fury a few hours ago and was walloping Southern Ontario.

"Dear, I know you'll be upset with me, but there's something I just have to ask you," her mother said as she started pouring the tea using the family silver teapot.

Here it comes, Parish thought, looking outside and watching the wind and snow lash the mullioned dining room windows.

"I do understand that it's your job," her mother said. "But of all the cases, I mean . . . Really, dear. Do you have to take this one?"

"Mom, this is what I do. Defend people. Whether they're charged with shoplifting or murder."

I'm trapped in this case, Parish thought, watching the snow pile up on the driveway. Just like Larkin St. Clair, stuck in his jail cell. At least the food's better in this prison.

"But a child murderer?"

"Right now he's only accused of murder." She couldn't resist sneaking a peek at her father.

Her mother tossed her fork on the table in frustration. "Well, someone has to say it. You both think I'm unsophisticated. But what will you say to this poor family who lost their little son?"

Take a deep breath, Parish told herself. Don't get angry. "I'll never speak to them personally. If one of them takes the stand to testify, I'll have to cross-examine them. That's how the system works. It's horrible what happened—"

"That's my point," her mother said. "Why in the world would you want to be a part of it?" She pushed back her chair and ran into the kitchen.

Parish's father looked at her, opened his hands, and shrugged. I'm going to throttle the twins, she thought, for making me face Mom's annual Christmas cry all alone. She stacked a load of dirty dishes in her arms and followed her mother back to the kitchen.

She put them down on the counter with care. The dishes were the family's good china and there were strict rules about how to handle them. They were not allowed anywhere near the dishwasher. Her mother was at the sink, wearing yellow plastic gloves, washing the silverware.

Parish put a hand on her shoulder. "I know it's hard for you."

Her mother stretched her neck. "I try not to interfere. But, Nancy Gale, we sent you to school in the States, and you were such a top student and . . ." She pulled her hands out of the soapy water and wiped her eyes with her sleeves.

"Mom. We both know if you'd been born thirty years later, you'd have been the one at law school."

Her mother pulled off one of her gloves and stroked her daughter's cheek. With her thumb she rubbed the little bump in the middle of Parish's nose. "All because of that silly little bump," she said.

When Parish was sixteen, her life obsession had been getting the bump on her nose removed. Her father didn't care, but her mother would have none of it. For two years their bitter arguments nearly tore apart the house. Secretly, Parish found a job on Saturdays at the nearby suburban hockey rink when she wasn't playing herself, selling stale popcorn and crappy coffee. On her eighteenth birthday she announced that she'd earned the fifteen hundred dollars for the operation. Her mother relented.

One outrageously cold February morning, mother and daughter

drove into the city. They had to leave home at six, and neither of them said a word the whole trip. Her mother parked the car in the hospital lot and refused to come inside. Instead, she left the motor running and picked up a trashy paperback novel.

Parish got out and slammed the door. For an hour she circled the hospital, her hands and feet getting colder by the minute. She couldn't make herself go inside. She walked south. She had been downtown a few times, but never when she was eighteen, alone, with money in her pocket and no parents around. Ending up at the big square in front of city hall, she wandered over to the open-air skating rink. She was amazed to see men and women in their business suits out on skates.

The most wonderful skater was a young man wearing long black robes. The garment flapped behind him in the wind, like a flock of geese in the fall. He soon stopped and rolled his robes into a luxurious blue velvet bag with his initials on it, pulled it closed with two twined ropes, slung it over one shoulder and the skates over the other. Picking up a large briefcase, he walked across the square, which was now filled with other men and women carrying similar velvet bags.

She followed the lawyers and minutes later was inside the first courtroom she'd ever seen. Behind the raised judge's bench was a massive coat of arms topped by a jewel-encrusted crown held up on one side by a gold lion and on the other by a white unicorn. Ribbons curled around and underneath the crest with the old French inscription HONI PENSE, DIEU ET MON DROIT written in gold letters. The lawyers all wore gowns—like the skater had worn—and gleaming white shirts with starched white tabs.

Parish had walked into a sexual assault trial. A well-dressed young female witness was giving evidence. While the Crown Attorney was asking her questions she seemed perfectly believable. Then a female defense lawyer rose to begin her cross-examination.

"You're an excellent student, Celia, correct?"

"Yes I am."

"Perfect attendance, never skip a class."

"That's right."

"In your initial statement to the police, you said my client, Duane, forced you into the back room behind the gym, correct?"

"Yeah," she said. "He did."

"And your mother was with you when you talked to the police, wasn't she?"

"Uh-huh."

"Your mother isn't in the courtroom today."

"No. She's not allowed."

"You didn't tell her that you skipped out of math because you wanted to meet Duane, did you?"

"I, I can't remember."

"This was the first time in two and a half years that you ever skipped a class. Wasn't it?"

The young woman balled her hands together.

"And your mother doesn't know you were bragging to your friends in the cafeteria a half hour before that you were going to be the first one to do it with my client, does she?"

The woman burst into tears.

"Your mom doesn't know that you told your friend Tina"—the lawyer opened a file and read—"'I win. I was the first to blow Duane.'"

The young woman bit her bottom lip but refused to answer.

"Once the rumor started, you had to deny it, didn't you? Otherwise when your mother found out—"

"You don't know what the kids are like at Caledonia!" Celia wailed. "I thought Tina wouldn't tell anyone. My mother is crazy that I don't become a teenage mom like her."

"And that's why you had to make up this story." The defense lawyer's voice was calm, comforting.

"All the other girls were saying they'd be the first and I . . . I . . ." She started to cry, big heaving sobs.

The judge leaned over and offered her a glass of water.

"Perhaps this is an appropriate time for the morning recess," he said.

As Parish got up to leave the court, a kindly old man in a blue uniform with medals across his chest came up to her. "Interesting, isn't it, dear?" he said. "The best lawyers understand that often you can catch more flies with sugar than with vinegar."

"Yes," she said, hardly able to speak.

"The court reopens at eleven thirty."

Parish looked at her watch. God, her mother would be panicking. She ran out. Racing through the city, she got lost twice before she found the parking lot.

Her mother was there, the remains of an egg salad sandwich crumpled up beside her. Parish yanked the door open. Their eyes met. Neither said a word. Parish reached into the pocket of her parka, pulled out a white envelope, and threw it in her mother's lap.

"I didn't do it," she said, stating the obvious. "There's the money. Save it for my tuition. I'm going to be a lawyer."

The water in the kitchen sink began to gurgle as it went down the drain. A sound Parish had grown up with. She took her mother's hand from her face and held it. There was a smell of soap suds. "No one can cook lamb like you do," she said.

"I miss the boys," her mother said. "And I can't stop thinking about how that poor woman must feel, losing her son that way."

Parish put her arms around her mother. And, for perhaps the thousandth time in her life, with her middle finger traced the bump on her nose. I took the bump less traveled by, she thought. And that has made all the difference.

29

His first day back from the Christmas break, and Ralph Armitage hadn't had a moment to himself. December twenty-seventh, he'd been warned when he took the job last year, was a perfect-storm day for the head Crown. The huge jail cell in the basement of old city hall court was packed with new arrests and people who'd been waiting for bail hearings for days. There were never enough Crowns around. Half of them were on holiday; those who showed up didn't want to be there. They were either hungover, or dying to sneak out and go sale shopping at the nearby Eaton Centre, or both.

He finally got back to his office at noon and was able to shut the door behind him. Somehow in the chaos of the day, he'd managed to find five minutes to sneak out to a newsstand and buy three copies of the new issue of the *Toronto Star,* with his picture on the front page. He'd slipped them into his briefcase but hadn't had time to read the story.

He sat behind his clean desk and pulled out the top copy. Admired it. The photograph of him was very good. And very large. On his way home, he planned to stop at the twenty-four-hour courier drop and overnight two copies down to Barbados, where his parents, sisters, and their broods were together for the annual gathering at the family compound.

This was the first time since he was a child that he hadn't spent Christmas on the island. It was impossible to get away with the new job and this big case. He'd never been in Toronto over the holidays and to his surprise found he liked how quiet the city was with just about everyone out of town. Still, he'd have loved to be there to see his father's face when he saw the newspaper.

The Armitage family was a family of rituals. In the summer they all gathered for the last week of July at their sprawling cottage on their own private lake in Northern Ontario. The fall was an apple-cider-making Thanksgiving weekend at Ralph's parents' rambling home. Christmas holidays and the New Year were spent in Barbados. Mid-February they went skiing at the family chalet in the Laurentians. And

Easter Sunday was an all-day event, starting with a massive egg hunt, followed by a round of golf at the club. But the climax was the Victoria Day weekend charity ball held in the estate's vast backyard, Ralph's favorite place in the world. Organizing the big event was an annual task that for more than a decade had rotated among his four older sisters

All this familial togetherness had seemed natural to him. When he was old enough to start dating, it amazed him to discover that most families didn't work this way. That parents and their grown children rarely got together, and when they did, instead of being fun and joyous, the occasions were often tense and difficult.

For his wife, Penny Wolchester, this ongoing "Armitage group hug," as she called it, was foreign territory. She was raised in what she laughingly referred to as the world's most boring family—her dad was a school librarian whose only hobby was refinishing furniture; Mom was a chemist who spent her spare time quilting and clipping coupons. Their home was in the cookie-cutter suburb of Don Mills, which she referred to as Don Nothing-Doing Mills. They never went on family trips. Didn't own a cottage. Didn't do any sports together. She moved out of the house when she was nineteen and after that saw her folks, and her younger sister, Lindsay, only two or three times a year.

When Penny was twenty-five, the year she dropped out of architecture school and started teaching spin classes full-time, her parents announced with great excitement that they'd sold the family home and bought a condo in Arizona, where they planned to spend six months every winter, and a mobile home they would travel around in for the other half of the year. A few months later, Lindsay got a nursing job in Saskatoon and within a year was married with her first child on the way.

She met Ralph at the gym a year later, and he was thrilled at the way she embraced his family. His four older sisters, who like Penny were all super-athletic, loved having another female around both as a play partner and to enjoy mocking "Little Ralphie." They'd grown close, and this year for the first time his sisters had passed the mantle of planning the May Two-Four charity event to Penny. This was the final step of her complete acceptance into the family fold. Penny was excited and terrified.

She'd been good about missing their holiday down south. Most of her rich clients were away, and she was glad to have the time to work on the party. In the newspaper article, the reporter asked him how, being so busy, they kept their marriage together, and he'd talked about their special Thursday night dates. Which reminded him. Penny was on to the menu planning now, and tomorrow night she'd arranged visits to three different caterers.

Armitage had just finished the article when he heard a knock on his door. He checked the time. Exactly four o'clock. He slipped the newspaper back in his briefcase.

"Hi, Albert," he said to Albert Fernandez, greeting him at the door. "Right on time."

Fernandez's arms were filled with two large black binders, and he had a pad of paper on top. There were five key witnesses to the shooting, and the plan was to interview them all this afternoon. Armitage wanted to meet beforehand to go over their evidence.

"I've put all the disclosure to date into both of these," Fernandez said, lifting the binders. "Officers' notes, forensic reports, photos of the scene, background and criminal records of all witnesses, CDs with all their statements on tape, and transcripts so you can just read them."

He wore a trim gray-green suit with the jacket buttoned up. Unlike most of the other Crowns, who wore pretty cheap, casual clothes, the guy dressed so formally, Armitage thought. I bet he doesn't even own a pair of jeans. And boy was he ever Mr. Organization.

"Good work," Armitage said. "We better get a copy over to the defense right away."

"Already done. I couriered a complete set to Nancy Parish's office and phoned to tell her. She was driving back into town from her parents' place. Appreciated the call."

Armitage closed the door behind them, clapped Fernandez on the back, and guided him to one of the two client chairs in front of his big desk.

"I read the article about you in the paper this morning," Fernandez said as he sat down. "I didn't know everyone calls you 'Ralphie.'" Fernandez sounded chipper for the first time.

Armitage sat beside him and laughed. "Call me Ralphie any time you want. All my old school buddies and camp friends do. But can I call you Albie?"

Fernandez cracked a smile. That's progress, Armitage thought.

"If you must," Fernandez said.

"Okay, Albie, but only behind closed doors." Armitage rubbed his hands together. "Witnesses all here and ready to go?"

Fernandez looked down at the pad of paper he had on top of the files and frowned.

"Adela Dobos. She's the one who bought a coffee and a maple-glazed doughnut and had just walked out the door when the shots started. From Serbia and hardly speaks a word of English. The translator is here, but we've only got him for an hour."

"I thought the Serbian woman was the one across the street."

"No, that was the Albanian. Edone Kutishi. We couldn't get a translator here today, but her English isn't too bad."

Armitage grinned. "Can't tell apart the witnesses without a program. I've got a headache already. Where was the Bangladeshi guy again?"

"Vikram Dalmar Abdul Mohammed. He was having hot chocolate with his grandson by the front window. His car got stuck in a snowbank, and he can't make it. Gandharvan Sundrilingham is the Tamil fellow. He's the one who'd just walked in the door. He was ahead of the Wilkinsons when the boy got shot. He's not coming also because his wife is sick."

"Neither of them speak English, do they?"

"No, but Nigel Jameson does. He's the South African who was the first to call 911."

"Great. Please tell me he's here."

"Stuck in New York because of the storm. He's a banker and travels a lot."

Armitage stood. "Let's start with these two," he said.

Fernandez remained seated. He looked up awkwardly at Armitage. "There's something I want to discuss with you."

"No problem, Albie," Armitage said, laughing as he sat back down. "Let's talk."

"You told me we had to keep this deal we made with Dewey Booth secret. But it's in the article." Fernandez pointed at the newspaper on Armitage's desk. "You told them all about it."

Armitage shrugged. "I had to wait until Greene moved in on Suzanne Howett and her boyfriend Jet."

Fernandez nodded reluctantly.

Armitage knew that other Crowns in the office thought he'd made a terrible move with this deal. It was further undermining their confidence in him as their leader. He had to nip this in the bud. "Albert, you don't think it's a good deal, do you?" he asked. No more "Albie" talk. This was serious.

"I mean"—Fernandez fidgeted with the corners of his pad of paper—"all you have is an affidavit. You didn't get Booth's sworn statement on video. He wasn't cross-examined. So—"

"So he might turn out to be a lousy witness for us at trial," Armitage said.

Fernandez exhaled loudly, relieved that Armitage had said it. "The affidavit's quite vague."

"I made a big mistake. That what you're saying?"

"Not really, but . . ."

Armitage turned to look Fernandez squarely in the eye. "Look. The key point is that Dewey Booth says in a sworn legal document that he wasn't the shooter, and that Larkin St. Clair was. If he changes his story in court, the deal's off. We charge him with perjury and first-degree murder."

"Do you really think the jury will believe him?" Fernandez asked.

"They might, probably won't," Armitage said, "but who cares? Once Booth says Larkin was the shooter, Larkin's got no choice but to take the stand. If he says he wasn't the shooter, how does he explain the gun? That's why I needed this deal. I needed that gun."

"What if Larkin says Dewey did it? And he was just hiding the gun for him?"

Armitage laughed. A big loud chuckle. "Even better. It's called a cutthroat defense. When two assholes like these punks get on the stand and point the finger of guilt at each other. Trust me, Albie, it never ever works. Jury would be out for less than an hour. But Cutter and Parish, they're too smart for that. Our biggest problem would be if they were both charged together and kept their mouths shut. We can't make an accused person talk or testify and how do we prove which one was the shooter?"

"Would it matter? Whoever shot the other one would be a party to the offense, equally guilty."

"That's the black-letter law. You're going to give me the greatest legal memo ever on parties to an offense. And I'll tell the jury that whichever one of those rats shot the gun, the other one is as guilty as sin. But you never know. First-degree murder, a jury wants certainty. And if they think Jet fired the first shots standing outside his Cadillac, that could be trouble for us."

Fernandez wasn't fiddling anymore. He was taking it all in.

"There's one more very important detail you might have overlooked. Here. Give me that pad of paper," Armitage said. "And your pen."

Fernandez handed them over. For the next twenty minutes, Armitage sketched out the Tim Hortons parking lot, the location of all the players, the direction of the gunshots. "Look at the autopsy report," he said when he was almost done. "You'll see the bullet hit the boy in the left side of the head, but Dewey and Larkin were standing to his right."

Detective Greene didn't think this was a big deal, but so what? He was just the cop. What was important was to get Fernandez on his side. He'd pass the word to the other Crowns.

Fernandez had the autopsy report perfectly tabbed in one of his binders. He inspected it. "I see your point," he said.

"James Trapper, aka Jet, has got a bad criminal record, including il-legal possession of an unregistered handgun." Armitage tapped the Ca-dillac in the drawing. "Only one shell casing was found at the scene. Crushed. It's useless for comparison with the gun we recovered. It was right here. If Jet was shooting, and remember the bullet mark on the wall behind where Dewey and Larkin were standing, this could be his shell." He drew a curved line in front of the car that showed it driving out of the lot.

He explained how, without finding the gun, the wound to the left side of the boy's head could have been used by Booth and St. Clair to claim that the fatal bullet wasn't fired by them.

Fernandez was silent. Like a witness whom Armitage had brow-beaten in court.

"Imagine what would have happened at trial if we couldn't match the bullet that killed the boy to the gun in St. Clair's hand. Sure, I hated having to make this deal, but without that gun we could easily have lost everything."

Fernandez nodded. Convinced.

"We're up against good defense lawyers in this case. I knew they'd put this together once they got the full disclosure. Cutter contacted me two days after the shooting. At that point all we had was that lousy video of St. Clair sticking some unknown thing down his pants and taking off."

"I see," Fernandez said.

Armitage ripped the page off the pad and crushed it into a ball. "We had to link St. Clair to the gun that was fired. Now Dewey's going to rat out his pal. It will force Larkin into the box and I can't wait to cross-examine him. And Cutter's deal was a one-time offer."

He had been a basketball star right through high school, university, and law school, and he still played with his high school friends every Tuesday night in the gym at their old private school. He took the rolled-up paper in his hand, pivoted, and eyed the garbage can in the corner.

"Listen, Albie. I know everyone in this office thinks I'm afraid to do a big trial and that all I can do is make deals." He raised his right arm above his head and flexed his wrist back, in perfect form for a jump shot. "Do me a favor. If we're going to work together on this case, I need you to back me up. Clear?"

"Clear," Fernandez said.

Armitage tossed the paper ball in a graceful arc. It landed squarely in the garbage can.

"Good." He allowed himself an unseen grin. "Now I've got to kick you out of here. *Canadian Lawyer* magazine is sending a reporter to interview me for another cover story."

30

"Merry Christmas, Nancy." Larkin St. Clair settled himself comfortably into his seat across from Nancy Parish in the interview room at the Toronto East Detention Centre. The East was a big, institutional jail and it felt as if the wind was blowing right through its thick concrete walls. "How's your mom's home cooking?"

"Delicious," she said.

"No family squabbles I hope."

A few years ago, in another weak moment, she'd complained to Larkin about her difficult relationship with her mother. Huge mistake. He never let her forget it. "It was a Kodak moment, wish you could have been there," she said.

"Me? No way. We got roast beef and mashed potatoes and peas. Special meal. My favorite prison guard, Rachel, even gave me an extra portion."

"I'm sure it was the highlight of her Christmas," she said.

He let out one of his patented guffaws. But his eyes were on her thick briefcase, which was bulging at the sides. "What've you got there?" he asked.

"I just picked up the disclosure and came right over here," she said.

"What took them so long?" he asked, stroking his hair. In the six weeks since his arrest it had grown back down close to his shoulders.

She hauled out two big evidence binders. "This is fast for a murder trial."

"I only care about one thing," he said. "What did that rat Dewey say?"

"Hold your horses," she told him. "I haven't even looked at this yet. Let's start from the beginning."

She'd come to visit him twice a week since his arrest and he'd steadfastly refused to discuss what had happened in the Tim Hortons parking lot until he saw what Booth told the cops. She was frustrated but experienced enough with Larkin to know that if she pushed him he'd just make up more lies.

Over the years she'd learned the best way to do a complex case was to go over every piece of evidence with her clients in painstaking detail. They always knew more than they told you, and sometimes they'd legitimately forgotten things. Besides, Larkin had made her wait long enough. She was going do this her way.

The first binder had all the technical stuff. Photos of the crime scene, the recovered bullet cartridges, a chip in the sidewalk by the side of the Tim Hortons, another in the wall behind, a third in the building across the way, a crushed empty bullet shell down at the corner of the lot, a scale drawing of the whole area, and lengthy medical reports.

On the last pages, she came to the photos of the young boy, including close-ups of where the bullet had entered his head. St. Clair, who'd been unusually subdued, grew quieter as he looked at the pictures.

She closed the binder.

"Shit," he whispered.

"You know how the jury's going to feel when they see this," she said.

He bobbed his head up and down. "They're going to hate me."

"With a passion."

He pointed to the second binder. "Let's see what Dewey the Rat said."

First there were witness interviews. Twenty-two people had been questioned, but most of their statements were only a page or two long. Only five had anything significant to say, and Parish went over these carefully with St. Clair.

"We need to map out the evidence against you at its highest," she said after they'd read the last statement. "They've got you and Dewey sitting at the table by the door. Only one witness sees you two leave, and he doesn't see you after that. The other witnesses are unclear on how many shots are fired, as many as nine, and no one can say for sure where they came from."

"Nine shots?" he said, perking up. "The gun's clip only held six bullets and one in the chamber. Seven max."

"I know. That's great evidence for us, if it stands up. I can argue there was another shooter. That the shots from the gun were fired in self-defense. The only shell they found was flattened by Jet's Cadillac and he took off right away. That helps."

He was nodding his head, fast.

"Don't get too excited. They've still got you on that video stuffing something in your pants and taking off."

"Doesn't help that they found the gun at my aunt's house, thanks to Dewey."

He was smart and bitter, she thought. His attitude would be a lethal combination in front of the jury. They'd smell his anger.

Next in the binder came a large collection of officers' notes that covered the night of the shooting, St. Clair's arrest, chasing down Booth, investigating various leads, and finding the gun. There was the gunshot residue report from the day of his arrest. She showed it to him. "GSR was on your right hand, your right sleeve, and inside the front of your pants."

His skin was dry and flaky. He picked at a scab on his hand. "It's not a problem," he said. "Pick a bunch of beautiful girls for the jury, and I'll tell them I stuffed a chocolate éclair down there and the thing was radioactive."

She started to shake her head at him, then she caught his grin. They both laughed.

Then came the forensic reports of the gun cartridges. This was bad news. X-ray photos of the barrel of the gun and the marks on the sides of the shell found in Kyle's brain at the autopsy were a perfect match. Conclusive proof that the gun found in St. Clair's aunt's backyard had fired the fatal shot.

In every case there was always one piece of damning evidence that stood out. Here it was: Larkin St. Clair had stuffed the gun that killed a four-year-old boy down the front of his pants, took off, and hid the murder weapon at his aunt's house. Unless they had an answer for this horrible fact, he was going to be convicted.

"Shit," he said.

"I agree," she said. "Shit."

They were almost at the end of the binder. The only windows in the jail were long and narrow, covered with bars on the outside. She could see the snow bashing away at the heavy glass.

Larkin closed his eyes and pressed his fingers into his forehead. "Where the fuck's Dewey's statement?"

"I don't know." She turned the pages and came upon a signed piece of paper titled "Agreement Re: Mr. Dewey Booth."

"Here it is," she said.

"Let me see, let me see," he said.

"Like I told you, Armitage signed a deal with Phil Cutter, Dewey's lawyer. Dewey's whole statement is a one-page affidavit sworn by Cutter's law partner."

"What's it say? What's it say?"

She read it slowly. "Your buddy told them you were the shooter. The deal is, Dewey takes them to the gun and if the gun tests, which it did, and he testifies in court against you, charges are dropped against him now and forever."

"Let me see."

"Be my guest." She turned the binder so he could read it. "The Crown didn't even cross-examine him or get a sworn video statement. Shows how desperate Armitage was to get the gun."

"No. Desperate to get me," St. Clair said after he'd read the affidavit. "That phony hates my guts."

"Maybe so . . ." Parish's mind was going in a thousand directions at once, trying to figure out what this would mean. "We knew this was coming. It's real bad."

She looked hard at Larkin.

"What if Dewey says in court that he was the shooter, not me?" Larkin asked.

"Was he?"

Larkin wouldn't meet her eyes. "I'm just asking."

"Then the deal's off. He gets charged too. With murder and perjury. There's no way he's going to change his story."

"What if I take the stand and say he was the shooter? What happens?"

"Depends. If the jury acquits you, the Crown might say, 'Hey, Dewey committed perjury,' and the deal will be off. Then they'd prosecute him."

"Oh."

Larkin looked even more unhappy.

"We call it a cutthroat defense when two accused point at each other. Only works one in a million times. There's a dead little boy lying in a Tim Hortons parking lot across the street from the courthouse. The jury's not going to give a shit if you pulled the trigger or if you were helping Dewey. Either way you were a party to the offense. Equally culpable in law."

St. Clair jumped out of his chair and clapped his hands to his head. He started rotating around his left leg, as if it were stuck to the ground.

Parish slammed the binder shut. "Time to talk the talk," she said.

"I'm not guilty," he said.

"You keep telling me that, but you haven't told me what happened. Dewey threw you to the dogs. Why are you protecting him?"

He stopped rotating. She could feel the tension coming from her oldest client. The competing calculations between the truth, whatever that was, and his survival, which would include making sure he didn't get on Dewey's bad side.

"If you lie to me again I'm getting off this case," she said. "I don't care how long I've been your lawyer."

He shook his head. "Then I'm not going to say anything. You've got to find some way of winning this case without me testifying."

"How am I supposed to do that?"

"I don't know. You're the lawyer."

She was acting shocked, but she'd expected this. "Okay. I've got a few theories."

He sat back down, stiller than she'd ever seen him.

"Theory one. You owed Dewey. Your last crime together, when you two robbed that pharmacy, he said you were outside as the lookout. He took the hit for three years and you only got a year plus probation. Jet's girlfriend Suzanne dumps him while he's in prison and starts dating Jet. Your payback to Dewey is to take a potshot at Jet. Not kill the guy, that's not your style, just scare him. But things go terribly wrong."

St. Clair folded his arms. "If the jury believes that, what happens?"

"Guilty of manslaughter, bare minumum. Even if you didn't mean it, once you're firing that gun whatever happens goes back to you."

"Theory two?"

"Same as one, but it's Dewey who's doing the shooting. Harder sell because you're the one who took off with the gun in your pants and hid it in your aunt's backyard. Maybe taking the gun was payback for Dewey taking the three-year rap."

"Where does that get me?"

"Same place. Even if you didn't pull the trigger, as long as you knew he was going to shoot then you're a party to the crime. And by the way, also guilty of accessory after the fact for hiding the gun."

"Any other brain waves?"

"Last one. Jet spots you two guys and fires first. There's a bullet hole in the wall behind where you and Dewey were standing and the only blank cartridge they find is a flattened-out one down at the end of the parking lot where his Cadillac was. He's shooting, and you or Dewey fire back in self-defense but slip on the ice. Et cetera, et cetera."

"Theory three have a chance?"

"A slight one."

St. Clair unfolded his arms and reached for the one-page affidavit. "Dewey doesn't say anything about Jet shooting first," he said.

"You're right. He's pretty vague about the whole thing." She stared at him. "Why won't you tell me what happened?"

"Because I'm not going to lie to you anymore."

She'd never seen him look so serious.

"I still don't get it," she said. "He ratted you out."

St. Clair leaned across the metal table, all sense of life drained from his face. "Nancy, you know why I've got to keep my trap shut. Dewey goes down for this because of me and I'm dead meat. You've got to find another way to get me out of this."

31

Ari Greene sat on the hard metal stool in the visitors' room of the Toronto East Detention Centre taking the measure of the man sitting across from him, who was wearing the standard prison-orange garb and a rather dirty turban. It was eleven thirty in the morning, and Officer Darvesh looked thin and tired. A large tinfoil package was in front of Greene. He unwrapped it to reveal a collection of East Indian breads—*paratha* and sesame naan, which was slathered with butter—as well as a plastic container of chicken curry and yellow Indian rice.

"Your mother asked me to bring you this."

Darvesh pulled off a tiny corner off the naan, dipped an edge in the curry sauce, and popped it in his mouth. Then he folded the foil back up to cover the food. "Tell her I ate it all," he said, passing the package over to Greene. "You can have it. I can't risk eating something this pungent."

The young officer was right. Inmates all ate the same bland, starch-rich diet. If the prisoner they knew as Alisander Singh went back to the range smelling of curry after he'd supposedly been meeting with the immigration board, the jig would be up.

"Has St. Clair said anything yet?"

"Nah. Nothing."

"Think he suspects you?" Greene asked.

Darvesh shook his head. "You made a smart move putting me in the wagon with him from day one. He'd never think a skinny brown guy like me would be a cop."

"What's he talk about?"

"Not much. The first few days he was the loudest guy on the range. Then day three he met with his lawyer, and since then he's hardly said a word."

"Day three he would have found out that his buddy Dewey had turned on him," Greene said.

"He met her again last night. Put him back in a foul mood."

"What did he say about it?"

"That he'd seen the disclosure and it was all bullshit."

"He would have seen the deal Armitage made with Dewey's lawyer all laid out in black and white."

"That must have been it. Boy, was he pissed. Throwing things around the cell. Screaming at the guards."

Greene stood up. Being in a jail cell always brought back to him the time he was arrested in the South of France. Trying to speak French. Trying to explain. Those few hours in custody on that horrible day never left him. Never would.

"Did Larkin say anything about Dewey?" Greene asked.

"Yeah. He said Dewey needed a brain transplant."

"Anything else?"

"No. I thought if I acted too curious it would be suspicious."

"Good call. Don't push him. I'm sure he's been warned to keep his trap shut. But people's basic personalities don't change. He won't be able to stay quiet forever."

Darvesh stretched.

"How're you doing?" Greene asked.

"I'm fine."

"I won't tell your mother how thin you look."

Darvesh laughed. He eyed the wrapped package of food by Greene's elbow. "I need another bite," he said.

Greene unwrapped it and Darvesh dipped a corner of bread in the curry. He lingered over the food, savoring the smell. "The worst part of this is the prison food. It's so bland."

"Dinner's on me anywhere you want in Little India, as soon as you get out," Greene said.

Darvesh folded up the aluminum foil. "How do you white people survive eating such boring food?" he asked.

"It's a challenge."

"You probably won't believe this," Darvesh said.

"Try me."

"I miss spices almost as much as I miss sex."

Greene laughed and stood to leave. "I guess," he said, "you've got a double incentive to get Larkin to talk."

32

Daniel Kennicott wasn't a joiner. He didn't care for team sports, preferring to run marathons, bike ride long distances, swim for miles up at the lake at his parents' cottage. He'd never been someone with many friends, in part because as a child he'd spent so much time with his family. Even when they were adults, he and his older brother Michael had spoken at least once a day, before he was murdered.

And then there was the question of women. The truth was, he much preferred their company to hanging out with a bunch of guys to play hockey, watch sports, or drink beer. In law school and at his law firm, he'd been popular enough, but leaving that all behind and becoming a police officer had mostly cut him off from his old life. And he didn't exactly fit on the police force: a cop who'd been a lawyer and lived in a funky neighborhood downtown instead of a cozy commuter suburb, to say nothing of his penchant for wearing quality clothes and handmade shoes.

Jeremy Pulver was the one exception. He and Kennicott had met in a philosophy class at university and gone to law school together. After graduating, Pulver headed straight to the Crown Attorney's office, where he'd been a very successful prosecutor for almost a decade.

Whenever his shifts allowed him the time, Kennicott would drop into Pulver's tiny office at the end of the court day. Usually just to say hello, but sometimes, like now, when he needed to think something through. For the last few weeks they'd been talking through the Wilkinson case, or "the Timmy's shooting" as the nonstop press insisted on calling it.

It was just before five in the afternoon, and Pulver was behind his desk. This was a hilarious sight because the government-issue furniture was small, and Pulver was six foot eight. Skinny, skinny, skinny, with a bleached white complexion and a crop of kinky, unmanageable hair. He was packing his briefcase and had to leave in fifteen minutes to meet his partner, Arthur, at the gym they went to every night.

"We've been looking for this Jose guy, the baker at the Tim Hortons who took off after the shooting." Kennicott leaned against the side wall. "We're pretty sure he's here illegally."

Pulver rolled his eyes. "Good luck. We had a seminar on illegals in Toronto a few weeks ago. The ministry estimates there are seventy-five thousand of them."

"Guy told his employer he was Portuguese, but we don't believe it. He speaks all sorts of languages, and it sounds as if he's real smart. Our hunch is that he's Romanian."

Pulver gave him a sardonic smile. "Well, that probably narrows your search from seventy-five thousand to about ten."

"You're a great help," Kennicott said.

"Philosophy 101, play it back from the beginning."

At university they'd had a demanding professor, Thompson Chamberlain, whose hobby was horses. "You train a horse one step at a time, always going back to the beginning and moving forward. Same thing with philosophy." He'd written those words on the blackboard the first day of class and had repeated them at the beginning of each lecture. After surviving his class, law school had been easy, mostly because Chamberlain had taught them how to analyze problems. How to think.

"Why did your man Jose take off?" Pulver asked.

Kennicott put a finger in the air. "First possibility is that he was somehow involved in the shooting. Doesn't add up. Dewey Booth is the one with motive to gun down his rival while Jet was picking up Suzanne, his ex-girlfriend."

"Keep going." Pulver rifled through a stack of files, jamming a few more into his briefcase.

Kennicott put another finger up. "Jose was threatened by the shooter. Years ago, Booth and St. Clair did a home invasion and scared the witness into not coming to court. There's a bullet mark in the wall behind where the two clowns were standing. Maybe they took a potshot at him. Scared him off."

"Then why didn't they kill him?"

Kennicott shrugged. "Too dark to see him? Too messy? However this went down, they couldn't have meant to kill that little boy."

Pulver looked up from his papers. "I buy that."

This was what made his friend such a good Crown, Kennicott thought. He had perspective. Didn't see every human foible as proof of some grand conspiracy of evil.

Third finger. "Sometimes the most obvious answer's the right one. Like I said, guy gave a false name to his employer. He's illegal, doesn't want to get deported."

"That works too." Pulver looked at his watch. He stood, towering now over the minuscule-looking desk. "Arthur keeps asking when are you coming over."

Pulver's partner Arthur loved trying to set Kennicott up with every woman he knew. He worked as a booker at a talent agency and was on a first-name basis with every actress and model in the city. Loved to brag that he had "access to the top tier." He was five feet tall, if he was lucky, which made Arthur and Jeremy the most mismatched pair you could imagine. And the happiest couple Kennicott knew.

"It's tough when I'm on a homicide like this," he said.

"Tomorrow night, no excuses. It's the holidays for goodness' sakes. Dinner at eight."

"On one condition. No more female friends of Arthur 'dropping by' just before it's time to eat."

"Then bring a date. Andrea tired of Paris yet?"

Kennicott had been involved in an on-again off-again relationship with a Toronto-born fashion model named Andrea for a very long time. Too long. They were very bad for each other in most ways, except in bed, where they'd been very good. He'd been relieved two years before when she had gone on an assignment to Paris and ended up living with a photographer. Relieved most of the time. Every once in a while, she'd show up on his doorstep, and he wasn't terribly good at kicking her out.

"Luckily not." Kennicott put up his fourth finger. "I thought maybe our pal Jose had been arrested before. I had the forensic guys take fingerprints from some pans in the kitchen and the butt of the cigarette he'd shared out back with Suzanne. We got some DNA from his hairnet that Greene found in the bushes. They ran everything through the police computer."

"Any luck?"

"Nada. Nothing matches."

Kennicott fanned out his fingers. "Where does that leave us?"

Pulver stuck out his thumb. "Five. Maybe he was arrested for some minor offense and he got released on a Form Ten."

This was a smart suggestion. A "Form Ten" was the piece of paper accused people signed when they were charged with minor offenses, such as mischief or shoplifting, and released by the arresting officer without having to be brought to court to get bail. They'd be required to sign another document, called a Promise to Appear. The promise was that they'd go the police station to get their photo and fingerprints taken, and then would go to court on the set date. "You're thinking that he never showed up for prints or court. There'd be a warrant out for his arrest," he said.

Pulver laughed. "When I first started at the Crown's office, I spent half a year processing fail-to-appear charges. Do you have any idea how many we get every month?"

Kennicott shook his head. "A hundred?"

Pulver spread out all the fingers in his massive hand. Wherever he went to school, gym teachers had tried to get him to join the basketball team. He never did. Said he was the least-coordinated person on the planet. "Five hundred on average. Way more in the summer. About six thousand a year. Assume your Jose could have been arrested any time in the last, say, five years—"

"Make it six. That's more than thirty-five thousand. Quite a haystack."

Pulver looked at his watch. "Happy hunting, amigo."

"Maybe now I have to work tomorrow night," Kennicott said.

"Nice try. The warrant office and everything else around here except a few emergency Crowns on duty is locked up until after the holidays," he said. "Got to go."

They walked together down the narrow hallway passing the office of a law school colleague of theirs, Jo Summers. Her door was closed. Kennicott had recently worked on a case in which her half brother was killed. They both had brothers who were murdered. It gave them something in common. That and a one-night stand they'd had years before at law school. The attraction hadn't gone away, but their timing was always off.

Kennicott had never mentioned any of this to Pulver, but Pulver didn't miss anything. "Jo took a bereavement leave," he said.

"Good idea." Kennicott worked hard to sound bored.

"Went back to South America, where she traveled a few years ago."

Actually, he knew she'd gone to Central America, but Kennicott wasn't about to correct him. And he hadn't heard from her in months. "Oh," he said, thinking he sounded foolish. He was tempted to ask, "When's she returning?" but he managed to hold himself back.

Pulver stopped walking. "She got back about a month ago."

"Oh," Kennicott said again. This time he really sounded stupid.

"Tomorrow night at eight," Pulver said. "With Arthur, anyone could drop in. And you know she'll be beautiful."

Kennicott thought to object, but the words didn't come.

33

This was turning into a really bad day. It was a Thursday, and right now Ralph Armitage was supposed to be on his way to tasting the fine foods of three of the city's best caterers with his beautiful wife, Penny. Instead, for the second time in the last two months, he'd had to cancel their weekly date. She was upset, but he'd assured her this was a one-time emergency and promised it wouldn't happen again. Now he was sitting once again at the Plaza Flamingo, in the exact same table where he'd met with Phil Cutter six weeks before and made their deal.

He'd decided this was a good place to meet the fellow who'd called him a few hours ago. The guy had insisted they meet privately and it had to be tonight. The restaurant was loud and crowded, and no one would notice them.

He had brought a copy of the *Toronto Star* with him to read while he was waiting. There wasn't any news. Not surprising three days after Christmas. Even the Maple Leafs weren't playing, so the sports page was a bore. The weather map showed another snowstorm was on the way. And the city was still shoveling out from the big one yesterday. He checked the temperature in Barbados. Sunny and warm. He could just picture his whole family spending the day at the beach, playing volleyball at sunset.

"Excuse me, sir."

He looked up. A small-boned man with short dark hair and a beard, but no mustache, was standing behind the chair at the other end of the table. Before coming here, Armitage had carefully inspected the composite drawing that had been done of Jose Sanchez, the baker who'd worked at the Tim Hortons. He could tell this guy had tried hard to change his appearance, but even in the bar's dim light the birthmark by his left eye was easy to spot.

"Have a seat."

"Thank you for meeting with me." The man's eyes flitted about the room before he sat across the table from Armitage. He had a slight accent, kind of Eastern European, but wasn't hard to understand.

"Most people call the cops, not the Crown," Armitage said.

"I don't want to talk to the cops." He put his hands on the sides of his head, as if he were trying to hide his face.

"At the Tim Hortons you gave your name as Sanchez," Armitage said. "Jose Sanchez. We've checked everyone in the city with that name. None of them is you. I'm assuming it's not your real name."

Sanchez, or whoever he was, nodded.

"What's your name?"

"Call me 'Jose,'" he said.

"Okay, Jose. What do you want to talk about?"

The man put his hands in front of him and meshed his fingers together. Armitage noticed his fingertips were brown. Looked like nicotine stains. He still didn't speak.

"You called me. I suggested we meet here because no one can overhear us," Armitage said. "I'm not taking any notes. Not taping this. Whatever you say will just be between you and me."

Jose stared straight ahead. "I was there," he said at last.

"We assumed that."

"No, no, I was right there. I heard them talking."

The restaurant was hot, but Armitage felt his skin go cold. Under the table, he balled his big hands into two fists. Don't talk, just listen, he told himself

"Sir," Jose said, shaking his head. "You've made a very big mistake."

Armitage felt as if he'd been punched in the head. Stay calm, he thought. "The police have investigated this very thoroughly. The lighting wasn't very good outside."

"I was right behind those two guys. They didn't know I was there. But I saw it all."

"We have a number of witnesses," Armitage said.

Jose, or whoever the hell he was, put his hands up. "I read the article in the *Star*. You're the one who made a deal with the short guy Dewey Booth's lawyer, aren't you?"

"I did." Armitage had a lump in his throat. "What are you saying?"

"The tall one with the hair."

"You mean Larkin St. Clair?"

Jose shook his head. "You picked the wrong guy."

A wave of heat spread across Armitage's body. Thank God it's dark in here, he thought. He unclenched his fists and wiped them on the top of his pants.

Jose stood and moved to the chair beside Armitage. He reached into his coat pocket and pulled out a piece of paper, which he unfolded and ironed out with his hand on the desk. "I drew everything out here for you," he said, and for the next five minutes traced out his story with his fingers as he spoke. It felt like five hours.

Armitage watched in horror. He thought of how he'd sat at this very same table when he'd signed off on the deal with Phil Cutter to let Dewey Booth walk free. How that asshole lawyer gloated afterward. Now he was thinking about the Wilkinsons and their dead child. About facing them. His staff. Everyone questioning what he'd done. And Larkin St. Clair and his smug, smiling face. Would he walk free again? This could give him a defense. And there was no guarantee this Jose character sitting across from him was telling the truth. He could just imagine Cutter slicing him to bits on the witness stand. Then Dewey would get off too. And forever more, Armitage would be known as the head Crown who blew the most important case in decades.

Anger surged through him. "Your name isn't Jose, is it?" he said.

The man exhaled. "Of course not."

"Who the hell are you?"

"Why do you need to know?"

"Because you've got a big problem. You ran away from the scene of a murder with material evidence. My guess is you did it because either there's a warrant out for your arrest for some other crime, or else you're in the country illegally."

He stared at Armitage for a long time. "Both," he whispered at last.

Good, Armitage thought. "You made a smart move contacting me first. Immigration finds out about this, they'll deport you the minute the trial's over. And the press would eat you alive."

Jose ducked his head down. "I don't want to be in the press. Dewey and Larkin both saw me." He pointed to his hand-drawn map. "That shot just above my head. I thought I was going to be killed."

Armitage thought of the bullet hole in the wall of the Tim Hortons. "You afraid?"

Jose nodded. "Wouldn't you be?"

"That's the real reason you ran?"

Jose shrugged. "I wish I'd stayed."

"I don't think you understand," Armitage said. "If you come forward with this now, so late, it will taint your testimony. The defense will discredit you in a minute. Say you made this up to play for sympathy, so you can stay in Canada."

Jose was back to being silent.

"I'm prosecuting the murder of a young boy. I don't need you to muddy the waters."

Jose was looking at his hands again. As if he'd retreated into himself.

This was like when he was in court and got going in a witness cross-examination, Armitage thought. "I might be able to help you with this."

Jose looked back up. In the low light, it was hard to read his eyes. Was he nervous or just curious?

"Tell me who you are, then I can look up your file. I'm the head Crown. How serious was it?"

Jose snorted. "Shoplifting. But then I never went to court."

Perfect. There were all sorts of ways he could bury a file like this. "I can take care of your charges," he said. "But you better keep quiet about it. Don't talk to anyone else but me. Understood?"

Jose nodded.

I've got him, Armitage thought. Thank goodness. He put his arm out and offered his hand. "Deal?"

Jose looked at the hand but didn't move. "I need to think about it." He stood up.

Armitage grabbed him by the wrist and jumped to his feet. He towered over the little guy. "I can take care of this for you," he said again. His voice was loud, and some patrons at the other tables looked over.

Jose stared up at him. Christ, he was a cool cookie.

"I don't think you want me to raise my voice, do you?" Jose whispered.

"I need an answer," Armitage hissed, his grip still firm.

"I'll call you."

"No," Armitage said. He knew he sounded desperate. "Don't call the office again. Give me your number. Or an address."

"I have a better idea. Meet me here in two weeks. Thursday night, same time, same table. We'll talk then."

Shit. Another Thursday night. Penny was going to kill him. "Okay," he said. He didn't have any other choice.

"Now let go of my hand," Jose said.

He released him. "But we have a deal?"

Jose reached back into his pants pocket and pulled out a folded-over piece of paper. "This is who I am. First, let's see what you can do for me."

Before Armitage could protest, the guy scampered away.

And with him, the fate of his whole career. Probably his marriage too. Worst day ever, he thought. Worst fucking day ever.

34

It was a key moment in the history of Toronto. Back in the 1970s, local politicians were about to drive an expressway right through the heart of the city, when a determined group of downtown residents brought construction to a screeching halt. The ill-fated project was about a third complete and huge tracts of land had been expropriated. The protesters returned to their protected neighborhoods, leaving behind a stump of a road and an open pit that carried on for miles, like tire marks left on a highway by a runaway truck suddenly forced to brake.

In the city's best tradition of political compromises leading to disastrous planning decisions, rails were laid across the open ground even though there was scant population on either side of the tracks. Decades later, the Subway to Nowhere, as it was soon nicknamed, was still a two-legged scar on the land. To make use of some of the vacant land, the Toronto Transit Commission built a huge rail yard where, every night, maintenance workers toiled on the fleet.

Ari Greene had grown up a few miles south of here, and as a teenager, on summer nights he and a few friends would ride their bikes to the yards and find ways to sneak in through the loose chain-link fence. He loved the size of the trains, the smell of the grease and the oil, and the adventure of it all.

Tonight he'd driven by the yard for the first time in years and of course now the place was surrounded by a formidable, fortified fence. No sign of kids poking around. He parked on a side street by the employee entrance and waited. It was four in the morning and the shift change was coming up in fifteen minutes. Greene preferred to take a good look at someone he was going to interview before he confronted them.

He had no trouble picking out Arlene Redmond as she strode out of the gate with her fellow employees. She was the only woman surrounded by a group of men. It reminded Greene of his days living in Paris, when groups of *clochards*—the romantic French name for what in North America would be called homeless people—would drift into the metro stations late at night. They were always in a group of six or seven, men and, without fail, only one woman.

Greene watched the TTC workers pile into their cars. With the streets empty, he followed Redmond's old Subaru at a good distance. She and three other cars pulled into a beat-up-looking little strip mall and sauntered into a Coffee Time doughnut shop. Back in university, Greene had a professor who once told the class that Canadians ate more doughnuts per capita than anyone in the world. This case seems to prove that, Greene thought as he walked in.

Redmond was a big-boned woman who wore a TTC Workers Local 113 leather jacket that looked at least ten years old. She had a hearty laugh that ricocheted around the room like a silver ball in a pinball machine. The Somali fellow behind the counter obviously knew this crew and brought them out their "regular" coffees and food.

Greene had brought a newspaper and read through the sports page and when Redmond got up to leave he followed her into the parking lot.

"Arlene, my name is Detective Ari Greene, Toronto homicide squad," he said to her just as she was out the door. "I'd like to chat with you about your nephew, Larkin St. Clair."

She turned around. He'd expected her to be surprised. Instead she let out a belly laugh. "Damn," she said, "I thought you were following me because you wanted to ask me out on a date."

He chuckled. "You seem to have enough men already."

She flicked her eyes back inside for a moment, looking serious all of a sudden. "I appreciate you being discreet. There's another Coffee Time at Bathurst and Wilson, meet me there in ten."

He followed her car through four or five yellow lights. She found a table near the window and he bought two bottles of water and gave her one.

She took a big swig. "I guess after I wouldn't talk to your pretty-boy sidekick you're the heavyweight."

Since Larkin St. Clair's arrest, he'd sent Daniel Kennicott to try to interview Redmond twice. Each time she'd politely but firmly refused. "Don't you think I'm pretty for a guy in his fifties?" Greene asked her.

She gave him an exaggerated once-over. "Bit rugged, little street-worn, natty dresser. Okay, you're a contender."

"A contender who's curious about your nephew."

Her eyes were back on him. Angry. "Really? That why you charged him with first-degree murder and let that little psychopath Dewey Booth walk free?"

"My question about Larkin," he said, locking eyes with her, "is how he would have turned out if the court had let you raise him."

She took another long drink of water. "You ever think you'd see the day Canadians would pay for water. The whole damn country's full of lakes."

"Seems pretty obvious to me," he said. "The judge who let your nephew go back to his mother made a huge mistake."

She capped the bottle. "You're a smart one. Bet you read the whole damn file."

He smiled at her.

"Larkin was on probation for eighteen months living at my house. He didn't breach once. First time ever he's stayed out of trouble for so long. Then Dewey gets out and four days later look what happens."

"I know." He opened his bottle and took a slow sip. "My dad ran a shoe-repair shop for about forty years. Didn't care if the people were good or bad, just fixed their shoes. The way you work on the trains all night. Make them run for everyone."

They stared at each other.

"I'm the one who convinced Larkin to surrender himself," she said.

"That's what I thought." He reached into his jacket pocket and pulled out a micro-recorder. He put it near him on the hard table top and flicked it on. Without losing eye contact he spoke into it: "This is Homicide Detective Ari Greene of the Toronto Police Service. It is Thursday, December twenty-nine, at"—he paused to pull his arm from his sleeve and check his watch—"four forty-four A.M. I am sitting at the Coffee Time doughnut shop at Bathurst and Wilson with Ms. Arlene Redmond, the aunt of Larkin St. Clair, a young man currently charged with first-degree murder."

She hadn't taken her eyes off him either.

He pushed the little recorder across the table toward her, like a passport control officer passing back documents to a traveler.

She looked down at it for a long minute, took another sip, and cleared her throat.

"I'm just going to say this once," she said at last, her eyes back on Greene. "I know my nephew better than anyone. Anyone. And Larkin is not a murderer." She reached down, flicked the machine off, then sat back and crossed her arms against her chest. Her eyes were defiant.

Greene put the recorder back in his pocket. "Thanks," he said.

"Right, thanks for nothing," she said. "Now I bet you'll toss that in the garbage."

"No," he said. "I'll keep it in a safe place."

PART THREE

JANUARY

PART THREE

35

"I think he's a cop."

"Who?"

"My cell mate."

"Shit."

"Don't worry."

"Hah," Nancy Parish said. She was so angry at Larkin St. Clair, she could almost feel the steam blowing out of her ears. She glared at him across the steel jailhouse table.

"It's cool," he said. It had been two months since his arrest, and now his hair was touching his shoulders. He stroked it lovingly, like an old lady would her favorite cat.

"There's nothing cool about it. What have you told him?"

"Believe it or not, nothing." He started to laugh, his big hearty chuckle.

"You think this is all just a big joke, don't you," she said.

He stopped laughing as abruptly as he'd started. She'd seen this before, his uncanny ability to switch moods at lightning speed. "You want to see how I'm going to cry in front of the jury?"

"Larkin, please."

"No. Watch." He placed his hands on the table and looked over her shoulder. His face turned passive. "Okay, this is me sitting in court beside you. The father of the little boy is testifying. What's his first name?"

"Cedric."

"Right. Mr. Cedric Wilkinson. Okay, take his statement out of your binder and read it."

She exhaled. "What's the point?"

"The point is, I already told you I'm not going to testify. But we both know the jury will be watching me like a hawk. Let's rehearse."

She sighed, but she grabbed the binder out of her briefcase. It was heavy. St. Clair was right about what would happen in court. The jury would be eyeing him, the silent accused, sneaking looks throughout the proceedings, searching for clues as to who he really was. Good luck, she thought, chuckling to herself. "Ready?"

"Yeah." Larkin's face had turned solemn. His eyes were fixed on the fictional witness with remarkable intensity.

"'My name is Cedric Wilkinson, father of Kyle,'" she read. "'I was born in California and lived my whole life there until my company moved our family to Canada this fall—'"

"No, no. Don't bother with all the background crap."

"If you insist." She scanned through a page and a half, and then started reading again. "'On November fourteenth, just before five o'clock, I was taking my son Kyle to see his mother, my wife, Madeleine, who was in the hospital. There were complications with her pregnancy, and she was there for observation. We parked the car, and, as we were walking over, Kyle saw the Tim Hortons. He wanted to go for a doughnut. Madeleine doesn't like me giving him sweets, but it was cold and I knew we'd be at the hospital for a while, so I foolishly—'"

"Come on, come on," St. Clair said. "Get to the shooting."

"Okay, Mr. Sensitive, okay." She flipped over to the next page. "'It had just turned very cold, and we were both wearing sneakers. I remember Kyle slipped on the sidewalk before we even got there. We were walking up through the parking lot when it started to snow. Kyle had never seen snow before. He'd been waiting for it. Asking every day: "Daddy, when's it going to snow?"'"

She looked up from the notes. St. Clair hadn't budged. His eyes were laserlike on the same spot. His face had softened somehow, and he looked genuinely upset.

"'Then I heard this loud sound. Again and again. I don't think I've ever heard a real gunshot before. I looked over, and Kyle was on the ground. Not moving. I saw the hole in the side of his head from the light from the window, and I started screaming.'"

She heard a sniffling sound in the concrete room, looked up again, and saw St. Clair's eyes tearing up. His shoulders began to tremble.

"'I'd given him a toy cell phone to play with, and he hadn't even had time to take off the wrapper.'"

The sniffing got louder.

She kept reading. "'The rest is a blur. I remember holding him. Screaming for help. Then an officer arrived. The ambulance.' Then after this part of the statement, Detective Greene asks him a few questions:

"Question: 'Any idea how many shots were fired?'

"Answer: 'None.'

"Question: 'Where they came from?'

"Answer: 'No idea.'

"Question: 'Did you see anyone else?'"

"Answer: 'It was already dark. I was focused on my son.'"

"Question: 'Just before the shooting, one witness heard someone say "Take that," or "Here, take this," something like that. Did you hear those words spoken?'"

"Answer: 'I might have. It's all a blur.'"

She looked at St. Clair again. " 'Take this.' You guys talk as if you're in some old-fashioned gangster movie."

He was still focused on the wall, like an actor who didn't want to get out of character. "Keep reading," he said,

"Another question by Greene. 'What happened next?' Answer: 'I remember hearing a car driving off. People yelling. On their cell phones. I didn't even think to call 911. Then a young officer ran up, the ambulance. I still can't sleep.'"

She put the book down. A flood of tears was streaming down St. Clair's cheeks. His eyes had never left the mythical witness box. Damn, it was moving.

He put one hand out, palm up, on the table. "At this point I'll tap you on the elbow. You fumble around in that little vest all you lawyers wear and find a fucking Kleenex," he said. "Only a single scrunched-up tissue. Pass it over to me. Here, do it now."

"Larkin, really—"

"It'll work, you'll see. Try it."

She pantomimed looking for a tissue, acted as if she pulled one out of her vest pocket, and pretend-passed it over.

His eyes still on the supposed witness, St. Clair nodded at her and rolled the fake tissue up in his hand.

She could imagine the jury being enthralled by his little performance.

He smacked the table, making a hollow sound. Broke off eye contact with the fictional witness, leaned back in his chair, and let out a loud whistle. The stream of tears stopped cold, like a faucet slammed shut. "Fucking good, don't you think?" he said, grinning from ear to ear.

"Larkin."

"What? It's perfect. Make sure you act surprised about that Kleenex. If you have it all ready to go, the whole thing will look staged."

"Really?" she said. "You think?"

She stood up.

St. Clair stood up with her. "What are you doing?"

"Leaving."

"What?"

"I can't do this case."

"Why not?"

She was mad again. It always happened. They were like a dysfunctional couple who couldn't live with or without each other. "I need to know what happened."

"I told you I'm innocent."

She shook her head. "I'll agree not to call you as a witness. And I'll play your charade with the Kleenex in court. But I need to know."

He teetered on his feet and picked at his fingernails.

"If you won't tell me, I'll have your aunt come in and talk to you. Bring in her little son."

"No!" he exploded. "Justin doesn't come near this place."

St. Clair had once told her that his first memory of seeing his father was visiting him in Kingston Penitentiary. "I said I'd bring him a spoon next time so he could dig his way out," he'd told her one tearful afternoon. Judging from his reaction today to the prospect of his five-year-old cousin coming to see him in prison, she thought that maybe, just maybe, those tears had been real.

She closed the binder. "Tell me or I walk."

Larkin shook his head. "What's it matter if I'm not going to testify?"

"It matters because I've put my whole life on hold to defend you. Because I fucked up my last relationship for this. Because everyone in the world, even my mother, thinks I'm some kind of monster for defending you. Because I get about twenty calls a day from reporters across the country desperate for an angle on the biggest and most horrifying shooting in the city's history." She could feel her cheeks flush. "Because I don't need this."

She grabbed the thick binder off the table.

He bent his head forward. "Why don't you hit me with it?"

"You have no idea how much I'd love to," she said.

St. Clair had once told a probation officer that his mother used to beat him on the back of the head. She'd thought this was another one of his stories, a typical Larkin play for sympathy. But then his mother showed up in court and said it was true. He showed Parish where part of one of his ears was torn off. This was the real reason for his long hair. And, now that she thought of it, why he hadn't shaved it all off.

She dropped the binder on the table.

He sat, his head still bent over. "Give me a pen and paper."

She sat and reached into her briefcase, gave him the pen and paper, and watched as he, at last, sketched out the truth.

For Ari Greene, there were many disadvantages to being a homicide detective. The shifts weren't regular and the hours were unpredictable. The first few days and nights on a murder investigation, when he'd go full-out with almost no sleep, didn't net him an extra penny in over-time pay. Beat detectives in the local divisions who worked on house break-ins and small-time domestic cases made a lot more money than the cops investigating murders. And the division guys didn't dress like Homicide, so they spent a lot less on clothes.

Still, everyone on the force wanted to make Homicide. It was the best job. And Greene liked working on his own, not susceptible to the whims of the division staff sergeant or tied to the police radio.

Yes, free to work a hundred hours a week, was the common joke, but it gave Greene time to do things for his father. It was the first Sunday in January and time for their annual pilgrimage to the German consulate. As a condition for reparations the German government paid for their years of slave labor in the Nazi camps, survivors were required to visit the consulate in person once a year. This was the only place where Greene had ever seen his father look afraid.

"You sure you have all the papers, Dad?" Greene asked as he opened the coat closet in his father's front hall and reached for a plastic folder neatly stacked at the back of the top shelf. "We don't want to have a problem like last year."

"The only problem was the death certificate," his father said. "The Germans were upset because your mother died on her own and they didn't get to kill her."

Greene opened the folder and began leafing through the papers. A certified copy of his father's birth certificate written in Polish, a three-page document headed "Declaration of Claimant," a copy of his original Canadian passport issued in 1948, a page entitled "Certificate of Reparations."

He pulled out a letter from the German consulate in Toronto. The letterhead featured dark, heavy type. It was dated January 5.

"Dad, when did you get this letter?"

His father looked over his shoulder. "Last January. A week after your mother died. Typical German efficiency. The moment they found out she was dead they couldn't wait to produce more paperwork."

Greene began to read the letter.

The Conference on Jewish Material Claims Against Germany, Inc.
(Claims Conference)
Article 2 Fund   Greene, Hanna   9-27953-9
(Deceased)

Dear Mr. Greene:

Ms. Hanna Greene, date of birth 07/10/22, was entitled to get monthly payments from the Article 2 Fund of the Claims Conference. We were informed she has passed away.

We are working under the rules of the German government. According to these regulations, the payments of Article 2 Fund are not inheritable. Therefore we are obliged to ask you to remit overpaid funds.

Please, upon your next annual attendance at the consulate for the purpose of reparations verification, present the following:
   1. Notarized copy of the death certificate of the claimant;
   2. Affidavit as to:
       a. your present marital status;
       b. complete listing of all your offspring and all surviving
           dependants.
Sincerely,
Ernst Schlüter
Claims Conference

Greene sighed. "Dad, we're going to have a hassle again. You need to get a lawyer to notarize Mom's death certificate and an affidavit that says you didn't run off and get married in the last twelve months and have another kid. The Germans are unbelievable."

"Here, give me that." Greene's father reached for the file. He fished out a sealed white envelope from the back. "I went to a lawyer and got it all done."

"You did? Where?"

"At the plaza. There's a law office above the jewelry store. Nice young man. Cost me a hundred bucks. He didn't want to charge me, but I made him. 'Don't worry,' I said, 'I'll give the bill to the Nazis and let them pay it.'"

"Good work, Dad." Greene reached for the sealed envelope.

His father pulled it back. "Don't worry, it's all there. You get the car warmed up."

Half an hour later, Greene was looking for a parking spot along Admiral Road, a tree-lined downtown street that featured some of the city's most beautiful old mansions. Tucked away, down a long driveway, was the German consulate, protected by a tall, dark iron gate. Greene cruised past. The gates were open. A black metal railing arched above the entrance, and the line of old people snaked its way out under it and partway down the sidewalk.

"Fewer people every year," his father said.

Greene had thought the same thing. As a young boy, when he came here with his dad each January, the line used to stretch all the way around the block. He remembered holding his father's hand, standing in the cold, amazed that all these people lived in Toronto and none of them spoke English, just Yiddish.

Holding his father's hand. Like Kyle Wilkinson. But there were no sugar doughnuts in the German consulate. Only heavy-looking bread rolls that Greene's father told him not to eat because they were made with something called lard. By the time Greene was a gangly teenager, the line only went to the end of the street, and he towered over the row of short, old people. Most carried shopping bags filled with documents. Like his father, these people were working-class.

The street was packed with cars.

"Use your pass and park close," his father said.

Greene pulled into a no-parking zone and tossed his Police Homicide card into the windshield. In years past, there were many couples, but now many of the old people were alone, accompanied by children whose faces were younger, healthier reflections of their parents.

"What is new with your case?" his father asked as they got out of the car.

The wind was strong, and they had to bend into it as they walked up the sidewalk. Greene went half a step ahead to provide his dad with a little shelter. "We're still looking for that baker who ran away. I figure he's illegal and that's why he hasn't come forward."

"After the war, I couldn't get a passport for two years," his father said.

They got to the end of the line. The old people seemed to get shorter every year, Greene thought. "Dad, why won't you let me see the affidavit?" he asked, laughing.

"There's Herschel." His father pointed to a short man up ahead in the line. Changing the subject was his way of saying no. "He's gotten pretty fancy."

Greene noticed a man with a fur-lined coat holding a black leather briefcase.

"Herschel," Greene said. "Isn't he the one who made a fortune in furniture?"

"Kitchens," his father said.

Greene looked at the folder in his father's hand. As independent and crusty as his dad was, it wasn't like him to go to a lawyer on his own. Why would he do that? What's going on? he wondered as the line moved forward and they approached the gate. His father looked up at the iron railing overhead, and Greene saw a shiver go through him.

Ah, stop being such a cop, he told himself. He laughed again. A nervous laugh. "Dad, I'm starting to feel as if I'm at work. Every time I ask you about those lawyer's papers, you change the subject."

"This cook. He said he was from Portugal?"

"That's what he told his employer. I don't believe it. He seems to speak four or five languages."

"So?" His father was unimpressed. After he'd escaped from Treblinka, the Nazi death camp where he'd been forced to work for six months, he'd spent two years living in the woods, picking up odd jobs and languages as he went.

"All we have to go on is a composite drawing done after the artist talked to his fellow employees."

"It's easy for a man to change what he looks like." Greene's father had gone through countless disguises before he was finally caught and thrown in Auschwitz six months before the liberation. "If he wants to hide, you're not going to find him unless he wants to be found. What kind of man is he?"

The wind shifted, coming from the north. Greene moved ahead again to shield his dad. "I think he's smart. I think he cares. He ran back outside to find the girl who he worked with and tried to warn her that her old boyfriend was out front."

His dad nodded. Taking it all in. He always had a surprising perspective on Greene's cases. "When the Americans came," he said, "some were afraid."

"Afraid of what?"

Greene's father swept his hand in front of him. "All this. Everything. Some people just ran away, and we never saw them again."

"He's got reason to be afraid. I think at least one of the shooters saw him. Maybe took a shot at him too."

Greene's father remained silent until they were almost at the front door.

"Even when I was in the deepest hiding," he said, "I always tried to find out the news. What was going on. You're looking for him. But maybe he's watching you."

37

Even Ralph Armitage was having trouble smiling. He and Albert Fernandez had been stuck all morning in the too-small Crown office boardroom, interviewing the three remaining eyewitnesses, and each one seemed more difficult than the last. Great way to spend a Sunday afternoon, especially when your wife wanted you to join her to go look at different florists for the party.

First there'd been the South African banker. He was the only one who spoke English, but he was a real blabbermouth. Next came the Tamil man, who was so frightened he had to go to the bathroom every ten minutes. They were nothing compared to Vikram Dalmar Abdul Mohammed, the Bangladeshi grandfather, their last interview of the day.

"Please, sir, listen carefully." Armitage tried to keep his voice calm. "We know that you understand a good deal of English, and you've explained to us twice already that you were a mathematics professor in Bangladesh. But when I ask a question, you must wait for the translator, and you must answer him in Bengali, not in English."

"Yes, sir, my most sincere apologies," Mohammed said. He was a tiny man, five feet tall if he was lucky.

"Or we can have no translator," Armitage said. "Then in court you will have to speak in English."

"No, no, must have translator."

"Then you must *use* translator," Armitage said. "Let's try this again. You told us that you and your grandson were at the Tim Hortons, sitting at a table near the door."

"Yes," Mohammed said in English, "we were having hot chocolate—"

Armitage thrust his hand at Mohammed, practically stuffing it in the little man's face. He pointed to the translator.

Mohammed cowered in his seat and, startled, spoke in Bengali to the translator for at least a minute.

Armitage rolled his eyes at Fernandez.

At last the translator turned to Armitage. "He says, 'Yes, we were having hot chocolate.'"

Armitage could feel the anger crawling up his skin. "I need to know every word Mr. Mohammed says," he said to the translator, who was short as well. Maybe five-two. "Understood?"

"Yes. But at first he was discussing the quality of the tea at the Tim Hortons. He does not like it. And he finds this Canadian habit of putting cream in hot drinks very peculiar. I didn't think it was relevant."

Armitage tapped his fingers on the table. "Mr. Mohammed. You told the police that you saw two young men at the table next to you. Please describe them for me."

"One had very long hair, like a Sikh man without a turban," Mohammed said through the translator. "The other had red hair, his skin extremely white, like a sari a bride might wear on her wedding day."

Armitage let out a sigh. This guy sure had colorful language for a math professor. He beamed his best smile at Mohammed, hoping to encourage him to stay on track. "Did you hear them speaking at all?"

"My grandson said the hot chocolate was too hot. I was in discussion with him at the time," Mohammed said through the translator. "The boy's name is Ramesh, and unfortunately his marks in geometry are not adequate."

"Sir. Did you hear anything?"

"I heard many things."

"Did you hear the two men, the one with long hair and the other one with the very white skin, say anything to each other or anyone else?"

"The gentleman with the long hair was speaking to some young women. They were black people. Am I allowed to say that?" Mohammed now had no problems using the translator.

"Of course you are allowed. What did he say to them?"

"I only heard him say that he could do fifty push-ups at one time. They seemed most impressed."

"Did he say anything to the other man, the one with the white skin?"

"No, sir, he did not."

"Did the one with the white skin say anything to the one with the long hair?"

"Yes, sir, he did."

Pulling teeth or what, Armitage thought. If Mohammed was this reluctant a witness in court, the jury would want to strangle him. They wouldn't remember a word of what he had to say. "And what did the white-skinned one say to the one with the long hair?"

"A bad word. I was concerned for my grandson."

"I can understand that."

"It was a short sentence."

Relax, Armitage told himself. After all, diversity is what makes Toronto such a special place to work and live and prosecute. "What was the short sentence the man with the white skin said to the man with the long hair? Including the bad word you didn't want your grandson to hear?"

"Must I tell you?"

"It is very important. Would you prefer to write it out?"

Mohammed started whispering into the translator's ear.

"No, no, no," Armitage shouted.

The two little men looked at him, shocked.

"No whispering," Armitage said. "Mr. Mohammed. Believe me, in this job there's nothing you could say that would surprise me."

Mohammed jutted his diminutive jaw out. His eyes flashed in anger. "I need a fucking cigarette," he muttered in English, his voice angry.

"I'm sorry." Armitage was taken aback by the man's abrupt change in mood. "There is no smoking allowed in these offices. If you want, we can take a break—"

"No, no." Mohammed slammed his small hand on the desk. It made a loud thwacking sound. "The man said that. The short one with the white skin. He was angry and spoke the way I just did. He said, 'I need a fucking cigarette.' Then the two of them walked outside. I didn't see them after that.'"

38

Nancy Parish stared at the stacks and stacks of paper that made up the case of *R. v. Larkin St. Clair,* charge: first-degree murder. The firm's boardroom, which she'd taken over a month ago, looked like it had been hit by a tornado.

It was only Monday and already she was exhausted. Today she'd run around to three different courts to deal with a bail hearing and a guilty plea and to receive judgment on a case that finished a month ago. She'd lost.

The upshot was she hadn't even got back to the office until six o'clock, and by the time she'd unpacked her files and cleared out her voice mails and e-mails, it was seven. Her other clients were feeling increasingly neglected.

Usually her partner, Ted DiPaulo, would jump in to pick up the slack. But these days he was constantly jetting off to some exotic locale to spend a night or two with Isabel, an Air France air hostess he'd met on a trip to Paris last spring. Suddenly, after being a widower for five years, and after a lifetime as a workaholic lawyer, now he spent every moment he could flying to France, or wherever his Parisian sweetheart was headed.

Even when he was in the office, he was spending hours online looking for cheap flights. All this from a guy who a year ago didn't even know how to use a computer and who hadn't been on holiday out of Canada for a decade. She didn't blame Ted. Was happy for him. And she'd gotten used to being in the office alone. Had started to like it.

The judicial pretrial, a meeting to discuss St. Clair's case with a high-court judge, was set for this coming Friday morning, and she needed to be ready.

Years ago, disclosure of the facts of a case was a cat-and-mouse game between prosecution and the defense counsel. The Crown Attorneys knew everything, and the defense lawyer had to guess what the evidence at trial would be. But as more and more unjust convictions of innocent people were uncovered, often due to the Crown Attorney's holding back exculpatory evidence, the courts imposed upon prosecutors an ironclad obligation to disclose every bit of information to the other side.

At first, defense lawyers were elated and the Crowns disheartened. But soon the prosecutors found, especially in a big case such as a first-degree murder trial, it was easier to pile everything into a stack of cardboard boxes and ship it out to the defense. Let them catalogue it. Figure the case out for themselves. Make them drown in the details.

On her way back to the office, Parish had stopped at an art-supply store and bought a few poster-size sheets of paper, some colored marking pens, and thumbtacks. She stuck one of the sheets on the back wall of the boardroom and drew an outline of the Tim Hortons parking lot on it.

"Let's see now," she said.

With Ted almost never around, she'd lost all inhibitions about speaking out loud when she was alone. Her plan was to select the five key prosecution eyewitnesses and, using a different color for each one, draw the key points of their evidence: where they were located when the shots rang out, how many shots they heard, who they saw run and in which direction, bits of overheard conversation.

"Adela Dobos, you're going to be red," she said. "You bought a coffee and had just got out the door and heard someone nearby say, 'Here, take this.' A moment later you heard the first shot."

She drew a red stick woman on her map. "You say there were 'maybe as many as nine gunshots.'" She put a red number nine behind the figure. "You saw Mr. Wilkinson turn to his son, who was behind him." To represent father and son, she used a big stick figure near the door and a smaller one a few steps away. "The little boy was on the ground. There was a big car in the corner of the lot and you heard it drive away real fast." She drew in the car. "You don't know where the gunshot sounds came from. You saw a guy with long hair and a much smaller man leave the doughnut shop but couldn't remember if that was before or after the shooting. People were running everywhere."

She assigned the Albanian, Edone Kutishi, the color green. For Vikram Mohammed she used yellow. Abdul Mohammed was blue. Nigel Jameson, black. She stood back to look at her handiwork. The whole paper was a mishmash of colors. It didn't seem to say anything. "The jury will think I'm nuts if I do this in court," she said.

Fortunately, she'd bought six sheets of paper. Each one was separately wrapped in a thin plastic that stuck as tight as CD packaging. It took her an hour to unwrap the other five, tack them on the wall, and methodically draw out the evidence of the individual witnesses, one per piece of paper. By the time she'd finished, she was tired, hungry, and discouraged.

She had to get some food, but she sat back down and took a last look at the drawings. Going back and forth between each one was confusing. Not at all illuminating.

"So much for that idea. You're supposed to be a criminal lawyer, not an artist," she scolded herself. There were six sheets of plastic in front of her, squarely stacked. She might have been a slob about a lot of things in her life, but when it came to art supplies she was ultra-neat. In the right-hand corner of each piece of plastic she'd written the name of each witnesses in their own color.

She stood up and flipped through the plastic sheets one last time. Wait. She flipped through them again. That's it, she thought. She grabbed two thumbtacks from the table, ran over to the wall of the original drawing she'd done, and stuck them through all five see-through sheets on top of it. Perfectly lined up.

"Yes," she shouted. "Yes, yes. That's it."

She looked at her watch. Eight thirty. The art-supply store stayed open until nine. She started to giggle, tapped her pockets until she found her car keys, and threw on her jacket. Who cared if she was here all night? She wasn't afraid of this trial anymore. Now she couldn't wait to pull on her robes and get started.

39

Some clichés were true, Daniel Kennicott thought, such as the one about good police work being mostly paperwork. And he should have been accustomed to paperwork. After all, he'd been a lawyer before becoming a cop.

But nothing in his experience prepared him for the warrant office at old city hall. It was nine o'clock on Tuesday morning, and he was in a windowless closet of a room that was filled to the ceiling with stacks of boxes. Each one held a year's worth of warrants for people who'd failed to come to court. Unless the file was a high-profile case, the only time these warrants were enforced was when one of the poor souls whose name was here got himself arrested. And then, only if his name had been entered into the police computer. The transfer of information from scratchy handwritten notes to digital police files was eighteen months behind schedule and falling farther back all the time as the onslaught of charges piled up and the police budget was cut. The cardboard boxes themselves were moist and soft and the whole place had the smell of molding paper.

He cleared off the only desk in the room and hauled out the box from six years ago. He was going to begin with that one and work his way forward in time. In her interview with Detective Greene, Suzanne Howett, the former server at the Tim Hortons, had estimated Jose's age as late twenties. She said he was smart, spoke many languages, wanted to be a professor. Kennicott was guessing that Jose had gotten a university degree in whatever country he came from, before getting to Canada. Had to start somewhere.

The only other clue Greene had given him was that Jose might be from Romania. Kennicott had downloaded from Google a list of the most common Romanian first and last names and printed them out. He pulled up the only chair in the room, put the list down on the desk, and dug in to the box.

The names on the warrants were an ad hoc social history of Toronto, he thought as he worked his way through them. There were long Tamil names, such as Padamandaman; piles of Vietnamese names, almost all with either Nguyen or Doan as the last name; Eastern European; North African; Caribbean; South American.

People came to Toronto from every corner of the world, it seemed, to shoplift at the Bay, pass rubber checks at Home Hardware, or snatch the money from the tip jar at Second Cup.

It took almost three hours to work through the box. He had found only four possible Romanian names, but two were men in their fifties, and one warrant had actually been enforced and the man was in jail. He put the last one on the concrete floor, packed up the box, and took out the one from five years ago.

Half a decade.

It amazed him to think of his life back then. He was working blocks from here, on the forty-fourth floor of a huge office tower with a stunning view of the lake. A rising star in Miller, Ford, one of the largest law firms in the country. He had been personally recruited by Lloyd Granwell, a lawyer who was unparalleled in the range of his knowledge and influence. He was dating Andrea and her modeling career had just taken off. His father was a semiretired judge working on a major inquiry; his mother was still one of the top investigative journalists in the country. And his older brother, Michael, had recently moved out to Calgary, where he headed up a major consulting firm.

How quickly it had all crumbled. That summer his parents were killed by a drunk driver, an impecunious ne'er-do-well named Arthur Rake, on their weekly drive to their cottage. Twelve months later, Michael was murdered the night he'd flown into Toronto to meet Daniel on his way to some still-unexplained trip to Gubbio, a small town in Italy. A year later Andrea took off for Paris.

He spent about two hours going through the next box of warrants and finished in an hour and a half. As with any repetitive task, there were shortcuts to be found. He did the last three in four hours. He'd brought some food with him and hadn't left the room all day. This kind of focused concentration had made him such a good lawyer. All his work had netted him four warrants with names and ages that were promising.

Cosmin Fidatov was a twenty-six-year-old student who'd been arrested for public mischief after he'd vomited on the sidewalk outside the Brunswick House, a pub that was popular with undergraduates at the University of Toronto. To top off his evening, he'd also smashed his beer bottle against the front door. Dorin Goga was twenty-four and had stolen an iPod from the Mac Store in Eaton Centre. He gave his occupation as computer analyst. Dragomir Ozera, age twenty-five, was caught stealing cheese, pâté, and crackers from Pusateri's, an expensive food chain in the city. Vasilica Neacsu, a twenty-eight-year-old auto mechanic, had passed a bad check at Creeds dry cleaning, a high-end service.

Kennicott stared at the four names and their meager profiles. He kept trying to picture the elusive "Jose Doe." Fidatov, the drunken beer-bottle smasher, didn't fit the bill. He crossed the name out. Goga, the student who'd stolen the iPod, and Neacsu, the guy who took his clothes to get dry-cleaned, were close. He put the numbers two and three beside their names. Something about the cheekiness of someone who would steal pâté from Pusateri's sounded like the same guy who'd hang out with the pretty server in back of the Tim Hortons.

He circled the name and opened up the warrant to find the officer who'd made the arrest. PC Arnold Lindsmore, metro Toronto police, badge number 1997, from 52 Division.

Let's hope the cop remembered this guy named Ozera.

40

For the third straight night in a row this week Nancy Parish was still at her desk, and her law office seemed more like a cage or a prison than a place where she worked. Especially since she spent way more hours here than at her little semidetached house. She couldn't even remember the last time she'd had anything close to a normal evening at home.

It was freezing outside, and after a day of running from overheated buildings to her cold car, again and again, layer after layer of frozen sweat had accumulated all across her body. What a lovely thought.

The garbage can below her desk was filled with empty take-out sushi packaging and three cans of Diet Coke. She'd been putting each witness statement in a separate folder and hand-labeling them. Yellow files were for the civilian witnesses. Red for the cops. Blue for the forensics, people who'd analyzed fingerprints, DNA, blood samples. White files she reserved for the most difficult witnesses: Suzanne Howett, the server at Tim Hortons, who although she hadn't said a lot had enough evidence to hurt their case badly; Jet, who'd told the cops to get lost and hadn't said a thing; and most important of all, Dewey Booth, his skimpy one-page statement and signed agreement between Ralph Armitage and Booth's lawyer, Phil Cutter. Plus his extensive criminal record.

The window of her Bay Street office looked north across Queen Street, and she could see the big square in front of the new city hall and her favorite winter place in Toronto—the open-air skating rink. On the other side of Bay Street, the old city hall clock tower began to ring out the hour, ten loud dongs for ten o'clock. She watched the city work crews turn off the overhead lights on the three concrete arches that lit the large white surface. A myriad collection of skaters—couples on first dates, gaggles of giggling girls and muscle-bound macho guys, and a few gray-haired figure skaters gliding with the veteran grace only gained by a lifetime of practice—headed off the ice.

Soon the hockey players would arrive, sticks slung over their shoulders like Robin's soldiers in Sherwood Forest. Their skates, tied together by their laces and wrapped around the end of the sticks, danced behind them in the clear night air. But instead of slipping through a wooded glen, the Gretzky wannabes would make their way to the open square by winding through myriad surrounding downtown office towers.

She stood and stretched. Peeled off her wool suit, silk shirt, and the damn pantyhose. They were ripped anyhow. In her corner closet she'd stacked long underwear, sweatpants, a thick sweatshirt, plus nylon pants and a shell to wear over it all as an extra layer. And her skates, her stick, her hockey gloves, her helmet, and a bag with a few pucks in it.

By the time the old city hall clock struck ten fifteen, she was sitting on a bench near the rink, tightening her waxed skate laces, her fingers freezing in the cold. Beside Parish, her friend the *Toronto Star* reporter Awotwe Amankwah was doing the same thing. They'd arranged to meet here tonight—this was their secret meeting place and a perfect one at that—and play.

"I need to find out what Dewey Booth is up to." Parish grunted in the cold as she tugged on her laces.

"Cutter is smart. From what I've been able to find out, he sent the kid home to live with his father on that island."

"Pelee Island."

"That's it. We went there once when I was a kid. All I remember is there were lots of birds and the place is real flat. We stopped in Chatham on the way down and went to a little museum about the underground railroad. I was amazed that there were black people living in Ontario so long ago."

"They sure never taught us that in school," Parish said. "Booth's going to have to be back in Toronto to go to court."

"Way I hear it, he's coming in the night before. Cops are putting him up in a hotel, he testifies, then he's gone. Cutter doesn't want him here a minute longer than he needs to be until this whole thing is over. The press is on this story like you've never seen before in this city."

She tied up her last lace and jammed her hands into her hockey gloves.

"Is Booth talking to the Crown?"

"No. Cutter's got him clamped shut. Armitage is going to throw him up in the box at the prelim and get his evidence solid under oath."

Parish had been thinking about the "prelim," the preliminary inquiry, a lower-court hearing that tested whether there was enough evidence for an accused to stand trial. Often the defense would "knock down" a first-degree charge to second-degree. That cut the minimum jail sentence from twenty-five to ten. Technically, the prelim was optional for an accused, but anyone charged with first-degree always had one.

"I figured Cutter would do that," Parish said.

Amankwah looked up at her. "Once Booth fingers your boy at the prelim, you're going to be in trouble."

She jogged in place on her blades to stay warm. "I know. I might waive it."

"The prelim? You crazy?" He tied up his last lace and shot to his feet.

"It's a radical move. But the Crown can't force the defense to have one. We can go straight to trial."

"But at the prelim you've got a good chance of getting this knocked down to second-degree. Could save your kid fifteen years behind bars."

"Right now all the prosecution has is Dewey Booth's sworn affidavit. There are all sorts of holes in his story."

"Such as?"

She smacked her stick on the rubber mats, for no real reason she could think of. But it was something hockey players did. She shook her head. "That, my friend, is something you'll have to wait to see in court."

He nodded. They understood that their friendship had professional limits. She would never disclose to him something that was covered by solicitor-client privilege. He would never reveal a source. "Still. Don't you want to see the evidence at the prelim? Hear from all those civilian witnesses?"

"And give the Crown a chance to clean up all their inconsistencies?"

"You have a point."

"And as you just said, Cutter's keeping his client under wraps. And once he's given evidence at the prelim, I'm up the creek."

"All true. But are you prepared to risk fifteen years of your young client's life? Still sounds crazy to me."

She exhaled a cloud of white steam and pointed her stick at a bank tower across the square where a big digital clock illuminated the temperature. "It's minus twenty degrees," she said. "You were born in Africa, and now you're outside playing hockey. So who's crazy?"

41

Ari Greene had taken a number of precautions to protect PC Darvesh while the young police officer spent time as the cell mate of Larkin St. Clair. Only three people at the Toronto East Detention Centre knew he was a cop, none of them guards. Greene had been concerned that if the regular guards knew, they might subconsciously treat him differently, just the kind of thing a smart prisoner such as St. Clair might pick up on. And Jennifer Raglan was the only person in the Crown's office who knew the case against him was a bogus file.

He'd only met with Darvesh once since the young officer had been incarcerated. That had been during regular prison visiting hours. Every week, Darvesh placed a collect call, as all the inmates did, from one of the two phones in the prisoners' range. His calls went directly to the homicide bureau, where they were answered by a receptionist. He pretended to speak to his family and always worked in a complaint about how bland the food was. It was a simple code that meant nothing new had happened.

This morning, Darvesh was going to be in old city hall court for a remand of his case. Greene was on his way there to meet him, in a side cell out of view. This was tricky and had to be done fast to make sure none of the other prisoners became suspicious.

It was ridiculously cold, and just before he got inside the courthouse, Greene's cell rang. "Your best friend just phoned from the cells in the bowels of the hall," the receptionist at Homicide said.

"What did he say?" Greene asked. The wind was howling and he could hardly hear. His ears were freezing.

"Pretended he was talking to his brother and told me he'd managed to find some spice for his food."

"Thanks," Greene said. It meant Darvesh had some news.

He was glad to get inside, and ten minutes later, in a small room out of sight from the hundreds of prisoners brought into the big "bullpen" jail cell, he was talking to the prisoner known as Alisander Singh. His ears stung as they defrosted from the cold.

"We only have a few minutes," Darvesh said. His arms looked muscular, the whole top of his torso more filled out.

"What have you got?" Greene asked. He'd bought a coffee at the concession stand in the basement, run by two old men who seemed to have been there for centuries, and passed it over to Darvesh.

He took a deep sip. "Thanks for this. Prison coffee is mostly water. St. Clair has been teaching me how to pump weights. We get gym twice a week."

"Good."

"Yesterday while we were doing curls he started talking."

"What'd he say?"

"That prison was no big deal, but it was shit being inside if you were totally innocent."

"Totally innocent?"

"That's what he said."

He offered Greene a sip. Greene laughed. "I can get as much fresh coffee as I want."

"Habit," Darvesh said. "When you come from a big family, you share everything."

"Do you think he knows you're a cop? Maybe he's playing you."

"Don't know. He's dumb like a fox. He might be trying to send you a message through me."

"Why do you think that?"

"Because he said there was another witness."

Greene felt the hairs on the back of his neck bristle. "What'd he say about that?"

"Some guy in a Tim Hortons uniform was out back when the shooting happened. 'I wish the fucking cops would find him.' Those are his exact words."

"He say anything else?"

"No. Just that he was going to turn me from a being skinny little brown runt into a muscle machine." Darvesh grinned at Greene. He was a good cop and smart enough to enjoy what he could from this assignment.

"Well then," Greene said, "I guess there's no hurry to get you out of there."

42

CFL.

For most people in Canada the letters stood for "Canadian Football League."

But for cops, they also meant "Constable for Life." That was their term for officers such as PC Arnold Lindsmore, metro Toronto police, badge number 1997, from 52 Division, a cop whose career had flatlined.

Daniel Kennicott had learned to recognize the telltale sign of a CFL from an officer's badge number and rank. Lindsmore's number, 1997, was low, which meant he'd been on the force for a long time. And he was still a PC, police constable. The lowest rank. In other words, he'd never been promoted. That made him a classic CFL.

Something about Lindsmore's name rang a distant bell for Kennicott, but he couldn't place it. For the last three days, he'd left messages for the constable saying that he needed to speak to him right away about an urgent matter. Lindsmore, who was on holiday, hadn't bothered to respond.

Now it was five to eight in the morning, and Kennicott had made a point of getting to 52 Division in time to catch Lindsmore coming in to work. The staff sergeant, a nice fellow named Finch, had cleared it so he could wait inside the cops' private entrance in back.

"Morning, Officer Lindsmore," he said at exactly eight o'clock, when Lindsmore ambled in. The man had to have weighed two hundred and fifty pounds. Probably more. "PC Daniel Kennicott." He held out his arm to shake hands.

"Hi," Lindsmore said, a little wary.

"I know you're just getting on shift, but I've got something fairly urgent to talk to you about."

"Oh." Lindsmore was doing his best to be unimpressed. "Kennicott. You're the guy who's been leaving me those messages, aren't you?" He gave a weak handshake back.

"Yes."

"The lawyer who joined up after your brother was shot, right?"

Kennicott had left the law to become a cop almost four years before, but unfortunately all that unwanted publicity still lingered in the minds of some of his fellow officers. Stuck in their craw like some old wound that refused to heal.

"That's me," Kennicott answered in a flat voice.

"I've got to get in uniform, do parade. Meet me in half an hour." Lindsmore cranked his head toward the window. "How about a large double-double from Timmy's and a maple glazed."

An hour later, Lindsmore meandered into the small back room where Kennicott was waiting for him. He carried a large blank envelope under his arm and put it on the table without comment. The large coffee, which Kennicott had double-cupped in an effort to keep it hot, was now lukewarm.

Lindsmore slurped a big sip and scowled.

Kennicott looked him straight in the eye. "It was steaming hot half an hour ago."

Lindsmore bit a large chunk out of the doughnut and gulped it down. "Finch says this is about a shoplifting arrest I made five years ago. He figures no way I'd remember it."

Kennicott took out his business card and handed it over. "I don't expect you would. But if you can get some free time maybe later in your shift, I'm wondering if you can go back to the property bureau and find your old notebook. I already gave Finch the details." He reached into his coat pocket and pulled out a piece of paper. "Here they are again."

Lindsmore took a lazy look at the paper. "I've got to tell you, Kennicott," he said, reaching into his own breast pocket, "the one thing I can't stand is an arrogant asshole."

Kennicott blanched. He knew that some veteran cops resented him, not only for the high-profile way he'd joined the force, but also because he had already worked on a few well-publicized homicides. He sat back in his chair. "Well, I'm—"

"And this kid Ozera was one of the most arrogant jerks I ever arrested." Lindsmore pulled out his narrow, police-issued notebook from the envelope on the table.

Kennicott could see he had an elastic band at a page halfway in.

Lindsmore slapped it open at that spot. "Let's see." He held the book at arm's length so he could read his own writing better. "This was five years ago next week. January fifteenth. I've got Dragomir Ozera,

age twenty-five, five foot seven, one hundred and forty pounds drip-
ping wet, black hair, mustache and long sideburns, birthmark by his
left eye. I did a drawing of his face, take a look."

Lindsmore showed Kennicott a page in his book. His fingers were
as fat at the rest of him, but, remarkably, the sketch was very good.
Close to the composite drawing.

"You're a talented artist," Kennicott said.

"A fucking Michelangelo," Lindsmore said. "My ex was always trying to get me to take art classes."

"Here's the composite." Kennicott pulled it out and put it on the table.

"That's him," Lindsmore said. "Caught stealing pâté and fancy French
cheese from the Pusateri's on Bay Street, the one just north of Bloor."

"You get an address, phone number?"

Lindsmore gave him a slow look that seemed to say, "What, you
think I'm an idiot?" and kept reading.

"Gave address as room twelve at Jilly's hotel on Broadview and
Queen."

"The strip bar?"

"They rent rooms out by the week. No phone number. He had no
driver's license. No social security or health card."

"How'd you identify him?"

"Library card. I wanted to hold him for bail, but the staff sergeant
told me to Form Ten him. No time for all the paperwork, and besides,
who gives a shit about some pâté? I knew the little fucker would never
show up in court."

"You thought he was illegal?"

Lindsmore shook his head. "No, I thought he was going to be the
next prime minister of Canada."

Kennicott started to laugh at himself. "Sorry I'm being such an idiot.
Can I get a copy of your notes?"

Lindsmore reached into the envelope on the table and pulled out
a sheaf of neatly stapled-together papers. "Made a copy for you." He
handed it over. "The kid was a charmer. Had half the women who
worked at Pusateri's eating out of the palm of his hand by the time
I arrived. Telling them recipes. Suggesting novels for them to read.
Spoke a few languages, I remember."

"This all helps a great deal," Kennicott said.

"This might help more." Lindsmore reached back into his envelope
and extracted a plastic evidence bag with a cigarette butt inside. "Like
I told you," he said in the same monotone drawl, "I knew he'd never

show up for court. So I gave him a smoke. Never know when we might need a DNA sample."

"That's great." Kennicott held the plastic bag with care, as if it were a crown jewel. "You got anything else for me?"

"About *this* case?"

The way Lindsmore said "this" made Kennicott stop. "What other case could there be?" he asked.

But the moment the words were out, he knew the answer. Lindsmore. The constable for life. He'd been one of the first cops on the scene the night Kennicott's brother was shot. He remembered now that Lindsmore had led the street canvass and gone straight through for twelve hours without a break. It had impressed him the first time he'd read the file. "I owe you a thanks for the work you did after my brother was shot."

"Frustrated the hell out of me. We knocked on doors all night for a twenty-block radius. By the book we're supposed to do ten."

"I know."

"I couldn't believe nobody saw anything. Right in the middle of Yorkville like that. Fuck. I can only imagine how you feel."

Kennicott didn't know what to say.

"Look. I've known Ari Greene for twenty-five years. We were in the same rookie class. He won't ever say it, but I can tell you it's eating him alive that he can't solve this case. It's his only outstanding homicide."

"I know," Kennicott said again.

"Don't you ever get pissed off at him?"

"Who?"

"Greene."

"Greene? Why?"

"Come on. You're no Boy Scout. Four years and where's he gotten?"

Kennicott felt himself nod involuntarily. Lindsmore had touched a secret sore spot, like a nerve that just got pinched. One that he hadn't even realized was there.

"Just because I'm a fat fart and a CFL doesn't mean I don't do my job," Lindsmore said. "You're going to make Homicide one day. Don't underestimate the cops on the beat."

43

Ralph Armitage knew that most of the Crown Attorneys in his office doubted his skill as a trial lawyer, but even his harshest critics down the hall had to admit that when it came to judicial pretrials, Ralphie boy had no peers.

A pretrial was a private, unrecorded meeting in a judge's office, or their chambers as they loved to call them, at which time both the defense lawyers and Crown Attorneys informally discussed the upcoming case. Often this was the turning point. Make a deal or prepare for trial.

And although Armitage, the consummate negotiator, rarely walked away without resolving even the toughest cases, this morning was going to be an exception. With the city ablaze with anger about the Wilkinson shooting, his secret marching orders from the political higher-ups were to go all the way with this case. No deals. No way.

Which meant this pretrial would be a formality. But it would be entertaining. Most of the jurists on the high court bench were a staid bunch, but not the assigned judge, His Honor Justice Oliver Rothbart. As a kid, Rothbart had been a famous child actor. When he was five years old, he'd won a tap-dancing competition on the local TV show *Tiny Talent Time,* and he was the Wonder Bread boy in a series of print and billboard advertisements at age eight. In 1964, when he was fourteen, he landed a role in the production of *Camelot,* which debuted in Toronto before the show went to Broadway.

"Come in, come in," Rothbart said to Armitage and Nancy Parish as the court constable escorted them to his office. His childhood falsetto voice had morphed into a booming baritone, which he was never afraid to use to effect in court. Most judges made a point of staying seated at their desks and waited for lawyers to arrive in their offices, but Rothbart was always at his door, big smile, hand extended.

Armitage had learned that despite his dramatic personality, Rothbart resented lawyers who thought he was a lightweight. So, although nothing would get resolved today, Armitage and Fernandez had put in the hours to get ready for this pretrial, and on Thursday morning they'd delivered an extensive brief.

Nancy Parish was a hard worker, well prepared and good on her feet. She'd also filed a large brief yesterday.

It was clear the moment they sat down that the judge had done his homework, because both briefs were stuffed with yellow sticky tabs poking out the sides. Armitage glanced around Rothbart's chambers, which looked more like the office of a musical theater producer than a place where serious legal matters were discussed. The walls were covered with signed publicity photos of movie stars, most made out to "Ollie." There were big framed stills from his various roles as a kid on TV. Most prominent of all was a blown-up photo taken backstage on the *Camelot* set of young Ollie standing in between Richard Burton and his then-new wife, Elizabeth Taylor. Rothbart's role in the show was something he somehow managed to insinuate into almost every conversation, no matter how obscure the topic.

"Okay, I just wanted to double-check something," Rothbart said, opening the Crown brief at a set page with an extralarge sticky attached to it. He had the nervous habit of strumming the fingers of his right hand in his left palm when he was anxious or bored. Like he was playing a tune to himself on his own piano.

Armitage and Parish sat patiently across the desk from him.

"This Dewey character." Rothbart turned to Armitage.

"Mr. Booth," Armitage said.

"'Mr. Booth' my ass. Save it for the jury. I looked at his record. Kid's a menace. But you've made this deal with him. He's your prime witness."

"One of them," Armitage said.

Rothbart stabbed at the open page. "His only statement is this affidavit. You don't have him on video, sworn under oath. Have I've got that right?"

"Correct."

"And if he changes his story, then you'll cross him on this?" His finger seemed almost stuck on the paper.

"Exactly." Armitage had expected this line of questioning, and he was doing his best to radiate calm and confidence. "It's no secret. We made full disclosure to the defense." Well, he thought, if you exclude the baker from Tim Hortons, my secret little friend. "If Booth doesn't commit perjury, he's never going to be charged."

"Mind my asking why you'd pull a first-degree murder case against a punk with a record like this and not get him tied down on video?"

Fuck you, judge, he thought, flashing his biggest grin. "I don't mind the question, sir. But I have no intention of answering."

Everyone chuckled. Then they all fell silent.

"I can tell you why." Nancy Parish spoke for the first time since they'd said their introductions. "The Crown needed to match the bullet with the gun that killed the boy."

Rothbart nodded.

He's starting to see how complicated this trial might become, Armitage thought.

Rothbart stared at Parish. "I see the bullet matches with the gun that was found at your client's aunt's house, where he'd been living on probation. Not great evidence for the defense."

Just like Rothbart, Armitage thought. He loved to grill both lawyers, show off how much work he'd done on the case.

"Could be better," she said. Everyone laughed again.

"Something else jumps out at me." Rothbart turned back to Armitage. "These witnesses are all over the map with the number of shots they heard. Three, six, one even says she thought there were eight or nine." He flipped back to another tab in the brief. "This gun was a Desert Eagle. The clip in the forty-four Magnum version only takes six bullets, and there's one in the chamber. That's seven. Where's the second gun?"

Rothbart was such a showoff. Couldn't wait to demonstrate his extensive knowledge of handguns and how smart he was. How I'd love to break his precious little fingers one by one, Armitage thought.

"Only one witness counts more than six shots, and we all know how unreliable civilians can be about such things," Armitage said. "There were buildings on both sides of the Timmy's. It's a natural echo chamber."

"Hmmm," Rothbart said. He started strumming his stupid fingers. "I don't see a direct eyewitness. Lots of people see little bits, hear a few things, but no one actually saw what happened. Do I have that right?"

He had been a very successful defense lawyer before being called to the bench, and he still loved trying to pick apart the case for the Crown. And he was right. The only one who saw it all was Armitage's unseen pal, who everyone else thought was named Jose. "All I can tell you," he said, "is that the investigation is ongoing."

"What about that kid in the Cadillac? I don't see a statement from him," Rothbart said. "I note he had a gun in his apartment, has a possession-of-handgun on his record. His nickname's easy to remember. Jet, like in *West Side Story*."

Everything reminded Rothbart of some musical or other, Armitage thought. But he laughed. Always humor the judge. Parish chuckled too. She was no fool.

"The kid clammed up as soon as he was arrested," Armitage said. "We'll call him at the preliminary inquiry and see what he has to say."

Rothbart took a long look at Parish.

She smiled back.

Neither said anything.

What was that all about? Armitage wondered.

"Okay," Rothbart said. He reached into his desk and pulled out a pile of forms. "Ralph, I know your answer, but I have to ask you anyway: Is there any way the Crown would take a plea to second-degree murder?"

"Not in a million years," Armitage said.

Rothbart laughed. "I wish I had a nickel for every time I heard that line." He closed the file in front of him and sat back. Relaxed now. "Ralph, did I ever tell you that when we took the show to New York, one night Elizabeth Taylor said to me, 'Can't Richard and I just kidnap you? If we let you go back to Canada your mother's going to make you become a doctor or a lawyer.'"

Only about fifteen times, Armitage thought. But he smiled. "Really?"

For the next ten minutes they worked their way through a series of technical questions about the trial. "Last but not least," Rothbart said, coming to the final page in the form. "When can we start this trial? First there's going to be the prelim in the lower court, and—"

"Won't be necessary, sir," Parish said. "My client is electing to go straight to trial, the sooner the better."

Armitage stared at her in stunned silence. Although accused people had the right to forgo their preliminary inquiry, which was essentially a vetting of the evidence, it was also a great opportunity for the defense to have charges reduced, or sometimes even thrown out. Waiving the prelim in a first-degree murder trial was unheard-of.

Rothbart grinned. He still had great teeth and a charming smile. "I see," he said.

Armitage saw it too. That's what she was smiling about a few minutes ago with him. At a prelim the Crown could force Jet to testify and find out what his evidence would be. Dewey too. They could test him out and fill in some of the holes left in his affidavit. By going straight to trial Parish was forcing the Crown to fly blind in front of the jury.

"The whole city is traumatized by this case," Rothbart said. "The sooner we can start this trial the better. But how long's it going to take? There's one thing on my calendar I never change. I'll be away the first week of May."

Yes, yes, I know, Armitage thought. The first week in May. The Tony Awards nominations came out, and Rothbart went down every year to hobnob with his old Broadway pals.

"Trial will only take a few weeks," Parish said. "If we start in early April we'll be fine."

Rothbart beamed. "Excellent. When I read through the briefs, it occurred to me the defense might waive the prelim. I've already got us the earliest possible trial date. April eleventh. Looks as if you two are going to have a very busy few months."

He hopped to his feet and pranced in front of them on the way to his door. Unlike many judges, who would summarily dismiss lawyers while seated behind their desks, Rothbart did this every time. Was it good manners, Armitage wondered, or did he just like to show how nimble he still was? He started strumming his fingers on his palm again.

What a disaster, Armitage thought. His witnesses were a bunch of civilians who couldn't speak English and some criminals who would probably lie their asses off on the stand. And April 11. A little more than a month before the party. Penny would be going crazy. It felt as if his life was getting squeezed from all sides.

Walking down the carpeted halls beside Parish, Armitage could just make out the sound of Rothbart humming a show tune. It was from *Camelot,* of course. That mythical land, where a young boy with a sword could save the kingdom. Just as Armitage had done for all those summers when he was a kid, playing make-believe in the dense woods behind his parents' estate.

44

"I found out who he is," Daniel Kennicott said the moment Ari Greene answered his cell phone.

"Hang on a minute," Greene said. He was walking up the staircase from the basement in Old City Hall, where the thick stone walls made reception difficult. He sprinted to the main floor, reaching into his coat pocket for pen and pad. "Okay, what have you got?"

"Name is Dragomir Ozera. Nabbed for theft under. Stole some pâté and brie from Pusateri's. Only had a library card for ID. Gave his address as a room at Jilly's, the strip joint over on Broadview. No phone."

"When did this happen?"

"Five years ago. An officer named Lindsmore arrested him."

"He's a good cop."

"Has a complete file. Even a drawing showing his birthmark. And a cigarette butt he left behind. Ozera never showed up for prints or court."

Five years ago, Greene thought after he hung up. The file would still be over in the Crown's office. He could easily go there and get it. Instead he dialed another number.

"Raglan," Jennifer Raglan said in that distracted voice that Crowns always had between nine and ten in the morning when they were getting ready for court.

"It's me," Greene said.

He heard an intake of breath on the line. Then the sound of papers being shuffled on her desk. The phone being put down. Footsteps walking away, and a door being closed. Footsteps coming closer again. "Hi," she said.

"Sorry to call like this."

"No. I'm real glad you did," she said. "I've been wanting to talk to you."

"This is about business. But first. Your mother?"

"That was one of the reasons I wanted to talk. It's a roller coaster. Last week I got an emergency call and had to boot out there in the middle of the day. She rallied but . . ." Her voice faltered.

He waited for her to speak again. His mind drifted to the other reasons she'd wanted to call.

"I'm having a real hard time with it," she said. "Makes me miss you."

"I need to see you today. But it's about work. A favor."

"Probably a good place to start."

"This is urgent," he said. "What's your day like?"

She exhaled. "Lucky you. I was supposed to start a three-day prelim on a carjacking The defense lawyer and I just made a deal. I'm going over an Agreed Statement of Facts he drew up. This will be done by ten thirty. What do you need?"

"I want you to pull a file for me. It should be in the Fail to Appear boxes. Five years old, and I know the boxes there go back almost a decade."

"What's this for?" she asked.

"Can't say, but it's important or I wouldn't ask. I'll wait for you at our usual place."

He gave her the details of Ozera's charges, then made his way over to the cafeteria at the new city hall and found a booth on the far wall. The morning rush had subsided, and the place was emptying out.

Greene tried not to keep looking at his watch as the time ticked by. His phone didn't ring. At a quarter to twelve, the cafeteria began to stir back to life. He ordered a grilled cheese sandwich and was biting into it when Raglan showed up. She smiled when she found him. He hadn't seen her since the last time he was here and the call came in about the shooting. She had nothing in her hands. Greene had expected her to be carrying her briefcase with the file inside.

Their eyes met. After all the years they'd known each other, working together on cases, then as lovers, now as whatever they were, they could communicate without words.

She sat and looked around. Made sure they were alone. "The file's not in the Fail to Appear box," she said.

"Where is it?"

"Both charges were pulled by the Crown. Cases dismissed."

"What? When?"

"A few weeks ago. December twenty-ninth. I tracked the records down. That's what took so long."

"You're kidding," Greene said.

"No. It was done in 112 court two Fridays ago. Probably took about a minute, and no one would have thought twice about it."

He'd eaten only about a quarter of his sandwich. He pushed the plate away.

She reached out and covered his hand. "I've been resisting calling you."

"It's okay."

"I couldn't have lasted another week without seeing you."

He felt her fingers intertwine with his.

"I don't know what to do," she said.

"How bad are things?"

"Mom's a quiet fighter. She's hanging on, but just barely."

"Anything I can do?"

She squeezed his hand harder but didn't say anything. Didn't have to.

"It might be easier if we talk business," he said. "Which Crown pulled the charges?"

"Armitage, of course," she said. "He's been combing through old files with minor charges and getting rid of them."

"This wasn't the only case?"

"No." She laughed. "There were more than a hundred. What's the big deal?"

"Not sure," he said. "Do you know when he started doing this?"

"Over the Christmas holidays. He sent a memo out when everyone got back saying he hoped we all felt sorry for him being stuck in the office, bored to death. That if anyone had ancient cases to get rid of, to pass them to him because he was doing a big purge."

His attention was drawn to someone approaching their table. He looked over and Johnathan Summers, a judge Greene knew very well, walked up. Raglan let go of his hand.

"Cops and Crowns, always going at it," Summers said with a big jolly laugh.

Greene and Raglan exchanged glances.

"Detective, I hear you're on the Timmy's shooting," Summers said.

Greene had been amazed how quickly the murder of young Kyle Wilkinson had been labeled "the Timmy's shooting." Like the way CNN came up with a banner headline for even the worst events, moments after they happened. And Kyle's name seemed to have been forgotten. "I am," he said.

Summers shook his head. Solemn. "Tough case," he said.

Gossip was a valuable currency for everyone in the criminal justice system—lawyers, judges, cops, court clerks, and most of all journalists. Insider tidbits of information about high-profile cases were liquid gold. People involved in trials weren't supposed to talk about them, but that didn't stop anyone. The unwritten code was if you were an outsider, you never asked directly. But right now, Judge Summers was fishing.

"They're all tough cases," Greene said. It was a platitude. And code for "Sorry, no dice. No gossip here."

Summers turned his ruddy red face to Raglan. "I heard your mom's sick. I'm very sorry."

"Thanks, Your Honor."

Summers rumbled away.

Raglan waited until he was out of earshot. "Ari, why do you care so much about us yanking this guy Ozera's case? It's just a stupid theft under a fail-to-appear charge from five years ago."

"We just figured out Ozera's the baker at Tim Hortons we've been looking for. Our missing witness."

"Really?"

He smiled.

She smiled back. "How did you do that?"

"Legwork."

"Great. But what does it have to do with Ralph withdrawing these charges?"

"I don't know yet. I'm a detective. I don't like coincidence."

"Well, this is a total coincidence. Ralph cleaned up hundreds of back files. I was a real popular head Crown with the troops but a disaster when it came to paperwork. When I left, the ministry wanted someone who could run the place efficiently. Ralph's a good civil servant."

"Whose idea was this cleanup?"

"Both of ours. Strictly between you and me, Ralph still calls me almost every day. It's a real pain. He was stuck here over the holidays. He told me he was going to do some housecleaning and I said, 'Great.' With all the cutbacks, we have a backlog of about eighteen months just getting all the information into the system."

Armitage initiated this, he thought.

Raglan had a way of running both hands through her hair at the same time that he loved to watch. "Did Ralph call you before he decided to take this case?"

She grinned at Greene. "I warned him, a trial like this can make or break his career," she said.

"He's in over his head. The deal he made with Cutter was a real rookie mistake."

"I know." She took her hands off her head and reached for his hand. "I told him he was very lucky it was your case."

He massaged her fingers.

"I've got to go," she said.

"I know."

He waited until she was gone before he reached for his cell phone. He touched an autodial number.

"Hi, detective," Kennicott answered almost immediately.

"Do you still have the actual warrant for the fail-to-appear and the theft-under charge?" he asked.

"It's right in my hand."

"Good. Find a brown paper bag, stick it inside, and staple the bag shut with an evidence time-date tag attached. And nobody, I mean nobody, hears about this but me. Understood?"

"Completely."

45

Ralph Armitage would have been happy if he never saw another soccer game on TV. Happier still if he never came back to the Plaza Flamingo, the restaurant where he'd had the two worst meetings of his life. Now it seemed a third one was about to take place.

To make matters worse, it was Thursday again. He had a hunch that this guy Ozera had read about his weekly date with his wife in that *Toronto Star* article and was testing him.

He took his seat at his usual table. Soccer games filled all the screens. It seemed strange to him that in Europe they played soccer in the winter, not the summer. Then again, they didn't get winters like the one Toronto was having right now.

A waiter, a short guy with a black cap, came by and asked for his order. He had such a thick Spanish accent he was hard to understand. Armitage ordered a Molson Canadian and waited.

Waiting sucked. But this time he had good news for this Dragomir Ozera, aka Jose Sanchez, aka the runaway witness who could fuck up Armitage's whole life.

The waiter came back with the beer. "That is four dollars please, sir," he said.

Armitage grabbed the bottle and took a swig. He needed a drink. "Here, keep the five." He handed over the bill.

"And the charges?" the waiter asked.

"Charges? For what?" The guy was hard to understand. "A cover charge?"

"No, my charges, Mr. Armitage." The waiter's voice had lost all its accent. Armitage took a second look. It was Ozera.

"You work here now?" he asked.

"I work wherever I can get paid cash, until I get a new identity. Or until you take care of things."

"I did. Both charges have been withdrawn."

"Where's the paperwork?"

Armitage pulled out a folded sheet from his coat pocket. "Here's what you need to do to get it. Go to the clerk's office, room 246 at old city hall. Ask for a certified copy of the court documents. It will cost you four or five dollars, takes a few weeks. I've written it all down here."

Ozera slipped it into his back pocket. "Why didn't you get it?"

Armitage laughed. "Thanks to you, I went through a few years' worth of old files for minor charges and withdrew more than a hundred dead cases. No one would see the connection. But it would be suspicious as hell if the head Crown were go to the clerk's office and order the documentation on one case. No reason for me to do it."

Ozera pondered this.

"It's no big deal. Just wait a few weeks before you go over there."

"What about the outstanding warrant for my arrest?"

Shit, this guy was smart. Armitage had been hoping he wouldn't ask. "I can't do anything about that. The cops are in charge of warrants. It will take a while to input everything into the computer, and then they'll toss it."

"How long?"

It would take eighteen months if not more, but Armitage wasn't going to tell him that. "I won't make a promise I can't keep. It's bureaucrats."

"Until then, if I get stopped by the cops I'll get arrested."

"If you were, they'd soon drop the charges."

"Thanks, that's a real help. What about immigration? You must have contacts there."

Armitage had wondered if this was going to be the next demand. He had lots of contacts at immigration, but it was too risky. Especially right now. Besides, he wasn't going to let this little guy with all his accents push him around anymore. He jumped to his feet, taking Ozera by surprise. Armitage had been in enough negotiations to know when to call someone's bluff.

"You know what? I'm done. You want to testify, come in and make a statement. I'll tell the folks at immigration you helped out." He shrugged, the biggest shrug in his repertoire for probably the biggest bluff of his life. "But I can't guarantee anything."

Just as he'd hoped, Ozera looked stunned. Time to push him.

"Besides, I should warn you. Detective Greene found out your real name."

"You told him?"

"No."

"Then how . . ."

"They interviewed some girl who worked with you at Tim Hortons. From that they figured out you were probably Romanian and traced you back that way."

"Suzanne," Ozera muttered.

"What about Suzanne?"

"She would have told them. When did you hear this?"

"A few hours ago."

It had been a close call. Greene came by the office this afternoon after court and asked him if he'd ever heard the name Dragomir Ozera. Armitage played dumb. "Sounds familiar," he'd said.

"I heard you went on blitz over the holiday and cleaned out a bunch of old charges," Greene had said.

"One hundred and forty-one to be exact." Armitage had laughed, trying to sound relaxed.

"Well, Ozera was one of those cases."

"Oh. That's why the name sounds familiar. So what?"

"We found the cop who arrested him for the original theft. Showed him the composite and he recognized him. He even had an old cigarette butt from the guy and we're doing a DNA test, ultra-high priority, with a strand of hair from a hairnet we found in the bushes beside the Tim Hortons. We'll know in twenty-four hours."

Armitage had said all the right things to Greene. *Great work. We have to tell the defense right away. What can we do to find this guy?* But now, looking at Ozera in the noisy restaurant, he could see the young guy was shaken.

"If my name and a picture of me gets in the newspaper, Dewey will know who I am," Ozera said.

That was Ozera's core fear: Dewey Booth. He'd terrorized this guy enough to guarantee he'd keep his trap shut. Probably, Armitage hoped, forever.

46

Outside Nancy Parish's office the wind was howling, pelting snow against the window in a repetitive *knock, knock, knock*. Like a raven with a broken wing, she thought. Friday night and here she was again, alone in the office, going through the seemingly endless e-mails from her other, increasingly irate clients. Then there was the deep pile of Legal Aid forms she'd tossed on the floor weeks ago and had steadfastly ignored.

Pain in the ass. Taking on a murder trial for a poor client such as St. Clair meant she'd be paid about a quarter of her usual rate, and she got to flirt with financial ruin while the rest of her practice dried up. As a bonus the best-case scenario with this trial? She wins, and forevermore the name "Nancy Parish" is synonymous with "the child-killer who beat the system."

Ignoring it all, she picked up a pad of paper. And to think I could have gone to art school, she thought. She began to draw a female lawyer meeting her male client in a prison cell. He was flipping a coin. "Heads I did it," the caption read. "Tails I didn't."

The office suite had an annoying bell that rang when the front door opened. Parish heard it and put down her pencil. Hadn't she locked the door? Ted constantly bugged her to do it when she stayed late and worked alone. Half the time she was so busy she forgot. Hopefully it was him.

DiPaulo had been out of town over the holidays and she was dying to talk to Ted about how Larkin wouldn't tell her what had happened. Refused to let her call him to testify.

One of the ironies about being a criminal lawyer was that, despite dealing with so-called hardened criminals, she never felt fearful of or threatened by her clients. Much to the consternation of her mother, she told everyone who asked if she was afraid of her clients, "No. They're the most polite people in the whole system. It's the cops and Crowns who scare me."

But now, alone in her office late at night, the silence was eerie. She felt nervous for the first time in years. Should she call out? That wasn't smart. Instead she clicked off her desk light, grabbed an old hockey trophy that doubled as a paperweight from her desk, and tiptoed behind her door. Thankfully it was open only a crack. She listened hard.

Steps started down the hallway. It sounded like more than one set of feet. Her office was the second door, one up from DiPaulo's. The footfalls were almost outside her door. She squeezed the trophy in her hand. It felt cold, even though her fingers were sweaty.

She heard a loud bang, just outside. Something fell hard against the wall.

She tensed.

"*Mon dieu,*" a woman's voice said. She had a heavy French accent. "I have the jet lag."

"And too much champagne," a man said.

Parish loosened her grip. Boy, did she feel like an idiot. It was Ted, with his French girlfriend Isabel. She'd never met the woman, and sure didn't want to start now.

"I'll carry you over the threshold," DiPaulo said on the other side of the wall.

She heard the sound of much fumbling.

"Very sexy," Isabel said. "I want to be seeing this office where you are spending so much of your lifetime."

Not as much time as he used to, Parish thought. His heavy footsteps stumbled past her door. She slipped off her shoes, tiptoed to her desk, and grabbed her coat, boots, scarf, mittens, cell phone, and keys.

"Is very comfortable," Isabel said.

Parish could hear they were inside his office, but the door was open. She slid out into the hallway. Behind her came the rustling sound of clothes being removed. "*Mon dieu, mon dieu.*" Isabel was moaning.

In the reception area, Parish stopped and collected herself. If she didn't open the door too wide, and was real fast, sometimes the stupid bell didn't ring. She grabbed the handle and threw her stuff outside, then squeezed through the gap. The bell stayed silent.

What a loser you are, she thought as she put on her shoes and coat in the deserted hallway. Just as she picked up her cell phone, it started to vibrate. She turned it over to look at the display. A text message from Zelda.

Cant make 2nite. Amanda the wman I met @ that confrnce in Bston jst
flew in. Think Im in luuuuuuv
Z

Great, Parish thought. Looks like an exciting evening home alone
watching *Law & Order* reruns.

Her phone buzzed again with another text.

PS. jst left Pravda w Amanda. The cute waitr asked whr r u??? hmm-
mmm. Luuuuuuv?

"No, Zelda, it's not love," Parish said as she pushed the Down button on the elevator. "But it's Friday night and any port in a storm."

PART FOUR
APRIL

47

"The first witness for the Crown will be Mr. Cedric Wilkinson," Ralph Armitage said. His long arms emerged from his freshly ironed black robes like a pair of muscular wings as he spread them to his sides and flashed his lightning smile at the jury seated directly to his right. It had taken all day Monday and Tuesday to pick six men and six women with backgrounds about as diverse as you could imagine. All had one thing in common. They wore wedding bands. That had been the only criterion Armitage had cared about. He wanted jurors who most likely had children.

With a flip of his blond hair, he swiveled his large head and looked back into the body of the court. He had strategically positioned the Wilkinson family right behind him in the seats closest to the jury box. He nodded at them, his face now solemn.

Wilkinson lumbered to his feet. In every photo taken of him before his son was shot, the big man's jowly face had fallen into a natural smile. But now, the stress of the last five months had stripped away the joy and replaced it with a ghostlike vacancy. He was much thinner, his skin stretched, as if pounds had fallen off him helter-skelter.

Armitage sat down to show his respect. The large courtroom was packed, but no one made a sound as Wilkinson plodded to the front and hoisted himself up into the witness stand.

Crown Attorneys had many different strategies for how to start a case. Some liked to call cops as their first witnesses, thinking this would give their evidence an official stamp of approval. Others preferred to begin with the civilian witnesses, to make the jury see what happened through the eyes of a stranger. The same way they would see the evidence.

He knew that every trial was a mixture of facts and emotions. To persuade the jury he had to find the right balance. With a highly charged case such as this one, he could either call the grieving father as his first witness, to hit the jury over the head with the tragedy, or save him for the end and send them out to deliberate on an emotional whirl.

"Good morning, Mr. Wilkinson," Judge Rothbart said, sliding his chair over beside the witness box. "We all appreciate your being here to testify."

During the previous two days of jury selection, Rothbart had kept his theatrical instincts in check, in keeping with the gravity of the case. But this little show of affection for the Crown's first witness was, judicially speaking, over the top. Armitage glanced across at the defense counsel table. Nancy Parish was grinding her teeth. Rothbart was letting the jury know where his sympathies lay, and she couldn't do anything about it.

Wilkinson looked at the judge and nodded. He was a quiet man.

The clerk swore him as a witness.

Armitage stood up. Everyone in the courtroom was watching him. He could feel it in his bones, that he'd made the right decision to call this witness first.

"I think we all understand how difficult this is for you, sir," Armitage said.

Wilkinson stared at him. Didn't say a word.

They'd met a number of times since the murder. The guy was pissed that he'd made the deal with Dewey Booth. And he wasn't happy about all the publicity that had centered on Armitage. It was important that the jury didn't get a whiff of this antagonism, but, by his stillness in the witness box, he could see Wilkinson didn't intend to make this easy.

"Let's keep it simple," Armitage said. "Take your mind back to the night of November fourteenth."

"Nothing simple about it," Wilkinson said. "My son was murdered."

Maybe it had been a bad idea to start with him, Armitage thought. Every victim went through a very angry stage, and it usually spilled out into their being mad at the whole legal process—all the technicalities, the objectification of their loved ones. Just as dying patients often lashed out at their doctors, witnesses like Wilkinson often took it out on the prosecutors.

He had to turn that anger to his advantage. Stop being charming, Ralphie, he told himself. Think of the TV show *Dragnet*—"just the facts, ma'am."

"Where were you earlier that day, Mr. Wilkinson?"

"At work."

Like pulling teeth. "And where do you work?"

"Lipton Industries." Wilkinson folded his arms in front of him.

"What type of company is it?"

"We manufacture pigment. I love colors."

To his side Armitage heard some jury members shuffle in their seats.

"What is pigment?"

Wilkinson unfolded his arms and glanced for the first time at the jury. "Pigment is a powdery material that changes the color of reflected or transmitted light. It's the basic material in most of the paint, clothes dye, and colored foodstuffs that we use every day. Pigment is an invisible product to most people, but it's crucial to our everyday life. The worldwide market in pigment is about twenty billion dollars." He spoke like a guest lecturer at a Kiwanis Club meeting.

"And your connection to Lipton Industries?" Armitage asked.

"I've worked at Lipton for eighteen years. We're based in California, where both my wife and I were born. Last August the company moved me up here to run the Canadian operation. We employ seventy-two people at our plant out in Scarborough."

The transformation was extraordinary. By getting Wilkinson to talk about normal things in his life, he'd turned into a perfect witness. Clear, cogent, trustworthy. The rustling in the jury box stopped.

For the next half hour, he led Wilkinson through the events of the evening and how every small and insignificant action ended up as an unintended yet fatal decision: if only he hadn't taken Kyle for a doughnut but instead had gone straight to the hospital as planned; if Kyle hadn't slipped on the sidewalk a minute before, they would have been safely inside when the shots rang out; if it hadn't started to snow at just that moment, Kyle wouldn't have stopped to look. If, if, if, if. The tragic horror of circumstance. The jurors were respectful and still. A few quietly cried.

He'd made the right decision to call Wilkinson after all, Armitage thought. Now the jury would think of this loving father and his enormous loss throughout the trial. "Finally, sir," he said once the whole story had been told, "do you have any idea how many shots were fired?"

Wilkinson shook his big head. "I keep replaying those moments over and . . ." For the first time since he'd started testifying, he faltered. He looked up toward the ceiling. Tears popped into his eyes, and one trickled down his wide cheeks. "At first I heard that bang sound, and I couldn't believe it was a gun. I mean we were downtown, going to buy a doughnut. Then there were more shots. I don't know how many."

The court had become still. People were crowded into every seat, and no one moved a muscle.

Armitage couldn't resist looking over to Nancy Parish to see how this was ruining her day. She was looking right at Wilkinson. Beside her, St. Clair was staring at Wilkinson too. Blinking his eyes. A tear, then another, rolled down his cheek. He tapped Parish on the arm. She looked surprised, fished around in her vest pocket, pulled out a scrunched-up piece of Kleenex, and slipped it over to him.

Someone cleared his throat.

He looked up. Judge Rothbart was trying to get his attention. He'd gotten distracted by the little drama at the defense table. The whole jury had been watching Larkin St. Clair cry. Up on the witness stand, Wilkinson was waiting for him.

He couldn't think of anything else to say. "Those are my questions." Armitage fluffed up his robes, sat down, and looked at Nancy Parish. "Your witness," he said.

He was sure she'd say, "No questions." What the hell could she gain from cross-examining this poor man?

Instead she stood and walked in front of the prosecution table, right up beside the jury, and looked at Wilkinson head-on.

She was a gutsy lawyer, but wasn't this a suicide move?

"Mr. Wilkinson," Parish said. "You studied engineering at Stanford University, correct?"

"Yes." He nodded.

"Then you got your MBA at Berkeley, correct?"

"Yes."

"You wrote a thesis entitled 'Everyone's Got a Job to Do,' about the importance of people understanding their various roles in the corporate structure."

"Yes," Wilkinson said again. He looked confused.

What the hell did this have to do with anything, Armitage wondered.

"Then you worked for Lipton in Sacramento for your whole career. You've been in various positions, including research, marketing, personnel. Always lived in California until you moved up here last September."

"That's right."

"When you were made president of Lipton Canada."

"Yes."

Armitage had to smile at himself. Some defense lawyers just had to hear themselves talk. She was making this grieving father even more likeable. This was only going to help the prosecution.

"Would I be correct if I said that last year was your first Canadian winter ever?" she asked.

Wilkinson smiled. He hadn't done that when Armitage questioned him.

"Sure was." In an instant his face turned sour. He threw his hands over his eyes. "That night, Kyle was so excited to see snow for the first time."

The man's emotions hit the courtroom with a wallop.

Armitage was sure Parish was going to sit down now and stop questioning him. But she waited, motionless.

"Excuse me," Wilkinson said, once he'd regained his composure.

"Nothing to apologize for," she said. "I'm sure you understand that I have to ask you a few questions."

"I know. You've got your job to do."

Now Armitage saw where she was going with this. "Everyone's got a job to do," and Parish was using Wilkinson to tell the jury, "Don't be mad at me, I'm just doing my job." Even worse, somehow she had a better rapport with Wilkinson than he did. Shit.

"You told us that Kyle slipped on the sidewalk as you were walking over to the Tim Hortons. Would I be right that the reason he fell was because of the sudden change in the weather? It had gotten very cold that afternoon, and there was ice on the ground."

"That's exactly what happened. Winter in Canada was all new to him. And me. We were both wearing sneakers."

Armitage could feel the shift in the courtroom. Parish had turned Wilkinson from being an emotional witness to an objective one. The engineer who was going to stick to the just the facts, ma'am.

"You remember that first gunshot."

"Yes."

"But after that, you can't tell how many more there were, can you?"

Parish was using Wilkinson to establish her best defense. That there were many shots, and therefore there could have been more than one shooter. And perhaps the shot that hit Kyle was fired in self-defense. Or some kind of accident. Or both.

"No idea," Wilkinson said.

"Some of the witnesses the Crown Attorney's going to call"—she looked back and waved her arm at Armitage—"say there were six gun-shots, one says there were nine. You can't say if that is right or wrong, can you?"

"No, I can't," Wilkinson said. "There were a lot of shots, that's all I know."

She's spelling out her whole case through my star witness, Armitage thought. Wilkinson looked strangely relaxed. Perhaps happier to be talking about the bits of objective evidence he was sure of. The jury was going to believe every word he said. Her tone was so gentle. He had to admit it was very effective. Just like the old adage about cross-examination: you catch more flies with sugar than with vinegar.

"I hate to ask you this, but I must. Do you have any idea which shot hit your son Kyle? Was it the first one?"

"I have no idea. It all happened so fast."

"I understand, Mr. Wilkinson. Thank you very much, I don't have any other questions," she said in a voice that was soft with compassion.

"Mr. Armitage, any questions in reexamination?" Judge Rothbart asked.

Armitage stood. He wanted to get Wilkinson off the stand as fast as possible. "None, Your Honor."

Wilkinson looked at the judge.

"Thank you, sir." Rothbart gave Wilkinson his most sympathetic look. An Oscar performance if I've ever seen one, Armitage thought.

"Is that all?"

"Yes." Rothbart was speaking in his most melodious baritone. "My deepest sympathies to you and your family."

A totally inappropriate thing for a judge to say in a first-degree murder trial. And great for the prosecution.

48

If a picture was worth a thousand words, then Nancy Parish knew that a real live object was worth ten times more. Something to show the jury. Something for them to not just see or hear about but feel. Touch. Bring back with them to the jury room as an exhibit at the end of the trial when they started to deliberate.

That was why, ten minutes before the trial was about to resume after the morning break, she was setting up a big easel in the courtroom at an angle where the judge, the jury, and the lawyers could all see it.

On the easel she placed a blown-up scale drawing of the scene of the murder, which showed the street in front of the Tim Hortons, the parking lot, and the doughnut shop itself. She then layered over the top of this the first of five see-through acrylic sheets that were at the end of her desk. Each piece had two holes on top that corresponded with little pegs at the top of the easel, guaranteeing that they would all sit as clear overlays in the exact same position.

Back at her counsel table, she unsheathed a collection of five different-colored markers and spread them out.

The special barrister's door beside her opened and Ralph Armitage and Ari Greene strode in.

"What do we have here, Nancy?" Armitage asked, coming right up to the display.

"You'll see soon enough," she said.

He fingered the pieces of acrylic and the markers. "Five see-through sheets, five colored markers, five eyewitnesses."

The man was not as dim as some defense lawyers assumed, she thought. Never underestimate your opponent. "Good counting, Ralphie."

"On good days, I can get all the way to twelve, so I can pick a jury," he said. Big grin on his face.

Well, the guy can laugh at himself, she thought.

The constable opened the main door, and like tap water filling an ice cube tray, a rush of people took every available seat in the courtroom. The big oak door beside the judge's dais swung open, and the clerk marched in, Judge Rothbart behind him. Both looked at Parish's display, but neither said a word as they took their seats.

The last people in were the jury. When they were settled, Mr. Mohammed, the first eyewitness who'd testified for the Crown before the break, went back to the witness box. Parish stood up to cross-examine.

"Ms. Parish," Rothbart said, still eyeing the display board but not commenting on it. "Proceed."

"Thank you, Your Honor." She grabbed the colored markers and walked directly up to the witness. Mr. Mohammed was a little man, almost hidden in the tall box. Beside him stood an equally small court translator.

"Sir, I have in my hand five different-colored markers." Parish showed them to him. With her free hand she pointed to the easel. "In a moment, I'm going to ask you to step down from the witness box and draw out for me exactly what you saw."

"I would be most pleased to do so," Mohammed said through the translator. Unlike many people she'd seen testify, Parish had noticed this morning that he had the patience to wait until his words were translated without trying to respond directly in English. It made him an impressive witness.

"Why don't you choose a color?" she asked.

"May I have blue?"

"Certainly." Parish noticed a few of the jurors smile for the first time since they were sworn in.

She had the little man and the little translator walk over to the easel. "Now, sir, you can write on this clear piece of plastic. Please put the number one where you were situated when you heard the first gunshot."

Mohammed drew the number in a precise hand, placing it inside the door.

"Now put number two where the little boy was shot, and a three where the father was located."

He wrote numbers for the location of the two men, one with long hair and one with extremely white skin; for the big car he saw drive into the corner of the lot; for the woman who ran across to the car.

"One final question, sir," she asked when Mohammed stood back to admire his handiwork. "How many shots did you hear?"

He shut his eyes. "Bang, then bang, bang, bang. Then one or two more."

Parish counted the bangs out on her hand for effect. "So you heard five or six shots," she said.

"Objection, Your Honor," Armitage shouted out behind her, bolting to his feet.

She turned toward him, feigning confusion for the sake of the jury, shrugged her shoulders, and turned toward the judge. "I'm only repeating what the witness said." She opened her palms by her sides, trying to act innocent.

Judge Rothbart might have been an actor in his day, but to her relief he was taken in by her routine. He turned to Armitage. "Mr. Crown, what's the problem?"

Armitage had turned beet red. "The problem, Your Honor, is this witness testified he heard 'bangs,' not 'shots.'"

Parish threw her hands up in mock frustration. "Bangs, shots," she said, trying to sound as dismissive as she could. Of course, there was a world of difference. A shot was a shot, but a bang could have just as easily have been an echo. Ralphie Armitage is no dummy, she told herself yet again.

Rothbart turned an angry eye at her. He didn't like being shown up this way in front of the jury. "Ms. Parish," he growled, "Mr. Armitage is right. Rephrase that immediately."

"Apologies, Your Honor," she said, all contrite, smiling inside because she knew the jury got it. Create doubt, Nancy, she told herself. Every chance you get, turn black and white into gray.

"Mr. Mohammed," she said with a smile on her face. "You heard five or six bangs, correct?"

"I did, ma'am."

"Please put '5–6' in the very bottom right-hand corner."

He obediently wrote in the numbers.

Parish took the pen from him, like a schoolteacher collecting her things at the end of a class. "Those are my questions," she told him as she took down the marked-up acrylic sheet from the display.

By now everyone in the courtroom knew what she was doing. The next four eyewitnesses would get different-colored markers to draw on their own see-through pieces of acrylic. They'd all seen things differently. For example, Mohammed had put the Cadillac on the right-hand side of the lot, whereas three others put it on the left. The last witness said there was no car at all. She knew that in her closing address to the jury, when she finally put them all together, the contradictions in the testimony would be manifest. Literally there for all to see.

The Crown's case, she thought as she sat down and fingered the second clear sheet, was going to look like a plate of spaghetti.

49

For three days now Ari Greene had sat at the Crown counsel table and watched Ralph Armitage call his five eyewitnesses, and for three days Nancy Parish had each one draw out their evidence on her see-through acrylic sheets. She was very precise in her questions, getting each one to agree that, yes, they weren't sure exactly how many gun-shots were fired; yes, it was dark; yes, the streets and sidewalks were slippery; and yes, everything happened so quickly they couldn't be sure about all sorts of things.

Greene could tell the jury couldn't wait to see how it would look when the five were put together. He already knew how bad it would be.

But it wasn't this evidence that bothered Greene about the trial so far. It was Ralph Armitage's performance. He seemed distracted, thrown off by Parish's gambit with the chart. Instead of his trademark confident swagger, Armitage was stumbling, even through routine stuff. Now, on Friday afternoon, he had Suzanne Howett on the stand. Last night they'd met with her and gone over the statement she'd made to Greene after he picked her up at the Petro-Can gas station. She was expected to be a solid witness. Hopefully, Armitage would fin-ish off the week on a more positive note.

"Ms. Howett, how old are you?" Armitage asked when everyone was settled back in court after the lunch break. The former Tim Hortons employee had taken the stand and been sworn.

"Twenty-two," Howett said. She'd cut her long curls and wore a conservative dress.

"Suzanne," Armitage said, softening his voice, switching to her first name to make her relax. "Do you have a criminal record?"

"No."

"Ever been arrested?"

"No. Never."

"Last November fourteenth, where were you working?"

"I was a server at the Tim Hortons." She pointed in the direction of the back of the courtroom with her right hand. Greene noticed she kept her scarred left baby finger curled up and hidden. "The one on Elm Street."

Armitage waved his hand in the same direction. "Right across the street, up only a block or two."

Smart move, Greene thought. Bring home to the jury how close the shooting was to the spot where they're sitting right now. Armitage had gotten into a relaxed conversation with Howett. Dealing with this witness appeared to have restored his confidence.

"Yeah. I worked there for a year. Until the shooting."

"Tell us about the night of the fourteenth." Armitage tilted his head a little to the side, as if he were hearing her evidence for the first time. The jury was rapt.

"My shift ended at five. Jet used to pick me up then," she said.

"Jet, what's his real name?" Armitage asked.

"Oh, it's James Trapper, but everyone calls him Jet. We grew up together on Pelee Island. That's in Lake Erie."

Howett was getting nervous, Greene thought. Everyone in the court could see it. But Armitage seemed completely nonchalant. He walked up to her. "Suzanne, take a second. You want a glass of water?"

"No thanks." She giggled a little.

"Have you ever been in court before to testify?"

"Me? No." She shook her head hard.

"Take a look at the jury. It's allowed. They're not going to bite."

She giggled again. "Yeah. I know."

He turned to the judge. "He's not going bite either."

She blushed. "Thanks."

Armitage looked at the defense table and pointed out Nancy Parish. "Now, she's the defendant's lawyer. I can't guarantee what she's going to do, you understand that?"

She was nodding now. "I guess so."

A few jury members chuckled.

Armitage moved back away. "You swore to tell us the truth. You can do that, right?"

"Sure.'

This was all done very smoothly. Greene was impressed. He'd seen many Crown Attorneys rush their own witnesses and turn good evidence into bad.

"Okay, Suzanne. You finished your shift and were waiting for Jet to come pick you up."

Good move, Greene thought, talking to her about Jet, not "Mr. Trapper."

"Yeah, I was having a smoke out back with Jose. He was the baker, and we used to do that."

"And what happened?"

"Well, I told him that my old boyfriend Dewey—Dewey Booth is his full name—had like just got out of prison, and how he hung out with his buddy Larkin, who had super-long hair."

"Larkin. Do you know his last name?"

"I didn't then, but I do now from the papers and stuff. It's him with the long hair. It used to be way longer."

She pointed to St. Clair, sitting at the defense counsel table beside Nancy Parish. He'd been staring straight ahead the whole time and didn't move a muscle. Well coached by his lawyer, Greene thought, to never look at the witness stand. Especially when one of the witnesses was someone he knew and who the jury might think he was trying to influence.

"What else did you say to Jose, while you were out back having your smoke? Before Jet came to pick you up?"

That was smart, Greene thought. Recap the key points to reinforce them to the jury. Make sure they know where she is in her story.

"I said I thought Dewey was looking for me. That I was afraid," she said. "I told him that Dewey and Jet hate each other."

"Objection, Your Honor." Nancy Parish came flying out of her seat.

Rothbart put his hand up as if to say, "I understand," then looked at Armitage with dagger eyes. "Mr. Crown, I don't want to hear this kind of highly prejudicial hearsay evidence." He turned to the jury. "Members of the jury, you will disregard this witness's last statement. What she thinks other people think of each other is not, I repeat, *not* evidence."

Greene wondered how Armitage would take this judicial rebuke.

He stood tall. "Apologies, Your Honor. We have an inexperienced witness here, but I'll be very careful."

Nicely done, Greene thought. And good move setting up right from the start that Howett has never been in court before.

"Suzanne, what happened next? Only what you saw and heard, and not what anyone else told you."

"Okay. We were sharing a cigarette, then Jose went inside."

"You two were alone?"

"Yeah."

"What did you do?" Armitage was in a smooth cadence with his witness, which made the story easy to follow, and to believe.

"I went around the far side of the building away from the lot where it's real dark. I heard Jose call me from out back and warn me that he'd seen Dewey and Larkin inside."

"Did you call back to him?"

"No."

"Why not?"

"I didn't want anyone to know where I was. Especially Dewey."

"Then what happened?"

"I hid beside the wall for another minute or two until I saw Jet's Caddy drive up. He owns an old Cadillac."

"What did you do?"

"Jet got out of the car and I ran across the lot to him. I didn't even see the father and the little boy."

"Just tell us what you did see." Greene saw Armitage look over to the jury. One of the jurors, a young woman, nodded at him. He smiled back at her, his best Ralph Armitage grin.

In the witness box, Howett had stopped speaking. Greene saw her start to shake, just as she'd done when he'd encountered her at the gas station. She reached down with her right hand and massaged her left baby finger. He could almost smell her fear.

It took Armitage a moment to hear the strained silence. He turned to her. "Suzanne, what did you see?"

Howett was nodding her head fast, gulping down air. "I didn't tell anyone this before," she said, speaking all in one breath. A sudden spurt of energy. "He, he, Jet I mean, he had a gun."

50

Ralph Armitage had a sick feeling. He knew what Suzanne Howett was going to say a moment before she blurted out her lie—that Jet had a gun. He might not have been the best legal eagle when it came to black-letter law, but as did most experienced prosecutors who faced this all the time, he knew everything about cross-examining his own witness when they recanted. Changed their earlier evidence and became a so-called hostile witness.

Nancy Parish had taken a big risk by waiving the prelim in this case, but now he could see another reason why she did it. Armitage had no way of knowing what Howett would say the first time she testified under oath. And a surprise such as this in front of the jury could be a disaster for his case.

Everyone in the court looked taken aback by what she'd said. He had to stanch the bleeding right away. He strode over to his counsel table, took three copies of the transcript of the initial statement Howett had given to Greene at the homicide bureau from a folder on his desk, and with a popping sound opened a yellow highlighter that was beside it.

Although he was acting shocked and outraged for the benefit of the jury, Armitage had half expected this to happen, so he had everything ready. If he played this right, it might actually help his case. Make it clear to the jury that Howett had been intimidated into changing her story. Probably by Larkin or Dewey or both. Didn't really matter. Juries hated this kind of thing and always took it out on the accused.

He highlighted a passage in each copy. The marker made an uncomfortable squeaking noise, the only sound in the packed, tense courtroom.

When he was done, he walked deliberately over to the defense table. Parish already had her copy of the transcript out and had turned to the same page as the one he'd highlighted. He showed her what he'd done and she nodded. She did not look happy. They both knew what was coming.

Then he turned back to Howett on the witness stand. Changing the pace to take her off guard, he barreled up to her and thrust a copy in front of her. He wanted the jury to think he was furious.

He rotated toward Rothbart. "Your Honor, I'm making an application before this court to have Ms. Suzanne Howett declared a hostile witness." He handed the second copy of the statement to the court clerk, who passed it up to the judge.

"On what grounds?" Rothbart asked.

"Contradiction of a previous signed, sworn, and videotaped statement given freely to a person in authority," he said. "I direct Your Honor to the highlighted portions on page four."

Rothbart drummed his fingers on his hand as he read the statement. Then he looked at the defense table. "Ms. Parish?"

Parish looked up from her copy of the statement and didn't even bother to rise. "I can see no grounds to object," she said.

She was a smart enough lawyer not to fight a losing legal battle, he thought.

"Proceed," Rothbart told him.

"Ms. Howett." He turned his gaze on her. No more calling her "Suzanne." No more Mr. Nice Guy. "Do you recognize this?"

She barely glanced at the papers. "I do."

"Take all six pages. Give them a good look." He was in very close, using his considerable height to dominate the space between them. "Tell the jury what this is."

She reached for the pages, her elbows tight to her sides, like a timid child about to get her hands slapped. "It's the statement I gave to Detective Greene," she said.

"That Detective Greene?" He pointed back to Greene, who was sitting placidly at the Crown's table.

"Yes, sir."

"At the Toronto police headquarters?"

"Yes, sir."

"On November seventeenth."

"Yeah, a few days after it happened."

"Under oath?"

"Yes."

"Videotaped?"

"Uh-huh."

"Is that a yes?"

"Yes. Yes, sir."

He ripped the document out of her hand and flipped to the last page. "And this signature," he said, jabbing at the paper, "is it yours?"

"It is," she said without looking at it.

"No, look," he demanded. "Is this your signature?"

Shaking now, she bent down. "Yes." She sounded absolutely defeated.

This was what he needed to do. Destroy this lie she'd just told. He wanted the jury to be as mad as he was. Or as mad as he was pretending to be.

He flipped to the fourth page. "Here." He pointed to the section he'd just highlighted. "I want you to read the parts in yellow. Including the name of the person asking or answering the question."

He jammed the papers into her hand and strode back, placing himself square in the middle of the jury box. Let her be alone with her lie. He flipped to page four of his copy, making it clear he was going to follow her every word.

She hesitated.

Armitage didn't. He had to keep the pressure on. "Your Honor, please tell this witness that she must read this passage out loud." He'd taken her from "Suzanne" to "Ms. Howett" to "this witness."

Rothbart put on a very stern face. "Ms. Howett," he said in his deep bass voice. Good to have an actor on the bench when you needed one, Armitage thought.

"Okay," she said. "Can I get a glass of water first?"

"Certainly." Rothbart poured one himself and handed it over to her.

She took a long sip, then started to read.

"'Detective Greene: "What happened next?"'

"'Suzanne Howett: "Someone said, 'Here, take this,' then I heard the shots. We jumped in the car and took off."'

"'Detective Greene: "How many shots?"'

"'Suzanne Howett: "I don't know. A lot."'

"'Detective Greene: "Did Jet have a gun?"'

"'Suzanne Howett: "No. He didn't have a gun."'"

Howett stopped reading. Her hands were shaking. She took another sip of water. She put the paper down and covered her face with her hands.

"Your Honor," Armitage said.

Rothbart leaned over to her. "Ms. Howett, please continue," he said gently.

She wiped her hands across her face and started to read again.

" 'Detective Greene: "You sure? You're under oath now and I'm going to get this statement typed out and have you sign it." ' "

"'Suzanne Howett: "I'm sure. Jet didn't have a gun." ' "

"'Detective Greene: "Where did the shots come from?" ' "

"'Behind me somewhere. Near the Timmy's.'"

She stopped and looked at Armitage.

"Ms. Howett," he said. "Were you asked those questions and did you give those answers?" he asked.

She tossed the paper down. "Yes. But I lied. I was afraid. Jet told me what to say."

This was a pivotal moment in this trial. If the jury believed her new evidence, that Jet had a gun, the case was in serious trouble.

Armitage looked back at Rothbart. "Permission to cross-examine this witness, sir?"

"Ms. Parish, any objections?" Rothbart asked.

"No objections," she said.

"Granted," Rothbart said.

Time for a change of pace, Armitage thought. He stroked his chin, smiled at her. "So, let me get this straight. Jet had a gun that night."

"Yes." She looked relieved by his less aggressive tone.

"What kind of gun was it?" he asked her, breaking rule number one in cross-examination: never ask a question when you don't know the answer. A rule he couldn't risk following right now.

"Umm. I'm not sure. I . . . I don't know much about guns."

"Was it real big"—he held his hands far apart at an exaggerated distance—"or teeny and small?" He moved his hands back so they were almost together.

"I didn't really see it."

"You didn't really see it? Or you didn't see it at all?"

"Just kind of saw it, you know. Like, I mean it was dark."

She was a bad liar. And he wanted to leave no doubt about that with the jury.

Back at the counsel table he retrieved a thick black binder. "When you were picked up and questioned by Detective Greene, he told you the police had recorded all your phone calls, monitored your e-mails and text messages."

"Yeah, they did." Her eyes were riveted on the binder. She would have read it all before testifying today.

"But you had no idea at the time, did you, that the police were listening in?"

"No, like I said, I don't really know about courts and stuff."

Perfect answer. He took the binder and strolled back up to her. "Every one of your conversations with your boyfriend Jet, texts and e-mails to him as well, and to your best friend, Cindy, who even came over to spend the night with you. They are all in here. And you've seen all this. Right?"

"Right."

"And in the three days between the shooting and Detective Greene picking you up and questioning you, in all your calls and messages, you never once mention anything to Jet or Cynthia about a gun. Correct?"

She stared at the black binder. Then at Armitage. She looked pathetic. "I guess I never talked about it. Wasn't important."

He lowered his voice to a stage whisper. "Do you expect this jury to believe that you, a twenty-two-year-old woman with no criminal record, never been arrested before, hear that a four-year-old boy was murdered inches from you, your boyfriend had a gun, and you didn't think it was important? Never talked about it?"

"I . . . I don't know."

He padded back to the counsel table. Put the binder down in front of him. Let the time and the tension accumulate. "Ms. Howett." His voice now was soft as silk. Sometimes soft was better than hard. "You haven't told us yet. Did Jet fire this gun you say he had? The one you never saw?"

Her eyes looked terrified. Clearly this was the one question she didn't want to be asked. She looked incapable of answering it.

He picked back up her sworn statement with one hand. The other he placed on Greene's shoulder. "You told Detective Greene the shots came from behind you. Didn't you?"

She nodded.

"That's a yes?"

"Yes, I said that."

"Because it was true, wasn't it?"

She was still nodding.

"Suzanne," he said, coming all the way back to using her first name. He was speaking gently, like a comforting adult talking to a disturbed child. "The shots came from behind you, didn't they?"

"Yes. Yes they did."

"And Jet never fired a gun, did he?"

She took a deep breath. "No. I mean I didn't see him shoot."

He put the statement down and touched the binder in front of him. "And you and Jet didn't say a word about him having a gun, because he didn't have one, did he?"

She started to cry. "I didn't know that little boy was shot," she blurted out. "And if I hadn't been there . . ."

He took a look over at the jurors. One of them caught his eye, then looked back at the witness stand. He had to watch out. If they felt he was yet another man pushing this weak young woman around, they'd start to feel sorry for her. Stuck as she clearly was between these two low-life men, Dewey and Jet.

On the witness stand, Howett started to shudder. Her breathing was halting. She was hyperventilating

Rothbart looked at Armitage. "Maybe we should give this witness five minutes," he said.

"That's okay, Your Honor," he said.

He wanted to leave it at this point. If she composed herself he had no way of knowing what she'd say. She might stick to her story that there was a gun. But this way, everyone knew she was at best completely unreliable, and at worst simply a liar.

"I'll just enter the binder as an exhibit. It says it all. No further questions."

This is a great way to end a lousy week in court, he thought as he walked up to the court clerk and delivered the binder, then returned to his counsel table. Cedric Wilkinson was sitting behind it and looked straight at him. For the first time since they'd met, Armitage saw something that he hadn't seen before from the grieving father.

Respect.

51

Her mother would not have approved of the language, but right now Nancy Parish felt like shit. No nicer way to describe it. Fourteen straight hours of working on the case. Her head was pounding. And she looked like hell too. Great way to spend Saturday night. Why oh why had she agreed to meet Ted DiPaulo for dinner tonight? And even worse, at Jump, one of the swish downtown restaurants he loved to frequent.

She'd spent the bulk of the day preparing her cross-examinations for next week, and most of all, her address to the jury. In a case where her client didn't testify—and Larkin St. Clair had not budged on that—it was the most important thing.

There was one advantage to St. Clair's not taking the stand: if the defense didn't call any evidence, she got to address the jury last. She had to make the most of the opportunity.

The jury address was the only thing Parish never typed out. Somehow the old-fashioned way of writing it by hand made her focus better. Problem was, every time she started to work on it, she found some way to get distracted. This was avoidance and she knew it. And having a pen and paper in hand made it too easy for her to start drawing cartoons instead.

She sighed, flipped over the pad to a fresh sheet, and sketched a picture of a courtroom. The judge was up on his dais. Twelve jurors were in the box. And the defense lawyer was standing in front of them. In one hand, she had a gun pointed at her head. With the other, she pulled a noose wrapped around her neck skyward. Parish smirked. She added a third arm, with a samurai sword pointed at her heart. A fourth with a lit bomb held to her chest. Fifth was an ice pick aimed at her ear. Sixth a razor blade about to slice one of the lawyer's many wrists.

What caption to give this? She put the paper down, stood up, and stretched. This reminded her of those back-page contests in the *New Yorker,* where they put in smart cartoons and people wrote in funny captions. She hated reading the witty lines she wished she'd thought of.

It was seven fifteen. DiPaulo's reservation was for eight. The last thing in the world she wanted to do was to go out in public, but it would be good to see Ted. Get his wise counsel. He'd just come back from his latest excursion with his Air France girlfriend. They'd been to Rio or Buenos Aires, she couldn't remember which one, only that it was someplace warm.

In the washroom she looked at herself in the mirror. The fucking fluorescent lights. Her skin, which had been among her best features, looked tired and splotchy. Her hair was a semi-disaster. In her haste to leave the house this morning, she'd forgotten her makeup. If she were like those smart and stylish career women who worked at one of those big law firms—the ones who'd be filling up the restaurant tonight— she'd have had an emergency makeup kit in the bottom drawer of her desk. Or at least some lipstick.

Thanks to Zelda, she had something decent to wear. One afternoon last year, she'd pried Parish out of the office and dragged her to some boutique down in the PATH—the underground walkway that snaked for miles under the downtown core. Zelda made her try on a "little black dress," and, to her surprise, Parish liked it. Cap-sleeved. Light wool. Then they'd gotten her a pair of leather pumps. Zelda had tried to get her into one with stiletto-like heels, but she'd opted for something more sensible. This way, she could look half-decent and run for the streetcar if she needed to.

Ten minutes of scrubbing her face with institutional soap and drying it off with harsh brown paper towels put some color back into her skin. She'd found a crappy old brush with a bunch of bristles missing, and after ten more minutes of hacking away at her hair, which she still wore down to her shoulders, it didn't look horrible. Thank goodness for the dress. All those years of playing hockey. She still had a good figure, and a woman could get away with a lot if her body was in shape and she had a dress that showed it off.

But wait. Parish couldn't believe it. She looked more closely at the mirror. "Fuck," she screamed, her voice echoing around the tiled bathroom. "Fuck, fuck, fuck." There it was. A gray hair. First one in her life. Off to the right, above her ear. Oh, no. She pictured a whole row in the pharmacy packed with women's hair-coloring products, which she'd managed to avoid. Until now.

Her hair was so thick it was hard to isolate the renegade strand. Zelda, who changed her hair color even faster than her lovers, had told her that this day would come. And warned her in advance that if she plucked a gray hair out, it would come back thicker and more wiry.

To hell with that. "I hate you," she screeched. She gave it a good hard yank. It took two pulls to get the thing out. What a way to spend a Saturday night, she thought.

"You look ravishing," DiPaulo said twenty minutes later when he greeted her on the marble steps outside Jump. He rarely met anyone without giving them a compliment. The restaurant was on the underground path, so she hadn't had to go outside in the storm.

"Yeah right," she said. "Nothing like working on a jury address all day before going out on the town."

The place was packed. Every other woman had on shoes with killer heels. Impossibly high, narrowing to a teeny-tiny point, yet somehow these female creatures managed to float about the hardwood floor, as graceful as ballet dancers. Their dresses were as minuscule as their heels and hardly covered anything. Perfect hair, flawless makeup, nails that looked as if they'd never touched a keyboard—or a dirty dish—in their lives. Somehow they were able to snack away on pristine little hors d'oeuvres without touching their carefully applied lipstick. Crunching them with their perfect white teeth.

The place was so bright. What the hell was she doing here?

DiPaulo loved the spotlight. The action. He had a regular table right in the middle of the floor.

The two lawyers couldn't have been more different, and that's what made their partnership work. He was the rainmaker, always out and about, meeting and greeting, stirring up business. So many very rich lawyers had messed-up kids. And it was amazing how much they'd pay DiPaulo & Parish to get their young charges out of trouble. Made it possible to do killer Legal Aid cases such as this Larkin St. Clair file.

"Don't fall over in shock," DiPaulo said. "But I had Emanuel save us that round table around back where we can talk in private."

"There is a God," she said, punching him in the arm.

"I'll take that as a compliment," he said.

Emanuel, the maître d', who treated DiPaulo as if they had been best friends since childhood, appeared out of the crowd with impeccable timing and led them to their private spot in back. He drifted along the polished wood floor as effortlessly as a king's courtier.

"How was the trip?" Parish asked after Emanuel seated them in the wonderfully high leather seats. She was hoping Ted would fill her in on the forgotten destination.

"Buenos is phenomenal. Eleven-hour direct flight, only one time zone east. No jet lag."

"Sounds warm."

He frowned. "I know I haven't been around. I'm going to stop traveling so much. It's been hard on Olivia too."

DiPaulo was referring to his second child, a very bright kid in her last year of high school. His son was away at university.

"You deserve some time off after all these years of hard work."

"Enough's enough," he said. "I've been a shitty partner for six months."

It was true. He'd hardly been around at all, leaving her strapped with her practice, his files to cover, and now this murder trial. But she'd made a point of not complaining. Since he'd teamed up with her a few years ago, after he left the Crown's office, he'd been extremely generous with his time, mentoring her.

"I've done fine on my own, but right now I need to talk through some things."

"I knew you would. And I knew you'd never leave the office if I didn't drag you out."

He insisted on ordering a very expensive meal—seared sea scallops for her, cedar-planked maple-glazed salmon for him, with a box of their delicious "Jump Fries" to start—as Parish talked him through the case.

"The worst thing," she said, crunching on one too many of the delicious fries after she'd got him up to speed on everything, "is that Larkin's not going to let me call him to testify."

"Hard to win a case where a little boy is killed if your guy doesn't testify. Juries like to hear an accused tell them he didn't do it."

"I know."

"What can I do?"

"Nothing," he said.

"Nothing?" she asked.

"In the end it's your client's case, not yours. Besides, if he testifies what's he going to say? That Dewey was the shooter? Then you've got a crossed-swords defense and the jury will convict him for sure. After that the Crown would probably say Dewey lied, the deal's off, and get him convicted too. How long do think your client would last in jail after that?"

She nodded. "Larkin told me the very first day that Dewey was connected inside."

"That's no surprise."

"So I'm stuck."

He pointed to the main courses that had just come. "Eat your scallops," he said. "I know they're your favorite."

She ate. Ted wasn't often very quiet, but he ate his salmon in silence.

"How did the boy's father do when he testified?" he asked when the dishes were cleared.

"Could have been worse. In ways he actually helped us. Still the jury was touched. Everyone was. He was the first witness. I keep hoping maybe they will forget about him. Stupid."

"They won't. No matter what you do, they're going to be thinking about that little boy and his dad."

"I know," she said again.

"Tell me about this missing witness, the baker," DiPaulo said when they started on dessert. White chocolate cheesecake for him, banana cream pie for her, and, at Ted's insistence, an assortment of orange, blackberry, and mango ices. This whole meal was a thousand miles away from the food-court sushi and pasta dishes she'd been living on for weeks.

"He's here in Canada illegally. Crown wants to find him as badly as I do. They have his name but aren't going to release it to the press. Figure it will drive him farther underground."

"How about your jury address?"

"Work in progress." She took her dessert fork and twirled it on the white tablecloth, making a small indentation in the linen.

"How's the rest of your life?" he asked after the waitress cleared away the dessert dishes.

"Horrible, pathetic, nonexistent. Take your pick." Her fling with Brett the waiter from the Pravda Vodka Bar had lasted about a month. Until he heard about the trial she was doing. In a nanosecond he lost all interest in going out with someone defending the child killer in the Timmy's shooting.

"Then let's get a drink at the bar. It's packed with smart, attractive, eligible young bankers and bond traders and lawyers at big firms who know how to make real money."

She shook her head. "After the trial. Right now this is my life."

He smiled. DiPaulo had one of those smiles that radiated happiness. She needed a few rays of his sunshine right now.

"There is no after this trial, Nancy," he said. "Don't you see that?"

"What do you mean?"

"What I mean is that you have the curse of true talent. It's easy to be a good lawyer. It's not that hard to be a very good lawyer. But there are no shortcuts to being great at this."

"Thanks, but—"

"You know, when I came out of the Crown's office, I could have gotten a job anywhere. Everyone was surprised when I picked you to be my partner. A young lawyer still establishing her practice. You have talent and drive. Not many people have both. And you see things other people don't. It's a blessing and a curse."

She stopped twirling the fork. The indentation was deeper than she thought it would be. She started to knead the tablecloth, hoping to restore the smooth surface. She didn't know what to say.

"Thanks for letting me drag you out for dinner," he said. "You're going back to the office, aren't you?"

"I've got to put in a few more hours."

"I know," he said. "You have to."

52

Despite all her confidence, independence, and considerable charm, planning this May Two-Four party had really taxed Ralph Armitage's wife, Penny. He hadn't helped by being so distracted with the new job and the St. Clair murder trial. And today, for the first time ever, he saw her lose it. Of all the times and all the places. She'd just dragged him into the downstairs washroom at his parents' estate, twenty minutes before she was set to do her big presentation to the family about the party plans she'd been working on the whole darn year. He was shocked by what he saw.

"I can't do it," she said. Her eyes bulged with tears. "They are going to hate this whole concept."

She'd spent weeks putting everything on a large piece of white Bristol board—this was another Armitage tradition. At the party all the adult guests signed the boards, which were then framed and put on the wall in the downstairs rec room. Penny's board was now ripped in half and tossed on the ground.

"No, they won't," he said, reaching out to her.

She batted his hand away. "Don't fucking patronize me."

"I've told you for months. I think bringing families from the shelter is an amazing idea."

"Amazingly dumb. I didn't know they'd need all these consent forms. Criminal record checks on all the employees. Fuck." She grabbed one of the two pieces of the presentation and went to rip it in half again.

He reached for it and stilled her hand. She didn't resist, instead crumpled into the corner of the floor. "The band canceled," she said.

"What? When?"

"Two days ago. I didn't want to bother you with this during the trial. They got a gig on some tour with a grunge group and left me high and dry. I called your sister Emma in a panic, and she said, 'But didn't you hire a backup?' How was I supposed to know about that?"

After Penny had dragged him to five different auditions, she'd decided to try a hip young group named the Bloor Baby Brats instead of one of the older bands that had been doing weddings, bar mitzvahs, and special events for decades. He'd worried something like this might happen. But he hadn't wanted to dampen her enthusiasm.

Penny's nose was running all over her sleeve. He grabbed a box of Kleenex and passed her some tissues. She blew hard with a big snort. "And the food, I didn't tell you about that either?"

"What's the problem?" After picking the band, there'd been another round of visits to caterers in every part of the city. Penny found all the traditional ones boring and had opted for a couple who ran a company called Local Locos. They served only organic produce grown within a fifty-mile radius of Toronto.

"Last week I had lunch with your sister Randy, and she just happened to mention that I shouldn't forget that some of the guests would be kosher or halal. Fuck. The second I got home I called Local Loco and they said look at the contract, it specifically says they can't do kosher, halal, lactose intolerant, peanut allergies, wheat allergies, and about fifty other fucking things I've never even heard of. I grew up in the boring burbs and ate meat and potatoes for the first eighteen years of my life. How am I supposed to know about all this crap?"

Her shoulders heaved, and her nose started running again. He'd never seen anyone cry so hard.

"And to top it all off, Lindsay's pregnant again."

Her younger sister, Lindsay, already had three kids. For the last year, Armitage and Penny had been "trying to get pregnant," as the stupid phrase went, with no luck. Although lately, with all the tension between them, their "efforts" had been few and far between.

"We're going through a rough time right now, that's all." He reached out to touch her hand again.

She smacked it away, harder this time. "Who is she, Ralph?"

"Who?"

"The woman you keep seeing on Thursday nights."

He started to laugh.

"Don't laugh at me."

"I'm laughing because you couldn't be more wrong."

"Well, who is it?"

"There's no 'she.' 'He' is a witness. And he is very afraid. Won't talk to anyone but me." He longed to share this with her. The whole story. But how could he tell Penny he was burying the one true eyewitness to this horrific crime, to protect himself and the bad deal he'd made with Cutter? "That's all I can say, and even that's more than I should tell you."

She pulled herself up. What an agile body she has, he thought for maybe the thousandth time. He had an indecent urge to yank her clothes right now.

Before he could stop her, she ripped the two other pieces of the Bristol board in half again.

"What are you doing?"

"Give me that box of Kleenex," she said. "And find some tape real fast. I'm making this the theme. Torn lives. A stripped-down party, no music, no fancy food. Broken people and how to start repairing them."

He burst out of the bathroom and rushed down to his father's basement workshop. He was filled with more admiration for his wife then he'd ever had. How would he live without her, if she ever found out that he'd turned himself into a liar?

53

"Ari."

He heard a voice whispering. It seemed very close.

"Ari."

Something soft was on his neck. Moist. Lips.

"Ari."

He opened his eyes, but the room was dark. Greene could hear a whirling sound overhead, which for a moment was confusing because he didn't have a fan in his bedroom at home. The lips moved to his cheek, then his forehead. He slipped his hand under Jennifer Raglan's arm and around her bare back. She eased her body on top of his, and he felt the roundness of her breasts curl across his chest.

"It's eight o'clock. I have to leave in forty-five minutes," she said before she directed a playful bite at his ear. "I'm leading the Sunday brunch seminar."

"Ah yes, I saw the topic: 'Dealing with Difficult Police Officers.'"

They were in a room at the Northlands Inn, where every Crown Attorney in the province—except those involved in major trials—met annually for their weekend conference.

She laughed, that deep guttural laugh of hers that he couldn't get enough of. It rang in his head at the most unexpected times.

"Wonder where I got the idea for the topic?" Raglan slipped her hips on top of him.

"You must have done a great deal of research," he said.

"Extensive." Her legs slid along the outsides of his, making a slithering sound on the thin sheet that covered them. "I told my colleagues at the bar last night I had to get to bed early to rest up for my presentation."

He laughed too. "You did get to bed early." He'd driven up in the evening, parked down the road, and, as prearranged, slipped up the back staircase into her room at ten o'clock.

"Mmmm." She curled up her toes and scratched his skin. "But I didn't get much sleep."

"Well then, why'd you wake up so early?"

"For this." She trailed her hands along both his arms and squeezed the insides of his elbows, hoisting herself up before she lowered herself down. Down. The whirl of the fan was the one constant sound in the room. The air on their skin.

By eight thirty she was getting dressed, and he was sitting up in bed watching her. Not staring, just watching.

"How's the trial going?" she asked.

"Hard to say," he said.

"Ralph stopped calling me all the time. How's he doing?"

"Good days and bad days."

She was wearing more casual clothes than she wore at work. She zipped up her jeans and pulled on a sweater. "You're pissed at him for making that stupid deal with Cutter. Aren't you?"

"A four-year-old boy was murdered," he said.

She sat at the end of the bed. "Do you have any idea how many nights I almost just drove over to your house, knowing you were dealing with this?"

"It's not just another trial."

She reached out and touched his face.

"I'll let myself out after nine," he said. "When everyone's gone downstairs."

"I know doing this was an absolutely crazy thing," she said, "but I so needed to see you."

It wasn't just crazy. They'd slipped through a new, silent barrier in their relationship. This was the first time they'd been together since she'd gone back home to her husband.

"I started cleaning out Mom's house last weekend," she said. "It was overwhelming."

"Did she have much stuff?" he asked.

"She was an unbelievable pack rat. You can't even imagine all the old magazines and newspapers stacked in the basement. You ever heard of a singer named Bobby Vee?"

"'The Night Has a Thousand Eyes.'"

"What do you mean?" she asked.

"That was the name of his hit record."

Raglan laughed. "Well, she has it. And tons more. *TV Guides* going back to 1965."

"What are you going to do with it all?"

"Kids want me to try to sell it on eBay. But I don't know." Her other hand was in a ball. She opened it up and showed Greene what was inside. "I think this was her only piece of jewelry." She started to cry, and he put his arms around her.

"My dad died such a long time ago, I've almost forgotten about him," she said. "What's up with your father?"

"He's hiding something from me."

"What do you mean?"

"Something from the war. He's always protected me in a way. Never wanted to me to know exactly what happened."

"I can't imagine what he had to live through to survive," she said. "What are you going to do?"

He shrugged. "I've learned. With my father, I have to wait him out. He'll tell me when he's ready."

She sat up.

"I don't know." She shook her head. Closed her eyes. "I just don't know."

"Death changes us," he said, "in ways we can't predict."

He took the brooch from her hand, held her at arm's length, and pinned it on, making sure it was straight before she got up to leave the room.

54

The lawyers' robing room was crowded, as it always was on Monday mornings. After the worst weekend of his life, Ralph Armitage was glad to be here, getting dressed for court.

He loved everything about wearing court robes, or silks, as they were called in Britain. The fine feel of the velvet carrying bag with his initials embossed in big letters on the front, slinging it over his shoulder walking to court. The twined ropes that held it together and opened so smoothly. The dark luxury of the robes themselves, worn over a freshly laundered white shirt, gold cuff links in his French cuffs, and starched white tabs.

Secretly, the robes reminded him of his favorite Batman suit, which he'd loved to wear as a child. They made him feel secure. Confident. In place. He needed that right now, because it seemed as if the rest of his life was falling apart.

Everything was riding on today. Phil Cutter had brought Dewey Booth back to Toronto last night and he'd be the first Crown witness. Armitage had spent hours this weekend preparing and he knew there was a very strong possibility that, like Suzanne Howett, Booth would try to change his story. If he did that, Armitage was ready.

The usual gaggle of journalists was waiting for him as he walked up to the courtroom. Zachery Stone, a short and particularly persistent reporter with the *Toronto Sun,* managed to sneak in right under his arm.

"We heard Dewey Booth is on the stand this morning," he said.

"You'll find out at ten o'clock," Armitage said.

"Come on, Ralphie, give me a quote."

He stopped dead in his tracks and looked Stone up and down. "You been going to the gym, Zach?"

Stone sucked in his belly. "Lost twenty pounds already. I'm becoming an online TV star. They got me doing these webcasts, forty-five-second hits every day. I gotta look good on camera."

"Your wife must be happy."

"She calls it a second honeymoon. Where's my quote?"

"Sorry, it has to be off the record."

"Come on," Stone said.

"Here's the quote, but it's embargoed. You can't publish it until I say so," Armitage said.

"Okay, okay." Stone had his pen and pad ready.

"'Whatever happens inside this courtroom today, I'm confident I made the right move.'"

"You mean making the deal with Cutter and his client Booth?"

"Exactly."

"Great," Stone said. "That's no big deal. Come on, let me use it."

"No, no, no. Let's see what happens in there."

Inside the courtroom, Booth was sitting in the back, next to his lawyer and Cutter's partner, Barb Gild. An older, well-groomed bald man wearing an earring sat next to Booth. Must be his father, Armitage thought.

Seeing Cutter again made Armitage feel ill. The guy would do anything to win. And getting his client out of this mess was just the kind of ego boost the bastard lived for.

Gild had sworn Booth's affidavit. Armitage had subpoenaed her to court, just in case Booth denied he'd signed the legal document. If that happened, he'd toss Gild up on the stand and bury Booth. Then he'd charge him with perjury and murder. Get him and St. Clair convicted. Wouldn't that be nice.

In short order, court started, and soon he was on his feet. "Good morning, ladies and gentlemen of the jury, and Your Honor. Today, the Crown calls as its first witness Mr. Dewey Booth."

Booth stood up. The jurors turned their heads in unison and watched him saunter through the rows of spectators, cut between the two counsel tables, and hop energetically up onto the witness stand. He was a little punk, Armitage thought. Cutter must have dressed him up, because he wore a white shirt with a blue tie and straight blue pants. The clothes all looked as if they'd been bought yesterday.

"Hello, Mr. Booth." With all his other witnesses, Armitage had immediately come out from behind his counsel table to talk to them. But now he stayed put. He wanted to send a message to the jury that he wasn't close to Booth in any way. He didn't bother to say, "Good morning," but kept it to a straight hello.

"Yeah," Booth said. "Hi."

Phil Cutter might have dressed his client up for court, but he couldn't repackage the punk's arrogant smirk and the "fuck you" attitude that radiated from every pore.

Armitage asked Booth about his background, walked him through his criminal record, inquired about his friendship with Larkin St. Clair and his relationship with Suzanne Howett.

"Suzie was my chick, then I got a three-year bit in Kingston," Booth said. "She came out for visits for about a year and a half, then she dumped me."

"How did that make you feel?" Armitage asked. He had to be careful. Thanks to Parish there had been no prelim, so he didn't know what Booth was going to say.

"Like shit." Booth looked over at the jury. "Sorry, I mean real bad."

"Angry?"

"Yeah. Especially when I heard she was going out with Jet."

"Jet. That would be Mr. Trapper."

"Mr. Trapper." Booth measured the words out one at a time in a way that sent a shiver down Armitage's spine. He could only imagine what the jury thought.

"Take us to November fourteenth. Where were you that day?"

"About noon I hooked up with Larkin." He pointed at the defense table. "We hung out at Kensington Market for a while and then drifted over to the Timmy's."

Armitage looked back at St. Clair, who was staring straight ahead at the judge.

"Larkin, that's Mr. St. Clair, the accused?"

"Larkin, yeah."

"And how do you know him?"

"We met in juvie and been best buds ever since."

Armitage looked over at the jury, but none of them looked back. They'd all zeroed in on Booth. "And Timmy's. That's the Tim Hortons? On Elm Street?" he asked.

"One and the same," Booth said in a slow drawl.

"Why did you go there?"

Booth looked remarkably comfortable. As if he were enjoying himself. Probably because, for once in his life, he was in court and only a witness, not the accused. "I'd found out Suzie was working there and that Jet picked her up every night."

"Suzie, that's Suzanne Howett, and Jet, that's Mr. Trapper?"

Booth gave Armitage a laconic look. "One and the same."

Armitage could feel the kid's cocky attitude starting to grate on his nerves. Time to get to work. "Mr. Booth, did you have a gun with you?"

"Me? No."

"How about Larkin St. Clair?"

Booth nodded vigorously. "Uh-huh. He was packing."

Armitage was relieved. It looked as if Booth was sticking to his story. He turned to the defense table and pointed to Larkin St. Clair.

St. Clair sat, stony still. Looking straight ahead.

"Just to be absolutely clear," Armitage said. He pointed at the defendant. "You are talking about that man, the accused, Mr. Larkin St. Clair. Correct?"

"That's right."

"On the afternoon of November fourteenth he was with you at the Tim Hortons on Elm Street, and he, Mr. St. Clair, had a gun with him. Correct?"

"One hundred percent."

"Did you see the gun?" Armitage asked.

"Yeah," Booth said. "I told him to bring it."

"You did?" This was new. Armitage had practically memorized Booth's affidavit, and this wasn't mentioned in it. "Why?" he asked instinctively. But the moment the question was out he realized he didn't know the answer. Not a good move with a witness like this.

"Jet. I didn't trust the guy."

Armitage didn't like that answer. Where was Booth going with this? Best to steer away. He'd gotten in the key point he needed: St. Clair was the one with the gun.

He poured a glass of water and drank it. Armitage wasn't thirsty, but he wanted to put some time between that last set of questions and the new ones he was about to ask. He picked up a different binder and opened it. This was another way to signal to the jury that he was heading in a new direction.

"Last week we heard from a witness, Mr. Vikram Mohammed. He said that before shots were fired, you were having a coffee inside the Timmy's with Mr. St. Clair. Do you recall that?"

"Sure. Two double-doubles, medium. Like we always get."

"Mr. Mohammed said you told Mr. St. Clair you wanted to go outside for a cigarette." This piece of evidence had troubled him. He was concerned that it would show Dewey as the one who planned this whole thing. He waited to see what Booth's answer would be.

"I might have."

"Did you say this to Larkin?" He looked down at his notes to emphasize to the jury that he was giving a direct quote. He didn't need to look. He'd memorized what Mohammed had said. But this way was more effective. "'I need a fucking cigarette.'"

"Sounds like me."

"Why did you need a cigarette at just that moment?"

"I saw Jet's Caddy drive up. I was planning to go talk to him. I wanted Larkin behind me, as backup."

This wasn't in the affidavit either. Not good. But he had to keep going. "What happened?"

"Jet pulls into the corner of the lot in his stupid Cadillac, and I see my girl, Suzie, running from the other side of the building toward him."

They were at the crucial point. He walked out from behind the counsel table for the first time and moved about halfway up to the witness box. This put the jury by his side. "What did you do?"

"Me? I see Jet get out of the car and start walking toward me. 'Long time no see,' I say. Even have my hand out to shake his. Instead, he yanks out a gun and, *pow*, fires right above my head." Saying this, Booth ducks down, like a sheriff in an old Western movie shoot-out. "I turn back and see Larkin. He's about to fire to protect me and he tumbles to the ground. It was slippery. Bullet flies off to the side. I hear the father screaming that his son's been hit. There's a few other shots, and I run out into the back alley and take off."

Armitage felt the blood beating against his temples. He was dying to barge up to the witness stand and throttle the arrogant little liar. Without saying a word, he marched back to the counsel table and grabbed Booth's affidavit. The asshole.

He rushed right up to the clerk below Judge Rothbart and handed him a copy of the affidavit. "The Crown seeks to have this witness declared hostile," he said.

"On what grounds?" Rothbart asked.

"Contradiction of a previous signed and sworn statement."

"Let me see that," Rothbart said to the clerk. He was drumming his fingers hard.

"The affidavit is all on one page," Armitage said.

Rothbart read it carefully. "Ms. Parish?" he asked at last.

Nancy Parish looked up from her copy of the affidavit that she'd been reading.

"Objection," she said. "He can only cross his own witness if there has been a clear contradiction. This witness's affidavit doesn't say anything about Jet and a gun."

"Exactly," Armitage said. "That's my point."

Rothbart read the document slowly. At last he looked up at Armitage. "It's also your problem. This witness never touches on the question of whether the man named Jet was armed or not armed. Looks as if he was never asked the question."

"That's right, nobody asked me," Booth piped in.

Rothbart gave him a withering stare. "No comments from you, sir."

But it didn't matter. The damage had been done. Armitage could see now that the affidavit was full of holes. All it said was that St. Clair brought a gun to the Tim Hortons and that he shot at Jet. Nothing about his slipping on the ice. And not a word about whether or not Jet had a gun or fired first, which gave Larkin the chance to say he only acted in self-defense. Rothbart had picked this up back at the pretrial. That's why he thought Parish was going to waive the prelim.

If there'd been a prelim, all this would have come out. And Armitage would have been prepared for it. But instead, here he was with his key witness, stunned into silence. Flat-footed in front of the jury.

Nancy Parish had risked fifteen years of Larkin St. Clair's life by waiving the preliminary inquiry for just this moment. Because of that move, Armitage hadn't been able to vet Dewey Booth's evidence before the young kid testified in front of the jury. It had worked. Armitage's deal with Phil Cutter was blowing up in his face.

He stared dumbly at the affidavit in his hand. Teetered on his feet. Armitage's considerable size, which he used to his advantage in court, suddenly made him look more vulnerable. Like a tall cedar tree, moments before it was felled.

The rules about cross-examining your own witness were very restrictive. The Crown could only attack the witness on explicit contradictions in his testimony, and Parish intended to hold Armitage to the letter of the law.

"Okay, Mr. Booth," Armitage said, recovering his breath. He pointed over to the defense table. "You and Larkin aren't just friends, you're best friends, aren't you?"

"Objection," Parish said, jumping to her feet. "He's cross-examining his own witness."

Rothbart looked down at Armitage. "Defense counsel's right."

Armitage paced. "Mr. Booth, how long have you known the defendant?"

"Since I was fourteen years old."

"Are you friends?"

"Best friends." Booth gave Armitage a cheeky grin.

"You'd do anything for him, wouldn't you?"

"Objection." Parish slammed back to her feet. "Cross-examining again."

"Sustained," Rothbart said without hesitation.

Armitage was bobbing his head up and down. His face was red with fury and frustration. He stopped, turned, and stared at the back of the court. Frozen.

Parish looked around and saw that Armitage was glaring down at Phil Cutter and Barb Gild.

"Mr. Armitage," Rothbart said from the judge's dais. "Do you have any further questions for this witness?"

Armitage snapped his head around. He stomped up to the witness box. For a moment Parish had a flashback. Seven years ago, in youth court, when she'd seen Armitage toss Larkin St. Clair up against the wall after an important case of his collapsed.

Booth must have remembered it too. He ducked down as the big Crown Attorney approached him. Was Armitage actually going to attack him? For the first time in her professional career, Parish was afraid during a trial.

At the last second, Armitage veered over to the court registrar's table. "Give me exhibit 4B."

The registrar, a tiny man with short fingers, fumbled with it for a moment, found the gun, and passed it to Armitage along with a pair of thin plastic gloves. He snapped them onto his big hands, grabbed the gun, and went right up to Booth. He held the weapon near his side.

"Do you recognize this gun?" Anger dripped from every word. Parish wanted to object again but she couldn't. His tone was all cross-examination, but his words were not.

"Yep. I think it's the one Larkin, my best friend, had." Booth's sarcasm was in lockstep with Armitage's anger. He flicked his hand toward the defense table. Parish kicked St. Clair under the table to make sure he didn't look at the witness stand.

"You ever hold this gun?" Armitage asked.

"Probably." Booth was as surly as ever.

"Here, take this," Armitage said. His voice softened. And despite what he'd said, he still held the gun close to his chest.

Booth looked confused. "The gun?"

"No, Mr. Booth, the words. 'Here, take this.' Did you hear your best friend Larkin St. Clair say those words?"

Parish felt a chill crease her whole body. This type of moment happened in every trial, when some small fact that everyone had overlooked now, in a different context, took on a whole new meaning. Oh no, she thought.

"Why would he say that?" Booth asked, sounding confused.

"I get to ask the questions," Armitage said. Still spooky calm. "On the night of November fourteenth, at just after five in the afternoon, in the Tim Hortons parking lot on Elm Street, did Larkin St. Clair say to Jet, also known as Mr. James Trapper, 'Here, take this'?" As he spoke, Armitage lifted the gun above Booth's head.

Parish could see by his eyes that Booth now understood the import of the words. "No," he said, defiant.

"You told us Larkin shot this gun."

"Okay."

"I'm asking you again, did St. Clair say, 'Here, take this,' to Jet before he pulled the trigger?"

Now Parish could object. Armitage had gone over the line into cross-examination. But she was afraid to. Didn't want to draw even more attention to this, the worst piece of evidence in the whole trial.

Booth jutted out his jaw. "No. It was Jet. He said it just before he shot at me."

Armitage turned his back on Booth and looked right at the jury. "You didn't mention that before."

"I forgot."

"You didn't forget." Armitage whirled around at Booth with lightning speed. He was shouting. His voice was louder than anything Parish had ever heard in a courtroom. "That's impossible. Adela Dobos, the witness who heard these words, was just outside the door. Steps from where you and Larkin St. Clair were standing. Jet was way over at the other side of the lot. No way she would have heard anything he said."

Parish was so taken aback that it took her a moment to stand up.

"It was your best friend, Larkin, wasn't it?" Armitage cast his free hand back at the defense table, pointing right at St. Clair. His voice at full volume. "'Here, take this.' That's what Larkin St. Clair said. Then he fired at Jet, didn't he?" He pointed the gun right at Booth's head.

"Your Honor," Parish said.

"But he slipped, just like the defense is saying," Armitage said. "That's why St. Clair fired all over the lot."

"This is cross-examination!" she yelled.

Rothbart was taken off guard too. "Yes, please, Mr. Armitage," he said at last.

"And he kept firing," Armitage spit out the words at Booth. "And killed Kyle Wilkinson."

"Mr. Armitage." Rothbart's baritone kicked into gear.

Armitage stomped back to the registrar's desk and slammed the gun down with a jolt. The sound bounced around the courtroom like a bullet pinging off steel. He pounded back to the edge of the witness stand and ripped the affidavit out of Booth's hands, half shredding it in the process.

"Those"—he huffed—"are"—he huffed again—"my"—an even bigger huff, like an angry black bear, Parish thought—"questions."

He spat out the last word, stalked back to his chair, and sat down.

The courtroom was stunned into silence. No one seemed to know what to do.

Parish was the only one standing.

Judge Rothbart, speechless for a moment, found his voice. "Ms. Parish? Any questions?"

The jurors swung their eyes to her. She had to make a split-second decision.

She felt like a character in an animated movie. A red devil was whispering into one ear, saying, Cross-examine him. He'll never admit he was the shooter, but he'll say anything to make it sound good for the defense. If you ask him, "Mr. Booth, you told Larkin to use the gun only in self-defense, didn't you?" he'll say, "Yes I did." Or if you say, "Jet was yelling and you thought he wanted to kill you, didn't you?" Booth will say, "He said, 'Here, take this,' and then he fired." And if you ask, "Larkin hid the gun afterward because you told him to, right?" he'll give you the answer that he thinks will help Larkin the most: "It was all my idea."

In her other ear the white angel was warning her to be careful. The jurors are going to think this whole thing was staged by the two best friends, Larkin and Dewey. Booth's pat answers will make this story too unbelievably perfect. Remember, Booth already said the key point when Armitage questioned him: that Jet had a gun and he fired first. That's the main course. The rest is dessert, dangerous dessert. You got a solid double here. Don't try to stretch it to a triple.

She glanced over at the witness box. Booth gave her a boastful, full-of-himself grin. Christ. If she asked Booth, "You and Larkin plan to join the Boy Scouts, become Big Brothers, and do charity work for old people after this trial?" he'd say yes to that too.

That was all she needed. Have Booth give a bunch of conveniently perfect answers. The jury wouldn't believe any of it. Instead, they'd be convinced he was the one pulling all the strings in this case and that he'd somehow intimidated Suzanne into changing her story so it fit. And since he wasn't on trial, they'd blame his best buddy. Larkin.

People called lawyers their mouthpieces, but sometimes the very best thing you could do as an advocate was keep your trap shut. And she wanted Booth off the stand. Now.

"Thank you, Your Honor," she said. "No questions."

Booth looked at her, disappointed.

Good, she thought. Now sit down nice and slowly, she told herself, confident that she'd made the right decision.

56

During the trial, lawyers were given small offices in the courthouse where they could keep their files, meet with witnesses, retreat from the melee in the hallways, and, when the time came, wait for the jury to return. Unlike Ralph Armitage's big, cozy digs in the Crown's office, the room Ari Greene shared with him now was small and cramped. And as the trial progressed and Armitage faltered in court, Greene began to feel as if the two of them were stuck together in a leaky lifeboat.

"I got you a grande caramel latte," he said, unpacking a Starbucks paper bag. He'd also got himself the same size cup of tea with two bags in it, "Awake" and "Calm." Seemed appropriate. It was Wednesday. Half an hour ago, court had finished for the day and they had work to do.

"Thanks," Armitage said, his voice flat and lifeless. He was looking out the only window in the room, which faced onto the wall of the adjoining building. Since Monday, the low point of the trial when he lost his cool with Dewey Booth on the witness stand, he'd been staring out the window whenever they were in the room.

To regain their footing in court, once Booth was off the stand, Greene had suggested they call the police witnesses, and for the last two days Armitage had paraded them before the jury.

He started with Daniel Kennicott, the first officer on the scene. He'd been an impressive witness. Nancy Parish cross-examined him on how slippery the sidewalks were that night and he described falling on the ice as he rushed to the scene.

Next came the officers who did the GSR tests on Larkin St. Clair. They described finding gunshot residue on his hands, the outside of his pants, and the inside front as well. Parish established that the GSR on his hands could have come from being near the shooter when the gun was fired or holding it afterward. Making the point that the results didn't prove St. Clair fired the gun.

Forensic Officer Harry Ho pointed out all the bullet holes at the scene, and Parish had him come to her diagram and mark on a separate one of her acrylic sheets the spot where the flatted shell casing had been found. Right where Jet's Cadillac had been. Then she got him to draw a straight line from that point to the bullet holes in the walkway beside the Tim Hortons and the wall behind it. Lined up perfectly.

A junior officer then played the video from the parking lot, and Armitage had him stop it at the point where St. Clair was stuffing something down the front of his pants. When combined with the GSR results, it was clear that he was stuffing a gun down there. Parish didn't ask any questions.

The two cops Greene had sent to get the gun from St. Clair's aunt's backyard testified that it was exactly where Dewey Booth said it would be. Parish remained silent again.

The scientist who'd compared the markings on the outside of the bullet in young Kyle Wilkinson's head with the inside of the gun did a demonstration for the jury. Perfect match.

"No questions of this witness," Parish said. She was smart enough to not contest the obvious: that her client had taken off with the gun that fired the fatal shot and hidden it. But throughout all of this evidence her body language had been relaxed, even bored. The message she was broadcasting to the jury, loud and clear, was that after Dewey Booth's testimony the case was over.

At the end of court today, Judge Rothbart had sent the jury out.

"Counsel," he said, "I'm concerned about timing. Mr. Armitage, do you have any more witnesses to call?"

"Detective Greene and I need to discuss that," he said, getting to his feet. "But if we do, it will only be one witness."

"Excellent," Rothbart said. "Ms. Parish, you have no obligation to tell us, but do you think you'll be calling a defense?"

This of course was the elephant in the room at every criminal trial. Was the defendant going to testify, or call other evidence?

Parish took her time standing up and gave Rothbart a sly grin. "Let's see what happens tomorrow," she said. "But if I had to guess, I'd put my money on us starting our jury addresses on Friday."

Rothbart beamed down at her. Looking as happy as an actor taking a curtain call. "That's very, very helpful," he said. "I'll see you all at ten o'clock tomorrow morning."

Greene sat with his still-hot tea in the only other chair in the little room he shared with Armitage and took a sip.

Armitage turned from the window. He hadn't touched his latte. He reached for a file folder with the label JAMES ERIC TRAPPER on the front. "What do you think? Should we call him?"

Greene knew this case desperately needed a reliable eyewitness who'd seen it all. And since they couldn't find Ozera, the baker from Tim Hortons, all they had was James Eric Trapper, aka Jet. "I subpoenaed him yesterday from jail. He'll be here in the morning."

"Without the damn prelim, I have no idea what he'll say," Armitage said.

"Probably just 'fuck you.'"

"But he'll be under oath. If I ask him if he had a gun, he's got to answer the question."

"What if he says, 'Yes, I had a gun'?" Greene asked. "'I fired the first shot.'"

Armitage sighed. "Look," he said, "if we don't call him, Parish will stand up in front of the jury and say, 'They had Jet as a witness, why didn't he testify? What are they afraid of? What are they hiding?'"

He was right.

Greene stood up with his cup in hand. "I'll go double-check with the prison transport. Make sure they get him here good and early."

Armitage nodded at Greene. "I know you think I messed up, making the deal with Cutter," he said.

Greene shrugged. "What's done is done. We have to move forward."

"I appreciate how hard you've worked on this."

"Thanks," Greene said as he opened the door. "It's a tough case."

Armitage turned back to the window and stared at the brick wall, cradling his warm drink in his hands. Still making no move to drink it.

57

Ted DiPaulo often told Nancy Parish about how, in the "bad old days," there used to be all sorts of surprises during trials. But in the new, "modern era," with full disclosure by the Crown, pretrial motions about most contentious issues, and extensive preliminary inquiries, the lawyers knew almost all the evidence that was going to come out during a trial—with the big exception of the testimony of the accused, if they testified—and what to expect from each witness.

But not this morning.

Parish watched James Trapper, aka Jet, shuffle into the courtroom, resplendent in his orange prison jumpsuit, and, like Ralph Armitage, she didn't know what he was going to say. Two guards, tightly at his sides, escorted him to the witness box. One stationed himself right beside it, the other backed off and sat beside the jury.

"What's your full name, sir?" Armitage asked once the new witness was sworn. He had moved out from behind the counsel table and for the first time in the trial was using the stand-up lectern. Almost as if he were hiding behind it.

"James Eric Trapper, but everyone calls me Jet." He gave his shoulders an exaggerated shrug.

"Thank you. To state the obvious, you are presently in prison, is that correct?" Armitage's whole demeanor had changed. No more being on a first-name basis with the witness. No more sucking up to the jury. Only cold clinical questions.

Trapper looked around the courtroom. "Possession of stolen property times ten. Proceeds of crime. Possession of an unregistered gun. Second time for that. Cops found it under my bed. Doing eighteen months. Four in already." He shrugged again as if to say, "Big deal."

Parish had warned St. Clair, especially with this witness, to never make eye contact. If the jury got even a whiff that Larkin or Dewey had intimidated him, they'd be furious.

Armitage had his notes in front of him and looked through them. "Where were you born, sir?"

"Pelee Island."

"Did you know Dewey Booth?"

Trapper snorted. "We were in a one-room class together from grade four when he showed up until he quit high school."

"How about Suzanne Howett?"

"Known Suzie since nursery school."

Parish could see that Armitage's body was unusually stiff. He gripped the podium. "Are you married, sir?"

"I am."

"What's your wife's name?"

"Charlene. We're separated right now."

"Last November, what was your relationship with Ms. Howett?"

"We were friends. I drove her around. She didn't have a car."

Here we go, Parish thought. Armitage was heading into dangerous waters. If Jet said he was afraid of Dewey because he was seeing Suzanne, Dewey's old girlfriend, then it made sense that he brought a gun to defend himself. And if the jury believed that Jet fired the first shot then the defense was in great shape.

She worked hard to keep her face neutral. But as a small self-indulgence, she cracked a tiny smile at the left corner of her mouth. The side the jury couldn't see.

Armitage paused and looked down at the podium again. He's using the notes as a prop, she thought. Buying himself time to decide which way to go. The reality was that he'd been forced to call Jet as a witness. Which meant that, since he didn't have the right to cross-examine, he'd be stuck with the answers he got.

"Do you know the accused, Larkin St. Clair?" He pointed at the defense table.

Smart, Parish thought. He's staying away from the question of Jet's relationship with Dewey. How Dewey must have hated him.

"I know Larkin," Jet said. He didn't bother to look over.

Armitage fiddled with his notes again. He was being painfully slow. Deliberate. "I'd like you to direct your mind to the afternoon of November fourteenth. Can you please tell the jury—"

"I don't remember much about it." For the first time since he'd been on the stand, Trapper's voice changed. Instead of sounding bored, it was firm, forceful. He flicked a look at St. Clair.

Bad move, Parish thought. Thankfully St. Clair kept following her instructions and looked straight ahead.

"Let's find out what you do remember," Armitage said. Parish could see his knuckles turning white. "Did you drive your Cadillac to pick up Suzanne when she got off shift at five?"

"Must have. I did it every day."

"Do you remember seeing her run toward you to get in the car?"

It was close to a leading question but Parish let it go. She didn't want to appear to be protecting this witness.

"Not really. November, it's dark already."

"Did you hear any gunshots?"

Trapper splayed out his hands in front of him and gave another exaggerated shrug. "It was a long time ago. I keep the car radio on real loud."

Armitage was getting stonewalled. Parish wondered how much longer he'd beat his head against this wall.

"Did you know Dewey was out of jail when you picked up Suzanne on November fourteenth?"

"Can't remember."

"Did you expect he was going to be at the Tim Hortons?"

"Can't remember."

"Did you bring your gun with you?"

"Can't remember."

Armitage walked back over to his table and picked up a set of papers. He was calm. Without all his big theatrics, Parish thought, he was a better lawyer.

"Do you recall that the police found an unregistered handgun in your apartment?"

"Right. Sure do. It's why I'm in jail."

"There was a forensic report done on it. Have you seen it?"

"I've seen it."

"It was dusty. There were cobwebs in the barrel."

Trapper crossed his arms. "My place is real dirty. Drove my wife crazy that I was such a slob."

He yawned and put his hands up to his mouth. As if he were bored with this, just a first-degree murder trial about the killing of an innocent four-year-old boy. The jury is going to hate him, Parish thought.

"Okay," Armitage said. He was back behind the podium. "Let's get right to the heart of the matter. On the night of November fourteenth, did you see Larkin St. Clair in the parking lot of the Tim Hortons, just across the street here on Elm?"

Parish sneaked a look at the jury. They were all staring at Trapper. Even Larkin couldn't resist looking over. She poked him in the side and he turned his head away.

Trapper raised his chin in defiance. "I have no recollection," he said.

"Dewey Booth? Did you see him?"

"No recollection."

"Did you fire a gun at Dewey?"

"No recollection."

Parish heard a strange rattling sound in the court. She looked over and saw Armitage was shaking the podium, anger dominating his face.

"You have a very clear recollection!" he shouted. "Because you didn't have a gun, and this man"—he pointed viciously at the defendant—"Larkin St. Clair was firing at you, wasn't he?"

"Objection." Parish was on her feet so fast she didn't even remember rising.

Armitage thrust the podium to the side and strode right up to the witness box. "And that's why you jumped in your car and took off, isn't it?"

"He's cross-examining his own witness again!" Parish shouted.

Rothbart looked stunned, confused.

"Because you were unarmed and Larkin was firing like a madman. Wasn't he?" Armitage growled. "You were scared for your life, just like you're scared right now."

Parish couldn't believe how Armitage had lost it. It looked terrible on him. Or did it?

Maybe this was deliberate. His only way to convey the message to the jurors: these old friends are all a pack of murdering liars. With a dead four-year-old boy, shots fired just blocks from where the jury was sitting, and Kyle's grieving family in the front row, that was probably all Armitage needed to get a conviction.

"I've heard enough of this." Judge Rothbart's baritone bashed down on Armitage like a weapon.

Armitage snapped a look at the judge, then turned to the jury. He shook his head in disgust and made his way, step by step, back to his seat. "No more questions," he said. "That's the case for the Crown."

58

Nancy Parish was used to talking to herself, so, logically, it should have made doing her jury address—essentially a speech to a silent audience of twelve—easier. But it didn't.

She'd done many of them and each time was struck by how strange the experience was. Talking away to twelve people who for days and weeks on end you had watched, and who'd watched you, but whom you'd never spoken to. A dozen strangers who couldn't talk back, no matter what you said. Limited to nodding, shaking their heads, making and breaking eye contact. The silence of it all was forever intimidating.

Every lawyer had a different theory about the best way to approach a jury. Some were long-winded, technical, and methodical. Others relied on emotion. Her favorite jury address story was about a crusty older lawyer who, after all the evidence was in during a very question-able sexual assault case, simply stood before the jury and said, "If that's rape then I'm a horse's ass. I ain't and it ain't," and sat down. The jurors laughed, and it only took them half an hour of deliberation to acquit his client.

But there was nothing funny about this case. A young boy killed by a stray bullet. A family broken. The peace and sense of well-being of the city shattered. Despite all this, she had to convince the jury to hold fast to the notion of reasonable doubt and acquit.

"Ladies and gentlemen," she said, standing squarely before the jury box. "There is one thing I am certain we can all agree on about this case. Me, and all twelve of you, believe it or not." That got one or two smirks from the jurors. A good start.

She turned toward the Crown. "I think even my friend Mr. Armitage will agree with me. Can you imagine that?"

This got a few full smiles. Good.

"We can all agree that my client, Mr. Larkin St. Clair, is probably guilty."

A dozen jurors' eyes snapped to her. After a moment a few grabbed glances back at St. Clair, their faces sad, as if to say, "My goodness, your own lawyer betrayed you."

She broke her position and walked with deliberate slowness to the end of the jury box nearest the judge. "He's probably guilty. I can see why you'd conclude that after hearing the evidence in this case."

She turned and walked to the other end of the jury box. "'Probably guilty' makes your job very easy. What does it mean that he is probably guilty?"

She turned again. When she'd gotten back to the middle, she turned to face the jurors. "'Probably' means"—she paused and looked at each of the twelve silent faces—"*not* guilty."

Her emphasis on the "not" was strong, the only time she raised her otherwise calm voice. And it had the intended effect. Some jurors looked at her, surprised, but a few gave her a little nod. Looking relieved. As if to say, "Yes, that's what I was thinking, he's probably guilty, but what does that mean for the verdict? It means that probably is *not* proof beyond a reasonable doubt."

She walked back to the easel with the outline of the Tim Hortons and the parking lot, then, one by one, placed the marked-up clear acrylic overlays on top, pausing each time to review the key evidence of each witness. At last, when she had all five in place, assembled together for the first time, she moved the easel right in front of the jury box.

The jurors hunched forward in their seats, like bidders at an art auction, getting their first glimpse of a rare piece of work they'd been dying to see for ages.

She said nothing, let the five colored contradictions speak for themselves.

"Excuse me, Ms. Parish," a voice said behind her.

It was a strict rule of jury addresses that the lawyer should never be interrupted by anyone in the court. She was so focused on the jury, she had no idea who was talking to her. She looked around the courtroom.

"Ms. Parish, I apologize," Judge Rothbart said. He was strumming his fingers on his hand at a frenetic pace. "But when the jury is done viewing, don't forget to turn the easel so the court can see it too."

Oh my, what a gift, she thought. By being so anxious to see the completed chart, he was practically giving the evidence the judicial stamp of approval. What song is he strumming to himself? she thought. How about "Let the Sunshine In"!

"Certainly, Your Honor. I was intending to do so once the jury has a little more time with it."

As she swung back around, she caught Ralph Armitage's eye. Sitting behind his counsel table, he looked as if his head was about to explode in frustration. Because the defense had not called any evidence, she got to address the jury last, and he had no opportunity to reply.

He'd made his jury address in the morning. It had been a good one, emphasizing the key parts of the evidence—the forensics had proved beyond any doubt that the gun found at Larkin St. Clair's aunt's place fired the bullet that lodged in little Kyle's brain. He played the video of St. Clair in the Tim Hortons parking lot, stuffing something down his pants, and reminded the jurors that the gunshot residue found on St. Clair's hands was consistent with someone who had recently fired a gun. He emphasized that St. Clair cut his hair to change his appearance and ran from the scene as evidence of his consciousness of guilt.

But now all he could do was listen and fume.

She had the floor. This was her moment.

59

"It is most lovely to see you, Mr. Kennicott."

"Excellent to see you as well, sir," Daniel Kennicott said, reaching out to shake hands with Lloyd Granwell, senior partner at the law firm of Miller, Ford. The man who had recruited him to come work there and had been his mentor during the five years he'd been a lawyer.

"And how is life these days at Metropolitan Toronto Police Services?" Granwell asked, leading Kennicott to the spot in his spacious corner office where they always sat in the two soft leather, high-back chairs around a square marble table.

Five years ago, they'd been in the very same seats.

"I've decided to leave the firm," Kennicott had said. "I want to become a police officer."

"Shall I contact Chief Charlton and enquire about a senior post?" Granwell had said without even flinching. As if it was the most normal thing in the world for his best associate to turn his back on his six-figure salary and promising legal career.

Granwell was a power broker, who had direct and personal contact with all the leading politicians, businesspeople, media folks, and anyone with real authority. He loved making things happen.

"Thanks, but that's the last thing I want you to do," Kennicott had said. "I'm going to be a beat cop. And hopefully stay under the radar."

"I wouldn't count on that. Your brother's very public murder is still a fresh wound in this city. I'm afraid this decision of yours will be too tempting a story for the local news publications."

Granwell had been right, of course. Charlton made a big deal about how Kennicott was the first lawyer turned cop in the city's history and the press ate it up. Now, every year the papers did one of their terrible anniversary-update stories, charting his rise through the ranks and noting that Michael's murder was still unsolved.

During that conversation, Granwell extracted a promise from Kennicott that he'd come back here for a chat once a year. In exchange, a spot would be held open for him at the firm. This was now their fifth annual get-together.

Granwell's corner office was pristine. The dark hardwood floors were covered in an exotic collection of Persian rugs. The walls were filled with stunning French impressionist art, the most prominent being a magnificent Monet painting of his lily gardens at Giverny. The large oak desk that dominated one end of the room was always empty except for one of his antique fountain pens and ten blank pieces of fine Florentine writing paper. Always ten. Always blank. Granwell refused to use lined paper, and he believed that any story that could not be reduced to ten pages of text was poorly told.

He always wore a combed cashmere gray suit, initialed fine cotton white shirts, Georg Jensen silver cuff links, and hand-made French leather shoes. He had no computer. No phone. No copier. He never carried a wallet. Had no credit cards. He had two secretaries—and he insisted on calling them secretaries, not legal assistants—who he kept busy at least sixty hours a week. He didn't "take exercise" and yet was always trim. His only concession to modernity was a CD player, discreetly hidden on his large bookshelf, from which opera and classical music played. This afternoon it was Beethoven's *Moonlight* sonata.

"How is this latest trial proceeding?" Granwell asked, after one of his secretaries had brought in the silver tea service and poured them both drinks in the Royal Albert bone china. "Terrible business. This shooting of that little boy at the coffee shop."

"The case is almost done," Kennicott said. "The lawyers are addressing the jury today."

"Tragic for the family. Tragic for the city. I am given to understand you were the first police officer to arrive."

Kennicott looked past Granwell through the big windows. The office had a magnificent view of the Toronto Harbor, the lagoon formed by the Toronto Islands, and Lake Ontario beyond. It was a warm April day, and a few boats were taking what looked like their first sails of the season. Jo Summers, the Crown Attorney who it looked like he wasn't going to see again, loved to sail. She lived on one of the islands that lay right in front of him. It seemed so close from up here, he felt like he could almost reach out and touch it. He fixed his eyes on a big boat gliding past and its billowing blue jib.

"It was a terrible night," he said. "Dark. November. The first time it snowed all year." For some reason, even though Granwell was so much older, and so extremely formal, Kennicott found it easier to talk to him than anyone else he knew. "The poor father. The look of horror on his face. I found the little boy's pulse and it was so weak."

He kept his eyes on the blue sail. He watched it round out through the gap between the islands and the shore and head out into the lake beyond. The blue sail matching the blue water.

"You've chosen a difficult path, Daniel," Granwell said.

Kennicott knew he had to get back to work. But the Beethoven was still playing. And Granwell's chair was comfortable. Just give yourself another minute, he thought, as his gaze was drawn back to the Monet. The tranquil lily pads. The color, so alive.

60

Ari Greene knew Nancy Parish the way cops get to know good lawyers in a big metropolis. The first case they'd had together was about a dozen years before. She had been a young lawyer, working at Grill & Partners. He was a detective on the Major Crime Unit.

Right from the beginning, she'd impressed him. Hardworking, tough but not stupid-tough, the way many lawyers tried to be. Knew when to pick her battles. Most of all she had that intangible thing you saw with very few courtroom lawyers, a certain presence. Made you want to listen to her. Made her arguments persuasive. She was like an athlete who had the same talent as all her teammates but possessed that little something extra—focus, charisma, ingenuity—hard to define, but it made her stand out.

Over the years, he'd occasionally had a case with her and he'd watched her mature as a lawyer. The cases she took on got tougher. She became more polished, without losing her enthusiasm for the job.

Last year, she'd taken on her first homicide. For defense lawyers, there are serious cases, then there are murder trials. The way with doctors there are surgeons and then brain surgeons, he imagined. It was Greene's case, and she'd done a good job.

He watched her move the easel back out of the way from the jury box. The courtroom was silent. She walked over and stood behind her client, put both hands on his shoulders, as if to say to the jury, "See, I'm not afraid of him. You shouldn't be either."

"You might be wondering," she said, not moving her hands, "why didn't Larkin St. Clair testify? Well, as you probably know, and as Justice Rothbart will certainly tell you, he has absolutely no obligation to do so. The burden of proof lies squarely with the Crown. But I'm not afraid to tell you why he didn't take the witness stand."

Greene always tried to keep his head down during key points in a trial. Take notes, appear neutral, confident, authoritative in front of the jury. But what Parish was doing right now was something he hadn't seen for a long time. He looked up. Neither the judge nor the Crown was permitted to comment on the failure of the accused to testify. It was the proverbial elephant in the room. But until a few years ago, when the law was changed, defense counsel was allowed to mention it to the jury, although few did.

Parish knew that, but she was doing it anyway.

"I told him not to testify," she said to the jury, pointing to herself. "There was no reason to."

Greene caught Armitage's eye. He could object right now. Even demand a mistrial. But he didn't move.

Greene was sure Parish had calculated that Armitage wouldn't want to have a whole new trial and have to do this case all over again. She'd decided to take the risk. Besides, Armitage had gone way over the top cross-examining his own witnesses. Now she was playing hardball back.

"If you're angry at Mr. St. Clair because he didn't take the stand, don't blame him. Blame me." She gave her client a comfortable tap on the shoulders and moved out to the space in front of the counsel table.

Everyone was watching her. All of a sudden, she threw her hands over her eyes. It was one of the most amazing things Greene had ever witnessed in a courtroom. Especially during a jury address. He couldn't stop looking.

"You know those three monkeys you always see in a toy store?" she said, still blinding herself in front of the jury. "See no evil." She took her hands away from her eyes and cupped them over her ears. "Hear no evil." She raised her voice a notch as she said the words. "And my favorite." She clapped her hands in front of her mouth, leaving a small space between her fingers that she could speak through. "Speak no evil," she said, her voice now muffled and deep.

Greene cast a look at the jurors. A few of them smirked. One of them laughed into her hands.

She had them following her every word.

"Number one Crown witness. Suzanne Howett, the server at Tim Hortons," she said, now standing erect, her hands at her sides. "Howett, let's call her 'See no evil.' Because does anyone really know what she saw? First she tells Detective Greene she didn't see a gun in Jet's hand. Then she comes to court, the Crown's star witness, and says, 'Oh yes, Jet had a gun.' He fired the first shot, at Dewey and my client Larkin. Was she telling the truth this time or the first time?"

A lot of lawyers paced when they addressed the jury. But Parish was absolutely still.

"It's simple. The facts in the Crown's case point to Jet shooting a gun. Remember he had a gun in his apartment when he was arrested."

Greene was always amazed at how lawyers picked the facts that helped their case and ignored the ones that didn't. Such as here. Parish made no mention that the gun was filled with cobwebs and obviously hadn't been fired the day before it was found.

Now she moved back to her easel, which was at an angle where both the jury and the judge could see it. With her finger she traced a line as she spoke. "The bullet hole in the wall of the building is a straight arrow from where Jet got out of his car to above the head of where my client Larkin St. Clair was standing. And the clincher." She pointed to the bottom part of the map, the spot where the Cadillac had been. "The only bullet shell found on the ground at the scene. Flattened. Right here, where Jet's Cadillac was before he took off, tires screeching."

Greene watched the jurors and was sure he saw more than one give little nods of their head.

"Next consider the Crown's witness Mr. Trapper, aka Jet. The man with no memory." This got more smirks and chuckles from the jury. Parish put her hands on her ears. "Let's call him 'Hear no evil.' He seems to have heard nothing. Not even the sound of his own gun going off."

Parish put her hands down and marched right back to the edge of the jury box. "Really." She lowered her voice to just above a whisper, as if she were telling a secret to a close friend. "Do you think if he fired that gun, like the two other witnesses say he did, that he'd come here as a Crown witness and admit it?" She shook her head. Amazingly, two jurors did the same.

"Put it in reverse." She was still whispering. Still shaking her head. "If he was firing, as you heard the other Crown witnesses say he was, do you really think he wouldn't remember?"

She started walking up along in front of the jury box, one hand on the railing, comfortable, like a kid trailing her fingers on a fence walking to school.

"Mr. Dewey Booth," Parish said when she got to the end of the rail. "I saved him for last." She put her hands over her mouth but didn't repeat her mumbling trick. Instead she removed them. "'Speak no evil.' The only witness who puts the gun in my client's hand. You might believe that. Or you might believe Dewey had the gun. But there's one thing about his testimony that is not in dispute. You've heard about it since the very first day of this trial. On the afternoon of November fourteenth the weather turned cold. It started to snow. And it was icy.

Mr. Wilkinson told us his son slipped on the sidewalk. And remember, Officer Kennicott tumbled running over. All five of the Crown's eyewitnesses agree with me about this. And that it was slippery is the only explanation that makes sense for this horrific tragedy."

She was brave and smart, Greene thought, not to shy away from what had happened here—the death of four-year-old Kyle Wilkinson. She'd handled it with sincerity and compassion and still made her argument. He promised himself he wouldn't peek at the jury again.

"Because here's the point that has not been mentioned in this trial. Not by any of the Crown's witnesses. Not by Mr. Armitage in his address to you this morning. The one thing that will make you realize that you not only should acquit my client, but you must find him not guilty."

Parish took in a few deep gulps of air. It looked like she'd gotten so caught up in what she was saying that she'd forgotten to breathe.

She walked back away from the jury to the court clerk, who handed her a pair of plastic gloves and then the gun. Greene had seen her arrange this before the jury came in. She pivoted back toward the jury, gun in gloved hands. You sure couldn't say this address was boring, he thought.

"If my client, or Dewey Booth, were trying to shoot Jet, why were no bullets fired at him or his car? Think of the place where Larkin and Jet were standing as being twelve on a clock face. We have evidence of shots fired at the top of the clock, behind them; to the left, hitting the building at nine o'clock; and to the right, striking Kyle at three o'clock. Not one stick of evidence a shot was directed at six o'clock. Where Jet was. No bullet holes in his car. No bullet holes in the concrete or the trees there. Nothing."

She was right. This was the part of the case that Greene knew had never fit. Always bothered him.

"Ask yourself," she was saying. "How many shots were fired? As many as nine. You've heard evidence that the gun found in my client's aunt's backyard had a clip that only took six bullets and there was room for one in the chamber. Only seven bullets maximum."

She turned toward the jury, brandishing the gun. "There are no bullets in this weapon. Believe me, I've triple-checked. Still, I'm going to point it well above your heads."

She's putting the jurors in the place of someone about to be shot at, Greene thought.

"Picture this scenario. It is the only one that fits with all the evidence. Dewey and Larkin are back against the wall. The Cadillac pulls up. A shot goes over their head. More shots. In a hasty effort at self-defense, this gun is fired."

Greene had to smile. Parish had been cagey enough with her words to not say who fired the gun. Since her client hadn't testified, she couldn't point the finger directly at Dewey. But this way she left it an open question for the jury.

She paused again. Greene knew where she was going with this. "Why in the world does this stray bullet go on such an odd angle and strike poor Kyle? There's only one explanation that makes sense. The ice."

Parish pretended to slip. Her outstretched arm and the gun in it turned a quarter of a clock face and aimed right at Ralph Armitage.

"That, I submit to you, ladies and gentlemen of the jury, is what happened. Tragic and horrible. Yes. But murder? No."

Parish brought the gun back to the registrar and pulled off the gloves with a snap.

For the thousandth time in the last few months Greene had played out in his head the different scenarios of what actually happened in the Tim Hortons parking lot. He didn't believe Parish had it right. But he thought she was closer than he'd ever come to the truth.

And that was what was the most frustrating thing about this case. With the civilian eyewitnesses not seeing much, everyone else lying, and Larkin St. Clair not talking, it meant the only one who knew the whole story was this Dragomir Ozera character. And he was nowhere to be found.

61

Five long, lousy days, and counting. Ralph Armitage was beginning to feel like a prisoner himself in the courthouse, waiting for the jury to come back. While the jury was deliberating, the trial lawyers were required to be on call, available to come back into court with just fifteen minutes' notice. They could leave the building only when the jurors weren't deliberating, meaning he and Greene were stuck here from nine in the morning until nine at night, with two hour-and-a-half breaks for lunch and dinner.

And every time he stepped out of their little courthouse office, a whole contingent of bored reporters, who were staked out in the hallway, desperate for any kind of a story, descended upon him. They peppered him with a barrage of questions and grew frustrated when he wouldn't give them a quote they could use.

Sitting in the room, staring at the wall outside his window, Armitage played over and over again in his mind every move that he'd made in the case: his deal with Cutter, the pretrial with Judge Rothbart, his cross-examination of all the witnesses, his addresses to the jury. And most of all Jose Sanchez, aka Dragomir Ozera, aka the guy who could totally and forever fuck up his life. This waiting was a strange and tortuous purgatory.

But now, just after the lunch break, his phone was ringing and he could see by the call display the court registrar was calling. Greene, who'd spent most of his time looking at another file, the murder of Officer Kennicott's brother Michael and the detective's only unsolved case, looked up at him.

"It's the registrar," he said, eyeing the phone display.

Greene closed his file.

Armitage swallowed hard and picked up the phone. "Ralph Armitage," he said. "What can I do for you, Mr. Registrar?"

"His Honor wants you back in court immediately."

"Does the jury have a question, are they deadlocked, or do we have a verdict?" he asked. His heart was fluttering.

"Sounds like they're still deadlocked," the registrar said, "but you didn't hear that from me."

Armitage chuckled. "Mum's the word. Thanks."

"Still deadlocked," he told Greene after he hung up.

"Rothbart's not going to be happy," Greene said.

That was for sure. Judges hated indecisive jurors and deadlocked juries.

This would be the third time they'd been called back to court. On day two the jury came back with a question: "Your Honor, could you please reread to us the definition of Parties to an Offence."

This question wasn't great for the Crown. It seemed to indicate the jury was thinking that Dewey was the shooter, not Larkin. He could still be convicted of first-degree murder, but it was tougher. Rothbart read them the law and explained, as he had done before, that being a party made St. Clair equally culpable.

Armitage had made the same point in his jury address: "You don't have to find that Larkin St. Clair pulled the trigger to convict him of first-degree murder." He thought it was one of his best lines. That was five days ago. Felt like five weeks.

Yesterday, a very unhappy Judge Rothbart called the lawyers back into court. The jury wasn't there.

"This is a message I received ten minutes ago from the jury foreperson," he said. "It reads: 'Your Honor, we are deadlocked.'"

He called the jurors back in and admonished them in his best, deep, judge's voice. Told them they were in a better position to find a verdict than any jury could be, that he was impressed at how hard they were working, how he was absolutely certain they could arrive at a just verdict, and how important it was that they, and not another jury, reach a decision. Blah, blah, blah.

"Rothbart's going to want a verdict soon," Greene said, as he packed up his file, tightened his tie, and pointed to a calendar on the wall. "He's supposed to be in New York tomorrow for his annual trip to see his Broadway buddies."

"Holy shit," Armitage said. "I forgot all about that."

"I bet our honorable high court justice remembered," Greene said.

Out in the hall the gang of reporters was thicker than ever. "Why do you think it's taking the jury so long?" Zachery Stone asked, perching himself right under Armitage's elbow.

"Maybe they like the free food," he said.

"Great quote," Stone said.

"No, no, Zack, that's off the record."

Everyone laughed.

Rothbart was already seated when they came into court. He was scowling. Nancy Parish rushed in, yanking on her robes, and took her seat. Rothbart drummed his fingers impatiently while Larkin St. Clair was led back in and his handcuffs were undone. He looked pale and distracted.

Rothbart unfolded a piece of paper that was the only thing on his desk. "I have another note from the jury. It says: 'Your Honor, we are hopelessly deadlocked.' The word 'hopelessly' is underlined." He threw up his hands. "What do counsel suggest?" he asked both lawyers.

"I think you send them back out to try again," Armitage said. As much as he feared losing the trial, the thought of having to do it all over again was even worse. Especially with Ozera still out there. God, he just wanted this to be over.

"I agree," Parish said. She looked exhausted too.

The unwritten rule with hung juries was "three strikes you're out." In other words, usually judges didn't let them off the hook and declare a mistrial until they'd complained at least three times that they couldn't reach a verdict. More often than not, the last go-round seemed to work.

But judges, who lived in fear of being overturned by a higher court, all knew that declaring a mistrial was the one thing they could do that could never be appealed. They could do it with impunity at any time.

"I disagree," Rothbart said, slapping his hand down on his desk. "Enough is enough. Bailiff, bring back my jury, I'm going to declare a mistrial. I've already got a new trial date lined up a month from now."

This nightmare's never going to end, Armitage thought, exchanging despondent glances with Parish. They had to do this all over again just so Ollie Rothbart could go down to New York for his little theater tour.

62

"Ms. Parish, how does your client feel about the hung jury?"

"Ms. Parish, is there any chance of a plea bargain now?"

"Ms. Parish, are you surprised Judge Rothbart didn't make the jurors keep deliberating? At least for a third time?"

"Ms. Parish."

"Ms. Parish."

"Ms. Parish."

Nancy Parish stood on the courthouse steps and looked across the sea of reporters in front of her. Others were on both sides of her, pushing in, shoving microphones in her face. The press called it a scrum, and their close proximity reminded her of her days playing rugby at her all-girls high school. A few weeks ago when the trial had started, she'd been shocked to have her personal space invaded in this way. Late at night, when she'd finally get home from the office and watched herself on the TV news, she'd looked like the proverbial deer caught in the headlights.

Fortunately, Ted DiPaulo and Awotwe Amankwah had been giving her some useful tips for handling the media: look directly at one camera at a time, keep her answers short, and always have one good quote. Give the reporters a six-second clip and they were happy. Her favorite trick was Awotwe's suggestions of how to handle a question she didn't want to answer. "Look the reporter straight in the eye and say nothing. Nothing is never news." So far today, she hadn't said a word.

"Ms. Parish, will you change your trial strategy next time?"

"Ms. Parish, will your client now apply for bail?"

"Ms. Parish, will you do the retrial or hand it off to another lawyer?"

Oh, how I'd love to get rid of this case, she thought. Be able to spend just one night at home. And in theory it would be a good idea to let another lawyer take a fresh look at everything. But Rothbart had set the trial date too soon. Besides, there was no way St. Clair would let her pass his file to another lawyer. A half an hour before, down in the jail cell minutes after the mistrial had been declared, he'd been in high spirits. "Hey, Nancy, look, we didn't lose," he told her. "We're still in the game."

"Ms. Parish, what do you think swayed the jurors either way?"

"Ms. Parish, how surprised are you that the jury was hung?"

"Ms. Parish, is it tougher to do a second trial?"

That was a good question, she thought. Usually the Crown did better on a retrial. They'd seen all the holes in their case and had time to fill them. But this time, the trial had exposed new and unexpected testimony, and now Dewey Booth's evidence was fixed under oath. This was much better for the defense than just having his affidavit. If only they could prove that he'd lied on the stand in this first trial, then Armitage's stupid deal with Cutter would be null and void and Booth could be charged with murder. That would change everything.

"Ms. Parish, will Ralph Armitage do the second trial for the Crown?"

"Ms. Parish, if you could ask one question of the jurors, what would it be?"

"Ms. Parish, how about you? How do you feel about doing this all again?"

She scanned the crowd and saw Awotwe's smiling black face. The only one in the all-white press corp. His was the best question of all. How did she feel about this? She put her hand up and everyone grew silent. What power I have, she thought, chuckling to herself. Amazing how suddenly everyone wanted a piece of her.

Yesterday Brett, the young waiter from the Pravda Bar who'd been scared off when he found out she was on this case, had sent her a text wishing her good luck and wondering when she was free "for a drink." Karl, the jerk from Cleveland, had left a message on her answering machine at the office, saying he'd been reading about her trial online and expected to be back in Toronto this summer. Even her ex-husband had e-mailed her while the jury was out and wished her *"courage, mon ami."*

She picked a TV camera to stare into. "I feel very enthusiastic about doing this trail again." It was a complete lie. She was exhausted. Dying to get back to a normal life. To stop living at the office. Find some new guy to go out with.

"My heart goes out to the Wilkinson family, who have to live through this all again. But I'm sure, like all of us, they don't want to see the wrong person convicted of this terrible crime."

There, she thought, that's your six-second clip.

"Ms. Parish."

"Ms. Parish."

"Ms. Parish."

"No more questions," she said. "I've got to get back to work." Actually Zelda had already texted her to meet at the Pravda and plan to take a cab home. Late.

She stepped forward and the reporters parted in front of her. It was quite remarkable how they fell away, like flies blown off by a strong wind.

By the time she got to the sidewalk, she was standing with her briefcase. Alone.

PART FIVE
MAY

63

"Hello, Detective Greene," Cedric Wilkinson said, standing in the doorway of his apartment, offering his hand to shake. "Nice of you to come over to say good-bye."

Ari Greene hadn't seen Wilkinson for a month, since the end of the trial. The man kept dropping pounds. It had been half a year since his son was murdered, and he looked as if he'd lost almost half his weight. "Least I could do." He reached out and grasped Wilkinson with his free hand. In the other he held his briefcase.

Wilkinson ushered him inside. Most of the furniture had been removed. The Persian carpets were all rolled up and stacked along the living room wall, and their voices and footsteps made a hollow sound. Rows of plastic bins were piled high in the hallway. "Madeleine and Kieran left on Monday, so I'm on my own for a week. Movers come on Friday morning and I fly out later that night. There's hardly any food here. Can I get you something to drink?"

"A glass of water's fine."

Greene followed him into the kitchen. All of the appliances were gone from the countertop, except a big coffeemaker that was almost full. The table had a setting for one.

Wilkinson opened the fridge. Inside were an unwrapped iceberg lettuce, brown around the edges; an opened packet of sliced salami; a bowl filled with precut mini carrots; half a loaf of bread; and a jar of peanut butter with no top on it. "I don't think I have any bottled water," he said.

"I prefer tap water." Greene pulled a glass from the overhead cupboard. "Tap water and public education, the only two things I believe in."

Wilkinson chuckled. "I wish. We were going to send Kyle to public school here, but back in California no way. I'm saving up for Kieran already." He poured himself a full cup of coffee and drank about half of it. "Figure I might as well drink as much as I want, since I don't sleep anyway."

Greene filled his glass over the sink.

Wilkinson took another big gulp. "If you are here to try to convince me to stay for the retrial, forget it," he said at last.

Greene took a sip. The new trial was set to go next Tuesday, after the upcoming long holiday weekend. "I understand why you want to leave," he said.

Wilkinson eyed the briefcase in Greene's hand. "I spoke to the company's lawyers and they got me a firm legal opinion. You have no legal grounds to make me stay in Canada, and once I'm in the States you can't force me to come back."

"Even if I could, I'd never force you." Greene motioned toward the outdoors with his glass. "Let's go on the balcony. Beautiful day. Not a cloud in the sky."

The porch furniture had been packed up as well. There was nowhere to sit. Not that it mattered. The trees had burst into bloom, covering the valley below in a spectacular canopy, and it was pleasant to look over the railing. Greene put his briefcase on the ground and tilted it against the barrier.

"You know, I never understood all this fuss people from up north made about the spring," Wilkinson said. "I have to admit, a beautiful day like this after such a long winter is special."

"Can't beat Toronto in May," Greene said.

Wilkinson took another big slurp of his coffee.

"I've got something for you." Greene pulled a large manila envelope from his briefcase that was bulging out at the sides. "These are the cards and letters people left at the shrine outside the Tim Hortons."

Wilkinson put his empty cup on the ground and took the package.

"Take one out. Any one," Greene said.

Wilkinson closed his eyes and put the envelope to his forehead.

A gust of wind rolled up from the valley, blanketing them in warm air. Greene smelled the scent of lilacs.

Wilkinson pulled the envelope back, reached in, and pulled out a handmade card with childlike writing in crayon. " 'Dear family,' " he read. " 'My mommy told me what happened and I am so, so sad for your family and we love you.' Love is spelled l-u-v." He slipped the card back in with the others.

Greene finished his glass of water and bent to set it on the ground.

Wilkinson reached for his hand. "Let me get you another glass," he said.

"It's okay," Greene said.

"I need more coffee anyhow." He put the envelope against his heart. "I want to put this in a safe place."

He took the glass and went back inside. Greene looked over at the impressive layer of foliage far below.

Wilkinson walked back onto the porch, coffee in one hand and water in the other. "Here," he said, handing the glass to Greene, "take this."

Their eyes locked.

"'Here, take this,'" Greene said as gently as he could. "Those were the last words you said to Kyle, weren't they?"

Wilkinson, his clothes hanging on his narrowing frame, standing against a backdrop of the blue sky, seemed suspended in space and time.

Greene picked up his briefcase.

Wilkinson watched in silence as Greene passed him a set of papers. He glanced at them for a moment, and then handed the pages back. He looked over the railing. "You know, detective, when we first got this place, I used to come out here in the mornings and stare at those trees. I've lived in California my whole life. I'd never seen that kind of fall color before. Like this amazing painting. Then winter came and the trees were bare. I could see all those streets, those houses. The people rushing to work. Now it's all covered up again."

Greene shuffled the papers in his hand. "I kept wondering about Kyle, holding that pretend cell phone, still in its wrapper. I got your cell phone records." He pointed to one entry that he'd highlighted in yellow. "November fourteenth at five-oh-one. You took a call from your office. Probably seconds before the shots were fired."

Wilkinson took his mug and poured the coffee over the edge. It swirled up in the wind for a moment before breaking up into liquid pieces and cascading earthward.

"You never told us you were on the phone when all this happened," Greene said.

Wilkinson's eyes were downcast, looking into the valley.

Greene put the papers in his case and zipped it up slowly, letting the ticking sound fill the silence between them. "Witnesses said that just before they heard the first gunshot, someone said, 'Here, take this,' and the voice was coming from near the front door. We assumed all along it was Dewey or Larkin."

Wilkinson put his free hand over his eyes. "I couldn't tell Madeleine," he said. "She didn't want me feeding Kyle junk food. Didn't want him to have a weight problem like his father. It was bad enough that this happened when I was taking him for a doughnut. But she hated the way I was on the cell all the fucking time."

Greene could picture how it had all unfolded. Wilkinson and his son walking up through the parking lot, holding hands. It starts to snow. Wilkinson's cell phone rings. He lets go of Kyle's hand for a moment to answer it and gives the boy a pretend phone. "Here, take this," he says. Now they both had cell phones. Like father, like son. Kyle turns to look at the snowflakes. In that magic moment, the bullet strikes.

"It was a stupid call about rescheduling a meeting," Wilkinson said. "Then I heard the bang. I've never been involved with guns before. I had no idea they were so loud. The bullet just missed me. Every night I think, If only I'd been beside him. I would have died and not my son. Kyle was having a hard time with his mom being in the hospital, a new baby on the way . . ."

His voice seemed to catch and his whole body shook.

"Whether you stay in Canada or not," Greene said, "I have to disclose this evidence to the Crown. They in turn have to disclose it to the defense."

"I understand," Wilkinson said. "And I know it means that St. Clair will almost certainly get off this time."

Greene rolled the glass in his hand, took another sip, and poured the rest of the water over the rail. "Yes," he said. "It does."

64

The smell was the first thing Daniel Kennicott noticed as he climbed the stairs to his second-floor flat. It wasn't really a smell, it was a perfume scent. One that he'd lived with, on and off, for years. Until Andrea, his fashion model ex-girlfriend finally, thankfully, moved to Paris to live with a photographer.

At the top of the stairs he saw a pair of tall leather boots tossed carelessly on the bare floor, erasing all hope that he'd been wrong about the damn perfume smell. Scent.

He had a two-bedroom flat and the door to the second room was shut. A note, written in red lipstick, was pinned to it with a sharp earring.

"D. Sorry to barge in. Photog was a jerk. Just need three days until I'm over the lag. Promise . . . A."

He could just imagine how she'd gotten in. Mr. and Mrs. Federico, his Portuguese landlords who lived downstairs, loved Andrea, who was half-Portuguese herself and perfectly fluent. It would have taken her less than a minute to talk them into opening his door.

This was the last thing he needed. Especially right now. The retrial of Larkin St. Clair was starting next week and he had a ton of work to do. As well, Detective Greene had asked him to set up a meeting at his old law firm later today, and he'd been there all morning getting things ready.

Coming home, he'd bought some vegetables on nearby College Street, and Mrs. Federico had left a shopping bag on the handle of his side-door entrance. It was filled with fragrant cuttings from the purple lilac tree in back. He made his way to the kitchen to unload everything. A very Parisian-looking blue Pastis 51 water pitcher was in the middle of the table. Typical Andrea. She always brought a gift.

He unclipped his cell phone and tossed it on the counter. The fridge was filled with French goat cheese and a wheel of Brie. More gifts. One thing about Andrea, he thought, was she knew the kind of food he liked.

"I mean it, Daniel, just three days," a familiar voice said behind him.

He turned and saw her. She was wearing one of his good dress shirts, half buttoned up, and was barefoot. The thing about a woman as beautiful as Andrea was that she looked stunning in almost anything.

He grabbed the Brie and flicked the fridge door shut a little too hard. It almost sounded like a slam. "I hope you didn't tell the Federicos that we are getting back together yet again."

She sat down and yawned. "No, actually I told them the truth."

He unwrapped the cheese and laughed. "Which is?"

She stared at him. It was her eyes that had made her a star. A stunning kind of green, blue with a strange and intriguing hint of yellow. She shook her head. "They say you're a very good cop. Working on murder trials now."

He broke off eye contact. "Thanks for the cheese, and the water pitcher is a nice touch."

She spotted the lilac cuttings in the bag and pulled them out. "God I miss that smell," she said, inhaling deeply.

"I don't have a vase," he said.

She pushed the Pastis 51 pitcher toward him. "Use this."

He filled it with water and sat back down across the table from her. She passed him half the cuttings and they both trimmed the lower twigs off with their hands before plunking them in the water.

"Photographer turned out to be an asshole," she said, as she worked. "Never told me he was married, and I caught him in bed with a young boy."

"Shit happens."

"Thanks for being so sympathetic."

He finished the last twig, went back to the kitchen, and pulled out a paring knife and small cutting board. Back at the table, he carved out a quarter of the wheel of Brie, then slicing back and forth from the tip, trimmed off a few thin pieces and passed one to her, attached to the end of the knife.

"I know," he said. "I should let the cheese come to room temperature."

She slid the piece onto her tongue. The ritual of food was one of the things that worked well between them. "Daniel, you've always been impatient."

He passed her another slice. "Three days. Promise."

Instead of taking the cheese, she took his hand. "You can put down the knife." She rubbed the inside edge of his palm. She was leaning over the counter and he could see she had nothing on under his shirt.

There was a buzzing sound in the room. She looked at him confused.

He smiled. "It's my phone," he said, letting go of her hand.

"Saved by the bell," she said.

Back at the counter he answered his phone without bothering to look at the call display. "Kennicott."

"Daniel?" It was a woman's voice he recognized instantly.

"Oh, hi, Jo," he said.

"I know it's been long time since we talked," Jo Summers said.

He thought back to the time in January when he'd visited his friend Jeremy Pulver at the Crown's office and discovered she was back from Central America. That was four months ago, and she had never called. He'd pretty much resigned himself to not hearing from her again.

"We're both busy." He forced a chuckle.

"I heard the St. Clair case starts again on Tuesday."

He looked back at Andrea. She was slicing up another piece of cheese. Smiling at him.

"Right after the Victoria Day fireworks."

"I didn't want to bug you during the first trial. But I wanted to say good luck."

"Well, thanks."

He looked out the back window. The Federicos were outside working in their garden. The lilac tree in full bloom.

"We should try to grab a coffee, sometime," she said. "I mean, after the case is done."

"Sure." Really he wanted to say something like "Yes, I'd like that." But he could feel Andrea's eyes on him.

"I'll call you when it's over," Summers said.

He said good-bye and put the phone back on the counter.

"Jo?" Andrea asked.

"Jo," he said.

"As in Joseph or as in Joanne?"

"As in, you're staying three days, no more," he said.

She took the last slice of cheese and sucked it slowly into her mouth. "Daniel, I only have one request. And I know you won't be able to resist."

He crossed his arms. "We both know where that leads." Sex and food. The two things that they did best.

She laughed. "Get your mind out of the gutter. I want to go with you to the Plaza Flamingo tomorrow to watch some soccer matches. The Euro Cup starts in a few weeks."

He laughed too. It had probably been the best part of their relationship. Spending their Saturday afternoons at the Flamingo, watching games from all over Europe, screaming and yelling with the crowd, eating lamb stew and beans, drinking Italian beer. Before going home. To bed.

65

"Do you have any idea what the divorce statistics are for couples after one of their children is killed?" Cedric Wilkinson asked Ari Greene. He was balancing his mug on the balcony railing.

"I think about eighty percent fail," Greene said.

"Closer to ninety." Wilkinson was focusing on steadying his cup as if that were the most important thing in the world.

"So, if you'd told your wife the whole story, she would have found out you let go of Kyle's hand to answer your cell phone," Greene said.

"When your family's attacked, you have to protect them first."

Greene tapped the metal barrier with his glass. It made a high-pitched pinging sound. "The Nazis killed my father's first family," he said. "Wife, children, parents, grandparents, aunts, uncles. Everyone."

They were both silent for a long time.

"My dad," Greene said at last, "still made a life for himself."

Wilkinson took his cup off the railing. "It happened just like you said. My cell rang, and I let go of Kyle's hand and gave him that toy cell phone. I said it. 'Here, take this.' Those were the last words I ever spoke to him."

"Did you see anything?"

"No. It was dark where those two were standing. I wasn't looking there anyway."

"Hear anything?"

"I was on the phone. Then there was the bang. I couldn't tell you about giving Kyle the cell phone when we met that first time at the hospital."

"I didn't ask."

"I know. You were kind."

"You were vague about it when you first gave me a statement," Greene said. He had gone back and looked again at the transcript of that initial interview.

Officer Greene: Just before the shooting, one witness heard someone say "Take this," or "Here, take this," something like that. Did you hear those words spoken?

Cedric Wilkinson: I might have. It's all a blur.

"I know. I was going to tell you when you came over after Christmas," Wilkinson said. "But when you told me the bullet that killed Kyle matched the gun and then I saw that picture of Armitage on the front page of the newspaper, I thought, What's the point? Bad enough one of the culprits was going to go free, why should I make it any easier for the other one?"

"And during the trial?" he asked.

Wilkinson shrugged. "No one ever asked me."

Greene thought about the time Wilkinson testified. He was never asked in court, "Mr. Wilkinson, did you say, 'Here, take this?'" Greene bent down and put his glass on the ground. "Don't you want to know what happened?" he asked.

"Does it matter? My son's dead."

"As frustrating as it is, there's one good thing about this mistrial."

Wilkinson stared at him. "What could possibly be good about it?"

"There was no preliminary inquiry before. But now we have Dewey Booth pinned down to all of his evidence under oath. Not just that half-baked affidavit Cutter hoisted on Armitage."

"So what? He'll just lie again like they all did."

"Yes, but if we can prove he lied at the first trial, we've got him for perjury. Then the deal's off. We can try him for murder."

Wilkinson's eyes looked exhausted. "I told you, I'm leaving Friday night. And I'm not going to court again, no matter what. What do you want me to do?"

"Stay until Tuesday morning."

"Why?"

"Your wife told me a long time ago that I'm the only person you can trust," Greene said. "From day one, we've been trying to find the baker from the Tim Hortons. I'm convinced he's the only eyewitness who saw what really happened."

"You said he'd gone underground. Who knows if he's still in Canada?"

"He's in Canada. We know his name. I alerted immigration right away. Passport records show he came in six years ago and hasn't left. He's an illegal immigrant who had a few minor charges and never went to court. My gut tells me he's smart. Afraid of Dewey and Larkin. Afraid of the police. Immigration. But maybe, just maybe, he'd talk to you."

"Me?"

"You."

"How?"

"I want you to give an interview to the *Toronto Star*."

"You told me to never talk to the press."

"Just one time. It might just smoke him out."

Wilkinson's breathing became very heavy.

"I'm not trying to trick you, and this is a real long shot. But it means you have to stay until Tuesday morning. You can leave first thing, before the trial even starts."

Wilkinson shook his head. Squeezed his eyes shut.

"I'm sure Madeleine would forgive you if she ever found out about the cell phone," Greene said. "But I don't think you'd ever forgive yourself if you didn't take this last chance to find out the truth."

Wilkinson steadied himself on the railing, still shaking his head. Greene didn't move. Just watched, until Wilkinson's head stopped going back and forth, and began to nod up and down.

66

Daniel Kennicott had spent countless hours in this fancy boardroom of Miller, Ford, his old law firm, where for five years he'd been a rising star in the litigation department. Nothing had changed. On the wall, prints of high-gloss modern photography. On the banquette, coffee, tea, sparkling water, fruit juices, cookies, sliced fruit, and a vase bursting with fresh-cut flowers. And out the south-facing windows the ubiquitous view of the blue harbor.

Detective Greene seemed totally unimpressed by this rarefied setting. He sat patiently in a chair in the middle of the table. Cedric Wilkinson was beside him, and beside Wilkinson was Lloyd Granwell wearing his usual perfectly tailored gray suit. He'd cleared his calendar immediately for this emergency meeting and insisted on acting for Wilkinson pro bono.

"How can I charge a man whose son was killed in the middle of our city?" he'd asked Kennicott.

"It's good of you."

"No. It's why I do this."

Granwell distributed business cards with the ease of an experienced croupier to Greene, Wilkinson, and Awotwe Amankwah, the *Toronto Star* reporter who sat alone across from them. Amankwah had a notebook in hand and a mini-recorder placed squarely in front of him.

Kennicott was the only one standing. Technically, he was here as a witness to the proceedings, and it was best that he stay far back.

"The ground rules for this interview must be clear," Granwell said to Amankwah. "You are the only reporter to whom my client, Mr. Wilkinson, will speak. In return for this exclusive interview, the *Toronto Star* agrees to run this as a front-page story tomorrow morning in the Saturday edition. Above the fold."

"That's right," Amankwah said.

"And you understand Mr. Wilkinson will not discuss any of his testimony in the case."

"I understand. But we need a photo of Mr. Wilkinson holding a picture of Kyle. I hate to ask for it, but my editors insist."

"We did not agree to that," Granwell said.

"I know," Amankwah replied. "I've only had a few hours to set this up. I don't like it, but it's a deal breaker. Mr. Wilkinson won't talk about his evidence, that weakens the story. We need the picture."

Kennicott watched Granwell furrow his otherwise perfectly smooth brow. He tilted sideways and whispered in Wilkinson's ear.

Wilkinson listened intently. Nodded. "It's okay," he said a few seconds later. "We want to make sure this story gets maximum coverage. I understand why they need the photo."

Amankwah clicked on his recorder. The sound seemed loud in the large room. "I'm recording everything," he said.

The air-conditioning was on very high, and the room felt unnaturally cold.

Kennicott concentrated on standing perfectly still.

"Mr. Wilkinson, how do you feel about the mistrial?" Amankwah asked.

"My wife and I are very disappointed," he said, still looking out the window. "We've decided to leave Toronto and don't plan to return. Detective Greene has told us that my evidence from the first trial, as much as it is relevant, can simply be read to the next jury."

Kennicott watched Amankwah's eyebrows rise. That the Wilkinsons were leaving Toronto and wouldn't be at the retrial, was big news. The reporter could smell a good story.

"I was at the first trial. I understand you didn't see what happened—"

Granwell put his hand in front of Wilkinson and leaned over to speak to him again. "We agreed no questions about my client's testimony."

"It's okay," Wilkinson said immediately, before Granwell had a chance to say anything to him. "I want to clarify something."

Granwell frowned and pulled his arm back.

Kennicott smiled to himself. Half an hour ago in Granwell's office, he'd watched the two of them rehearse this little act they'd just performed.

"We want to make the reporter believe that you are speaking spontaneously," Granwell had said, "not following your lawyer's instructions. It will impress him."

"As I said under oath in court," Wilkinson said to Amankwah, "I didn't see anything. But if I had, I would stay here for the new trial, no matter how stressful this would be for my family."

Amankwah had his notebook out and was writing furiously. "Thank you."

Wilkinson swiveled his head and caught Ari Greene's eye. "That's not all," he said. "I believe there is an eyewitness out there who saw exactly what happened. Who could answer all the unanswered questions."

"You think so?" Amankwah, already on high alert, looked as if he'd just gotten an extra bolt of energy. Wilkinson had given his story a banner headline, and everyone knew it: FATHER OF TIM HORTONS SHOOTING VICTIM CONVINCED THERE WAS AN EYEWITNESS.

"Yes. I'm convinced."

"Have the police been in touch with him?"

"No. I fear he's afraid to come forward to the police."

"What makes you think that?" Amankwah asked.

"Information I have learned from the detectives." Wilkinson was very calm.

Amankwah turned to Greene. "Do you know who this individual is?"

"We're very close to a positive identification of him," Greene said.

Kennicott had agreed with Greene that it was better to not give out Ozera's name.

There followed a series of standard questions and answers.

"How's your wife doing?"

"As well as can be expected."

"How's the new baby?"

"Wonderful."

"Are you going for counseling?"

"No."

"Has your company been supportive?"

"Remarkably."

"What do you think of the Canadian judicial system?"

"Off the record?"

"Okay."

"No comment."

With that last answer, the tension in the room broke, and everyone chuckled.

"If this potential witness did want to contact you," Amankwah said, "how would he get in touch?"

"He could call Detective Greene, who has promised to pass along any message to me without question," Wilkinson said.

"How much longer are you staying in Toronto?"

"I'm leaving on Tuesday morning, before the trial begins. Monday night, I plan to attend the Armitage family celebration. I've heard a lot about it, and it would be a way for me to thank Ralph Armitage for all his hard work on this case."

Kennicott was watching Amankwah's pen. He hadn't bothered to write this down. He clicked off the recorder. "Thank you very much, sir. Our photographer is in reception."

Wilkinson glanced at Greene again, then back at Amankwah. "That last fact must be in the story," he said to Amankwah.

Amankwah looked surprised. "The Armitage May Two-Four celebration? Well, I don't think it's—"

"Turn that recorder back on," Wilkinson said. All traces of his passive civility throughout the interview vanished, replaced by a startling streak of anger and determination. This was a man whose son had been murdered.

Amankwah clicked on the recorder.

Lloyd Granwell, who had hardly moved during the whole interview, put up his hand and pointed his finger right at Amankwah's face. "Let me be very clear," he said in his patient, confident voice. "If you do not agree to put in your newspaper article the fact that Mr. Wilkinson will be attending the annual Armitage Victoria Day festivities this Monday evening, then he will not pose for a photograph. If you run the story without this fact being mentioned, please expect to face a crushing lawsuit aimed at both your newspaper and yourself. Is that clear?"

Amankwah shook his head sagely. "Perfectly clear."

"State for the record that you will include Mr. Wilkinson's attendance at these festivities in your newspaper article," Granwell said. It wasn't a statement but a command.

Kennicott smiled. Granwell had taught him, never go into a meeting where the answer will be no. And wait. Wait for the right moment and then pounce. Make sure you get your yes.

"For the record, I agree to include in my story the fact that Mr. Wilkinson will go to the Armitage party on Monday night."

"Excellent," Granwell said, retracting his finger.

"It would mean a great deal to my wife and me if I could meet with this missing witness," Wilkinson said. "For us, not knowing what really happened to Kyle has made this tragedy much worse. I just pray this man finds it in his heart to make contact with us."

Amankwah wrote in his notebook and no one said a word. Now it was obvious to the reporter why he'd been granted this exclusive interview. They were using him to try to reach out to the missing witness.

Ozera. Greene had thought up the idea and it was the best chance they had.

Amankwah clicked off his recorder. "Well," he said, "let's hope this smokes him out."

"Thanks for doing this," Greene said. It was the first time he'd spoken and he had everyone's attention. "I'm glad we chose you to write this story."

Amankwah said to Wilkinson: "I hate how trite this sounds, but I'm so sorry for what you've gone through. I have two children. I'm divorced and don't get to see them as much as I'd like."

Wilkinson reached across the table and shook his hand.

"Awotwe, what are you doing Monday night?" Greene asked.

Amankwah smiled. "Fortunately, I have the kids this weekend. I was thinking of taking them to a fireworks display."

"I think," Greene said, standing to leave, reaching across to shake hands with him, "that the Armitage party could be the best fireworks around."

67

Albie Fernandez to the rescue, Ralph Armitage thought.

After the hung jury, he had suggested to Fernandez that the young lawyer take over the case and do the retrial. He said he had to get back to running the office. That it was better to have someone with a new approach. Blah, blah, blah.

Fortunately Albie readily agreed. Armitage was just happy to be done with the file. The trial had been such a roller coaster; thank goodness he was off it. The worst moment was that first time the jury came back. He'd been sure they had a not-guilty verdict. Boy, was he relieved when he found out they just wanted to ask the judge a question. Five days later, when Rothbart finally declared a mistrial, he knew he'd dodged a bullet. Well, that wasn't really a good way to put it. But if he had lost the case that would have been a disaster. And now he'd palmed it off on Fernandez.

But he wasn't entirely in the clear. Ozera. Who knew where the guy was? He might show up at any time and demand to know if the warrant was still outstanding. A few days ago, Armitage was so nervous about it he signed back into the warrant office to have a look.

He'd made a point of going through a number of the boxes, sprinkling his fingerprints everywhere. But when he came to the one that should have had the Ozera warrant, it was missing. He felt sick. Someone had the warrant. Someone was looking. For what? A connection back to him?

As if this weren't bad enough, Penny was going crazy with all her party preparations. Every night she was up on the computer, working on lists and lists of things she had to do. He could hardly remember the last time they'd had sex.

It was Saturday morning, and he'd told her he needed to go to the office to help out Fernandez, who was in his final weekend of trial preparation. This was true, but what he really wanted was to be alone. To think. Figure out what else he could do to keep a lid on everything.

At exactly eleven, Fernandez came in. Mr. Right on Time, Armitage thought. He had a copy of the Saturday *Star* in his hand. "Have you seen this?" he asked, tossing the paper on Armitage's desk.

Of course Armitage had seen it. That was why he was so worked up. But he pretended he hadn't. "No." He felt his stomach lurch, just as it had done when he read the story this morning. A front-page exclusive interview with Cedric Wilkinson.

"Mr. Wilkinson is putting out a personal plea to find that missing witness," Fernandez said.

"Let's hope it works." Armitage felt the bile rise in the back of his throat. The Saturday *Star* was the widest-circulation paper in Canada. No way Ozera wouldn't see this.

"Sounds like Greene planted this story," Fernandez said. "Smart move."

"That's Greene for you," Armitage said. The walls were closing in on him. He could feel it.

"If he finds this guy, it could be a game changer," Fernandez said.

"You said it," Armitage said. "A fucking game changer."

68

The Plaza Flamingo hadn't changed. Sure, the actual faces were all different, but the people were the same. Mostly guys, dark, big chested, friendly, loud. A sprinkling of women, long hair, lots of makeup, nails done to the nines. The occasional blonde.

He wasn't only here to bring Andrea back. He had another motive. A few months before, Greene had tracked down the Ozera file and discovered that Ralph Armitage had withdrawn the charges against him. Sounded suspicious until it turned out Armitage had been on a binge, cleaning up old files and that the previous Head Crown Jennifer Raglan had agreed. Still.

Greene had told him to hold on to the original arrest warrant for Ozera. Kennicott pulled in a favor with the forensic officer Harry Ho, who printed the warrant and found a match to a fingerprint of Armitage's, which they'd lifted from a legal brief Greene had provided. Kennicott had gotten excited about this until Greene suggested they print the other warrants in the same box. Sure enough, most of them had also been handled by Armitage. Logic dictated that this was a dead end. Even Greene thought there was probably nothing to it.

But Kennicott kept racking his brain. And he kept hold of the warrant. There was a book you needed to sign to get into the warrant room, and he'd check it every few days and yesterday Ralph Armitage had signed in. What was he looking for and why? That's when this idea had come to him. Armitage had told Greene that he'd made the original deal with Dewey's lawyer at the Plaza Flamingo. Detective 101: go back to the beginning and follow the trail.

Outside a pink banner said "Lunch Buffet only $8.95. Dinner, Show, and Dance lessons package available!"

Lunch had cost $5.95 when they used to come here, he thought.

"Table for two?" the dark-haired hostess inside the door asked when she saw Kennicott and Andrea.

"Yeah, please," he said.

"Lunch special?"

"Always," Andrea said.

The food setup was exactly as he remembered it. Short, heavyset women toiled behind a row of steam trays and piled chicken, sliced sausage, shrimp, rice, vegetables, and bread onto large Styrofoam plates. One of them recognized Andrea and rushed around to give her a big hug.

He'd told her that he would need to speak to the manager alone. She chatted away with the older lady as he took a seat by the wall. It gave him a good view of the place. Chelsea was playing Birmingham. Their fans were all wearing blue-and-white striped scarves. Just like Dewey Booth, he thought.

A young female in a sleeveless dress showed up. A long cobra tattoo ran down her right arm. "What can I get you?" she asked.

"I used to come here a lot. Do you still serve Moretti?'

"Sure."

"Get me two. And who's the manager on shift today?"

She looked at him. "Something wrong?"

"No." He laughed. "Just the opposite. I want to compliment who-ever's in charge."

"That's sweet." She touched his shoulder.

Seconds later a tall brute of a man showed up. He bent down to talk without taking a seat. "Hi, sir," he said in a voice that was as deep as a mine shaft. "I'm Severino. Francesca said you want to chat with me."

Kennicott gave him a big smile. "I'm an old customer, and wanted to tell you how nice it is to be back here."

"Thanks. You need anything?"

He made sure there was no one in earshot. "I'm also a police of-ficer. Working on a homicide case. I wonder if you would help me for a minute."

Severino swiveled and surveyed the area around the table.

"Don't worry," Kennicott said, "no one here's in trouble."

"Thanks for being discreet." Severino sat.

"Always. I'm going to show you a picture. Let me know if this per-son is familiar."

Severino's eyes darted around the restaurant again before he looked back at the table, where Kennicott had laid out the *Toronto Star* story from a few months ago about Ralph Armitage, with a big picture of him.

"The tall blond guy," Severino said without a moment's hesitation.

"You recognize him?"

"Yeah. He's been here before."

Kennicott could feel his heartbeat speed up. Keep calm, he told himself. "Do you know how often?"

"Three times."

"Any reason you remember him."

Severino laughed. "Tall, blond, white guy in a business suit. Not our usual clientele."

"Who'd he come in with?"

"First time, a short, bald guy in a suit too. Guy had a real big head, like a bowling ball. Looked like they were arguing, so I kept an eye on their table."

That would be Dewey Booth's lawyer, Phil Cutter, Kennicott thought. "And after that?"

"Second time he met a skinny, short guy named Pedro. Pedro came to work for me after their first meeting."

"He did?"

"Showed up a few days later. Kid spoke about ten languages. Said he'd wait on tables for free and live off his tips. I hired him on the spot."

"How long did he work for you?'

"About ten days. The women loved him. Guy made a fortune."

"Can you describe him to me?"

"Like I said. Short, thin. Skin color like me. He was from Brazil. Real thick accent."

"Facial hair?"

"He had a twirly little mustache. Wore dark-framed glasses. Girls said he looked like Johnny Depp."

"Anything else?"

"No. Oh yeah. He had this funny little birthmark on the side of his face."

Kennicott pulled out the composite sketch of Ozera and showed it to Severino. "Recognize him?"

He didn't hesitate. "That's Pedro. No mustache and glasses, but it's him. See the mark?"

Unbelievable, Kennicott thought. Here he and Greene were busting their asses to try to find Ozera, and Armitage had met with him before the trial started. And never disclosed this to anyone. Greene was going to have a fit when he found out.

Francesca the waitress arrived with the two bottles of beer. Severino plunked them off her tray. Kennicott reached into his pocket for some money, but the manager waved him off.

"You have an employment file on him?" Kennicott asked, once Francesca was out of earshot. "Address? Social security number?"

Severino pulled out a white towel that was looped around his belt and wiped down the chair by his side. "Come on, officer. What do you think? Look around—half the people in here are illegals. Working their balls off. Construction. Paving. Building the whole fucking city. You try running a business in this town. Bylaws for everything. I get charged twenty-five bucks for every stupid garbage bag we put out on the sidewalk."

"So you've got nothing on this guy?"

"Nada. He worked for tips. And one day Mr. Blondie came back in. Looked like they fought again, and then Mr. Suit stormed out."

"What did this Pedro say about it?"

Severino shrugged. His focus had shifted back to other tables, like a searchlight that had temporarily paused, then started up again. "He said the guy was a demanding customer and a lousy tipper. Pedro didn't show up the next day and that was it."

This Ozera was a slippery fish, Kennicott thought. He seemed to be able to talk himself into any kind of job. Especially when it had something to do with serving food. He'd tell Greene about this too as soon as he got home.

"Anything else you can tell me about him?"

Severino stood. Anxious to get back to the work. "Guy could sell ice to the Eskimos. Talk his way into anything. I'd hire him again in a heartbeat. You still drink Moretti, eh?"

"Still?"

"I remember," Severino said. "You and your model girlfriend drank it here Saturday afternoons." He pointed to the food stand, where a small crowd had gathered around Andrea." I see her picture now on the cover of all the fashion magazines the girls bring in."

Kennicott put a five-dollar bill on the table.

Severino hovered for a moment. "Hope you don't mind my asking, but they never found the guy who killed your brother, did they?"

Kennicott took a sip of his beer. It was cold and good. "Not yet," he said.

"Don't be a stranger. You're welcome here anytime. With or without your model girlfriend."

Ari Greene's most vivid memory of Victoria Day had to be when he was in grade seven. He and some friends rode their bikes through the city as dusk settled in, the spring trees in bloom everywhere around them. They took over a patch of ground on the steep hill at Earl Bales Park among the crowd filing in for the fireworks display. A few kids had brought blankets, which they spread out on the tilted lawn. Somehow in the jumble of people Karen O'Hara ended up sitting beside him. Very close.

Although there had been some debate among the grade-seven boys as to whether O'Hara or Lane Wilson was the prettiest girl in class, there'd been no question at all that she had the best body. It was a remarkable thing, and Greene had spent a good deal of the school year sneaking looks at her from many different angles.

She was smart and friendly, one of those people who touched you on the shoulder when she talked. He always felt comfortable around her, but he'd never been this close. Especially on a blanket, with the late-spring darkness falling all around them.

"Ooooh." "Ahhh." "Wow." The crowd reacted as one to every burst of color in the blackened sky when the fireworks display began.

"They're so beautiful," O'Hara said after a particularly spectacular one.

Tongue-tied, Greene could only nod. He felt her hand slide into his. Perspiration erupted across his skin and all he could think of was how sticky his fingers must have felt. She'd angled her body and rubbed against him. The only light was the sporadic flashes of color in the sky. She moved his palm over to her flat stomach, then upward. Rising.

There was a dryness in his mouth that he'd never felt before as she brought his hand to her breast.

"Detective Greene, Mr. Wilkinson, great of you both to come," Ralph Armitage said, extending his large hand, a huge grin pasted in place. They'd just stepped onto the backyard stone patio.

Greene shook his hand. He'd read about the Armitage estate, which was always described in various articles as "vast" or "sprawling," but looking down into the valley, the sheer scale of it took him by surprise. There was nothing but trees for as far as the eye could see. Below, a gigantic gazebo had been set up, as well as tents, a playground, and even a set of bleachers. More than a dozen buses were parked over to the side. Piles of children poured out of them, amazed that they'd been transported to this wonderland.

"I wanted to thank you personally for all the work you did on the case," Wilkinson said to Armitage.

Right on script, Greene thought. Just as they'd practiced on the drive up here.

"I'm sure Albert Fernandez will do a great job on the retrial," Armitage said. "Don't you think so, detective?"

"Absolutely." Greene pointed to the cascade of children running into the backyard. "Every Canadian kid has great memories of Victoria Day."

"We've brought in more than a thousand children this year," Armitage said. "I'd love you to meet my wife, Penny. She's down below, the woman with the clipboard. You wouldn't believe how much work goes into all of this. A million details. And something always goes wrong."

He pulled his cell phone from his pocket. "Two minutes ago she called me all in a panic because some new waiter had shown up. I told her relax, we can use all the help we can get."

A waiter, Greene thought, recalling a conversation he'd had with Daniel Kennicott yesterday. "We'll keep an eye out for your wife," he said.

"Great. Grab your seats in the bleachers. I've reserved spots for you in the first row."

"Thanks," Greene said.

"Penny's got me working up here as the official greeter. Awotwe Amankwah from the *Star* told me he's coming and I want say hello, but I'll be there before the fireworks start.

Greene had worked closely with Armitage for months. It was hard to tell if the man was nervous. He was always so smooth, but something about him seemed off. Even more forced than usual. Maybe he had a hunch that there might be another kind of fireworks tonight.

The air was warmer in the valley, and there was only a thumbnail of a moon on the horizon. Wilkinson walked beside him. Greene could see his eyes were fixed on the children at play.

Dusk came slowly near the end of May, adding a touch of magic to late-spring Canadian nights. They took their seats on the bottom row of the bleachers. Penny Armitage was impossible to miss. Tall and willowy, she flitted about chatting with everyone, ticking notes off on her clipboard. The bleachers behind them filled up with guests, the grass on both sides with children. Greene scanned the crowd. He saw Awotwe Amankwah walking in with his two kids and waved.

"Welcome, everyone, welcome," Ralph Armitage said, stepping onto the pieces of plywood flooring that had been placed on the ground as a temporary stage. A few spotlights had been set up, and he had a microphone in hand.

"I am thrilled to welcome everyone to the twenty-fifth annual Armitage Family Victoria Day Celebration."

An enthusiastic roar went up from the crowd of children.

"Fireworks start in about five minutes," he said. "But first I want to say a special word of thanks to my amazing wife, Penny, who's spent countless hours putting this all together."

Penny walked tentatively into the light and took the microphone. The clipboard was still in her other hand. "Thanks, Ralph," she said, her voice quavering. "I'm not a public speaker like my husband, but I just want to thank the whole Armitage family so, so, so, much. My wonderful sisters-in-law, I couldn't have done this without you. Ralph's parents, Bill and Sandra. You're the greatest."

Another cheer went up from the crowd.

Penny passed the microphone back to her husband and looked relieved to go to the back of the stage.

Greene touched Wilkinson on the shoulder. "I think you should go up and introduce yourself to Penny Armitage."

"Okay," he said.

Greene watched him walk up to the side of the stage. Even though Wilkinson had lost so much weight, he still lumbered along like a big man.

Armitage took the mike back from Penny. "Are you kids ready?" he shouted in full camp counselor mode.

"Yes!" a chorus of children screamed back.

"No?" he asked theatrically.

"Yes!" the kids yelled louder.

Greene had heard "Ralphie" had spent years being a camp counselor, and you could see why he'd been good at it. He looked genuinely happy.

"Are you sure about that?"

"Yes!" The voices were almost hysterical.

"Okay. Without any further ado," he said, "let the show begin."

Wilkinson came into the light by the back of the stage. Armitage saw him and rushed over, extending his hand in his usual greeting. Greene watched him tap Penny on the shoulder and direct her attention to Wilkinson.

Penny's vibrant smile turned sad. She touched Wilkinson on the shoulder with compassion. It was easy to read her lips. "I'm sorry, I'm so, so sorry for your loss," she said.

Wilkinson nodded with the fatigue of a longtime mourner.

A small man in a black and white waiter's uniform popped onto the back of the lit stage. He had a tray in one hand with a few glasses of water on it. No one noticed him.

Greene stood up.

The waiter came up behind the three of them. He said something to Ralph Armitage, but Greene couldn't see his lips.

It didn't matter.

Because he saw Ralph Armitage's face fall when he turned to look at the short man.

And Greene knew.

70

Every night for the last month, Ralph Armitage had had nightmares about this moment. Two days before, when he read that front-page article in the Saturday *Toronto Star*, his sense of impending doom had heightened to the point where he couldn't sleep at all. He'd told Penny it was because of his excitement about the big party, combined with the St. Clair trial starting up. How could he say to her, "I can't sleep because at any moment I could be arrested?"

And now it was happening. He was watching Detective Greene's mouth move; the words seemed unreal. But he could feel Greene's hand on his arm, couldn't he?

"You have the right to remain silent," the homicide detective was saying.

Armitage felt himself nod. But it seemed like someone else. Penny was clutching him. Digging her fingers into his arm.

"You have the right to retain a lawyer." Greene kept talking. Blah, blah, blah. Like I don't know my legal rights, Armitage thought.

Greene had waited until the lights were turned off on the stage to arrest him. The fireworks were exploding above them. The whole thing had happened so fast. But slowly, in a weird way.

"I'm the baker. The witness you've been looking for," Ozera had told Greene moments before. "You arrested the wrong man."

"Why's that?" Greene asked.

Ozera looked right at Wilkinson. "I saw everything. Dewey was the shooter. When Larkin saw he was about to fire at Jet and Suzanne, he knocked Dewey's hand away. He probably saved Jet's life. Suzanne's too. But Dewey slipped, and that's why the bullet hit your son."

"And the other shots?" Greene asked.

"Dewey kept firing as he fell. One shot went into the ground. He rolled over and the next one went in the other direction, into the building across the lot."

"What about the bullet behind where you were standing?" Greene asked.

Ozera shrugged. "Dewey walked out a few steps toward where the Cadillac had been, didn't even go into the light, and fired right over my head. I saw him stomp on the shell casing and kick it across the lot to where Jet's car had been."

Armitage watched Greene nod, the way you nod when a mystery is solved for you. Like those Hardy Boy books he'd loved to read, back here in the woods. In his secret fort.

"Dewey set it all up to make it look like Jet was firing at him."

Armitage heard the voice saying the words. It was flat. Lifeless. It sounded like someone else. Who was talking? But he knew it was his voice. Maybe this was who he really was, he thought. What he really sounded like.

Everyone stared at him. Were they surprised that he knew all this? Penny looked shocked, but Greene didn't.

"Mr. Ozera here told me everything after I made the stupid deal with Cutter," he heard himself saying. Still that same voice. This is what Ralph sounds like, not Ralphie. "I tried to shut him up. I pulled his charges."

Penny lifted her hand from his arm. He couldn't blame her. The woods around them were dark. Lovely, dark, and deep, he thought. He knew them better than anyone. He had grown up without any brothers to play with. Dad was always at work. He'd spent hours, days, summers, playing pretend Cowboys and Indians back there, acting like Davy Crockett. Hidden in his old bedroom, he still had that fake coon hat he got for his sixth birthday.

A new set of fireworks lit up the sky.

"Oooh! Wow!" the kids screamed.

He loved to hear the sound of happy children playing. He had so many secret forts and special hiding places. They'd never find him there. Never.

The light started to fade. Penny had let go. Nothing was holding him now. Quick, before there was another burst. He stepped back quietly. Stepped again. One more. Almost there.

It was getting dark. Real dark.

Another step. Okay, Ralphie, he told himself, last step and . . .

He heard the *click* sound before he felt the cold metal on his wrist.

A huge fireworks display exploded, and he saw that a Toronto police officer wearing a blue turban behind him. That was so Toronto. So multicultural. Where had the guy come from? Before he could react, the cop had his second hand behind his back and had bolted them together in the handcuffs.

Instinctively, he tried to pull them apart.

The hard steel dug into his wrists. He felt the pain, and he knew this was no dream. His real-life nightmare had begun.

71

"What kind of vodka do you have?" Nancy Parish asked the server.

He was cute. Not quite as cute as Brett from the Pravda Bar had been, but not unattractive. She laughed to herself for using a lawyer's double negative. The guy had already told them that his name was Stuart, and he'd be their server for the night.

"Stoli, Grey Goose, Absolut, Blue Ice," Stuart the almost-cute waiter said.

She grinned. "Grey Goose. Double shot, with a glass of water on the side."

Stuart smiled back. Had a sweet little dimple in his cheek.

"And you, sir?" He turned to Larkin St. Clair.

They were sitting on the outdoor patio at Pappas Grill. All of St. Clair's attention was focused on the seemingly endless parade of scantily dressed females promenading on the Danforth on this warm summer night.

"Sir?" Stuart asked again, his pen poised above his little waiter's notepad.

"Ah, a Coke." St. Clair peeled his eyes from the short skirts and long legs voyaging past on the other side of the wrought-iron railing. "No ice."

Stuart scampered off to get their drinks, and St. Clair went back to staring.

"See," Parish said, "there are advantages to not living your life in jail."

St. Clair's hair had grown about half a foot since his arrest. It was inching its way down his back and lovingly coiffed.

He turned his attention back to her. "Can you believe it? We are actually here at Pappas, having drinks on the patio. Did you ever think it would happen?"

"I'm going to remain silent, on the grounds it might incriminate me." She didn't want to break the moment for him—considering he'd just gotten out of jail this morning—by mentioning that St. Clair still had three more years of probation to get through before he was truly a free man. Three more years of drug and alcohol testing. Three more years of "keeping the peace and being of good behavior." "Being of good behavior" was stretching things a tad for Larkin, she thought, especially when it came to women.

Stuart came with the drinks.

Parish and St. Clair both sipped in silent appreciation of the moment. The sun was bright and the temperature perfect. The long winter she'd been through was a dark memory.

"Sorry I made you miss that trip to Mexico." St. Clair was wearing a black T-shirt, his sleeves rolled up over his shoulders, exposing his prison-hard biceps.

"Guy wasn't worth it," she said.

"I keep telling you, guys are jerks," he said.

"So I keep hearing."

He took his eyes off the parade of exposed female flesh and looked at Parish. "You did an amazing job at my trial."

"It helps that you weren't guilty for a change."

"Only me," he said. "I try to save someone's life and almost end up going to jail for twenty-five years. Would have without you."

Parish hadn't exactly won the trial. But getting a hung jury had turned out to be the key. When Greene found Ozera, the baker from the Tim Hortons, he told the police the exact same story St. Clair had told Parish months before in jail. With this new evidence, Dewey Booth had been charged with perjury at the first trial and first-degree murder.

Parish and Albert Fernandez, the new Crown on the case, quickly worked out the obvious deal. St. Clair, who'd already been in jail for half a year, pled guilty to accessory after the fact for hiding the gun and got three years' probation. The maximum amount, and maybe, just maybe, enough time for his aunt Arlene to keep him on the straight and narrow. Especially with Dewey now looking at twenty-five years in jail for the murder of Kyle Wilkinson..

Ralph "Just call me Ralphie" Armitage was still in jail because no one would bail him out. His wife had left him and his family wanted nothing to do with the son who had soiled the family name. Ralph Armitage Senior let it be known in the press that he had cut Ralph Junior out of his will "one hundred percent. He'll get one dollar and not a penny more." There wasn't a lawyer in the whole province who wanted to touch the case. Jennifer Raglan, the former head Crown, had been brought back in to clean up the mess and run the office again.

Behind her Parish heard a child's voice screaming above the hustle and bustle on the street. "Uncle Larkin, Uncle Larkin!"

St. Clair's always-animated face lit up another notch. His aunt Arlene and her son were steps away.

"Holy cow, Justin, is that you?" He stood and hopped over the wrought-iron fence, his long hair flowing behind him, every strand in place.

"Who's that?" Justin asked, pointing to Parish. He had an incredibly loud voice, just like his uncle. "She another girlfriend?"

St. Clair gave a loud chuckle. "No, silly. Her name's Nancy, and she's my lawyer," he said.

"The good one or the bad one?" the little boy asked.

"The good one. Real good. Just like you're going to be one day."

There was a little vodka left in her glass. Parish downed it and stood up as the three of them came around to the table.

Arlene gave her a hug, and Justin held out his hand for a formal handshake. She shook it and couldn't resist patting him on the top of his head. "Have a great meal," she said.

"What do you mean?" St. Clair asked. "Where you going?"

"We always dreamed of a summer night, having our drink together on the patio at Pappas. No charges outstanding against you. And we did it. You have dinner with your family."

"But . . ."

She put her hand on his shoulder. "It's time for me to go home."

They stared at each other.

"Do they have chicken fingers here?" Justin shouted.

Larkin wrapped his arms around her in a powerful embrace. "Love you, Nancy," he whispered into her ear.

She smiled as she let go of him. Smiled as she walked down the crowded avenue. People, dogs, strollers, all crisscrossing in front of her. The wind was still fresh and warm, and the sun hovered high in the sky, as if it were in no hurry at all to go down.

ACKNOWLEDGMENTS

Walk downtown in most Canadian cities, and you'll find aging stone bank buildings on the street corners of major intersections. Decades ago these tall-columned and high-ceilinged structures projected financial power and confidence. Today, all too many have been turned into money marts and hamburger joints.

But some have been lovingly restored. At this moment I'm sitting in the magnificent yet comfortable law library at the office of Edward L. Greenspan, Q.C., in what was once an impressive branch of the Dominion Bank of Canada. Eddie, as he's known to everyone, is one of North America's leading criminal lawyers, and for the last few years he's been my landlord.

After two decades of practicing law in the high-rise towers of Toronto's downtown core, it's been a great relief for me to hang my shingle, and park my laptop, in a building where there are no parking garages, packed elevators, or a downstairs food court. And where the windows actually open.

Finding the right office to continue my dual career of defending people and writing these novels has been important, especially since I am now taping out a book a year.

Thanks, then, go to a long list of people for their assistance this time around. They are, in no particular order: Kevin Hanson; Alison Clarke; Amy Cormier; Amy Jacobson; Anneliese Grosfield; Victoria Skurnick; Elizabeth Fisher; Angela Hughes; Patricia Bandeira; Susan Petersen; Michael Lacy; Joe Wilkinson; Andras Schreck; Donald Schmidtt; Dr. Jan Ahuja; Douglas Preston; David Flacks; Ron Davis; Julie Lacey; Christine Jenkins; Tom Klatt; Kate Parkin; Stan Klich; Travis West; and, of course, Eddie.

And a special thanks to my daughter, Helen, and her junior high school friends (bffs) Elizabeth, Claire, and Amelia for translating my English words into . . . OMG! . . . proper texting language.

Toronto
January 13, 2012

ABOUT THE AUTHOR

Robert Rotenberg is a criminal lawyer in Toronto, where he lives with his family. *Stray Bullets* is his third novel.

Visit his website: www.robertrotenberg.com.
Follow Robert on Twitter @robertrotenberg.
Keep up with Robert at Facebook/robertrotenberg.